Jeff Kerwin walked swiftly now through the dark, deserted streets of Thendara. He heard a step behind him—a slow, purposeful step, but told himself not to be suspicious; he wasn't the only man who might have a good reason to be out in the rain tonight! The step kept pace with him, then quickened to over-take him, and Kerwin stepped side to let the follower pass in the narrow street.

That was a mistake. Kerwin felt a searing pain; then the top of his head exploded and from somewhere he heard a voice crying out strange words:
Say to the son of the barbarian that he shall come no more to the plains of Arilinn! The Forbidden Tower is broken and the Golden Bell is avenged!

THE BLOODY SUN

PLUS *To Keep the Oath*
—a new Free Amazon story
  never before published anywhere!

The Bloody Sun

MARION ZIMMER BRADLEY

SF

ace books

A Division of Charter Communications Inc.
A GROSSET & DUNLAP COMPANY
360 Park Avenue South
New York, New York 10010

For showing me universes without number;
in loving memory,
Henry Kuttner.

The stranger who comes home
does not make himself at home
but makes home strange.

Prologue: Darkover

The Leronis

Leonie Hastur was dead.

The ancient *leronis*, sorceress of the Comyn, Keeper of Arilinn, telepath, trained with all the powers of the matrix sciences of Darkover, died as she had lived, alone, sequestered high in the Tower of Arilinn.

Not even her priestess-novice-apprentice, Janine Leynier of Storn, knew the hour when death came quietly into the Tower and took her away into one of the other worlds she had learned to walk as skillfully as within her own enclosed garden.

She died alone; and she died unmourned. For, although Leonie was feared, revered, worshipped almost as a Goddess throughout all the Domains of Darkover, she was not loved.

Once she had been greatly loved. There had been a time when Leonie Hastur had been a young woman, beautiful and chaste as a distant moon, and poets had written of her glory, comparing her to the exquisitely shining face of Liriel, the great violet moon of Darkover; or to a Goddess come down to live among men. She had been adored by those who lived under her rule at Arilinn Tower. Once, despite the austerity of the vows under which she lived (which would have made it blasphemy unspeakable for any

1

man to touch her fingertips) Leonie had been loved. But that had been long ago.

And now, as the years had passed over her head, leaving her more and more alone, further from humanity, she was loved less; and feared and hated more. The old Regent Lorill Hastur, her twin brother (for Leonie had been born into the royal house of the Hasturs of Hastur, and if she had not chosen the Tower, she would have stood higher than any Queen in the land), was long dead. A nephew she had seen but a few times stood behind the throne of Stefan Hastur-Elhalyn and was the real power in the Domains. But to him Leonie was a whisper, an old tale and a shadow.

And now she was dead and lay, as the custom was, in an unmarked grave within the walls of Arilinn, where no human being save those of Comyn blood might ever come; in death no more secluded than in life. And there were few left alive to weep.

One of the few who wept was Damon Ridenow, who had married years ago into the Domain of Alton, and briefly been Warden of that Domain for the young Heir to Alton, Valdir of Armida.* When Valdir had come of age and taken a wife, Damon and all his household, which was large, had removed to the estate of Mariposa Lake, which lay in the pleasant upland country in the foothills of the Kilghard Hills. When Leonie was young, and Damon was young, and he a mechanic in the Tower of Arilinn, he had loved Leonie; loved her chastely, with never a touch or a kiss or any thought of breaking the vows that bound her. But he had loved her, nonetheless, with a passion that had given form and color to all

*This story is told in *The Forbidden Tower*.

his life afterward; and when he heard of her death, he went apart to his own study and there he shed the tears he would not shed before his wife or his wife's sister, who had once been Leonie's novice-Keeper at Arilinn, or before any of his household. But if they knew of his grief—and in a household of Comyn telepaths such things could not well be hidden—no one would speak of it; not even his grown sons and daughters asked why their father grieved in secret. Leonie, to them, of course, was only a legend with a name.

And so, when the news spread throughout the Domains, there was much excited speculation, even in this most distant of remote corners in the Domains, about the question that now quickened and burned all over the Domains, from the Hellers to the Plains of Arilinn: *Who now will be Keeper of Arilinn?*

And to Damon, one day soon after that, in the privacy of his own study, came his youngest daughter Cleindori.

She had been given the old-fashioned name, legendary and traditional, of Dorilys: *Golden-flower.* But as a child her hair had been pale sunny gold, and her eyes so big and blue that her nurses dressed her always in blue frocks and blue ribbons; her fostermother, Damon's wife Ellemir, said that she looked like a blue bell of the *kireseth* flower, covered with its golden pollen. So they had nicknamed her, when she was only a toddler, Cleindori, *Golden Bell,* which was the common name for the *kireseth* flower: And as the years passed, most people had all but forgotten that Dorilys Aillard (for her mother had been a *nedestro* daughter of that powerful Domain) had ever borne any other name but Cleindori.

She had grown into a tall, shy, serious young woman, thirteen years old now, her hair sunny, copper-golden. There was Drytown blood in the Ridenow clan, and her mother's father, too, had been, it was whispered, a Drytown bandit from Shainsa; but that old scandal had been long forgotten. Damon, looking up at the womanly body and serious eyes of his last-born daughter, felt for the first time in his life that he was approaching old age.

"Have you ridden all the way from Armida today, my child? What had your foster-father to say to that?"

Cleindori smiled and went to kiss her father on the cheek. "He said nothing, for I did not tell him," she said gaily, "but I was not alone, for my foster-brother Kennard rode here with me."

Cleindori had been sent to fosterage at nine years old, as the custom was in the Domains, to grow to womanhood under a hand less tender than that of a mother. She had been fostered by Valdir, Lord Alton, whose lady, Lori, had only sons and longed for a daughter to rear. There was a distant understanding that when Cleindori was old enough to marry, she might be wedded to Lord Alton's elder son, Lewis-Arnad; but as yet, Damon supposed, there was no thought in Cleindori of marriage; she and Lewis and Valdir's youngest son Kennard were sister and brothers. Damon greeted Kennard, who was a sturdy, broad-shouldered, grey-eyed boy a year younger than Cleindori, with a kinsman's embrace, and said, "So I see my daughter was well-guarded on her way here. What brings you here, children? Were you hawking and late returning, and chose to ride this way, thinking there would be cakes and sweets for runaways here when there would be only the bread and water of punishment at home?" But he was laughing.

"No," Kennard said seriously. "Cleindori said she must see you; and my mother gave us leave to ride, but I do not think she knew fully what we asked or what she answered, for there was such hullabaloo at Armida on this day, ever since the news has come."

"What news?" Damon asked, leaning forward, but already he knew, and felt his heart sink. Cleindori curled herself up on a cushion at his feet, looking up at him. She said, "Dear Father, three days ago the Lady Janine of Arilinn came riding to Armida on her search for one to bear the name and dignity of the Lady of Arilinn who is dead; the *leronis* Leonie."

"It took her long enough to come to Armida," Damon commented with a curl of his lip. "No doubt she had tested in all the Domains before this."

Cleindori nodded. "I think so," she said, "for after she knew who I was, she looked at me as if she smelled something bad, and said, 'Since you are from the Forbidden Tower, have you been taught in any of their heresies?' For when Lady Lori told her my name, she was angry, and I had to tell her that my mother had given me the name of Dorilys. But Janine said, 'Well, by law I am required to test you for *laran*. I cannot deny you that.'"

She screwed up her face in imitation of the *leronis*, and Damon put his hand across the lower part of his face, as if in thought, but actually to conceal a grin; for Cleindori had a knack for mimicry and she had caught the sour tone and disapproving stare of the *leronis* Janine. Damon said, "Aye. Janine was among those who would have had me burned alive or blinded when I fought with Leonie for the right to use the *laran* the gods had given me as I myself chose, and not only as Arilinn demanded. It would not make her love you, child, that you are my daughter."

Cleindori smiled again, gaily. "I can live well enough without her love; I can well believe that she has never loved even a pet kitten! But I was trying to tell you, Father, what she said to me and what I said to her . . . she seemed pleased when I told her that you had taught me nothing as yet, and that I had been fostered since I was nine at Armida; and so she gave me a matrix and tested me for *laran*. And when she had done, she said that she wanted me for Arilinn; and then she frowned and told me that she would not have chosen me for this, but that there were few others who could bear the training; and that she wished to train me as Keeper."

Damon's breath caught in his throat; but the cry of protest died unspoken, for Cleindori was looking up at him with her eyes shining. "Father, I told her, as I knew I must, that I could not enter a Tower without my father's consent; and then I rode away here to ask for that consent."

"Which you shall not have," said Damon harshly, "not while I am above ground and unburied. Or after, if I can prevent it."

"But Father—to be Keeper of Arilinn! Not even the Queen—"

Damon's throat tightened. So after all these years the hand of Arilinn was reaching out again toward one that he loved. "Cleindori, no," he said and reached out, touching her fair curls, which shone with the light of alloyed copper and gold. "You see only the power. You do not know the cruelty of that training. To be Keeper—"

"Janine told me. She said that the training is very long and very cruel and very difficult to bear. She told me something of what I must vow and what I must give up. But she said also that she thought I was capable of it."

"Child—" Damon swallowed hard. He said, "Human flesh and blood cannot endure it!"

"Now that is foolish," Cleindori said, "for you endured it, Father. And so did Callista, who was once Leonie's novice-Keeper at Arilinn."

"Have you any idea what it cost Callista, child?"

"You made sure I should know, before I was out of childhood," Cleindori said. "And so, too, did Callista, telling me before I had come to womanhood what a cruel and unnatural life it was. I cut my teeth on that old tale of how you and Callista fought Leonie and all of Arilinn in a duel that lasted nightlong. . . ."

"Has the tale grown so much?" Damon interrupted with a laugh. "It was less than a quarter of an hour; though indeed the storm seemed to rage through many days. But we fought Arilinn; and won the right to use *laran* as we would and not as Arilinn should decree."

"But I can see, too," Cleindori argued, "that you, who were trained in Arilinn, and Callista, too, trained in the Way of Arilinn, are superbly skilled; while those who have been taught *laran* here have fewer skills and are clumsy in the use of their gifts. And I know, too, that all the other Towers in this land still hold to the Way of Arilinn."

"These powers and skills—" Damon paused and collected himself, trying to speak calmly, for he was

shouting. Then he said, "Cleindori, since I was a
young man I have believed that the Way of Arilinn—
and of all the other Towers on whom the people of
Arilinn force their will—is cruel and inhuman. I believed this; and I fought, laying my life as forfeit, so
that men and women in the Towers need not give up
all their lives to a living death, sealed within Tower
walls. Such skills as we have can be learned by any
man or woman, Comyn or Commoner, if they
possess the inborn talent. It is like playing the lute;
one is born with an ear for music and can learn the
way of plucking the strings, but even for that difficult
vocation no one should be asked to give up home and
family, life or love. We have taught much to others;
and we have won the right to teach them without
penalty. A day will come, Cleindori, when the ancient matrix sciences of our world will be free to any
who can use them, and the Towers will be no more
needed."

"But we are still outcaste," argued Cleindori.
"Father, if you had seen Janine's face when she
spoke of you, calling it the Forbidden Tower. . . ."

Damon's face tightened. "I do not love Janine so
much that her evil opinion of me will lose me any
sleep of nights."

"But Cleindori is right," Kennard said. "We are
renegades. Here in the countryside people hold to
your ways; but all over the Domains they turn only
to the Towers to know of *laran*. I too am to go to a
Tower, Neskaya perhaps, or perhaps to Arilinn itself,
when I have done my three years' service in the
Guards; if Cleindori goes to Arilinn, they said I could
not go until she had completed her years of seclusion, for a Keeper in training cannot have a foster-

brother near, or anyone to whom she is bound by affection—"

"Cleindori is not going to Arilinn," Damon said, "and there's an end of it." And he repeated, even more vehemently, "Human flesh and blood cannot endure the Way of Arilinn!"

"And again I say that is foolish," Cleindori said, "for Callista endured it; and the lady Hilary of Syrtis; and Margwenn of Thendara; and Leominda of Neskaya; and Janine of Arilinn; and Leonie's self; and nine-hundred-and-twenty-odd Keepers before her, so they say. And what they endured, I can endure if I must."

She leaned her chin on her folded hands, looking up at him seriously. "You have told me often enough, since I was only a child, that a Keeper is responsible only to her own conscience. And that everywhere, among the best of women and men, conscience is the only guide for that they do. Father, I feel it is laid upon me to be a Keeper."

"You can be Keeper among us, when you are grown," said Damon, "without such torment as you must endure at Arilinn."

"Oh!" She rose angrily to her feet and began to pace in the chamber. "You are my father, you would keep me always a little girl! Father, do you think I do not know that without the Towers of the Domains, our world is dark with barbarism? I have not been very far abroad, but I have been to Thendara, and I have seen the spaceships of the Terrans there, and I know that we have resisted their Empire only because the Towers give our world what we need, with our ancient matrix sciences. If the Towers go dark, Darkover falls into the hands of the Empire like a ripe plum, for the people will cry out for the technology and the trade of the Empire!"

Damon said quietly, "I do not think that this is inevitable. I have no hatred for the Terrans; my closest friend was Terran-born, your uncle Ann'dra. But it is for this I am working, that when every Tower is dark, there will be enough *laran* among the populace of the Domains that Darkover may be independent, and not go begging to the Terrans. That day will come, Cleindori. I tell you, a day will come when every Tower in the Domains stands bare and empty, the haunt of evil birds of prey—"

"Kinsman!" Kennard protested swiftly, and made a quick sign against evil. "Do not say such things!"

"It is not pleasant hearing," Damon said, "but it is true. Every year there are fewer and fewer of our sons and daughters with the power or the will to endure the old training and give themselves over to the Towers. Leonie once complained to me that she had trained six young girls and of them all, only one could complete the training to be Keeper; this was the *leronis* Hilary, and she sickened and would have died if they had not sent her from Arilinn. Three of the Towers—Janine would not tell you this, Cleindori, but I who am Arilinn-trained know it well— three of the Towers are working with a mechanic's circle because they have no Keeper, and their foolish laws will not allow them to take a Keeper to their circles unless she is willing to be a cloistered symbol of virginity. They say her strength and her *laran* powers are less important than that she should be a virgin goddess, sequestered and held in superstitious awe. There are, at a guess, a hundred women or more in the Domains who could do the work of a

Keeper, but they see no reason to undergo a training that will make them, not women, but machines for the transmission of power! And I do not blame them! The Towers will go. They must go. And when they are gone, standing bare as ruined monuments to the pride and the madness of the Comyn, then *laran* power, and the matrix stones that help us to use it, can be used as they were meant to be used; science, not sorcery! Sanity, not madness! I have worked for this all my life, Cleindori."

"Not to overthrow the Towers, Uncle!" Kennard sounded shocked.

"No. Never that. But to be there when they have been abandoned or forsaken, so that our *laran* sciences need not perish for lack of Towers to work them."

Cleindori stood beside him, her hand lightly on his shoulder. She said, "Father, I honor you for this. But your work is too slow, for they still call you outcaste and renegade and worse things. And that is why it is so much more important that young people like I, and like my half-sister Cassilde, and Kennard—"

Damon said, shocked, "Is Cassilde, too, going into Arilinn? It will kill Callista!" For Cassilde was Callista's own daughter, four or five years older than Cleindori.

"She is too old to need consent," Cleindori said. "Father, it is necessary that the Towers shall not die until the time has come, even if the day must come when they are no longer needed. And I feel it laid upon my conscience to be Keeper of Arilinn." She held out her hand to him. "No, Father, listen to me. I know *you* are not ambitious; you flung away the chance to command the City Guard; you could have been the most powerful man in Thendara; but you threw it away. I am not like that. If my *laran* is as powerful as the Lady of Arilinn told me, I want to be Keeper in a way that will let me *do* something useful with it; more than ministering to the peasants and teaching the village children! Father, I want to be Keeper of Arilinn!"

"You would put yourself into that prison from which we freed Callista at such great price!" Damon said, and his voice was unspeakably bitter.

"That was *her* life," Cleindori flared, "this is *mine*! But listen to me, Father," she said, kneeling beside him again. The anger was gone from her voice and a great seriousness had taken its place. "You have told me, and I have seen, that Arilinn declares the laws by which *laran* is used in this land, save for you few here who defy Arilinn."

"They may be doing things otherwise in the Hellers or at Aldaran and beyond," Damon qualified. "I know little of that."

"Then—" Cleindori looked up at him, her round face very serious. "If I go to Arilinn and learn to be Keeper, by their own rules the most orthodox of the ways by which *laran* can be used—if I am Keeper by the Way of Arilinn, then I can change those laws, can I not? If the Keeper of Arilinn makes the rules for all the Towers, then, Father, I can change them, I can declare the truth; that the Way of Arilinn is cruel and inhuman—and because I have succeeded at it, they cannot say I am simply a failure or an outcaste attacking what I myself cannot do. I can change these terrible laws and cast down the Way of Arilinn. And when the Towers no longer give men and women over to a living death, then the young men and women of our world will flock to them, and the old matrix sciences of Darkover will be reborn. But these laws will never be changed—not until a Keeper of Arilinn can change them!"

Damon looked at his daugher, shaken. It was indeed the only way in which Arilinn's cruel laws could be changed; that a Keeper of Arilinn should herself declare a new decree that should be binding on all the Towers. He had tried his best, but he was renegade, outcaste; he could do nothing from outside the walls of Arilinn. He had accomplished little—no one knew better than he how little he had accomplished.

"Father, it is fated," Cleindori said, and her young voice trembled. "After all Callista suffered, after all you suffered, perhaps it was all for this, that I should go back and free those others. Now that you have proven that they can be freed."

"You are right," Damon admitted, slowly. "The Way of Arilinn will never be thrown down until the Keeper of Arilinn herself shall throw it down. But—oh, Cleindori, not you!" Agonized, despairing, he clasped his daughter to him. "Not you, darling!"

Gently she freed herself from his embrace, and for a moment it seemed to Damon that she was already tall, impressive, aloof, touched with the alien strength of the Keeper, clothed in the crimson majesty of Arilinn. She said, "Father, dear Father, you cannot forbid me to do this; I am responsible only to my own conscience. How often have you said to all of us, beginning with my foster-father Valdir, who never tires of repeating it to me, that conscience is the only responsibility? Let me do this; let me finish the work you have begun in the Forbidden Tower. Otherwise, when you die, it will all die with you, a little band of renegades and their heresies perishing unseen and good riddance. But I can bring it to Arilinn, and then all over the Domains; for the Keeper of Arilinn makes the laws for all the Towers and all the Domains. Father, I tell you, it is fated. I *must* go to Arilinn."

Damon bowed his head, still reluctant, but unable to speak against her young and innocent sureness. It seemed to him that already the walls of Arilinn were closing around her. And so they parted, not to meet again until the hour of her death.

Chapter One: The Terran

Forty Years Later

This is the way it was.

You were an orphan of space. For all you knew, you might have been born on one of the Big Ships; the ships of Terra; the starships that made the long runs between stars doing the business of the Empire. You never knew where you had been born, or who your parents had been; the first home you knew was the Spacemen's Orphanage, almost within sight of the Port of Thendara, where you learned loneliness. Before that somewhere there had been strange colors and lights and confused images of people and places that sank into oblivion when you tried to focus on them, nightmares that sometimes made you sit up and shriek out in terror before you got yourself all the way awake and saw the clean quiet dormitory around you.

The other children were the abandoned flotsam of the arrogant and mobile race of Earth, and you were one of them, with one of their names. But outside lay the darkly beautiful world you had seen, that you still saw, sometimes, in your dreams. You knew, somehow, that you were different; you belonged to that world outside, that sky, that sun; not the clean, white, sterile world of the Terran Trade City.

You would have known it even if they hadn't told

15

you; but they told you, often enough. Oh, not in words; in a hundred small subtle ways. And anyway you were different, a difference you could feel all the way down to your bones. And then there were the dreams.

But the dreams faded; first to memories of dreams, and then to memories of memories. You only knew that *once* you had remembered something other than this.

You learned not to ask about your parents, but you guessed. Oh, yes, you guessed. And as soon as you were old enough to endure the thrust of a spaceship kicking away from a planet under interstellar drives, they stuck your arm full of needles and they carried you, like a piece of sacked luggage, aboard one of the Big Ships.

Going home, the other boys said, half envious and half afraid. Only you had known better; you were going into exile. And when you woke up, with a fuzzy sick headache, and the feeling that somebody had sliced a big hunk out of your life, the ship was making planetfall for a world called Terra, and there was an elderly couple waiting for the grandson they had never seen.

They said you were twelve or so. They called you Jefferson Andrew Kerwin, Junior. That was what they'd called you in the Spacemen's Orphanage, so you didn't argue. Their skin was darker than yours and their eyes dark, the eyes you'd learned to call animal eyes from your Darkovan nurses; but they'd grown up under a different sun and you already knew about the quality of light; you'd seen the bright lights inside the Terran Zone and remembered how they hurt your eyes. So you were willing to believe it, that these strange dark old people could have been your father's parents. They showed you a picture of a Jefferson Andrew Kerwin when he was about your age, thirteen, a few years before he'd run away as cargo boy on one of the Big Ships, years and years ago. They gave you his room to sleep in, and sent you to his school. They were kind to you, and not more than twice a week did they remind you, by word or look, that you were not the son they had lost, the son who had abandoned them for the stars.

And they never answered questions about your mother, either. They couldn't; they didn't know and they didn't want to know, and what was more, they didn't care. You were Jefferson Andrew Kerwin, of Earth, and that was all they wanted of you.

If it had come when you were younger, it might have been enough. You were hungry to belong somewhere, and the yearning love of these old people, who needed you to be their lost son, might have claimed you for Earth.

But the sky of Earth was a cold burning blue, and the hills a cold unfriendly green; the pale blazing sun hurt your eyes, even behind dark glasses, and the glasses made people think you were trying to hide from them. You spoke the language perfectly— they'd seen to *that* in the orphanage, of course. You could pass. You missed the cold, and the winds that swept down from the pass behind the city, and the distant outline of the high, splintered teeth of the mountains; you missed the dusty dimness of the sky, and the lowered, crimson, blazing eye of the sun. Your grandparents didn't want you to think about Darkover or talk about Darkover and once when you saved up your pocket money and bought a set of

views taken out in the Rim planets, one of them with
a sun like your home sun of Darkover, they took the
pictures away from you. You belonged right here on
Earth, or so they told you.

But you knew better than that. And as soon as you
were old enough, you left. You knew that you were
breaking their hearts all over again, and in a way it
wasn't fair because they had been kind to you, as
kind as they knew how to be. But you left; you had
to. Because you knew, if they didn't, that Jeff
Kerwin, Junior, wasn't the boy they loved. Probably,
if it came to that, the *first* Jeff Kerwin, your father,
hadn't been that boy either, and that was why *he* had
left. They loved something they had made up for
themselves and called their son, and perhaps, you
thought, they'd even be happier with memories and
no real boy around to destroy that image of their
perfect son.

First there was a civilian's job in the Space Service
on Earth, and you worked hard and kept your tongue
between your teeth when the arrogant *Terranan*
stared at your height or made subtle jokes about the
accent you'd never—quite—lost. And then there was
the day when you boarded one of the Big Ships,
awake this time, and willingly, and warranted in the
Civil Service of the Empire, skylifting for stars that
were names in the roll call of your dreams. And you
watched the hated sun of Earth dwindle to a dim
star, and lose itself in the immensity of the big dark,
and you were outward bound on the first installment
of your dream.

Not Darkover. Not yet. But a world with a red sun
that didn't hurt your eyes, for a subordinate's job on
a world of stinks and electric storms, where albino

women were cloistered behind high walls and you never saw a child. And after a year there, there was a good job on a world where men carried knives and the women wore bells in their ears, chiming a wicked allure as they walked. You had liked it there. You had had plenty of fights, and plenty of women. Behind the quiet civil clerk there was a roughneck buried; and on that world he got loose now and then. You'd had good times. It was on that world that you started carrying a knife. Somehow it seemed right to you; you felt a sense of completion when you strapped it on, as if somehow, until now, you had been going around half dressed. You talked this over with the company Psych, and listened to his conjectures about hidden fears of sexual adequacy and compensation with phallic symbols and power compulsions; listened quietly and without comment, and dismissed them, because you knew better than that. He did ask one telling question.

"You were brought up on Cottman Four, weren't you, Kerwin?"

"In the Spacemen's Orphanage there."

"Isn't that one of the worlds where grown men wear swords at all times? Granted, I'm no comparative anthropologist, but if you saw men going around wearing them, all the time. . . ."

You agreed that probably that was it, and didn't say any more, but you kept on wearing the knife, at least when you were off duty, and once or twice you'd had a chance to use it, and proved quietly and to your own satisfaction that you could handle yourself in a fight if you had to.

You had good times there. You could have stayed there and been happy. But there was still a compulsion driving you, a restlessness, and when the Legate died and the new one wanted to bring in his own men, you were ready to leave.

And by now the apprentice years were over. Until now you'd gone where they told you. Now they asked you, within reason, where you wanted to go. And you never hesitated.

"Darkover." And then you amended: "Cottman Four."

The man in Personnel had stared awhile. "God in heaven, why would anyone want to go *there*?"

"No vacancies?" By now you were half resigned to letting the dream die.

"Oh, hell, yes. We can never get volunteers to go there. Do you know what the place is *like*? Cold as sin, among other things, and barbaric—big sections of it barred off to Earthmen, and you won't be safe a step outside the Trade City. I've never been there myself, but the place, from what I hear, is always in an uproar. Added to which, there's practically no trade with the Darkovans."

"No? Thendara Spaceport is one of the biggest in the Service, I heard."

"True." The man explained gloomily, "It's located between the upper and lower spiral arms of the Galaxy, so we have to recruit enough personnel to staff a major re-routing station. Thendara's one of the main stops and transfer points for passengers and cargo. But it's a hell of a place; if you go there, you might be stuck for years before they could locate a replacement for you, once you get tired of it. Look," he added persuasively, "you're getting on too well to throw yourself away out there. Rigel 9 is crying out for good men, and you could really get ahead there—

maybe work up to Consul or even Legâte, if you wanted to get into the Diplomatic branch. Why waste yourself on a half-frozen lump of rock way out at the edge of nowhere?"

You should have known better; but you thought, for once, maybe he really wanted to know; so you told him.

"I was born on Darkover."

"Oh. One of *those*. I see." You saw his face change, and you wanted to smash that smirk off his pink face. But you didn't do it; you only stood there and watched him stamp your transfer application, and you knew that if you had ever had any intention of transfer to the Diplomatic Branch, or any hopes of working up to Legate, whatever he had stamped on your card had just killed them off; but you didn't care. And then there was another of the Big Ships, and a growing excitement that gnawed at you so that you haunted the observation dome, searching for a red coal in the sky that grew at last to a blaze haunting your dreams. And then, after a time that seemed endless, the ship dropped lazily toward a great crimson planet that wore a necklace of four tiny moons, jewels set in the pendant of a carmine sky.

And you were home again.

Chapter Two: The Matrix

The *Southern Crown* made planet-fall at high noon on dayside. Jeff Kerwin, swinging efficiently down the narrow steel rungs of the ladder from the airlock, dropped to the ground and took a deep breath. It had seemed that the very air should hold something rich and different and familiar and strange.

But it was just air. It smelled good, but after weeks of the canned air inside the spaceship, any air would smell good. He inhaled it again, searching for some hint of his elusive memory in the fragrance. It was cold and bracing, with a hint of pollen and dust; but mostly it held the impersonal chemical stinks of any spaceport. Hot tar. Concrete dust. The stinging ozone of liquid oxygen vaporizing from bleeder valves.

Might as well be back Earthside! Just another spaceport!

Well, what the hell? He told himself roughly to come off it. *The way you built it up in your mind, getting back to Darkover, you made it such a big deal that if the whole city came out to meet you with parades and fanfares, it would still fall flat!*

He stepped back, out of the way of a group of Spaceforce men—tall in black leather, booted, blasters concealing their menace behind snug holsters—with stars blazing on their sleeves. The sun was just a fraction off the meridian—huge, red-orange, with little ragged fiery clouds hanging high in the thin sky. The saw-toothed mountains behind the spaceport cast their shadows over the Trade City, but the peaks lay bathed in the sullen light. Memory searched for landmarks along the peaks. Kerwin's eyes fixed on the horizon, he stumbled over a cargo bale, and a good-natured voice said, "Star-gazing, Redhead?"

Kerwin brought himself back to the spaceport, with a wrench almost physical. "I've seen enough stars to last me awhile," he said. "I was thinking that the air smells good."

The man at his side grinned. "That's one comfort. I spent one tour of duty on a world where the air was high-sulfur content. Perfectly healthy, or so the Medics said, but I went around feeling as if someone had thrown a whole case of rotten eggs at me."

He joined Kerwin on the concrete platform. "What's it like—being home again?"

"I don't know yet," said Kerwin, but he looked at the newcomer with something like affection. Johnny Ellers was small and stocky and going bald on top, a tough little man in the black leather of a professional spaceman. Two dozen stars blazed in a riot of color on his sleeve; a star for every world where he had seen service. Kerwin, only a two-star man so far, had found Ellers a fund of information about almost every planet and every subject under the sun—any sun.

"We'd better move along," Ellers said. The process crew was already swarming over the ship, readying it for skylift again within a few hours. Favorable orbits waited for no man. The spaceport was already jammed with cargo trucks, workhands, buzz-

ing machinery, fuel trucks, and and instructions were
being yelled in fifty languages and dialects. Kerwin
looked around, getting his bearings. Beyond the
spaceport gates lay the Trade City, the Terran
Headquarters Building—and Darkover. He wanted
to run toward it, but he checked himself, moving
with Ellers into the line that was forming, to verify
their identities and assignments. He gave up a fingerprint and signed a card verifying that he was who he
said he was, received an identity certificate, and
moved on.

"Where to?" asked Ellers, joining him again.

"I don't know," Kerwin said slowly. "I suppose
I'd better report to the HQ for assignment." He had
no formal plans beyond this moment, and he wasn't
sure he wanted Ellers butting in and taking over.
Much as he liked Ellers, he would have preferred to
get reacquainted with Darkover on his own.

Ellers chuckled. "Report? Hell, you know better
than that. You're no greenie, still bug-eyed about his
first off-planet assignment! Tomorrow morning is
time enough for the red tape. For tonight—" He
waved an expansive hand toward the spaceport
gates. "Wine, women and song—not necessarily in
that order."

Kerwin hesitated, and Ellers urged, "Come on! I
know the Trade City like the back of my hand.
You've got to fit yourself out—and I know all the
markets. If you do your shopping at the tourist traps,
you can spend six months' pay without half trying!"

That was true. The Big Ships were still too weight-
conscious to permit transshipping of clothing and
personal gear. It was cheaper to dispose of everything
when you transferred, and buy a new outfit when you

landed, than to take it along and pay the weight allowances. Every spaceport in the Terran Empire was surrounded with a ring of shops, good, bad, and indifferent, all the way from luxury fashion centers to second-hand rag markets.

"And I know all the high spots, too. You haven't lived till you've tried Darkovan *firi*. You know, back in the mountains they tell some funny stories about that stuff, especially its effect on women. One time, I remember—"

Kerwin let Ellers lead, listening with half an ear to the little man's story, which was already taking a familiar turn. To hear Ellers talk, he had had so many women, on so many worlds, that Kerwin sometimes wondered vaguely how he'd had time in between to get into space. The heroines of the stories ranged all the way from a Sirian bird-woman, with great blue wings and a cloak of down, to a princess of Arcturus IV surrounded by the handmaidens who are bound to her with links of living pseudoflesh till the day she dies.

The spaceport gates opened into a great square, surrounding a monument raised on high steps, and a little park with trees. Kerwin looked at the trees, their violet leaves trembling in the wind, and swallowed.

Once he had known the Trade City fairly well. It had grown some since then—and it had shrunk. The looming skyscraper of Terran HQ, once awesome, was now just a big building. The ring of shops around the square was deeper. He did not remember having seen, as a child, the loom of the massive, neon-fronted Sky Harbor Hotel. He sighed, trying to sort out the memories.

They crossed the square and turned into a street paved with hewn blocks of stone, so immense in size that it paralyzed his imagination to guess who or what had laid down those vast slabs. The street lay quiet and empty; Kerwin supposed that most of the Terran population had gone to see the starship touch down, and at this hour few Darkovans would be on the street. The real city still lay out of sight, out of hearing—out of reach. He sighed again, and followed Ellers toward the string of spaceport shops.

"We can get a decent outfit in here."

It was a Darkovan shop, which meant that it spilled out halfway along the street and there was no clear distinction between outside and in, between the merchandise for sale and the owner's belongings. But this much concession had been made to custom of the alien Terrans, that some of the goods for sale were on racks and tables. As Kerwin passed beneath the outer arch, his nostrils dilated in recognition of a breath of the familiar; a whiff of scented smoke, the incense that perfumes every Darkovan home from gutter to palace. They hadn't used it, not officially, in the Spacemen's Orphanage in the Trade City; but most of the nurses and matrons were Darkovan, and the resinous fumes had clung to their hair and clothing. Ellers wrinkled his nose and made an "Ugh!" sound, but Kerwin found himself smiling. It was the first touch of genuine recognition in a world gone strange.

The shopkeeper, a little withered man in a yellow shirt and breeches, turned and murmured an idle formula: *"S'dia Shaya."* It meant *you lend me grace,* and without thinking about it, Kerwin muttered an equally meaningless polite formula; and Ellers stared.

"I didn't know you spoke the lingo! You told me you left here when you were just a kid!"

"I only speak the City dialect." The little man was turning to a colorful rack of cloaks, jerkins, silken vests and tunics, and Kerwin, exasperated with himself, said curtly in Terran Standard, "Nothing like that. Clothing for *Terranan*, fellow."

He concentrated on picking out a few changes of clothing—underwear, nightgear, just what he could get along with for a few days until he found out what the job and climate would demand. There were heavy mountain-weight parkas, intended for the mountains in the climbing preserves of Rigel and Capella Nine, lined with synthetic fibers, guaranteed to safeguard body heat down to minus thirty Centigrade or well below, and he shrugged it aside, though Ellers, shivering, had already bought one and put it on; it wasn't *that* cold even in the Hellers, and here in Thendara it felt like shirtsleeve weather to him. He warned Ellers in an undertone against buying shaving gear.

"Hell, Kerwin, going native? Going to grow a beard?"

"No, but you'll get better ones in the Service canteens inside the HQ: Darkover is metal-poor, and what metals they have aren't as good as ours, and cost a hell of a lot more."

While the shopkeeper was making up the parcels, Ellers drifted to a table near the entry-way.

"What sort of outfit is this, Kerwin? I've never seen anyone on Darkover wearing anything quite like *this*. Is it native Darkovan costume?"

Kerwin flinched; *native Darkovan costume* was a concept, like *the Darkovan language,* which consisted only in the simplifications of Empire outsiders. There were nine Darkovan languages he knew about—although he could speak only one well, with a smattering of words from two others—and costume on Darkover varied enormously, from the silks and fine-spun colors of the lowlands to the coarse leathers and undyed furs of the far mountains. He joined his friend at the table, where a tangle of odd garments, all more or less worn, most of them the utilitarian coarse breeches and shirts of the city, were flung at random there; but Kerwin saw at once what had attracted Ellers's eye. It was a thing of beauty, green and dull yellows blended, richly embroidered in patterns that seemed familiar to him; he suspected he was more fatigued than he realized. He held it up and saw that it was a long, hooded cloak.

"It's a riding-cape," he said. "They wear them in the Kilghard Hills; and from the embroidery it probably belonged to a nobleman; could be his house colors, though I don't know what it signifies, or how it came here. They're warm and they're comfortable, especially for riding, but even when I was a kid, this kind of cloak was going out of fashion down here in the city; stuff like that—" he pointed to the offworld synthetic parka Ellers was wearing—"was cheaper and just as warm. These cloaks are handmade, hand dyed, hand embroidered." He took the cloak from Ellers. It was not a woven fabric, but a soft, supple leather, fine as woven wool, flexible as silk, and richly embroidered in metallic threads: The rich dyes were a riot of color spilling over his arm.

"It looks as if it had been made for a prince," commented Ellers in an undertone. "Look at that fur! What kind of beast is *that* from?"

The shopkeeper burst out into a voluble sales pitch

about the costliness of the fur, scenting customers; but Kerwin laughed and cut him off with a gesture.

"Rabbithorn," he said. "They raise them like sheep. If it was wild *marl*-fur, this *would* be a cloak for a prince. As it is, I suppose it belonged to some poor gentleman attached to a nobleman's household—one with a talented and industrious wife or daughter who could spend a year embroidering it for him."

"But the embroideries, nobles, the patterns, fit for *Comyn,* the richness of the dyed leather . . ."

"What it looks, is *warm,*" Kerwin said, settling the cloak over his shoulders. It felt very soft and rich. Ellers stepped back, regarding him with consternation.

"Good lord, are you going native already? You aren't going to wear *that* thing around the Terran Zone, are you?"

Kerwin laughed heartily. "I should say not. I was thinking it might be something to wear around my room in the evenings. If bachelor quarters in HQ are anything like they were at my last assignment, they're damn stingy with the heat, unless you want to pay a double assessment for energy use. And it gets fairly cold in the winter, too. Of course it's nice and warm here now—"

Ellers shivered and said gloomily, "If this is *warm,* I hope I'm at the other end of the Galaxy when it gets *cold* ! Man, your bones must be made of some kind of stuff I don't understand. This is *freezing*! Oh, well, one man's planet is another man's hell," he said, quoting a proverb of the Service. "But man, you aren't going to spend a month's pay on that damn thing, are you?"

"Not if I can help it," Kerwin replied out of the

corner of his mouth, "but if you don't shut up and let me bargain with him, I just might!"

In the end he paid more than he had expected, and told himself he was a fool as he counted it over. But he wanted the thing, for no reason he could explain; it was the first thing that had taken his fancy after his return to Darkover. He wanted it, and in the end he got it for a price he could afford, though not easily. He sensed, toward the end of the bargaining, that the shopkeeper was uneasy, for some reason, about haggling with him, and gave in much easier than Kerwin had expected. He knew, if Ellers didn't, that he had really gotten the thing for somewhat less than its value. Considerably less, if the truth be told.

"That kind of money would have kept you happily drunk for half a year," Ellers mourned as they came out on the street again.

Kerwin chuckled. "Cheer up. Fur isn't a luxury on a planet like this, it's a good investment. And I've still got enough in my pocket for the first round of drinks. Where can we get them?"

They got them in a wineshop on the outer edge of the sector; it was clear of tourists, although a few of the workhands from the spaceport were mingled with the Darkovans crowded around the bar or sprawled on the long couches along the walls. They were all giving their attention to the serious business of drinking, talking, or gambling with what looked like dominoes or small cut-crystal prisms.

A few of the Darkovans glanced up as the two Earthmen threaded their way through the crowd and sat down at a table. Ellers had cheered up by the time a plump, dark-haired girl came to take their order. He gave the girl a pinch on her round thigh, ordered wine in the spaceport jargon, and, hauling the Darkovan cloak across the table to feel the fur, launched into a long tale about how he had found a particular fur blanket particularly worthwhile on a cold planet of Lyra.

"The nights up there are about seven days long, and the people there just shut down all their work until the sun comes up again and melts off the ice. I tell you, that babe and I just crawled inside that fur blanket and never put our noses outside . . ."

Kerwin applied himself to his drink, losing the thread of the story—not that it mattered, for Ellers's stories were all alike anyhow. A man sitting at one of the tables alone, over a half-emptied goblet, looked up, met Kerwin's eyes, and suddenly got up—so quickly that he upset his chair. He started to come toward the table where they were sitting; then he saw Ellers, whose back had been turned to him, stopped short and took a step backward, seeming both confused and surprised. But at that moment Ellers, reaching a lull in his story, looked round and grinned.

"Ragan, you old so-and-so! Might have known I'd find you in here! How long has it been, anyhow? Come and have a drink!"

Ragan hesitated, and it seemed to Kerwin that he flicked an uneasy glance in his direction.

"Ah, come on," Ellers urged. "Want you to meet a pal of mine. Jeff Kerwin."

Ragan came and sat down. Kerwin couldn't make out what the man was. He was small and slight, with a lithe sunburnt look, the look of an outdoor man, and callused hands; he might have been an undersized mountain Darkovan, or an Earthman wearing

Darkovan clothes, though he wore the ubiquitous climbing jacket and calf-high boots. But he spoke Terran Standard as well as either of the Earthmen, asking Ellers about the trip out, and when the second round of drinks came, he insisted on paying for them. But he kept looking at Kerwin sidewise, when he thought he wouldn't be noticed.

Kerwin demanded at last: "All right, what is it? You acted as if it was me you recognized, before Ellers called you over—"

"Right. I didn't know Ellers was in yet," Ragan said, "but then I saw him with you, and saw you wearing—" He gestured at Kerwin's Terran outfit. "So I knew you couldn't be who I thought you were. I *don't* know you, do I?" he added, with a puzzled frown.

"I don't think so," Kerwin said, sizing the man up, and wondering if he could have been one of the kids from the Spaceman's Orphanage. It was impossible to tell, after—how long? Ten or twelve years, Terran reckoning; he'd forgotten the conversion factors for the Darkovan year. Even if they'd been childhood friends, that amount of time would have wiped it out. And he didn't remember anyone named Ragan, although that didn't mean anything.

"But you're not Terran, are you," Ragan inquired.

The memory of a clerk's sneer—*one of those*—rushed through Kerwin's mind; but he shoved it aside. "My father was. I was born here, brought up in the Spaceman's Orphanage. I left pretty young, though."

"That must be it," Ragan said. "I spent a few years there. I do liaison work for the Trade City

when they have to hire Darkovans: guides, moun-
taineers, that kind of thing. Organize caravans into
the mountains, into the other Trade cities, whatever.''

Kerwin was still trying to decide whether the man
had a recognizably Darkovan accent. He finally
asked him. ''Are you Darkovan?''

Ragan shrugged. The bitterness in his voice was
really appalling. ''Who knows? For that matter, who
cares?''

He lifted his glass and drank. Kerwin followed
suit, sensing that he would be drunk fairly soon; he
never was much of a drinker and the Darkovan
liquor, which of course as a child he had never tasted,
was strong stuff. It didn't seem to matter. Ragan was
staring again and that didn't seem to matter either.

Kerwin thought, *Maybe we're a lot the same. My mother was probably Darkovan; if she'd been Terran, there'd have
been records. She could have been anything. My father was in
the Space Service; that's the one thing I know for sure. But
apart from that, who and what am I? And how did he come
to have a halfbreed son?*

''At least he cared enough to get Empire citizenship for you,'' Ragan said bitterly, and Jeff stared,
not realizing that he had actually been saying all this
aloud. ''Mine didn't even care that much!''

''But you've got red in your hair,'' Jeff said and
wondered why he had said it, but Ragan seemed not
to hear, staring into his glass, and Ellers interrupted,
with an air of injury:

''Listen, you two, this is supposed to be a celebra-
tion! Drink up!''

Ragan leaned his chin in his hands, staring across
the table at Kerwin. ''So you came here, at least part-

ly, to try and locate your parents—your people?"

"To find out something about them," Kerwin amended.

"Had it ever occurred to you that you might be better off not knowing?"

It had. He'd been all the way through that and out the other side. "I don't care if my mother was one of those girls," he said, nodding toward the women who were coming and going, fetching drinks, stopping to chaff with the men, exchanging jokes and innuendos. "I want to *know* about it."

To be sure which world can claim me, Darkover or Terra. To be certain . . .

"But aren't there records at the orphanage?"

"I haven't had a chance to look," Kerwin said. "That's the first place to go, anyhow. I don't know how much they can tell me. But it's a good place to start."

"And if they can't tell you anything? Nothing else?"

Kerwin fumbled, with fingers made clumsy by drink, at the copper chain that had been around his neck as long as he could remember. He said, "Only this. They told me, in the orphanage, that it was around my neck when I came there."

They didn't like it. The matron told me I was too big to wear lucky charms, and tried to get it away from me. I screamed . . . why had I forgotten that? . . . and fought so hard that they finally let me keep it. Why in the hell would I do that? My grandparents didn't like it, either, and I learned to keep it out of sight.

"Oh, nuts," interrupted Ellers rudely. "The long-lost talisman! So you'll show it to them and they'll recognize that you're the long-lost son and heir to the Lord High Muckety-Muck in his castle, and you'll live happily ever after!" He made an indescribable sound of derision. Kerwin felt angry color flooding his face. If Ellers really believed that rubbish. . . .

"Can I have a look at it?" Ragan asked, holding out his hand.

Kerwin slipped the chain off his neck; but when Ragan would have taken it, he cradled it in his palm; it had always made him nervous for anyone else to touch it. He had never wanted to ask them, in Psych, just why. They probably would have had a pat and ready answer, something slimy about his subconscious mind.

The chain was of copper, a valuable metal on Darkover. But the blue stone itself had always seemed unremarkable to him; a cheap trinket, something a poor girl might treasure; not even carved, just a pretty blue crystal, a bit of glass.

But Ragan's eyes narrowed as he looked at it, and he gave a low whistle. "By the wolf of Alar! You know what this is, Kerwin?"

Kerwin shrugged. "Some semiprecious stone from the Hellers, I suppose. I'm no geologist."

"It's a matrix jewel," Ragan said, and at Kerwin's blank stare, elaborated, "a psychokinetic crystal."

"I'm lost," Ellers said, and stretched out his hand to take the small gem. Quickly, protectively, Kerwin closed his hand over it, and Ragan raised his eyebrows.

"Keyed?"

"I don't know what you're talking about," Kerwin said, "only I somehow don't like people touching it. Silly, I suppose."

"Not at all," Ragan said, and suddenly seemed to make up his mind.

"I have one," he said. "Nothing like that size; a

little one, the kind they sell in the markets for suit-case locks and children's toys. One like yours—well, they don't just lie around in the street, you know; it's probably worth a small fortune, and if it was ever monitored on any of the main banks, it won't be hard to tell who it belonged to. But even the little ones like mine—" He took a small wrapped roll of leather out of an inside pocket and carefully unrolled the leather. A tiny blue crystal rolled out.

"They're like that," he said. "Maybe they have a low-level form of life, no one has ever figured out. Anyway, they're definitely one-man jewels; seal a lock with one of them, and nothing will ever open it except your own *intention* to open it."

"Are you saying they're magic?" Ellers demanded angrily.

"Hell, no. They register your brainwaves and their distinct EEG patterns, or something like that; like a fingerprint. So somehow you are the only person who can open that lock; a great way to protect your private papers. That's what I use this one for. Oh, I can do a few tricks with it."

Kerwin stared at the small blue jewel in Ragan's palm. It was smaller than his own, but the same distinctive color. He repeated it slowly: "Matrix jewel."

Ellers, sobering briefly, stared at Kerwin and said, "Yeah. The big secret of Darkover. The Terrans have been trying to beg, borrow, or steal some of the secrets of matrix technology for generations. There was a big war fought here about that, twelve, twenty years ago—I don't remember, long before my time. Oh, the Darkovans bring little ones into the Trade City, like Ragan's there, and sell them; trade them off for drugs, or metals, usually daggers, or small

tools, or camera lenses. Somehow, they transform
energy without fission by-products. But they're so
small; we keep hearing rumors of big ones. Bigger
ones even than yours, Jeff. But no Darkovan will talk
about them. Hey," he said, grinning, "maybe you *are*
the lost heir to the Lord High Muckety-Muck in his
castle after all! It's for sure no bar girl would be
wearing a thing like that!"

Kerwin cradled the thing in his hand, but he did
not look at it. It made his eyes blur with a strange
dizzy sickness. He tucked it inside his shirt again. He
did not like the way Ragan was staring at him.
Somehow it *reminded* him of something.

Ragan shoved his own small crystal—it was no
longer than the bead a woman might braid at the end
of a long tress—toward Kerwin. He said, "Can you
look into it?"

*Someone had said that to him before. At some time someone
had said,* Look into the matrix. *A woman's voice, low. Or
had she said,* Do not look into the matrix. . . . His head
hurt. Pettishly he pushed the stone away. Ragan's
eyebrows went up again in appraisal. "That much,
huh? Can you use yours?"

"Use it? How? I don't know *one damn thing* about
it," he said rudely. Ragan shrugged; he said, "I can
only do tricks with mine. Watch."

He up-ended the rough green-glass goblet to drink
the last few drops from it, then turned it bottom-up
and laid the tiny blue crystal on the foot of the goblet.
His face took on an intent, concentrated stare;
abruptly there was a small eye-hurting flash, a sizzling sound, and the rigid stem of the goblet melted,
sagged sidewise, slid into a puddle of green glass. Ellers gasped and swore. Kerwin passed his hand over

his eyes; the goblet sat there, bowed down with the wilted stem. There was a Terran artist, he remembered from a course in art history, who had painted things like fur teacups and limp watches. History had judged him a lunatic, rather than a genius. The goblet, stem lolling to one side, looked just as surrealistic as his work.

"Could I do that? Could anybody?"

"With one the size of yours, you could do a hell of a lot more," Ragan said, "if you knew how to use it. I don't know how they work; but if you concentrate on them, they can move small objects, produce intense heat, or—well, other things. It doesn't take much training to play around with the ones this size."

Kerwin touched the lump at his chest. He said, "Then it isn't just a trinket."

"Hell, no. It's worth a small fortune—maybe a big one; I'm no judge. I'm surprised they didn't take it away from you before you left Darkover, considering how hard the Terrans have been trying to get hold of some of the larger ones, to experiment with them and test their limits."

Another of those dim memories surfaced. Drugged, on the Big Ship that had taken him to Terra, a stewardess or attendant of some sort fumbling with the jewel; waking, screaming, nightmares. He had thought it a side-effect of the drugs. He said somberly, "I think maybe they tried."

"I'm sure the authorities at the HQ would give a lot to have one that size to play around with," Ragan sad. "You might consider turning it over to them; they'd probably give you anything you wanted for it, within reason. You might be able to get a really good assignment out of them."

Kerwin grinned. He said, "Since I feel like hell whenever I take it off, that would present—some difficulties."

"You mean you never take it off?" Ellers demanded drunkenly. "That must present some troubles. You don't take it off even in the bath?"

Kerwin said, with a chuckle, "Oh, I *can*. I don't like to; I feel—oh, I don't know, *weird*—when I take it off. Or leave it off for any amount of time." He had always berated himself for being superstitious, irrational, compulsive, treating the thing as a fetish.

Ragan shook his head. "Like I say, they're a strange kind of thing. They—hell, this makes no sense, but it *happens:* I don't know how it works, I just know it does; maybe they *are* a low form of life. See, they *attach* themselves to you; you can't just walk away and leave them behind, and nobody I heard of ever lost one. I know a man who kept losing his keys until he got one of these to tag on his keyring, and whenever he left it behind, believe me, he *knew* where it was."

That, Kerwin thought, explained a lot. Including a child, screaming as if he were half his age, when a Terran no-nonsense matron deprived him of his "lucky charm." They had had to give it back to him in the end. He wondered, with a shiver, what would have happened if they had *not*. He didn't think he wanted to know. He touched the hidden jewel again, shaking his head, remembering his childish sureness that this held the key to his hidden past, to his identity and the identity of his mother, to his obscured memories and half-forgotten dreams.

"Of course," he said with heavy irony, "I was hoping it was that amulet that really *would* prove I was the long-lost son and heir of your Lord-High-

Something-or-Other. Now all my illusions have been shattered." He raised the goblet to his lips, calling the Darkovan girl to bring them more of the same.

And as he did so, his eyes fell on the goblet whose stem Ragan had melted. Hell, was he drunker than he'd ever believed?

The goblet stood upright on a solid green stem, unbroken, unsagging. There was nothing whatever wrong with it.

Chapter Three: The Strangers

Three drinks later Ragan excused himself, saying he had a commission at the HQ and had to report on it before he could get paid. When he had gone, Kerwin scowled impatiently at Ellers, who had matched Ragan drink for drink. This wasn't the way he had wanted to spend his first night back on the world whose image he'd carried in his mind since childhood. He didn't know quite what he *did* want— but it wasn't to sit in a spaceport bar all night and get drunk!

"Look, Ellers—"

Only a gentle snore answered him; Ellers had slid down in his seat, out cold.

The plump Darkovan bar girl came with refills— Kerwin had lost track of how many—and looked at Ellers with a professional mixture of disappointment and resignation. Then, with a quick glance at Kerwin, he could see her shift her focus of interest; bending to pour, she brushed artfully against Kerwin. Her loose robe was unpinned at the throat so that he could see the valley between her breasts, and the familiar sweet smell of incense clung to her robe and her hair. A thread of awareness plucked a string deep in his gut, as he breathed in the scent of Darkover, of woman; but he looked again and saw that her eyes were hard and shallow, and the music of her voice frayed at the edges when she crooned, "You like what you see, big man?"

She spoke broken Terran Standard, not the musical idiom of the City dialect; that, Kerwin knew afterward, was what had bothered him most. "You like Lomie, big man? You come 'long with me, I nice and warm, you see . . ."

There was a flat taste in Kerwin's mouth that wasn't just the aftertaste of the wine. Whatever the sky and sun, whatever they called the world, the girls around the Terran Trade City bars were all the same.

"You come? You come—?"

Without knowing quite what he was going to do, Kerwin grabbed the edge of the table and heaved himself up, the bench going over with a crash behind him. He loomed over the girl, glaring through the dim and smoky light, and words in a language long forgotten rushed from his lips:

"Be gone with you, daughter of a mountain goat, and cover your shame elsewhere, not by lying with men from worlds that despise your own! Where is the pride of the Cahuenga, shameful one?"

The girl gasped, cowered backward, a convulsive hand clutching her robe about her bared breasts, and bent almost to the ground. She swallowed, but for a moment her mouth only moved, without sound; then she whispered, *"S'dia shaya . . . d'sperdo, vai dom alzuo. . . ."* and fled, sobbing; the sound of the sob and the scent of her musky hair lingered in the room behind her.

Kerwin clung, swaying, to the edge of the table. *God, how drunk can you get! What was all that stuff I was spouting, anyway?* He was bewildered at himself; where did he get off anyway, scaring the poor girl out of her wits? He was no more virtuous than the next man. What Puritan remnant had prompted him to rise up in wrath and demolish her that way? He'd had his share of the spaceport wenches on more worlds than one.

And what language had he been speaking, anyway? He *knew* it hadn't been the city dialect, but what *was* it? He could not remember; try as he might, not a syllable remained of the words that had come into his mind; only the form of the emotion remained.

Ellers, fortunately, had snored through the whole thing; he could imagine the ribbing the older man would have given him, if he hadn't. He thought, *We'd better get out of here while I can still navigate—and before I do something else that's crazy!*

He bent and shook Ellers, but Ellers didn't even mumble. Kerwin remembered that Ellers had drunk as much as Kerwin and Ragan put together. He did this in every spaceport. Kerwin shrugged, set the bench he'd knocked over back on its legs, lifted Ellers's feet to them, and turned unsteadily toward the door.

Air. Fresh air. That was all he needed. Then he'd better get back inside the Terran Zone; at least, inside the spaceport gates, he knew how to behave. But, he thought confused, I *thought* I knew how to behave here on Darkover. What got into me?

The sun, bleared and angry-looking, lay low over the street. Shadows of deep mauve and indigo folded the huddled houses in a friendly gloom. There were people on the streets now, Darkovans in colorful shirts and breeches, wearing heavy woven capes or the commonplace imported climbing jackets; women muffled to the eyebrows in fur; and once, gliding along, a tall form invisible beneath a hood and mantle of strange cut and color; but the gliding form was not human.

And even as he paused, looking up at the flaming sky, the sun sank with a rush and the swift dark came swooping across the sky, a darkness like great soft wings, folding to blot out the brilliance; the fast-dropping night that gave this world its name. Leaping out in a sudden glare came the crown of vast white stars; and three of the small jeweled moons were in the sky, jade-green, peacock-blue, rose-pearl.

Kerwin stood staring upward, his eyes wet, unashamed of the sudden tears that had started to them. It was not illusion, then, despite the commonplace spaceport bars and the disillusion of the streets. It was real; he was home again; he had seen the falling dark over the sky, the blaze of the crown of stars they called Hastur's Crown after the legend . . . He stood there until, with the sudden cooling of the air, the thick nightly mist gathered and the blaze dimmed, then vanished.

Slowly, he walked on. The first thin misty traces of rain were stirring; the tall beacon of the HQ in the sky gave him his bearings, and he moved, reluctantly, in that direction.

He was thinking of the Darkovan girl in the bar, the one he had rebuffed so unexpectedly—and so strangely. She had been warm and lissome, and she was clean, and what more could a man want for a welcome home? Why had he sent her away—and sent her away like *that*?

He felt strangely restless, at loose ends. Home? A home meant more than a familiar sky and stars overhead. A home meant people. He had had a home on Earth, if that was what he wanted. No, he thought soberly; his grandparents had never wanted him, only a second chance to remake his father in their own image. In space? Ellers, perhaps, was the closest friend he had, and what was Johnny Ellers? A bum of the spaceports, a planet-hopper. Kerwin felt the sudden hunger for roots, a home, for a people and a world he had never known. Never been allowed to know. The words he had said, self-deriding, to Ellers, came back to his mind: *I had hoped it was the amulet that would prove I was the long-lost son and heir.* . . .

Yes; he knew it now, that was the dream that had lured him back to Darkover, the fantasy that he would find a place where he belonged. Otherwise, why should he have left the last world? He'd liked it there; there had been plenty of fights, plenty of women, plenty of easygoing companionship, plenty of rough and ready adventure. But all the time, driving him, there had been that relentless compulsion to get back to Darkover; it had caused him to turn down what he knew, now, had been a sure route to advancement; and further, to kill off any hope of serious promotion.

And now that he was back, now that he had seen the four moons and the swift dark of his dreams, would all the rest be anticlimax? Would he find that his mother was just such another spaceport wench as the one who had rubbed up against him tonight, eager to take home some of the plentiful spaceport pay? If so, he didn't admire his father's taste. His father? He had heard a lot about his father, in those seven years he'd stuck it out with his grandparents, and the picture he'd gotten from them wasn't quite like that. His father, he assumed, had been a fastidious man. But that was only, perhaps, how he had seemed to his grandmother. . . . Well, at least he had cared enough to get Empire citizenship for his son.

Well, he'd do what he'd come here to do. He would try to trace his mother, and decide why his father had abandoned him in the spaceport orphanage and how and where he had died. And then? *What then?* The question nagged him—what would he do then?

I will fly that hawk when his pinions are grown, Kerwin said to himself, realizing afterward that he had spoken the Darkovan proverb without thinking about it.

The nocturnal mist had condensed now, and a thin cold rain was beginning to fall. It had been so warm during the day that Kerwin had almost forgotten how swiftly daytime warmth, at this season, was blotted out in sleety rain and snow. Already there were little needles of ice in the rain. He shivered and walked faster.

Somehow he had taken a wrong turning; he had expected to come out into the square fronting on the spaceport. He was on an open square, but it was not the right one. Along one edge there was a line of little cafés and cookshops, taverns and restaurants. There were Terrans there, so it was certainly not off limits to spaceport personnel—he knew that some of them were, he had been carefully briefed about that—but horses were tethered outside, so there was a Darkovan clientele also. He walked along outside them,

picked one that smelled richly of Darkovan food, and
walked inside at random. The smell made his mouth
water. Food; that was what he needed, good solid
food, not the tasteless synthetics of the starship. In
the dim lights faces were all a blur, and he didn't
look for any of the men from the *Southern Crown*.

He sat down at the corner table and ordered, and
when the food came, he sank his teeth into it with
pleasure. Not far away a couple of Darkovans, rather
better dressed than most, were idling over their food.
They wore gaily colored cloaks and high boots, jeweled belts with knives stuck into them. One had a
blazing red head of hair, which made Kerwin raise
his eyebrows; the city Darkovans were a swarthy lot,
and his own red hair had made him an object of
curiosity and stares when, as a child, he'd gone out
into the city. His father and grandparents, too, had
dark hair and eyes, and he had blazed like a beacon
among them. In the orphanage they'd called him
Tallo—copper; half in derision, half, he recognized it
now, in a kind of superstitious awe. And the Darkovan nurses and matrons had been at such pains to
suppress the nickname that even then it had surprised him. He had collected the notion somehow,
though the Darkovan nurses were forbidden to talk
local superstitions to the children, that red hair was
unlucky, or taboo.

If it was unlucky the redhead certainly didn't seem
to know about it or care.

On Earth, perhaps because red hair was really not
all that uncommon, the memory of that superstition
had dimmed. But maybe that explained Ragan's early stare. If red hair was all that uncommon, obviously
you would assume, if you saw a red-haired man at a

distance, that he was the man you knew, and be surprised when it turned out to be a stranger.

Though, come to think of it, Ragan's own hair had a rusty dull-red look to it; he might have been redheaded as a child. Kerwin thought again that the little man had looked familiar, and tried again to remember if there had been any redheads, other than himself, in the orphanage. Surely he had known a couple of them when he was very small. . . .

Maybe before I went to the orphanage. Maybe my mother was redheaded, or had some relatives who were. . . . But try as he might, he could not uncover the blankness of the early years. Only a memory of disturbing dreams . . .

A loudspeaker on the wall hiccuped loudly, and a metallic voice remarked, "Your attention please. All spaceport personnel, your attention please."

Kerwin lifted his eyebrows, staring at the loudspeaker with definite resentment. He'd come in here to get away from things like that. Evidently some of the other patrons of the restaurant felt the same way; there were a couple of derisive noises.

The metallic voice remarked, in Terran Standard, "Your attention please. All HQ personnel with planes on the field report immediately to Division B. All surface transit will be cancelled, repeat, will be cancelled. The *Southern Crown* will skylift on schedule, repeat, on schedule. All surface aircraft on the field must be moved without delay. Repeat, all HQ personnel with private surface aircraft on the field . . ."

The redheaded Darkovan Kerwin had noticed before said in an audible and malicious voice—and in the City dialect everyone understood—"How poor these Terrans must be, that they must disturb us all with that squawking box up there instead of paying a few pennies to a flunkey to bring their messages." The word he used for "flunkey" was a particularly offensive one.

A uniformed spaceport official near the front of the restaurant stared angrily at the speaker, then thought better of it, settled his gold-lace cap on his head and tramped out into the rain. A blast of bitter cold blew into the room—for he had started a small exodus—and the Darkovan nearest Kerwin said to his companion, *"Esa so vhalle Terranan acqualle . . ."* and chuckled.

The other replied something even more insulting, his eyes lingering on Kerwin, and Kerwin realized that he was the only Terran left in the room. He felt himself trembling. He had always been childishly sensitive to insults. On Earth he had been an alien, a freak, a Darkovan; here on Darkover, suddenly, he felt himself a Terran; and the events of the day hadn't been calculated to sweeten his disposition. But he only glared and remarked—to the empty table at his left, "The rain can only drown the mud-rabbit if he hasn't the wit to keep his mouth shut."

One of the Darkovans—not the redhead—pushed his bench back and swung around, upsetting his drink in the process. The thin crash of the metal goblet, and the bleat of the waiter, drew all eyes to them, and Kerwin edged out of his seat. Inside he was watching himself with dismay. Was he going to make *two* scenes, in *two* bars, and would this rip-rousing welcome to Darkover end up by getting him hauled off to the local brig for being drunk and disorderly?

Then the man's companion grabbed his elbow and

said something urgent that Kerwin didn't hear. The first man's eyes traveled slowly upward, rested on Kerwin's head, now clearly illumined by a lamp in a bracket over him, and he said with a little gulp, "No! I want no trouble with Comyn. . . ."

Kerwin wondered what in the hell he was talking about. The would-be fighter looked at his companion, found no encouragement there; then he flung up his arm before his face, mumbled something that sounded like *"Su serva, vai dom . . ."*, barged across the room, avoiding tables like a sleepwalker, and plunged out into the rain.

Kerwin realized that everybody left in the little restaurant was staring at him; but he managed to meet the eyes of the waiter long enough to drive him away. He sat down and picked up his cup, which contained the local equivalent of coffee—a caffeine-rich beverage tasting remotely like bitter chocolate—and sipped. It was cold.

The remaining well-dressed Darkovan, the redheaded one, got up, came over, and slid into the empty seat across from Kerwin.

"Who the hell are you?"

He spoke Terran Standard, to Jeff's surprise; but he spoke it badly, forming each word with care.

Kerwin set his cup down wearily.

"Nobody you know, friend. Go away, will you?"

"No, I am serious," the red-haired man said. "What is your name?"

And suddenly Kerwin was exasperated. What right did this chap have to come over and demand that he give an account of himself?

"Evil-eye Fleegle, a very ancient god," he said. "And I feel every millennium of it. Go away or I'll put the whammy on you like I did on your friend."

The red-haired man grinned—a mocking, unfriendly grin. "He's no friend of mine," he said, "and it's obvious you're not what you seem; you were more surprised than anyone when he ran out of here. Obviously, he thought you were one of us." He broke off and amended: "One of my relatives."

Kerwin said politely, "What is this, Old Home Week? No, thank you. I come from a long line of Arcturian lizard-men." He picked up the coffeelike stuff and buried his head in his mug again, felt the redhead's puzzled gaze on the top of his head. Then the man turned away, muttering, *"Terranan"* in that tone that made the single word into a deadly insult.

Now that it was too late, Kerwin wished he had answered more politely. That was the second time tonight that someone had thought they recognized him. If he closely resembled someone in Thendara, wasn't this what he had come here to find out? He had a tardy impulse to go after the man and demand an explanation. But the sure knowledge that this would only mean a new rebuff prevented him. Feeling frustrated, he put some coins down on the bar, picked up the bundle from the spaceport shop—and went out again.

By now the rain had become icy sleet; the stars were gone. It was dark and cold, with a howling wind, and he fought his way along, shivering in the thin uniform jacket. Why hadn't he brought along something warm to wear after dark? He knew what the weather was like here at night! Hell—he *had* something warm with him. A little peculiar-looking, perhaps, but he could put it on till he got out of this wind. With stiff fingers he fumbled with the bundle and got out the fur-lined, embroidered cloak. He settled it over his shoulders with a shrug, feeling the supple warmth of the fur closing around him like a caress.

He turned into a side street and there was the open square fronting on the spaceport, the neon lights of the Sky Harbor Hotel facing it across from the gates. He should go into the HQ, get assigned to quarters; he hadn't reported, he didn't even know where he was going to sleep. He walked toward the gates; then, on impulse, turned back toward the hotel for a final drink and some time to think before going back into the world of white walls and yellow lights. Maybe he would take a room here for the night.

The clerk, busily sorting records, hardly glanced up at him.

"You go through there," he said curtly, and returned to his book.

Kerwin, startled—had the Civil Service reserved accommodations here?—started to protest, then shrugged and went through the indicated door.

And stopped, for he had stepped into a room prepared for a private party; a long table was laid in the center with some kind of buffet supper and there were flowers in tall crystal vases; at the far end of the room a tall red-headed man in a long embroidered cape stood hesitantly looking at him—then Kerwin realized that the black wall was a pane of glass opening on night, and darkness behind it made it a mirror; the cloaked Darkovan was himself. He looked as if he had never seen himself before; a big man, with red hair flattened from the rain, and a lonely and introspective face, the face of an adventurer who has for some reason been cheated of adventure. The sight of his own face rising above the Darkovan cloak arrested him with a strange surge of—of memory? When had he seen himself dressed like this before? Or—or *someone else*?

Kerwin scowled, impatient. Of course he looked familiar to himself. What was the *matter* with him? And this was the answer, too; the clerk had simply taken him for a Darkovan, perhaps someone he knew by sight, and directed him into the reserved room. In fact, that would explain Ragan, too, and the redhead in the restaurant; he had a double, or near-double on Darkover, some big redhead of about his size and coloring, and that deceived people, with a quick look.

"You're here early, *com'ii,*" said a voice behind him, and Kerwin turned and saw her.

He thought at first that she was a Terran girl, because of the red-gold hair clustered in curls atop her small head. She was slight and slim, wearing a simple gown that clung to dainty curves. Kerwin quickly averted his eyes—staring at a Darkovan woman in public is insolence punishable by a beating or worse, if any of the woman's relatives are around and care to take offense—but she returned his gaze frankly, smiling with welcome, and so, even on second thoughts, he believed for a moment she was a Terran, despite her Darkovan speech.

"How did you get here? I thought we had decided to come with our respective Towers," she said, and Kerwin stared. He felt his face heating, and not from the fire. "My apologies, *domna,*" he said in the language of his childhood. "I didn't realize that this was a private room; I was directed here by mistake. Forgive the intrusion; I will go at once."

She stared at him, her smile fading. "But what are

you thinking of?" she demanded. "We have many
things to discuss—" She stopped. Then she said, un-
certainly, "Have I made a mistake?"

Kerwin said, "Somebody's made one, that's for
sure." His voice trailed away on the last words, realizing that she was *not* speaking the language of
Thendara, but some language he had never heard
before. And yet he had understood her, so well that
for a moment he had not realized that she had
spoken an unfamiliar language.

Her mouth dropped open, and she said, "In the
name of the Son of Aldones and his divine Mother,
who are you?"

Kerwin started to say his name; then realized it
could not possibly mean anything to her, and that
red imp of anger, held in abeyance for a few moments
because he was talking to a beautiful woman, deviled
him again. This was the second time tonight—no,
the third. Damn it, that double of his must be quite
a fellow, if he was recognized simultaneously in a
spaceport dive, and in the private reserved suite of
Darkovan aristocracy—for the girl could not possibly
be anything else.

He said, with the heaviest irony he could manage,
"Don't you recognize me, lady? I'm your big brother
Bill, the black sheep of the family, who ran away to
space when he was six years old and I've been held
captive by space pirates in the Rim Worlds ever
since. Find out in the next installment."

She shook her head, uncomprehending, and he realized that language, and satire, and the allusions he
had made, would mean less than nothing to her.
Then she said in that language he understood, if he
didn't think too hard about it, "But surely you are

one of us? From the Hidden City, perhaps? Who are you?"

Kerwin scowled impatiently, too annoyed to carry the game any further. He almost wished that the man she had mistaken him for would walk in right now so he could punch him in the face.

"Look, you're mistaking me for someone else, girl. I don't know anything about your Hidden City—it's hidden too well or something. What planet is it on? You're not Darkovan, are you?" For her manners were certainly not those of a Darkovan woman.

If she had seemed startled before, now she appeared thunderstruck. "And yet you understood the language of Valeron? Listen to me," she began again, and this time she was speaking the City dialect of Thendara. "I think we must have this clearly understood. There is something very strange here. Where can we talk together?"

"We're doing fine, right here and now," Kerwin said. "I may be new to Darkover, but not *that* new; I'm not crazy about having your relatives file an intent-to-murder on me before I've been here twenty-four hours, in case you have some touchy male relatives. If you *are* Darkovan."

The small pixielike face screwed up in a puzzled little smile. "I can't believe this," she said. "You don't know who I am, and what's worse, you don't know *what* I am. I was sure that you must be from one of the remoter Towers, someone I have never seen before face to face, but only in the relays. Perhaps someone from Hali, or Neskaya, or Dalereuth. . . ."

Kerwin shook his head.

"I'm no one you know, believe me," he said. "I

wish you'd tell me who you mistook me for; I'd like to meet him, whoever he is, if I have a double in this city. It might answer a few questions for me."

"I can't do that," she said, hesitant, and he sensed that now, under his opened Darkovan cloak, she had seen the Terran uniform. "No, please don't go. If Kennard were here—"

"Tani, what is this?" A low, harsh voice broke in, and in the mirrored wall Kerwin saw a man walking toward them. He turned to face the newcomer, wondering—so mad had the world become—if he would see a mirror image of himself. But he didn't.

The newcomer was slight, tall, fair-skinned, with thick red-gold hair. Kerwin detested him on sight, even before he recognized the red-haired man with whom he'd had that brief and unsatisfactory confrontation in the bar. The Darkovan took in the scene at a glance, and his face took on the look of scandalized conventionality.

"A stranger here, and you alone with him, Taniquel?"

"Auster, I only wanted—" the girl protested.

"A *Terranan!*"

"I thought, at first, he was one of us, perhaps from Dalereuth."

The Darkovan favored Kerwin with a contemptuous glance. "He's an Arcturian lizard-man— or so he told me," he said with a sneer. Then he spoke to the girl, a rush of words in, Kerwin thought, the same language she had spoken, but so rapidly that he could not understand a single word of what the man said. He didn't need to; the tone and gestures told Kerwin all he needed to know. The redhead was mad as hell.

A deeper, mellower voice interrupted. "Come, Auster, it can't be as bad as all that. Come, Taniquel, tell me what this is all about, and don't tease, child." A second man had come into the room. And he too was one of the redheads. Where were they all coming from, tonight? This one was heavy-set, a burly man, tall and strongly built; but his red hair was dashed with long streaks of grey, and a close-cut, greying beard surrounded his face. His eyes were almost hidden behind ridged brows so thick as to approximate deformity. He walked stiff-legged, leaning on a thick, copper-headed walking stick. He looked straight at Kerwin and said, *"S'dia shaya;* I'm Kennard, third in Arilinn. Who is your Keeper?"

Kerwin was sure he said *Keeper.* It was a word that could also be translated as *Warden,* or *Guardian.*

"They usually let me out without one," he said dryly. "At least they have so far."

Auster said, quickly and mockingly, "You're wrong too, Kennard. Our friend is an—an Arcturian crocodile-man, or so he claims. But, like all Terrans, he lies."

"Terran!" Kennard exclaimed, "but that's impossible!" And he seemed as shocked as the girl.

Kerwin had had enough of this. He said sharply, "Far from being impossible, it is perfectly true; I am a citizen of Terra. But I spent my early years on Darkover, and I learned to think of it as home, and to speak the language well. Now, if I have intruded or offended, please accept my apologies; and I wish you good night." He turned on his heel and started to leave the room.

Auster muttered something that sounded like "crawling rabbithorn!"

Kennard said, "Wait." Kerwin, already halfway out the door, paused at the man's courteous, persuasive voice. "If you have a few minutes, I'd really like to talk with you, sir. It could be important."

Kerwin glanced at the girl Taniquel, and almost yielded. But one look at Auster decided him. He didn't want any trouble with that one. Not on his first night on Darkover. "Thank you," he said pleasantly. "Another time, perhaps. Please accept my apologies for intruding on your party."

Auster spat out a mouthful of words, and Kennard gave in gracefully, bowed, and spoke a polite formula of farewell. The girl Taniquel stared after him, sobered and stricken, and he hesitated again, on an impulse, realizing that he should stop, change his mind, demand the explanation that he suspected Kennard could give. But he had gone too far to back down and keep any dignity at all. He said, "Again, good night," and felt the door swing shut between himself and the redheads. He felt a curious sense of defeat and apprehension as he crossed the lobby. A group of Darkovans, most of them in long ceremonial capes like his own—no surrender here to the cheap imported clothing—crossed the lobby in the other direction and went through the door he had just vacated. Kerwin noticed that there were some redheads among them, too, and there was murmuring among the crowd in the lobby; again he caught the murmured word *Comyn*.

Ragan had spoken that word, about the jewel he had around his neck; *fine enough for Comyn*. Kerwin searched his memory; the word meant, only, *equals*— those who stood in rank equal to one's own. That wasn't how they had used the word, though.

Outside, the rain had dissolved into stinging mist. A tall man in a green and black cape, red head held high, brushed past Kerwin and said, "Inside, quick, you'll be late," and went on into the Sky Harbor Hotel. It seemed like a curious place for a group of Darkovan aristocrats to hold a family reunion, but what did he know about it? A wild thought darted into his mind that perhaps he ought to crash the party and demand to know if anyone had lost a young relative about thirty years ago. But it was only a wild notion, dismissed as soon as it had arisen.

In the dark street, glazed underfoot now with the icy rain, which froze as it fell, the thick sleet cut off moon or stars. The lights of the HQ gates burned with a yellow glare. Kerwin knew that there he would find warmth and familiar things, shelter, assigned place and even friends. Ellers had probably wakened, found him gone, and returned to the HQ.

But what would he find there if he did return? A set of assigned rooms exactly like those on his last planet, cold and bare with the antiseptic institutional smell; a library of films carefully censored so as not to raise too many unmanageable emotions; meals exactly the same as he would have had on any other Terran Empire planet, so that the workers likely to be transferred at any moment would not have to suffer any digestive discomforts or period of adjustment; and the society of other men like himself, who lived on fantastically alien worlds by turning their backs on them, to live in the same dull familiar world of the Terrans.

They lived on alien worlds under alien suns just as they lived on Terra—unless, that was, they wanted to go out and raise hell; when they sought the worst, not the best, of that alien beauty. Potent drink, women who were willing, if not too appealing, and a place to spend their spare pay. The real worlds lay, would always lie, a million miles out of their reach. As far out of their reach as the red-haired, smiling girl who had smiled and greeted him as *com'ii,* friend.

He turned, again, away from the gates of the HQ. Outside the circle of spaceport bars, tourist traps, whorehouses, and exhibitions, there must be a real Darkover out there somewhere, the world he had known when he was a boy in the city, the world that had haunted his dreams and jerked him out from his new roots on Terra. But why had he ever had those dreams? Where had they come from? Certainly not from the clean, sterile world of the Spacemen's Orphanage!

Slowly, as if wading through mud, he walked toward the old town, his fingers knotting the fastenings of the Darkovan cloak about his throat. His Terranmade boots rang hard on the stone. Whatever people took him for, it wouldn't hurt to go looking around a little. This was his own world. He had been born here. He was no naive Terran spaceman, unsafe outside the spaceport quarter. He knew the city, or had known it once, and knew the language. All right, so Terrans weren't specially welcome in the Old Town. He wouldn't go as a Terran! Wasn't it a Terran who had once said, *Give me a child till he is seven years old, and anyone who wants him can have him after that.* That grim old saint had the right idea; by that reckoning, Kerwin was Darkovan and always would be, and now he was home again and he wasn't going to be kept away!

There were not many people in the streets now. A

few, in cloaks and furs, moving head-down against the bitter biting wind. A shivering girl, hugging an inadequate fur smock about her, gave Kerwin a hopeful glance and murmured to him in the old tongue of the city, which Kerwin had spoken before he could lisp three words of nursery Terran (how did he know that?). And he hesitated, for she was shy and soft-voiced and wholly different from the hard-eyed girl in the spaceport bar, but then her eyes raised to his red hair and she murmured unintelligibly and fled.

A little dwarfed creature pattered by, giving Kerwin a swift upward glance from green eyes that glowed, catlike, in the dark, but had unmistakable human intelligence behind them; Kerwin moved quickly aside, for the *kyrri* were strange creatures who fed on electrical energy and could give unwary strangers painful, though not fatal, shocks if they were jostled or crowded.

Kerwin walked on through the market of the Old Town, savoring the unfamiliar sounds and smells. An old woman was selling fried fish in a little stall; she dropped the bundles of fish into a thick batter, then into the bowl of clear green oil. She looked up and with voluble words in a dialect too thick for understanding, handed him the fresh fish. He started to shake his head, but it smelt good and he shrugged and fumbled for coins in his purse, but she looked at him, startled, and the coins dropped on the ground as she backed away. In her babble he caught again the word *Comyn,* and frowned. The devil! He seemed to have the knack, tonight, of innocently scaring people half to death. Well, with the city full of redheaded men and women on some kind of family reunion,

Kerwin decided red hair was even unluckier than
they'd told him in the orphanage!

Maybe it was this fantastic nobleman's cloak he
was wearing. He'd take it off, but it was too cold for
his thin Terran uniform; besides, he surmised that in
his Terran clothes he couldn't be really safe in this
part of the city.

He admitted it to himself, now; he had had just
this kind of imposture in mind when he bought the
cloak. But too many people were staring. He turned,
deciding he had better take the fastest route back to
the HQ.

He walked swiftly now through dark, deserted
streets. He heard a step behind him—a slow, purposeful step; but told himself not to be suspicious; he
wasn't the only man who might have a good reason
to be out in the rain tonight! The step kept pace with
him, then quickened to overtake him, and Kerwin
stepped aside to let the follower pass in the narrow
street.

That was a mistake. Kerwin felt a searing pain;
then the top of his head exploded and from somewhere he heard a voice crying out strange words:

*Say to the son of the barbarian that he shall come no more
to the plains of Arilinn! The Forbidden Tower is broken and
the Golden Bell is avenged!*

That didn't make sense, Kerwin thought in the
split second before his head struck the pavement and
he knew no more.

Chapter Four: The Search

It was dawn, and it was raining hard, and somebody somewhere was talking right in his ear.

"Lie still, *vai dom*, no one will hurt you! Vandals! What has come to the city, when Comyn can be attacked . . ."

And another voice, rougher: "Don't be a donkey; can't you see the uniform? The man's *Terranan* and somebody's head will roll for this. Go and call the watch, quickly!"

Someone tried to lift his head, and Kerwin decided it was his head that was going to roll, because it exploded and he slid back into unconsciousness again.

Then, after confused noises and pain, a bright white light seemed to shine into the innermost recesses of his brain. He felt someone mauling his head, which hurt like hell, and grunted in pain, and someone took the light out of his eyes.

He was lying in an antiseptic white bed in an antiseptic white room, and a man in a white smock, wearing the caduceus emblem of Medic and Psych, was bending over him.

"All right now?"

Kerwin started to nod, but his head exploded again and he thought better of it. The doctor handed him a small paper cup of red liquid; it burned his mouth and stung all the way down, but his head stopped hurting.

"What happened?" Kerwin asked.

Johnny Ellers put his head around the door; his eyes looked bloodshot. "You ask that? *I* pass out— but you're the one gets slugged and rolled! The greenest kid, on his first planetside assignment, ought to know better than that! And why the hell were you wandering around in the native section? Didn't you study the off-limits map?"

There was a warning in his words. Kerwin said, slowly, "Yeah. I must've got lost."

How much of what he remembered was true? Had he dreamed all the rest—his bizarre wanderings in the Darkovan cloak, all the people who had mistaken him for *someone else*. . . . Had it all been wishful thinking, based on his desire to belong?

"What day is this?"

"Morning after the night before," Ellers said.

"Where did it happen? Where did I get knocked out?"

"God knows," the doctor said. "Evidently someone found you and got scared; dragged you to the edge of the spaceport square and dumped you there about dawn." The doctor moved out of eye range and Kerwin found that it hurt his head to try and follow him, so he went back to sleep. Ragan, the girl in the wineshop, the redheaded aristocrats and the strange encounter in the Sky Harbor Hotel drifted in his mind as he slipped away. If he'd started by thinking that this return to Darkover was an anticlimax to his dreams, at least he'd had enough adventure now to last him fifty years.

No satirical demon whispered in his ear that he hadn't started yet.

* * *

His head was still bandaged when he reported to the Legate for assignment the next morning, and the Legate regarded him without enthusiasm.

"I need Medics and technicians, mapmakers and linguists, and what do they send me? Communications men! Hell, I know it's not your fault, they send me what they can get. I hear you actually requested transfer out here, so maybe I can keep you a while; usually what I get are greenies who transfer out as soon as they have enough seniority credits. I hear you got yourself smashed up a little, wandering around alone in the native quarter. Didn't they tell you that's not smart, here?"

Kerwin just said, "I got lost, sir."

"But why the hell were you wandering around outside the spaceport area anyhow? There's nothing interesting back there." He scowled. "Why would you want to go exploring on your own?"

Kerwin said doggedly, "I was born here, sir." If they were going to discriminate against him because of that, he wanted to know it right away. But the Legate only looked thoughtful.

"You may be fortunate," he said. "Darkover is not a popular assignment; but if it's home to you, you won't hate it quite as much. Maybe. I didn't volunteer, you know; I got in with the wrong political crowd, and I'm serving—you might say—a sentence here. If you actually like the place, you might have quite a career ahead of you; because, as I told you, under normal conditions nobody stays much longer than they have to. So you think you'll like it here?"

"I don't know. But I did want to come back." He added, feeling somehow that he could trust this man,

"It was almost a compulsion. What I remembered as a child."

The Legate nodded. He was not a young man, and his eyes were sad. "God, don't I know!" he said. "The longing for the smell of your own air, the color of your own sun. I know, lad. I've been out for forty years, and I've seen Alpha twice in that time, and I hope I die there. What's the old saying . . . *Though stars like weeds be thickly sown, no world of stars can match your own . . .*" He broke off. "Born here, huh? Who was your mother?"

Kerwin thought of the women in the spaceport café and then tried not to think about them. At least his father had cared enough about his son to get citizenship for him, to leave him in the Spacemen's Orphanage.

"I don't know, sir. That's one of the things I hoped would be recorded here."

"Kerwin," the Legate mused. "I seem to have heard the name. I've only been here four or five years, local time. But if your father had married here, it would be in Records, downstairs. Or the Orphanage would have records. They're fairly careful who they take in there; ordinary foundlings get turned over to the Hierarchs of the City. And then, you were sent back to Earth; that's *very* rare. Normally you would have been kept here and given work or training by the Department, mapping worker, interpreter, something where it would be an advantage to you to know the language like a native."

"I've thought I was probably Darkovan . . ."

"I doubt that; your hair. We Terrans have a lot of redheads—hyperadrenal types, we go in for the adventurous life. With certain exceptions, there aren't many redheaded Darkovans . . ."

Kerwin started to mention that he'd run into at least four, last night, and then could not speak the words. Literally he *could not;* it was like a fist rammed at his throat. Instead he listened to the Legate talking about Darkover.

"It's a funny place," he said. "We hold scraps of it for trade, Trade Cities here and in Caer Donn up in the Hellers, the spaceport here and the big airfield out at Port Chicago, just as we do elsewhere. You know the routine. We leave governments alone, usually. After the people of the various planets have seen what we have to offer in the way of advanced technology and trade, membership in a galactic civilization, they start to get tired of living under primitive or barbarian conditions and hierarchies and monarchies and autarchies; and they petition to come into the Empire. And we're here to enforce plebiscites and protect them against entrenched tyrannies. It's almost a mathematical formula; you can predict the thing. A class-D world like this will hold out maybe a hundred, hundred and ten years. But Darkover isn't following the pattern, and we don't quite know why."

He struck his clenched fist on his acres of desk. "They say we just don't have a damned thing they want. Oh, they trade with us, sometimes; give us silver, or platinum, or jewels, or small matrix crystals—you know what they are?—for things like cameras and medical supplies and cheap down or synthetic mountain gear, ice axes, that sort of thing. Metal tools, especially; they're metal-starved. But they don't have the faintest interest in setting up industrial or technological exchange with us, they haven't asked for technological experts or advice, they don't have anything resembling a commercial system. . . ."

Kerwin remembered some of this from his briefing on the ship. "Are you talking about the government or the common people?"

"Both," the Legate snorted. "The government's a little hard to locate. At first we thought there wasn't any. Hell, there might as well *not* be!"

The Darkovans, according to the Legate, were ruled by a caste who lived in virtual seclusion; they were incorruptible and, especially, unapproachable. A mystery, a riddle.

"One of the few things they do trade for, is *horses*," the Legate told him. "Horses. Can you figure that? We offer them planes, surface transit, roadbuilding machinery—and what do they buy? Horses. I gather there are big herds of them, out on the outer steppes, the plains of Valeron and Arilinn, and in the uplands of the Kilghard Hills. They say they don't want to build roads, and from what I know of the terrain, it wouldn't be easy, but we've offered them all kinds of technical help and they don't want it. They buy a few planes, now and then. God knows what they do with them. They don't have airstrips and they don't buy enough fuel, but they do buy them." He leaned his chin on his hands.

"It's a crazy place. I never have figured it out. To tell the truth, I don't really give a damn. Who knows? Maybe you'll figure it out some day."

When he next had free time, late the next day, Kerwin went out through the more respectable section of the Trade City, toward the Spacemen's Orphanage. He remembered every step of the way. It rose before him, a white cool building, strange and alien as it had always been among the trees, set back at the end of a long walk from the street; the Terran star-and-rocket emblem blazed over the door. The outer hall was empty, but through an open door he saw a small group of boys working industriously around a globe. From behind the building he could hear the high cheery sound of children playing.

In the big office that had been the terror of his childhood, Kerwin waited until a lady dressed respectably in muted Darkovan clothing—loose skirt, furred jacket over all—came out and inquired in a friendly manner what she could do for him.

When he told her of his errand, she held out her hand cordially. "So you were one of our boys? I think you must have been before my time. Your name is—?"

"Jefferson Andrew Kerwin, Junior."

Her forehead ridged in a polite effort at concentration. "I may possibly have seen the name in Records, I don't remember offhand. I think you must have been before my time. When did you leave? At thirteen? Oh, that is unusual. Mostly our boys stay until they are nineteen or twenty; then, after testing, we find them work here."

"I was sent to my father's family on Earth."

"Then we will surely have records on you, Jeff. If your parents are known—" She hesitated. "Of course, we try to keep complete records, but it's possible we may only have one parent's name; there have been—" She hesitated, trying to find a courteous way to phrase it. "—unfortunate liaisons—"

"You mean, if my mother was one of the women of

the spaceport bars, my father may not have bothered telling you who she was?"

She nodded, looked ruffled at this plain speaking. "It does happen. Or one of our young women may choose to have a child without informing us of the father, though in your case that wouldn't seem to apply. If you'll wait a minute." She went into a little side office. Through the open door he caught a glimpse of office machines and a trim Darkovan girl wearing Terran uniform. After a few minutes the lady came back looking puzzled and a little annoyed, and her voice was curt.

"Well, Mr. Kerwin, it seems there is no record of you in our orphanage. It must have been some other planet."

Kerwin stared, in amazement. "But that's impossible," he said reasonably. "I lived here until I was thirteen years old. I slept in Dormitory Four, the matron's name was Rosaura. I used to play ball on that field back there." He pointed.

She shook her head. "Well, we certainly have no records of you, Mr. Kerwin. Is it possible you were registered here under another name?"

He shook his head. "No, I was always called Jeff Kerwin."

"Furthermore we have no record of any of our boys being sent to Terra in his thirteenth year. That would be very unusual, not our regular procedure at all, and it would certainly have been carefully recorded. Everyone here would certainly remember it."

Kerwin took a step forward. He leaned over the woman, a big man, menacing, furious. "What are you trying to say? What do you *mean*, you have no records on me? In God's name, what possible reason would I have for lying about it? I tell you, I lived here thirteen years, do you think I don't *know?* Damn it, I can prove it!"

She shrank away from him. "Please—"

"Look," Kerwin said, trying to be reasonable. "There has got to be some kind of mistake. Could the name be misfiled, could your computer have malfunctioned? I need to know what kind of records were kept on me. Will you check the spelling again, please?" He spelled it again for her, and she said coldly, "I checked that name, and two or three possible spelling variations. Of course, if you had been registered here under another name—"

"No, damn it," Kerwin shouted. "It's *Kerwin*! I learned to *write* my name—in that schoolroom right at the end of that corridor, the one with a big picture of John Reade on the north wall!"

"I am sorry," she said. "We have no record of anyone called Kerwin."

"What kind of half-headed, fumbled-fingered idiot have you got tending your computer, then? Are they filed under names, fingerprints, retinal prints?" He had forgotten that. Names could be altered, changed, misfiled, but fingerprints did not change.

She said coldly, "If it will convince you, and you know anything about computers . . ."

"I've been working in CommTerra with a Barry-Reade KSO4 for seven years."

Her voice was icy. "Then, sir, I suggest you come in here and check the banks yourself. If you feel the name may have been misrecorded, misspelled, or misfiled, every child who has passed through the Orphanage is coded for fingerprint access." She bent silently and handed him a card form, pressed his fingers, one by one, against the special molecular-sensitive paper that recorded, invisibly, the grooves and whorls of the raised lines, pore-patterns, skin type and texture. She faced the card into a slot. He watched the great silent face of the machine, the glassy front, like blind eyes staring.

With uncanny speed a card was released, slid down into a tray; Kerwin snatched it up before the woman could give it to him, disregarding the cold outrage on her face. But as he turned it over his triumph and assurance that she had, for some reason, been lying to him, drained away. A cold terror gripped at his stomach. In the characterless capitals of mechanical printing it read

NO RECORD OF SUBJECT

She took the card from Kerwin's suddenly lax fingertips.

"You cannot accuse a machine of lying," she said coldly. "Now, if you please, I'll have to ask you to leave." Her tone said clearer than words that unless he did she would have someone come and put him out.

Kerwin clawed desperately at the counter edge. He felt as if he had stepped into some cold and reeling expanse of space. Shocked and desperate, he said, "How could I be mistaken? Is there another Spacemen's Orphanage on Darkover? I—I *lived* here, I tell you—"

She stared at him until a sort of pity took the place of her anger. "No, Mr. Kerwin," she said gently. "Why don't you go back to the HQ and check with Section Eight there? If there is a—a mistake—

maybe they could help you."

Section Eight. Medic and Psych. Kerwin swallowed hard and went, without any further protest. That meant she thought he was deranged, that he needed psychiatric help. He didn't blame her. After what he had just heard, he kind of thought so himself. He stumbled out into the cold air, his feet numb, his head whirling.

They were lying, lying. Somebody's lying. She was lying and he knew it; he could feel her lying. . . .

No; that was what every paranoid psychotic thought; somebody was lying, *they were all lying, there was a plot against him.* . . . Some mysterious and elusive *they* was conspiring against him.

But how could he have been mistaken? Damn it, he thought as he walked down the steps, *I used to play ball over there; kickball and catch-the-monkey when I was little, more structured games when I was older.* He looked up at the windows of his old dormitory. He had climbed into them often enough after some escapade, aided by convenient low branches of that very tree. He felt like climbing up into the dormitory to see if the initials he had carved into the windowframe were still there. But he abandoned the notion; the way his luck was running, they'd just catch him and think he was a potential child molester. He turned and stared again at the white walls of the building where he had spent his childhood . . . *or had he?*

He clasped his hands at his temples, searching out elusive memories. He could remember so much. All his conscious memories were of the orphanage, of the grounds where he stood now, running around these grounds; when he was very small he had fallen

on these steps and skinned his knee . . . how old had
he been then? Seven, perhaps, or eight. They had
taken him up to the infirmary and said they were
going to sew up his knee, and he had wondered how
in the world they would get his knee into a sewing
machine; and when they showed him the needle, he
had been so intrigued at how it was done that he had
forgotten to cry; it was his first really clear memory.

Did he have any memories *before* the orphanage?
Try as he might, he could remember only a glimpse
of violet sky, four moons hanging like jewels and a
soft woman's voice that said, "Look, little son, you
will not see this again for years. . . ." He knew, from
his geography lessons, that a conjunction of the four
moons together in the sky did not come very often;
but he could not remember where he had been when
he saw it, or when he had seen it again. A man in a
green and golden cloak strode down a long corridor
of stone that shone like marble, a hood flung loose
over blazing red hair; and somewhere there had been
a room with blue light . . . and then he was in the
Spacemen's Orphanage, studying, sleeping, playing
ball with a dozen other boys his age, in a cluster of
kids in blue pants and white shirts. When he was ten,
he had had a crush on a Darkovan nurse called—
what had been her name? Maruca. She moved softly
in heelless slippers, her white robes moving around
her with fluid grace, and her voice was very gentle
and low. *She tousled my hair and called me Tallo,
though it was against the rules, and once when I had
some kind of fever, she sat by me all night in the infirmary, and put cold cloths on my head, and sang to
me. Her voice was deep contralto, very sweet.* And
when he was eleven he'd bloodied the nose of a boy

named Hjalmar for calling him *bastard*, yelling that
at least he *knew* his father's name, and they'd been
pulled apart, kicking and spitting gutter insults at
each other, by the grey-haired mathematics teacher.
And just a few weeks before they bundled him,
scared and shaking and listless from the drugs,
aboard the starship that would take him to Terra,
there'd been a girl named Ivy, in a class higher than
his. He had hoarded his allotment of sweets for her,
and they had held hands shyly, walking under those
trees at the far edge of the playground; and once,
awkwardly, he had kissed her, but she had turned
away her face so that he had kissed only a mouthful
of fine, pale-brown, sweet-scented hair.

No, they couldn't tell him he was crazy. He remembered too much. He'd go to the HQ, as the
woman said, only not to Medic and Psych, but
Records. They had a record there of everyone who
had ever worked in the Empire service. Everyone.
They'd know.

The man in Records sounded a little startled when
Kerwin asked for a check, and Kerwin couldn't exactly blame him. After all, you don't usually walk up
and ask for your own record, unless you're applying
for a job transfer. Kerwin fumbled for an excuse.

"I was born here. I never knew who my mother
was, and there might be records of my birth and
parentage. . . ."

The man took his fingerprint and punched buttons disinterestedly. After a time a printer began
clattering, and finally a hard copy slid out into the
tray. Kerwin took it up and read it, at first with satisfaction because it was obviously a full record, but

with growing disbelief.

KERWIN, JEFFERSON ANDREW. WHITE. MALE. CITIZEN TERRA. HOME MOUNT DENVER. SECTOR Two. STATUS single. HAIR red. EYES grey. COLORING fair. EMPLOYMENT HISTORY age twenty apprentice CommTerra. PERFORMANCE satisfactory. PERSONALITY withdrawn. POTENTIAL high.

TRANSFER age 22. Sent as warranted CommTerra certificate junior status, Consulate Megaera. PERFORMANCE excellent. PERSONALITY acceptable, introverted. POTENTIAL very high. DEMERITS none. No entanglements known. PRIVATE LIFE normal as far as known. PROMOTIONS regular and rapid.

TRANSFER age 26. Phi Coronis IV. CommTerra ratings expert. Legation. PERFORMANCE excellent; commendations for extraordinary work. PERSONALITY introverted but twice reprimanded for fights in native quarter. POTENTIAL very high, but in view of repeated requests for transfer possibly unstable. No marriages. No liaisons of record. No communicable diseases.

TRANSFER age 29, Cottman IV, Darkover. (requested for personal reasons, unstated.) Request approved, granted, suggest Kerwin not be transferred again except at loss of accumulated seniority. PERFORMANCE no records as yet, one reprimand for intrusion into quarter off limits. PERSONALITY APPRAISAL excellent and valuable employee but significant personality and stability defects. POTENTIAL excellent.

There was no more. Kerwin frowned. "Look, that's my employment record; what I wanted was birth records, that kind of thing. I was born here on Cottman IV."

"That's your official transcript, Kerwin. It's all the computer has on you."

"No birth records at all?"

The man shook his head. "If you were born outside the Terran Zone—and your mother was a native—well, it wouldn't be recorded. I don't know what kind of birth records they keep out there—" He waved an inclusive hand at the view of distant mountains—"but it's for sure they're not in *our* computer. I'll try you in Birth Records; and I can try pass rights for orphans. If you were sent back to Terra at thirteen, that would be under Section Eighteen, the Repatriation of Spacemen's Orphans and Widows Act." He punched buttons for several minutes, then shook his head.

"See for yourself," he said. It kept coming up: NO RECORD OF SUBJECT.

"Here are all the birth records we have for Kerwin; we have an Evelina Kerwin, born to one of our nurses here, died at six months. And there's an employment record on a Henderson Kerwin, black, male, age 45, who was an engineer in Thendara spaceport and died of radiation burns after an accident to the reactor. And under pass rights for orphans I found a Teddy Kerlayne, who was sent to Delta Ophiuchi four years ago. Not relevant, huh?"

Kerwin mechanically shredded the paper into bits, his fingers knotting with the frustration he felt. "Try one more thing," he said. "Try my father. Jefferson Andrew Kerwin, senior." He crushed his own printout in his hands, remembering it had said, no marriages, no recorded liaisons. His father's marriage, or liaison, with his unknown mother, would have *had* to be recorded, in order for the older Jeff Kerwin to get Empire citizenship for his son. The procedure had been carefully explained to him when he joined the Civil Service; how to record native marriages—few Empire planets were as tough on fraternization and mixing with natives as Darkover—and how to legitimize a child, with or without Terran marriage. He knew how it would have to be done. "See when and where my father filed a 784-D application, will you?"

The man shrugged. "Buddy, you sure are hard to convince. If you had ever been listed on a 784, it would have showed up on that employment record."

But he started to punch buttons again, staring at the glassed-in surface where the information appeared before the hard copy was printed. Abruptly, he started; his lips pursed. Then he turned and said civilly, "Sorry, Kerwin; no records. Somebody's steered you wrong; we don't have any record of a Jeff Kerwin in Civil Service. Nobody but you."

Kerwin snapped, "You've got to be lying! Or what are you gawping at on that screen? Damn it, move your hand and let me see it myself!"

The clerk shrugged. "Suit yourself." But he had punched another button and the screen was blank.

Fury and frustration surged up in Kerwin like a cresting wave. "Damn it, are you trying to tell me I don't exist?"

"Look," the clerk said wearily, "you can erase an entry in a ledger. But show me anybody who can tamper with the memory banks of CommTerra records, and I'll show you a cross between a man and a crystoped. According to official records, you came to Darkover for the first time two days ago. Now go down and see Medic and Psych, and quit bothering me!"

How naive do they think I am? CommTerra can be fudged so no outsider can get at the records, if you have the right codes for access. Someone, for some obscure reason, had fixed it so that he couldn't get access to the data.

But why would they bother?

The alternative was what the woman had said. She had thought he was crazy, confabulating, that he had never been on Darkover before, that for some reason he was inventing an elaborate Darkovan past for himself. . . .

Kerwin reached into his pocket, extended a folded bill.

"Try my father again. Okay?"

The clerk looked up, and now Kerwin knew that his guess had been right. It was worth the money, though he couldn't afford it, to know that he wasn't crazy. Greed and fear wavered in the man's face, and finally he said, whisking the bill quickly into his pocket, "Okay. But if the banks are being monitored, it could be my job. And whatever we get, that's *it;* no more questions, okay?"

Kerwin watched the programming this time. The machine burped slowly to itself. Then the panel flashed a red light, blink-blink-blink, an urgent panic signal. The clerk said softly, "Shunting circuit."

Red letters flashed on the panel.

REQUESTED INFORMATION AVAIL-
ABLE ON PRIORITY CODE ONLY:
CLOSED ACCESS. GIVE VALID ACCESS
CODE AND AUTHORITY FOR FURTHER
ACCESS.

The letters flashed on and off with hypnotic intensity. Kerwin finally shook his head and motioned and the clerk shut off the lights. The screen stared back at them, blank and enigmatic.

"Well?" the clerk asked. Kerwin knew he wanted another bribe to try and break the access code, but Kerwin had as good a chance of breaking it as the clerk did. Anyhow, that proved there was *something* there.

He didn't know what. But it explained the way the woman at the Orphanage had acted, too.

He turned and went out, resolve slowly hardening in him. He had been drawn back to Darkover—only to find greater mysteries awaiting him. Somewhere, somehow, he would find out what they were.

Only he didn't know where to start.

Chapter Five: The Technician

He let it alone for the next few days. He had to; breaking in on a new job, however simple the job was, and however similar to the one on his last planet, demanded all his attention. It was a highly specialized branch of Communications—the testing, calibrating, and occasional repair of the intercom equipment both in the HQ building itself and from point to point in the Terran Zone. It was time consuming and tedious rather than difficult, and he often found himself wondering why they bothered to bring Terran personnel in from outside, rather than training local technicians. But when he put the question to one of his associates, his friend only shrugged:

"Darkovans won't take the training. They don't have a technical turn of mind—no good with this sort of thing." He indicated the immense bank of machinery they were inspecting. "Just naturally that way, I guess."

Kerwin snorted brief, unamused laughter. "You mean something inborn—some difference in the quality of their minds?"

The other man glanced at him warily, realizing that he had trodden on a sore place. "You're Darkovan? But you were brought up by Terrans—you take machinery and technology for granted. As far as

I know, they don't have anything resembling it—never have had." He scowled. "And they don't want it, either."

Kerwin thought about that, sometimes, lying in his bunk in the bachelor quarters of the HQ building, or sitting over a solitary drink in one of the spaceport bars. The Legate had mentioned that point—that the Darkovans were immune to the lure of Terran technology, and had kept out of the mainstream of Empire culture and trade. Barbarians, beneath the veneer of civilization? Or—something less obvious, more mysterious?

During his off-duty hours, sometimes, he strolled down into the Old Town; but he did not wear the Darkovan cloak again, and he made sure that his headgear covered the red head. He was giving himself time to work it through, to be sure what his next move would be. If there was a next move.

Item: the orphanage had no record of a boy named Jefferson Andrew Kerwin, Junior, sent to Terran grandparents at the age of thirteen.

Item: the main computer banks at the HQ refused to disclose any information about Jefferson Andrew Kerwin, Senior.

Kerwin was debating what these two facts might have in common—added to the fact that the Terran HQ computer was evidently set in such a way as to give the casual inquirer no information whatever—not even that such a person as his father had ever existed.

If he could find someone he had known at the orphanage, presumably that would be proof, of a sort. Proof at least that his memories of a life there were real—

They were real. He *had* to start from there because there was no other place to start. If he began doubting his own memories, he might as well open the door right now to chaos. So he would go on the assumption that his memory was real, and that for some reason or other, the records had been altered.

During the third week he became aware that he had seen the man Ragan just a little too frequently for coincidence. At first he thought nothing of it. In the spaceport café, when he saw Ragan at a far table each time he entered, he nodded a casual greeting and that was that. After all, the place was public, and there were doubtless many steady customers and habitués. He was well on the way to being one himself, by now.

But when an emergency failure in the spaceport dispatch office kept him on duty overtime one evening, and he saw Ragan in his usual place at well past the usual hour, he began to notice it. So far, it was just a hunch; but he began to shift his mealtimes and eat at odd hours—and four times out of five he saw the swart Darkovan there. Then he did his drinking in another bar for a day or two; and by now he was sure that he was being shadowed by the man. No, shadowed was the wrong word; it was too open for that. Ragan was making no effort to keep out of Kerwin's sight. He was too clever to try to force himself on Kerwin as an acquaintance—but he was putting himself in Kerwin's path and Kerwin had the curious hunch that he wanted to be charged with it, questioned about it.

But why? He thought it through, long and slowly. If Ragan was playing a waiting game, perhaps it was tied in somehow with the other oddities. If he held aloof, and seemed not to notice, maybe they—whoever "they" were—would be forced to show a little more of their hand.

But nothing happened, except that he settled down to the routine of his new job and his new life. In the Terran Zone, life was very much like life in the Terran Zone of any other Empire planet. But he was very conscious of the world beyond that world. It called to him with a strange hunger. He found himself straining his ears in the mixed society of the spaceport bars for scraps of Darkovan conversation; absentmindedly heard himself answer one too many casual questions in Darkovan. And sometimes at night he would take the enigmatic blue crystal from its place around his neck and stare into its strange cold depths, as if by wanting it fiercely he could bring back the confused memories to which it now seemed a key. But it lay in his palm, a cold stone, lifeless, giving back no answer to the pounding questions in him. And then he would thrust it back into his pocket and walk restlessly down to one of the spaceport bars for a drink, again, straining ears and nose for a whiff of something beyond. . . .

It was three full weeks before the waiting suddenly snapped in him. He spun around from the bar on impulse, not giving himself time to consider what he would do or say, and strode toward the corner table where the little Darkovan, Ragan, sat over a cup of some dark liquid. He jerked out a chair with his foot and lowered himself into it, glowering across the ill-lighted table at Ragan.

"Don't look surprised," he said roughly. "You've been on my tail long enough." He fingered in his pocket the edges of the crystal, drew it out, slapped it on the table between them. "You told me about this, the other night—or was I drunker than I think? I've got the notion you have something more to say. Say it."

Ragan's lean, ferret face looked wary and guarded. "I didn't tell you anything that any Darkovan couldn't have told you. Almost anyone would have recognized it."

"Just the same, I want to know more about it."

Ragan touched it with the tip of a finger. He said, "What do you want to know? How to use it?"

Briefly, Kerwin considered that. No; at present, at least, he had no use for such tricks as Ragan had done with the crystal, to melt glasses or—whatever else it might do. "Mostly I'm curious to know where it came from—and why I happened to have one."

"Some assignment," Ragan said dryly. "There are only a few thousand of them, I should imagine." But his eyes were narrowed, not casual at all, although his voice was elaborately casual. "Some of the people at the Terran HQ have been experimenting with the small ones. You could probably get a sizable bonus, or something, by turning this one over to them for experimental purposes."

"No!" Kerwin heard himself speak the negative before he even knew he had rejected the idea.

"But why come to me?" Ragan asked.

"Because lately I've stumbled over you every damn time I turn around, and somehow I don't think it's just because you've got a yen for my company. You know something about this business, or you want me to think so. First of all, you might tell me who you mistook me for, that first night. Not just

you. Everybody who saw me thought I was somebody else. That same night I got slugged and rolled
in an alley. . . ."

Ragan's mouth dropped open; Kerwin could not
doubt that he was genuinely shocked.

". . . and pretty obviously, it was because I looked
like that same *somebody*—"

"No, Kerwin," Ragan said. "There you're wrong.
That would have protected you, if anything. It's a
messy business. Look," he said, "I've got no grudge
against *you*. I'll tell you this much; it's because of
your red hair—"

"Hell, there are redheaded Darkovans. I've met
them—"

"You have?" Ragan's eyebrows lifted. "*You*?" He
snorted brief, unamused laughter. "Look, if you're
lucky, you got yours from the Terran side. But I'll
tell you this much; if I were you, I'd be on the first
ship offplanet, and I wouldn't stop till I was halfway
across the Empire. That's my advice, dead sober."

Kerwin said with a bleak smile, "I like it better
when you're drunk," and signaled the waiter for refills. "Listen, Ragan," he said when the waiter had
gone, "if I have to, I'll put on Darkovan clothes and
go down in the Old Town—"

"And get your throat cut?"

"You just said red hair would protect me. No. I'll
go down in the Old Town and stop everybody I meet
on the street and ask them whom they think I am, or
whom I look like. And sooner or later I'll find *somebody* to tell me."

"You don't know what you're monkeying with."

"And I won't, unless you tell me."

"Stubborn damned fool," Ragan said. "Well, it's

your neck. What do you expect *me* to do? And what's in it for me?"

Now Kerwin felt on safer ground. He would have distrusted it if the shrewd Darkovan had offered to help him.

"Damned if I know, but there must be something you want from me, or you wouldn't have spent so much time hanging around waiting for me to ask you questions. Money? You know how much a Communications man makes with the Empire. Enough to live on, but no big rakeoffs. I expect—" his mouth twisted—"that you'll be expecting some pickings whatever happens. And that you have a good reason to expect them. Start with this." He picked up the matrix crystal on its chain. "How do I find out about it?"

Ragan shook his head. "I gave you the best advice I could; I'm not going to get mixed up in that part of it. If you have to know more, there are licensed matrix mechanics, even in the Terran Zone. They can't do much. But they can give you some answers. I still say keep out of it. Get as far away as you can. You haven't the slightest idea what you're monkeying with."

Of all of this Kerwin had fastened only on the strange knowledge that there were licensed matrix mechanics. "I thought it was this big secret the Terrans didn't know anything about!"

"I told you; they trade for the little ones. Like mine. And the small ones, almost anybody can learn to handle. The way I do. A few tricks."

"What does a matrix mechanic do?"

Ragan shrugged. "Say you have legal papers you want to lock up, and you don't even feel safe about trusting them to a banker; you buy one of the smaller matrixes—if you can afford it, they're not cheap, even the tiny ones—and get the mechanic to key it to your personal pattern; your own brainwaves, like a fingerprint. Then you decide to shut that box, and the matrix will seal those edges so that nothing in the world, not a sledgehammer or a nuclear explosion, will ever open them again; nothing except your own personal decision, your own mental 'Open Sesame.' You think *Open* at it, and it opens. No combination to remember, no secret bank-account number, nothing."

Kerwin whistled. "What a gadget! Come to think of it, I can imagine some pretty dangerous uses for that kind of thing."

"Right," Ragan said drily. "I don't know a lot of Darkovan history, but the Darkovans aren't letting any of the bigger matrixes out of their hands. Even with the little ones you can do some fairly nasty tricks, even though they can't handle more than the smallest measure of energy. Suppose, for instance, you have a business rival who owns some sensitive machinery. You concentrate on your crystal—even a little one like mine—and raise the heat in a thermostat, say, three degrees Centigrade, and melt the most important circuits. You want to put your competitor out of business? You hire an unscrupulous matrix mechanic to sabotage him, mess up his electrical equipment, short out his circuits, and you can still prove you never went near the place. I think they're scared green, up at HQ, that the Darkovans will play some trick with matrixes—wipe the memory banks of their computers, mess up the navigational control center of their starships. The

Darkovans have no reason to do such a thing. But the very fact that that kind of technology exists, indicates to the Terrans that they ought to know how it works and how to guard against it." Again he grinned, wry-ly. "That's why I say they'd probably give you a small fortune, or let you write your own ticket, if you turned that one of yours over to them. It's the biggest one I ever saw."

Kerwin recalled fragmentary memories; a Terran starship's stewardess, fumbling at the shirt of a drugged and screaming child. "So tell me, how the hell did *I* get one that size?"

Ragan shrugged. "Kerwin, my friend, if I knew the answer to that, I'd go to the Terran Zone and let them beg me to write *my* own ticket. I'm no fortune-teller."

Kerwin thought about that for a minute. He said, "Maybe a fortuneteller or something like it is what I need. Well, I've heard there are telepaths and psy-chics all over Darkover."

"You don't know what you're playing around with," Ragan said, "but if you're bound and de-termined to risk it, I know a woman, down in the Old Town. She used to be—well, no matter. If anybody can tell you, she can. Give her this." He fumbled in his pocket for a bit of paper, scribbled briefly on it. "I've got contacts in the Darkovan Zone; it's how I make my living. I warn you; it'll cost you plenty. She'll be risking something, and she'll make you pay for it."

"And you?"

Ragan's brief, dry chuckle sounded loud. "For a name and an address? Hell, you bought me a drink, and maybe I've got a score to settle with another redhead or two. Good luck, *Tallo.*" He raised his hand and Jeff watched him go, wondering. What was he being steered into? He studied the address, realizing that it was in the most unsavory part of Thendara, in the Old Town, the haunt of thieves and pimps and worse. He wasn't anxious to go there in Terran uniform. He wasn't anxious to go there at all. Even as a kid, he'd known better.

In the end he made cautious inquiries about matrix mechanics in the better part of town and found out that they operated quite openly; he found the names of three licensed and bonded ones in the most respectable part of the city, and chose one at random.

It lay in a district of wide, high houses, with walls of translucent building stone; here and there he saw a park, a public building of some sort, a walled compound bearing a small placard saying it was the Guild House of the Order of Renunciates—he wondered if that was something like a convent or monastery—and the streets were wide and well-kept without paving stones. In an empty square men were working on an unfinished building whose walls rose gaunt, half completed; men laying stones with mortar, sawing, hammering. In the next street was a market where shawled women bargained for food, small children clinging to their skirts, or sat in little clusters at a stall selling fried fish and deep-fried sweet cakes and mushrooms. The very commonplace minutiae of everyday life were reassuring; women gossiping, children playing catch-the-monkey in and out of the stalls and teasing their mothers for sweets or fried mushrooms. They called this culture *barbarian,* Jeff thought resentfully, because they had no complicated transit or technology and felt no need for it. They had no rocket-cars, no great roadways and skyscrapers, no spaceports; but they had no steel factories, or stinking chemical refineries, none of what some Terran writer had called "dark Satanic mills," no dark mines filled with slave labor or robot machinery. Kerwin chuckled dryly to himself; he was romanticizing. Looking at a livery stable where horses were being packed and saddled, he reflected that shoveling horse manure on a morning when the snow lay three feet deep wasn't all that much better than working in a mill or a mine, either.

He located the address he was looking for and was admitted by a quietly dressed woman, who showed him into an enclosed room, a kind of study hung with pale draperies. *Insulating draperies,* Jeff found himself thinking, and raised a mental eyebrow at himself. What the hell! A woman and a man came toward him; they were tall and stately, fair-skinned with grey eyes and an air of quiet authority and poise. But they both seemed startled, almost awed.

"Vai dom," said the man, "you lend us grace. How may we serve you?"

But before Kerwin could answer the woman curled her lip in swift disdain. *"Terranan,"* she said with flat hostility. "What do you want?"

The man's face mirrored the change in hers. They were enough alike to be brother and sister and Kerwin noted in the fluid light that although both were dark of hair and grey-eyed, there were pale reddish glints, hardly noticeable, in the hair of both. But they had nothing like the red hair and aristocratic bearing of the three redheads in the Sky Harbor Hotel that night.

He said, "I want information about this," and extended the matrix to them. The woman frowned, motioned it away, went to a bench and picked up a length of something sparkling, like a silk shot with metallic or crystalline glitter. She shrouded her hand carefully with the stuff, and as she returned and carefully picked up the matrix out of his hand so that her bare hands did not touch it, Kerwin was struck with a brief, painful *déjà vu*.

I saw someone do that, before, that gesture . . . but where? When?

She scanned it briefly, the man looking over her shoulder. Then the man said, with sharp hostility, "Where did you get this? Did you steal it?"

Kerwin knew perfectly well that the accusation did not have quite the force it would have had in the Terran Zone; just the same it made him angry. He said, "No, damn it. I have had it ever since I can remember, and I don't know how I came by it. Can you tell me what it is or where it came from?"

He saw them exchange a glance. Then the woman shrugged and sat down at a small desk, the matrix in her hand. She examined it carefully with a hand lens, her face thoughtful and withdrawn. Before the desk was a heavy glass plate, opaque, dark, with small lights glittering deep inside the glass; the woman made another of those familiar-strange gestures and lights began to wink on and off inside the glass with a hypnotic effect. Kerwin watched, still in the grip of the *déjà vu*, thinking, *I have seen this before.*

No. It's an illusion, something to do with one side of your brain seeing it a split second before the other side, and the other side, catching up, remembers seeing it. . . .

The woman said, her back to Kerwin, "It is not on

the main monitor screen."

The man bent over her, wrapped his hand in a fold of the insulating stuff, and touched the crystal. Then he looked at the woman, startled, and said, "Do you suppose he knows what he has here?"

"Not a chance," the woman said. "He is from off-planet; how would he know?"

"Is he a spy sent to draw us out?"

"No; he is ignorant, I sense it. But we cannot afford to risk it; too many have died who were touched even by the shadow of the Forbidden Tower. Get rid of him."

Kerwin wondered with a little annoyance if they were going to keep talking right past him. Then, in shock, he realized that they were not speaking the dialect of Thendara, nor even the pure *casta* of the mountains. They were speaking that language whose form he somehow knew without being able to understand consciously a single syllable.

The woman raised her head and said to the man, "Give him a chance. Perhaps he is really altogether ignorant and he could be in danger." Then she said to Kerwin in the language of the spaceport, "Can you tell me anything about how you came by this crystal?"

Kerwin said slowly, "I think it was my mother's. I don't know who she was." Then, hesitantly, aware that it was relevant, he repeated the words he had heard the night he was struck down in the Old Town.

"Say to the son of the barbarian that he shall come no more to the plains of Arilinn, that the Golden Bell is avenged. . . ."

The woman suddenly shuddered; he saw her

perfect poise split and crack. Hastily she stood up and the man extended the crystal to Kerwin as if their movements were somehow synchronized.

"It is not for us to meddle in the affairs of the *vai leroni*," she said flatly. "We can tell you nothing."

Kerwin said, shocked, "But—you know something —you can't—"

The man shook his head, his face blank and unreadable. *Why do I feel as if I ought to be able to know what he was thinking?* Kerwin wondered.

"Go, *Terranan*. We know nothing."

"What are the *vai leroni?* What—"

But the two faces, so alike, distant and arrogant, were closed and impassive; and behind the impassivity, frightened; Kerwin knew it.

"It is not for us."

Kerwin felt as if he would explode with frustration. He put out his hand in a futile, pleading gesture, and the man stepped back, avoiding the touch, the woman withdrawing fastidiously.

"But, my God, you can't leave it like that, if you know something—you have to tell me—"

The woman's face softened slightly. "This much, I will say; I thought *that*—" she indicated the crystal, "had been destroyed when—when the Golden Bell was broken. Since they saw fit to leave it with you, they may some day see fit to give you an explanation. But if I were you, I would not wait for it. You—"

"*Latti!*" The man touched her arm. "Leave it! Go," he added to Kerwin, "you are not welcome here. Not in our house, not in our city, not on our world. We have no quarrel with you; but you bring danger on us even with your shadow. Go." And from that, there was no appeal. Kerwin went.

Somehow he had halfway expected this. Another door slammed in his face; like the computer, coded so he could not read the records of his own birth. But he could not drop it here, even though he wanted to, even though he was beginning to be frightened.

He took the precaution of covering his hair; and although he didn't wear the Darkovan cloak, he carefully took off all the insignia of the Service, so that when he went into the Old Town there was nothing that could identify him with the spaceport people.

The address was in a crumbling slum; there was no bell, and after he knocked he stood waiting a long time. He had half resolved to turn away again when the door opened and a woman stood there, holding to the doorframe with an unsteady hand.

She was small and middle-aged, clad in non-descript shawls and bundled skirts, not quite rags and not really dirty, but she gave a general impression of unkempt slovenliness. She looked at Kerwin with dreary indifference; it seemed to him that she focused her eyes with difficulty.

"Do you want something?" she asked, not caring.

"A man named Ragan sent me," he said, and handed her the scribbled slip. "He said you were a matrix technician."

"I was once," she said, still with that deadly indifference. "They cut me off from the main relays years ago. Oh, I can still do some work, but it'll cost you. If it was legal, you wouldn't be here."

"What I want's not illegal, as far as I know. But maybe it's impossible."

A faint spark of interest flickered behind the dull eyes. "Come in." She motioned him into the room.

Inside it was clean enough; it had a pungent-familiar smell, herbs burning in a brazier; the woman stirred the fire, sending up fresh clouds of the pungent smoke, and when she turned, her eyes were more alert.

But Kerwin thought he had never seen so colorless a person. Her hair, coiled loose on her neck, was the same faded grey as her bundled shawl; she walked wearily, stooping a little as if in some chronic pain. She lowered herself carefully into a chair and gestured him, with a tired, abrupt motion of her head, to sit.

"What do you want, *Terranan?*" At his look of surprise, her faded lips stretched faintly, not quite a smile. "Your speech is perfect," she said, "but remember what I am. There is another world in your walk and the set of your head, in what you do with your hands. Don't waste our time in lies."

At least she hadn't mistaken him for his mysterious double somewhere, Kerwin thought thankfully, and pushed back his headgear. He thought, *Maybe if I level with her, she'll level with me.* He fumbled at his neck and laid down the crystal in front of her.

"I was born on Darkover," he said, "but they sent me away. My father was Terran. I thought it would be very simple to find out more about myself."

"It should be, with this." she said, "Fit for a Keeper, it is." She leaned forward; unlike the other mechanics, she did not shroud her hand when she touched it. Kerwin flinched; he hated to have it touched, for some reason. She saw the gesture and said, "So you know *that* much. Is it keyed?"

"I don't know what you mean."

She raised her eyebrows. Then she said, "Don't

worry; I can guard against it, even if it is. I'm not superstitious, and I learned a long time ago, from the old man himself, that any halfway-competent technician can do a Keeper's work. I've done it enough. Let me take it." She picked it up; he felt only a faint shock. The hands were beautiful, younger than the rest of her, smooth and supple and the nails well-kept; he had expected them, somehow, to be gnawed and dirty. Again the gesture seemed familiar.

"Tell me about it," she said, and Kerwin told her everything, feeling suddenly secure; the way in which he had been mistaken for some mysterious *other*, the attack in the street, the failure to find records in the orphanage, the refusal of the two matrix mechanics to tell him anything. At that she frowned scornfully.

"And they say they are free of superstition! Fools," she said.

"What can you tell me?"

She touched the crystal with one beautifully manicured fingertip. She said, "This much: It's not on the main banks. It may have come from one of the Forbidden Tower people. I don't recognize it offhand," she said. "But it's hard to believe you have any Terran blood at all. Though there have been a few, and once I saw old *Dom Ann'dra*. . . . But that's neither here nor there." She went to a cupboard and rummaged in it, taking out something wrapped in a length of the insulating silk. Before her on the table she placed a small wicker-wood frame, then carefully untwisting the silks, she laid something in the frame. It was a small matrix; smaller than his own, but considerably larger than the one Ragan had showed him. Small lights played in it; Kerwin, looking at them, felt sick and nauseated. The woman looked

into her own matrix, then into Kerwin's, rose, stirred
the brazier again so that clouds of the choking smoke
rose, and Kerwin's head began to swim. The smoke
seemed to contain some potent drug, for the woman,
inhaling it deeply, stared at him with a sudden live
glitter in her eyes.

"You," she said, "you are not what you seem."
Her words slurred strangely. "You will find what
you seek, but you will destroy it too. You were a trap
that missed its firing, they sent you away to safety,
from the blizzard to feed the banshee. . . . You will
find the thing you desire, you will destroy it but you
will save it, too. . . ."

Kerwin said rudely, "I didn't come here to have
my fortune told."

She seemed not to hear, muttering almost in-
coherently. It was dark in the room, except for the
dim glow of the brazier, and very cold. Impatient,
Kerwin stirred; she made an imperative gesture and
he sank back, surprised at the authority of the movement. *Muttering, drugged old witch! What the hell was she
doing now?*

The crystal on the table, his own crystal, glowed
and shimmered; the crystal in the wicker frame, between the woman's slender hands, began slowly to
glow with blue fire.

"The Golden Bell," the woman muttered thickly,
slurring the words and making them one, *Cleindori*.
"Oh, yes, Cleindori was beautiful, long, long they
sought her in the hills across the river, but she had
gone where they could not pursue, the proud superstitious fools preaching the Way of Arilinn. . . ."

All the light in the room, now, was focused on the
woman's face, the light that seemed to pour from the

blue center of the crystal. Kerwin sat there a long, long time, while the woman stared into the crystal and muttered something to herself. Finally he wondered if she had gone into a trance, if she were a clairvoyant who could answer his questions.

"Who am I?"

"You are the one they managed to send away, the brand snatched from the burning," she said thickly. "There were others, but you were the most likely. They didn't know, the proud Comyn, that you had been snatched away from them. That they had hidden the prey inside the hunter's door, hidden the leaf inside the forest. All of them, Cleindori, Cassilde, the *Terranan,* the Ridenow boy. . . ."

The lights in the crystal seemed to coagulate into a brilliant flash of flame. Kerwin flinched as it knifed through his eyes, but he could not move.

And then a scene rose before his eyes, clear and distinct, as if imprinted on the inside of his eyelids:

Two men and two women, all of them in Darkovan clothing, all seated around a table on which lay a matrix crystal in a cradle; and one of the women, very frail, very fair, was bending over it, gripping the cradle so tightly that he could see the knuckles of her hands whitened by that desperate grip. Her face, framed in paling reddish hair, seemed eerily familiar. . . . The men watched, intent, unmoving. One of them had dark hair and dark eyes, animal eyes, and Kerwin heard himself thinking, The Terran, *and knew at the back of his mind that he looked on the face of the man whose name he would bear, and they all watched spellbound while the cold lights played on the woman's face like some strange aurora; and then the tall redheaded man suddenly wrenched the woman's hands from the cradle; the blue fires died and the woman sank back senseless in the dark man's arms. . . .*

The scene swept away; Kerwin saw moving
clouds, cold drenching rain falling in a courtyard. A
man strode through a high-pillared corridor, a man
in a jeweled cloak fastened high at the neck; a tall
arrogant man, and Kerwin gasped, recognizing the
dream-face of his earliest memories. The scene narrowed again to a high-walled chamber. The women
were there, and one of the men. Kerwin seemed to
see the scene from a strange perspective, as if he were
either up very high or down very low, and he realized
that he was *there*, horror and sudden dread making
him tremble. He seemed to look away from the four
grouped around the matrix, at a closed door, a turning door-handle that moved slowly, very slowly, then
was suddenly flung back, blotted out by dark forms
that filled the doorway and blotted out the light,
rushing forward . . .

Kerwin screamed. It was not his own voice, but the
voice of a child, thin and terrible and terrifying, a
shriek of utter despair and panic. He slumped forward across the table, the scene darkening before his
eyes, remembered screams ringing and ringing on
and on in his ears long after his cry had jolted him up
to consciousness again.

Dazed, he straightened and passed his hand slowly
across his eyes. His hand came away wet with clam-
my sweat—or tears? Confused, he shook his head.
He was *not* in that high-walled room filled with vague
shapes of terror. He stood in the stone-walled cottage
of the old matrix technician; the fire in the brazier
had burned out, and the room was dark and cold. He
could just see the woman; she had collapsed forward,
her body lying across the table and atop the wicker
frame, which had turned sidewise and spilled the

crystal out on to the table. But there was no blue
light in her crystal now. It lay blank, grey, a featureless piece of glass.

Kerwin looked down at the woman, angry and
puzzled. She had shown him *something*—but what did
it mean? Why had he screamed? He felt cautiously at
his throat. His voice felt frayed.

"What the hell was that all about? I suppose the
dark man was my father. But who were the others?"

The woman neither stirred nor spoke, and Kerwin
scowled. Drunk, drugged? Not gently, he reached to
shake her shoulder. "What was that? What did it
mean? Who were they?"

With nightmarish, slow grace, the woman slid
down and toppled sideways to the floor. Swearing,
Kerwin vaulted the table and knelt at her side, but he
already knew what he would discover.

The woman was dead.

Chapter Six: Re-Exile

Kerwin's throat still hurt, and he felt a ragged hysteria gripping at him.

All the doors keep closing in my face!

Then he looked down at the dead woman with pity and a painful guilt. He had dragged her into this, and now she was dead. This unknown unlovely woman, whose name he didn't even know, and he had involved her in the mysterious fate that was tracking him.

He looked at her matrix, lying grey and featureless on the table. Had it died when the woman died, then? Gingerly, he picked up his own and put it into his pocket, looked down at the dead woman again with regret and futile apology, and then, turning away, he went and called the police.

They came, green-clad, cross-belted Darkovans of the City Guard—the equivalent of metropolitan police, what there was of it on Darkover—not at all happy to see a Terran there, and they showed it. Reluctantly, with rigid politeness, they allowed him the legal privilege of summoning a Terran consul before questioning, a privilege Kerwin would just as soon have waived. He wasn't at all eager for the HQ to know he had been making inquiries down here.

They asked him questions, and then they didn't

like the answers. Kerwin held back nothing, except the fact of his own matrix, or why he had been there to consult the woman in the first place. But in the end, because there wasn't a mark on her, and because the woman had obviously not been sexually molested, and because a Terran medic and a Darkovan both gave their independent opinion that she had died of a heart attack, they let him go, and escorted him formally to the edge of the spaceport. They said goodbye to him there with a certain grim formality that warned him, without words, that if he was found in that part of the city again, they wouldn't be responsible for what happened.

He thought, then, that he had seen the worst of it, when the blind alley led to a dead end and a dead woman. Alone in his quarters, pacing the floor like a caged animal, he reviewed it again and again, trying to make sense of it.

Damn it, there was *purpose* behind it! Some one, or something, was *determined* he should not trace down his own past. The man and woman, refusing to help him, had said, "It is not for us to meddle in the affairs of the *vai leroni*."

That word was unfamiliar to him; he tried to puzzle out the component parts. *Vai*, of course, was simply an additional honorific, meaning something like *worthy* or *excellent;* as in *vai dom,* which meant, roughly, *worthy lord, good sir, your Excellency,* depending on context. *Leroni* he found under *leronis* (singular; mountain dialect) and defined as "probably derived from *laran,* meaning power or inheritance right, especially inherited psychic power; *leronis* can usually be translated *sorceress*."

But, Kerwin wondered, frowning, who then were

the *vai leroni*, the worthy sorceresses, and why in the world—*any* world—should anyone believe he was entangled in their affairs?

An intercom buzzer struck through his preoccupation; he growled response into it, then braced himself, for the face of the Legate, in the screen, looked very grim indeed.

"Kerwin? Get yourself up to Administration—on the double!"

Kerwin did as ordered, riding the long elevators to the high, glass-walled penthouse that was the Legate's staff quarters. As he waited outside Administration, he stiffened, seeing through the open door two of the green cross-belted uniforms of City Guardsmen; they came out, walking stiffly on either side of a tall, straight, silver-haired man whose rich dress and short, jeweled, blue-and-silver cloak betokened high Darkovan aristocracy. All three of them looked straight through Kerwin, and Kerwin felt a nagging sensation that the worst had yet to come.

The receptionist motioned him in. The Legate scowled at him and this time did not ask him to sit down.

"So it's the Darkovan," he said, not kindly. "I might have known. What the hell have you been getting yourself into now?"

He didn't wait for Kerwin's answer.

"You were warned," he said. "You got yourself into trouble before you'd been here a full twenty-eight hours. That wasn't enough; you had to go looking for trouble."

Kerwin opened his mouth to answer, but the Legate gave him no time. "I called your attention to

the situation on Darkover; we live here under an uneasy truce at best; and, such as it is, we have agreements with the Darkovans. Which includes keeping
nosey tourists out of the Old Town."

The injustice of that made Kerwin's blood boil.

"Look here, sir, I'm not a tourist! I was born and
brought up here—"

"Save it," the Legate said. "You got me just
curious enough to investigate that cock-and-bull
story you told me about having been born here.
Evidently you made the whole thing up, for some obscure reason of your own; there's no record of any
Jeff Kerwin anywhere in the Service. Except," he
added grimly, "the damned troublemaker I'm looking at right now."

"That's a lie!" Kerwin burst out in anger. Then
he stopped himself. He had seen it himself, the red
priority circuit for coded access warning. But he had
bribed the man; and the man said, *it's my job on the
line*.

"This is no world for snoops and troublemakers,"
the Legate said. "I warned you once, remember; but
I understand you had to do some pretty extensive
nosing around. . . ."

Kerwin drew breath, trying to present his case
calmly and reasonably. "Sir, if I made this whole
thing up out of whole cloth, why would anyone be
bothered by what you call my 'nosing around'? Can't
you see that if anything this proves my story—that
there's something funny going on?"

"All it proves to me," said the Legate, "is that
you're a nut with a persecution complex; some notion that we're all in a plot to keep you from finding
out something or other."

"It sounds so damned logical when you put it that way, doesn't it?" Kerwin said, and his voice was bitter.

"Okay," the Legate said, "just give me one good reason why anyone should bother plotting against one small-time civil servant, son of—as you claim—a spaceman in the Empire, somebody nobody ever heard of? Why would you be that important?"

Kerwin made a helpless gesture. What could he say to that? He knew his grandparents had existed, and he had been sent back to them, but if there was no record on Darkover of any Jeff Kerwin except himself, what could he say? Why would the woman at the orphanage lie? She had said herself that they were eager to retain contact with their boys. What proof did he have? Had he built the whole thing up from wishful thinking? His sanity reeled.

With a long sigh he let the memories go, and the dream.

"All right, sir, I'm sorry. I'll stay out of it; I won't try to find out anything more—"

"You won't have the chance," the Legate said coldly, "you won't be here."

"I won't—" Something struck, grim and knife-cold, in Kerwin's heart. The Legate nodded, his face rigid.

"The City Elders put your name on a list of *persona non grata*," he said. "And even if they hadn't, official policy is to take a dim view of anybody who gets too mixed up in native affairs."

Kerwin felt as if he had been pole-axed; he stood motionless, feeling the blood drain from his face, leaving him cold and lifeless. "What do you mean?"

"I mean I put you down for transfer out," the

Legate said. "You can call it that if you want to. In plain words, you've stuck your big nose into too many corners, and we're making damned sure you don't do it again. You're going to be on the next ship out of here."

Kerwin opened his mouth and then shut it again. He steadied himself against the Legate's desk, feeling as if he might fall over if he didn't. "You mean I'm being deported?"

"That's about it," the Legate confirmed. "In practice, it's not that bad, of course. I signed it as if it were a routine transfer application; God knows, we get enough of them from out here. You have a clean record, and I'll give you a clean-sheet recommendation. Within limits, you can have any assignment you've got the seniority for; see the Dispatch board about it."

Kerwin said, through a queer thickening lump in his throat, "But sir, Darkover—" and stopped. It was his home. It was the only place he wanted to be.

The Legate shook his head, as if he could read Kerwin's thoughts. He looked tired, worn, an old man, a weary man, struggling with a world too complex for him. "I'm sorry, son," he said, kindly. "I guess I know how you feel. But I've got a job to do and not an awful lot of leeway in how I do it. That's the way it is; you're going to be on the next ship out of here. And don't put in an application to come back, because you won't get it." He stood up. "I'm sorry, kid," he said, and offered his hand.

Kerwin did not touch it. The Legate's face hardened.

"You're relieved from duty as of now; inside twenty-eight hours, I want a formal transfer request

filled out, with your preferred routing for assignment; if I have to do it for you, I'll put you through
for the penal colony on Lucifer Delta. You're con-
fined to quarters till you leave." He bent over his
desk, shuffling the papers there. Without looking up,
he said, "You can go."

Kerwin went. So he had lost, then—lost entirely. It
had been too big for him, the mystery he faced; he
had run up against something entirely beyond him.

*The Legate had been lying. He had known that, when the
man offered him his hand at the last. The Legate had been
forced to send him into exile, and he didn't particularly want
to. . . .*

Going back into his bleak rooms, Kerwin told
himself not to be a fool. Why would the Legate lie?
Was he a dreamer, a fool with delusions of persecution, compensating for his orphan childhood
with dreams of grandeur?

He paced the floor, went restlessly to the window,
staring at the red sun dipping toward the hills. *The
bloody sun.* Some romantic poet had given Cottman's
Star that name a long time ago. As the swift dark
came rushing from the mountains, he clenched his
fists, staring into the sky.

*Darkover. It's the end of Darkover for me. The world I
fought for, and it's kicking me out again. I worked and
schemed to get back here, and it's all going for nothing. All
I get is frustration, closed doors, death. . . .*

*The matrix is real. I didn't dream that, or invent it. And
that belongs to Darkover. . . .*

He put his hand into his pocket and drew out the
blue jewel. Somehow this was the key to the mystery,
the key to all the closed doors slammed in his face.
Maybe he should have shown it to the Legate . . . no.

The Legate knew perfectly well that Kerwin was telling the truth; only, for some reason, he had chosen not to admit it. Faced with the matrix, he would simply have invented some other lie.

Kerwin wondered how he knew the man had been lying. But he *knew*. Beyond a doubt, without hesitation, he knew the man had been lying, for some obscure reason of his own. But *why*?

He drew the curtains against the blackness outside, the lights of the spaceport below, and set the crystal on the table. He paused, hesitant, seeing in his mind's eye the picture of a woman sprawled in unlovely death, the terror that had risen in him. . . .

I saw something when she was looking into the matrix, but I can't remember what it was. I only remember that it scared the hell out of me. . . . A woman's face flickered in his mind, dark forms against an opening door. . . . He set his teeth against the surging panic, battering against the closed door of his memory, but he could not remember; only the fear, the scream in a child's voice and darkness.

He told himself sternly not to be a fool. The man Ragan had used this crystal and it hadn't hurt him. Feeling self-conscious, he laid the crystal on the table and shaded his eyes as the woman had done, staring into it.

Nothing happened.

Damn it, maybe there was a special knack to it, maybe he should have hunted up Ragan and persuaded him, or bribed him, to teach him how to use it. Well, too late for that now. He stared fiercely into the crystal, and for a moment it seemed that a pale light flickered inside it, crawling blue lights that made him feel vaguely sick. But it vanished. Kerwin shook his head. He had a crick in his neck and his eyes were playing tricks on him, that was all. The old "crystal-gazing" trick was just a form of self-hypnosis, he'd have to guard against that.

The light remained. It crept, a small faint pinpoint of color moving inside the jewel. It *flared,* and Kerwin jumped; it was like a red-hot wire touching something inside his brain. And then he heard something, a voice very far away, calling his name . . . no. There were no words. But it was speaking to *him,* to no one else who had ever existed, a vastly *personal* message. It was something like, *You. Yes, you. I see you.*

Or, even more, *I recognize you.*

Dizzily he shook his head, gripping at the edge of the table with his fists. His head hurt, but he could not stop now. It seemed that he could hear speech, just random syllables . . . a low murmuring voice, or voices, that went on and on just below the threshold of awareness, like a running, whispering stream murmuring over sharp stones.

Yes, he is the one.

You cannot fight it now.

Cleindori worked too hard for this to waste it.

Does he know what he has or what is happening?

Be careful! Don't hurt him! He's not accustomed . . .

A barbarian, Terranan . . .

If he is to be any good to us, he must find his way alone and unaided, that much of a test I must insist upon.

We need him too much for that. Let me help . . .

Need that? A Terranan—

That voice sounded like the redhead in the Sky Harbor Hotel, but when Kerwin whirled, half expecting to find that the man had somehow made his way into the very room, there was no one there and the bodiless voices were gone

He leaned forward, staring into the crystal. And then, as it seemed to expand, to fill the room, he saw the face of a woman.

For a moment, because of the glint of red hair, he thought it was the small, pixielike girl they had called Taniquel. Then he realized that he had never seen her before.

Her hair was red, but a pale red, almost more golden than red; she was small and slender, and her face was round, childish, unmarred. She could not, Kerwin thought, be very far out of her teens. She looked straight at him, with wide, dreamy grey eyes that seemed to look, unfocused, *through* him.

I have faith in you, she said somehow, wordlessly, or at least the words seemed to reverberate inside his head, *and we have such need of you that I have convinced the others. Come.*

Kerwin's hands clenched on the table.

"Where? *Where?*" he shouted.

But the crystal was blank and blue again, and the strange girl was gone; he heard his own cry echo foolishly on empty walls.

Had she ever been there? Kerwin wiped his forehead, damp with cold sweat. Had his own wishful thinking tried to give him an answer? He swept the crystal into his pocket. He couldn't waste time on this. He had to pack for space, dispose of his gear, and leave Darkover, never to return. Leave his dreams behind, and the last of his youth. Leave behind all those vague memories and teasing dreams, those will-o'-the-wisps that had led him halfway to destruction. Make a new life for himself somewhere, a smaller life somehow, bounded by the KEEP OUT sign of the old dead hopes and longings, make a life somehow out of the fragments of his old aspirations, with bitterness and resignation. . . .

And then something rose up inside Jeff Kerwin, something that was not the meek CommTerra employee, something that stood up on its hind legs and pawed the ground and said, cold and clean and unmistakable: *No*.

That wasn't the way it was going to be. The *Terranan* could never force him to go.

Who the hell do they think they are, anyway, those damned intruders on our world?

The voice from the crystal? No, Kerwin thought, the inner voice of his own mind, flatly rejecting the commands of the Legate. This was *his* world, and he'd be damned if they were going to force him off it.

He realized that he was moving automatically, without thought, like a long-buried other self. Kerwin watched himself moving around the room, discarding most of his gear; he thrust half a dozen minor keepsakes into a pocket, left the rest where they were. He put the matrix on its chain around his neck and tucked it carefully out of sight. He started to unbutton his uniform, then shrugged, left it the way it was, but went to a wardrobe and got out the embroidered Darkovan cloak he had bought his first night in Thendara, drew it around his shoulders and did up the fastenings. He glanced briefly in the mirror. Then, without a backward glance, he walked out of his quarters, the thought dimly skittering across the surface of his mind that he would never see them again.

He walked through the central living rooms of bachelor quarters, took a short cut through the deserted dining commons. At the outer door of the section he paused; a clear and unmistakable inner voice said, *no, not now, wait.*

Not understanding, but riding the hunch—what else was there to do?—he sat down and waited. He felt, oddly, not impatient at all. The waiting had the same wary certainty of a cat at a mousehole; a secureness, a—a *rightness.* He sat quietly, hands clasped, whistling a monotonous little tune to himself. He did not feel restless. Half an hour, an hour, an hour and a half went by; his muscles began to feel cramped and he shifted automatically to relieve the tension, but he went on waiting, without knowing what he was waiting for.

Now.

He stood up and stepped out into the deserted corridor. As he walked swiftly down the hall, he found himself wondering if there would be a pickup order out for him if he should be missed from his quarters. He supposed so. He had no plans, except the very basic one of refusing to obey the deportation order. This meant he must somehow get out, not only of the HQ, but of the Spaceport Zone and the entire Terran Zone unobserved. What would come after he did not know and, strangely, did not care.

Still riding the strange hunch, he turned out of the main corridor where he might meet off-duty acquaintances heading for the quarters, and went toward a little-used freight elevator. He told himself that he ought, at least, to take off the Darkovan cloak; if anyone met him wearing it, inside the HQ, it would lead to question and discovery. He put up his hand to unfasten the clasps and sling it over his arm; back in uniform, he'd just be another invisible employee walking in the halls.

No.

Clear, unmistakable, the negative warning in his mind. Puzzled, he dropped his hand and let the cloak be. He emerged from the elevator into a narrow walkway and paused to orient himself; this part of the building was not familiar to him. There was a door at the end of the walkway; he pushed it open and emerged into a crowded lobby. What looked like a whole shift of maintenance workers in uniform was milling around, getting ready to go off duty. And a large group of Darkovans in their colorful dress and long cloaks were making their way through the crowd toward the outer door and the gates. Kerwin, at first taken aback by the crowd, realized quickly that no one was paying the slightest attention to him. Slowly, unobtrusively, he made his way through the crowd, and managed to join the group of Darkovans. None of them took the slightest notice of him. He supposed they were some formal delegation from the city, one of the committees that helped administer the Trade City. They formed a random stream in the crowd, going in their own special direction, and Kerwin, at the edge of the group, streamed along with them, into the street, outside the HQ, through the gateway that led out of the enclosure. The Space-force guards there gave them, and Kerwin, only the most cursory of glances.

Outside the gate the group of Darkovans began to break up into twos and threes, talking, lingering. One of the men gave Kerwin a polite look of non-recognition and inquiry. Kerwin murmured a formal phrase, turned quickly and walked at random into a side street.

*   *   *

The Old Town was already shadowed with dimness. The wind blew chill, and Kerwin shivered a little in the warm cloak. Where was he going, anyhow?

He hesitated at the corner of the street where, once in a restaurant, he had faced Ragan down. Should he seek out the place and try and see if the little man could be useful to him?

Again the clear, unmistakable *no* from that inner mentor. Kerwin wondered if he was imagining things, rationalizing. Well, it didn't matter much, one way or the other, and it had gotten him out of the HQ; so whatever the hunch he was riding, he'd stay with it a while. He looked back at the HQ building, already half wiped out in the thickening mist, then turned his back on it and it was like the slamming of a mental door. That was the end of that. He had cut himself adrift and he would not look back again.

A curious peace seemed to descend over him with this decision. He turned his back on the known streets and began to walk quickly away from the Trade City area.

He had never come quite so far into the Old Town, even on that day he had sought out the old matrix mechanic, the day that had ended with her death. Down here the buildings were old, built of that heavy translucent stone, chill againt the blowing wind. At this hour there were few people in the streets; now and then a solitary walker, a workman in one of the cheap imported climbing jackets, walked head down against the wind; once a woman carried in a curtained sedan chair on the shoulders of four men; once, moving noiselessly in the lee of the building, a silver-mantled, gliding nonhuman regarded him with uninvolved malice.

A group of street gamins in ragged smocks, barefoot, moved toward him as if to pester him for alms; suddenly they drew back, whispered to each other, and ran off. Was it the ceremonial cloak, the red hair they could see beneath the hood?

The swift mist was thickening; now snow began to fall, soft thick heavy flakes; and Kerwin became quickly aware that he was hopelessly lost in the unfamiliar streets. He had been walking almost at random, turning corners on impulse, with that strange, almost dreamish sensation that it didn't matter which way he went. Now, in a great and open square, so unfamiliar that he had not the slightest idea how far he had come, he stopped, shaking his head, coming up to normal consciousness.

Good God, where am I? And where am I going? I can't wander around all night in a snowstorm, even wearing a Darkovan cloak over my uniform! I should have started out by looking for a place to hide out for a while; or I should have tried to get right out of the city before I was missed!

Dazed, he looked around. Maybe he should try and get back to the HQ, take whatever punishment was coming. No. That way lay exile. He had already settled that. But the curious hunch that had been guiding him all this way seemed to be running out, and now it deserted him entirely. He stood staring this way and that, wiping snowflakes from his eyes and trying to decide which way he should go. Down one side of the square there was a row of little shops, all fast-shuttered against the night. Kerwin mopped his wet face with a wet sleeve, staring through the thick snow at a solitary house; a mansion, really, the town house of some nobleman. Inside there were lights, and he could see, through the translucent walls, dark blurred forms. Drawn almost magnetically to the lights, Kerwin crossed the square and stood just outside the half-open gate. Inside was a flight of shallow steps, which led to a great carved door. He stood there, fighting the invisible pull of that door.

What am I doing? I can't just walk in there, into a strange house! Have I gone completely crazy?

No. This is the place. They're waiting for me.

He told himself that was madness; but his steps carried him on, automatically, toward the gate. He put a hand on it, and when nothing happened, he opened it and went through and stood on the lower step. And there he stopped, sanity and madness fighting in him, and the worst part of it was, Kerwin wasn't quite sure which was which.

You've come this far. You can't stop now.

You're being an awful God-damned fool, Jefferson Andrew Kerwin. Get out—just turn right around and get the hell out of here before you get yourself into something you really *can't handle. Not just something predictable like being slugged and rolled in an alley.*

Step by slow step, he went up the sleet-slipperied steps toward the lighted doorway. *Too late to turn back now.* He grasped the handle, noticing peripherally the design, in the shape of a phoenix. He twisted it slowly, and the door opened and Kerwin stepped inside.

Miles away, in the Terran Zone, a man had gone to a communicator and requested a specially coded priority circuit to speak with the Legate.

"Your bird's flown," he said.

The Legate's face on the screen was composed and smug.

"I thought so. Push hard enough and they'd have to make a move. I knew they wouldn't let us deport him."

"You sound awfully sure, sir. He sounds like an independent cuss. Maybe he just walked off on his own; went over the wall. He wouldn't be the first. Not even the first one named Kerwin."

The Legate shrugged. "We'll soon find out."

"You want him tailed any further, then?"

The answer was immediate. "No! Hell, no! These people are nobody's fools! In the state he was in he might not have spotted a tail; it's for damn sure *they* would. Let him go; no strings. It's their move. Now —we wait."

"We've been doing that for more than twenty years," the man grumbled.

"We'll wait twenty more if we have to. But the catalyst's working now; somehow I don't think it will be that long. Wait and see."

The screen went blank. After a while the Legate pushed another button and hit a special access code marked KERWIN.

He looked satisfied.

Chapter Seven: Homecoming

Kerwin stood blinking against the warmth and light of the spacious hallway. He mopped snow from his face again, and for a moment all he could hear was the wind and snow outside, slapping against the closed door. Then a bright tinkle of laughter broke the silence.

"Elorie has won," said a light, girlish voice, somehow familiar to him. "I told you so."

A thick velvet curtain parted, just before him, and a girl stood there; a slender young woman with red hair in a green dress with a high collar, and a pixie-pretty face. She was laughing at him. Behind her two men came through the curtains, and Kerwin wondered if he had somehow wandered into a daydream —or nightmare. For they were the three redheads from the Sky Harbor Hotel; the pretty woman was Taniquel, and behind her, the feline and arrogant Auster, the thickset, urbane man who had introduced himself as Kennard. It was Kennard who spoke now.

"Did you doubt it, Tani?"

"The *Terranan*!" Auster stood glowering; Kennard gently moved Taniquel out of his way, and came toward Kerwin, who stood bewildered, wondering if he ought to apologize for this intrusion. Kennard stopped a step or two from Kerwin and said, "Welcome home, my boy."

Auster said something sarcastic, curling his lip in an ironic smile.

Kerwin said, shaking his head, "I don't understand any of this."

"Tell me," Kennard countered, "how did you find this place?"

Kerwin said, too baffled for anything but the truth, "I don't know. I just came. Hunch, I guess."

"No," Kennard said gravely, "it was a test; and you passed it."

"A *test?*" Suddenly Kerwin was both angry and apprehensive. Ever since he landed on Darkover, somebody had been pushing him around; and now, when he made what he thought was an independent move to break away, he found himself led here.

"I suppose I ought to be grateful. Right now all I want is an explanation! Test? What for? Who *are* you people? What do you want with me? Are you still mistaking me for someone else? Who do you think I am?"

"Not who," said Taniquel, "what." And at the same time Kennard said, "No, we knew *who* you were all along. What we had to find out—" And the two of them stopped, looked at each other and laughed. Then the girl said, "You tell him, Ken. He's *your* kinsman."

Kerwin jerked up his head and stared at them, and Kennard said, "We are all your kinsmen, if it comes to that; but I knew who you were, or at least I guessed, from the beginning. And if I had not known, your matrix would have told me, because I have seen it before and worked with it before. But we had to test you, to see if you had inherited *laran,* if you were genuinely one of us."

Kerwin frowned and said, "What do you mean? I am a Terran."

Kennard shook his head and said, "That's as may be. Among us the child takes the rank and privilege of the parent of higher caste. And your mother was a woman of the Comyn; my foster-sister, Cleindori Aillard."

There was a sudden silence, while Kerwin heard the word *Comyn* echo and re-echo in the room.

"Remember," Kennard said at last, "that we mistook you for one of ourselves, that night in the Sky Harbor Hotel. We were not so wrong as we thought —not so wrong as you told us we were."

Auster interrupted again with something unintelligible. It was strange how clearly he could understand Kennard and Taniquel, and hardly a word of Auster's speech.

"Your foster-sister?" Kerwin asked. "Who are you?"

"Kennard-Gwynn Lanart-Alton, Heir to Armida," the older man said. "Your mother and I were fostered together; we are blood kin as well, though the relationship is—complicated. When Cleindori—died—you were taken away; by night and by stealth. We tried to trace her child; but there was, at that time, a—" Again he hesitated. "I'm not trying to be secretive, I give you my word; it's only that I can't imagine how to make it clear to you without giving you a long history of the political complications of forty-odd years ago in the Domains. There were—problems, and when we knew where you were, we decided to leave you there for a time; at least you were safe there. By the time we could try and reclaim you, they had already sent you to Terra, and all we could do was wait. I was reasonably sure of who you were, that night in the hotel. And then your matrix turned up on one of the monitor screens . . ."

"What?"

"I can't explain just now. Any more than I can explain Auster's stupidity when he met you in the bar, except that he'd been drinking. Of course, you weren't exactly cooperative, either."

Again Auster exploded into unintelligible speech, and Kennard motioned him to silence. "Save your breath, Auster, he's not getting a word of it. Anyway, you passed the first test; you have rudimentary *laran*. And because of who you are, and—and certain other things—we're going to find out if you have enough of it to be useful to us. I gather you want to stay on Darkover; we offer you a chance at that."

Dazed, still off balance, and feeling somewhere inside himself that Kennard's explanations were only confusing the issue further, Kerwin could do nothing but stare.

Well, he had followed his hunch; and if it had led him from the trap to the cookpot, he had only himself to thank.

Well, here I am, he thought. *The only trouble is, I haven't the foggiest notion of where "here" is!*

"What is this place?" he asked. "Is it—" He repeated the word he had heard Kennard say: "Armida?"

Kennard shook his head, laughing. "Armida is the Great House of the Alton Domain," he said. "It's in the Kilghard Hills, more than a day's ride from here.

This is the town house belonging to my family. The rational thing would have been to bring you to Comyn Castle; but there were some of the Comyn who didn't want anything to do with this—" he hesitated—"this experiment until they knew what was going to happen, one way or another. And it was better that we shouldn't let too many people in on what was happening."

Kerwin looked around at the rich draperies, the walls hung with panels of curtain. The place seemed familiar, somehow, familiar and strange, out of those long-ago, half-forgotten dreams. Kennard answered his unspoken thought:

"You may possibly have been here once or twice. As a very young child. I doubt if you would remember, though. Anyhow—" He glanced at Taniquel and Auster. "We should go, as soon as we can. I want to leave the city as quickly as possible. And Elorie is waiting." His face was suddenly somber. "I don't have to tell you that there are—some people— who will take a very dim view of all this, and we want to present them with something already accomplished." His eyes seemed to go right through Kerwin as he said, "You've already been attacked once, haven't you?"

Kerwin didn't waste time wondering how Kennard knew that. He said, "Yes," and Kennard looked grim. He said, "I thought, at first, that Auster was behind it. But he swore to me that he wasn't. I had hoped—those old hates, superstitions, fears—I had hoped a generation would quiet them down." He sighed, turned to Taniquel.

"Let me just say goodnight to the children. Then I'll be ready to go with you."

*　　*　　*

A little airship, buffeted by the treacherous winds and currents of flowing atmosphere above the crags and ridges of the mountains, flew through the reddening dawn. They had left the storm behind; but the rough terrain, a dizzy distance below, was softened by layers of mist.

Kerwin sat with legs folded up uncomfortably beneath him, watching Auster manipulate the unseen controls. He would not have chosen to share the small forward pilot-cabin with Auster, but there was barely room for Kennard and Taniquel in the small rear cabin, and he had not been consulted about his preference. He was still baffled by the speed with which events had moved; almost at once they had hurried him to a small private landing field at the far edge of the city, and put him aboard this plane. At least, he thought wryly, he now knew more than the Terran Legate, who couldn't imagine what use the Darkovans had for aircraft.

Kerwin still didn't know what they wanted with him; but he wasn't frightened. They weren't exactly friendly; but they somehow—well, they *accepted* him, much as his grandparents had done; it had nothing to do with his character and personality, or whether they liked him—and Auster, at least, definitely *didn't* —they accepted him, like family. Yes, that was it; like family. Even when Kennard had brusquely cut off his flood of questions with "Later, later!" there had been no offense.

The ship had no visible instruments except for some small calibrator dials. One of these Auster had adjusted when they boarded, apologizing curtly for the discomfort—an unpleasant vibration that made

Kerwin's ears and teeth ache. It was necessary, Auster told him in a few grudging words, to compensate for the presence of an undeveloped telepath inside the aircraft.

Since then Auster had barely leaned forward, now and then, from his folded-up kneeling posture, stirring a hand languidly as if signaling some unseen watcher. Or, thought Kerwin, as if he were shooing away flies. He had asked, once, what powered the ship.

"Matrix crystal," Auster said briefly.

This made Kerwin purse his lips in a soundless whistle. He had not even remotely guessed that the power of these thought-sensitive crystals could be so enormous. It wasn't psi power alone. He was sure of that. Kerwin had guessed, from what Ragan had told him and what little he had seen, that matrix technology was one of those sciences that Terrans lumped together under the general name of *non-causative sciences;* cyrillics, electromentry, psychokinetics; and Kerwin knew very little of these. They were usually found on nonhuman worlds.

Kerwin was, despite all his fascination, plainly and unequivocally scared. And yet—he had never thought of himself as Terran except by accident of birth. Darkover was the only home he had ever known, and now he knew that he really belonged here, that he was somehow related to their highest nobility, to the Comyn.

The Comyn. He knew very little about them; just what every Terran assigned to Cottman Four knew, which wasn't much. They were a hereditary caste who chose to have as little as possible to do with the Terrans, though they had ceded the spaceport lease and allowed the building of the Trade Cities. They were not kings, autocrats, priesthood, or government; he knew more about what they were *not* than what they were. But he had had a taste of the fanatical reverence with which they were treated, these red-haired noblemen.

He tried cautiously to unkink his legs without kicking out a bulkhead. "How much further is this city of yours?" he asked Auster.

Auster did not deign to look at him. He was very thin, with a suggestion of the feline in his shoulders and the curl of his arrogant mouth; but he looked familiar somehow, too, in a way Kerwin couldn't quite identify. Well, they were all related somehow; Kennard had said they were all his kinsmen. Maybe Auster looked like Kennard.

"We do not speak the Cahuenga here," Auster said tersely, "and I cannot understand you, or you me, with the telepathic damper adjusted." He made a small gesture toward the calibrator.

"What's wrong with Cahuenga? You can speak it all right—I heard you."

"We are capable of learning any known human tongue," said Auster, with that unconscious arrogance that irritated Kerwin so much, "but the concepts of our world are expressible only in the nexus of our own semantic symbology, and I have no desire to converse in crocodile with a half-breed on trivial matters."

Kerwin fought an impulse to hit him. He was thoroughly tired of his offhand statement about lizardmen, and tireder of having Auster throw it back at him every time he opened his mouth. He'd never known a man quite so easy to dislike as Auster, and if the man was his kinsman, he decided blood relationships didn't mean as much as they were supposed to mean. He found himself wondering just how closely they were related. Not too closely, he hoped.

The sun was just touching the rim of the mountains when Auster stirred slightly, his satirical face relaxing a little, and pointed between twin mountain peaks.

"It lies there," he said, "the plains of Arilinn, and the City, and the Arilinn Tower."

Kerwin moved his cramped shoulders, looking downward at the city of his forefathers. From this altitude it looked like any other city, a pattern of lights, buildings, cleared spaces. The little craft slanted downward in response to one of those shoofly motions of Auster's hands; Kerwin lost his balance, made a wild grab to recover it, and involuntarily fell against Auster's side.

He was wholly unprepared for Auster's reaction. The man forgot the operation of the ship and with a great sweep of his arm, jerked backward, his elbow thrusting out to knock Kerwin away from him, hard. His forearm struck Kerwin a hard blow across the mouth; the aircraft lurched, swerved, and behind them, in the cabin, Taniquel screamed. Auster, recovering himself, made swift controlling movements.

Kerwin's first impulse—to swat Auster in the teeth and be damned to the consequences—died unacted. He held himself in his seat by an act of will, clenching his fists to keep control. He said in Cahuenga, "Fly the damn ship, you. If you're spoiling for a fight, wait till we get landed, and it will be my pleasure to oblige you."

Kennard's head appeared in the narrow doorway

between control and rear cabin; he said something questioning, concerned, in a language Kerwin didn't know, and Auster snarled, "Then let him keep his crocodile's paws to himself, damn him!"

Kerwin opened his mouth—it was Auster's sharp movement that had flung him against the other man —and then shut it again. He hadn't done anything to apologize for! Kennard said in a conciliating tone, "Kerwin, perhaps you did not know that any random movement can throw the aircraft off course, when it is being operated by matrix control." He looked at Kerwin thoughtfully, then shrugged. "We'll be landing in a minute, anyway."

The little ship came down smoothly on a small landing field where a few lights were blinking. Auster unfastened a door and a swart Darkovan in a leather jerkin and breeches threw up a short ladder.

"Welcome, *vai dom'yn*," he said, throwing up one hand in a courtly gesture vaguely like a salute. Auster stepped down the ladder, gesturing Kerwin to follow, and they repeated the salute for him. Kennard came down the ladder, fumbling with his feet for the rungs. Kerwin had not realized how excruciatingly lame the older man was; one of the men came, deferentially, to assist Kennard, who accepted the man's arm with good grace. Only a little tightening of his jaw showed Jeff Kerwin what Kennard really thought of accepting the man's help. Taniquel scrambled down the ladder, looking sleepy and cross; she said something to Auster with a scowl and they stood talking together in an undertone. Kerwin wondered if they were married, or lovers; they had a sort of easy intimacy that he associated only with long-term couples. Then she looked up at Kerwin, shaking her head.

"There's blood on your mouth. Have you and Auster been fighting already?"

There was a teasing malice in her voice; she tilted her head to one side, looking first at one of them and then the other. Auster glowered.

"An accident and a misunderstanding," Kennard said quietly.

"*Terranan,*" Auster muttered.

"How can you expect him to be anything else? And whose fault is it that he knows nothing of our laws?" Kennard asked. Then he pointed, drawing Kerwin's gaze with the gesture.

"There it lies; the Tower of Arilinn."

It rose upright, squat, and yet, on closer look, incredibly high, fashioned of some brown and glareless stone. The sight seemed to stir in Kerwin some buried *déjà vu* again, as he looked at the Tower rising against the sky, and he said, his voice shaky, "Have I—have I been here before, sir?"

Kennard shook his head. "No, I don't think so," he said. "Perhaps the matrix—I just don't know. Does it seem so familiar to you?" He laid his hand briefly on Kerwin's shoulder—a gesture that surprised the younger man, in view of the taboo that seemed to surround a random touch among these people. Kennard withdrew his hand quickly, and said, "It is not the oldest, or even the most powerful of the Comyn Towers. But for a hundred generations and more our Keepers have worked the Arilinn Tower in an unbroken succession of Comyn blood alone."

"And," said Auster behind them, "with the hundred and first we bring the son of a Terran and of a renegade *leronis* here!"

Taniquel turned on him fiercely. She said, "Are you going to question the word of Elorie of Arilinn?"

Kerwin swung angrily on Auster. He had taken enough from him already; now the man had started on his parents! *The son of a Terran and a renegade leronis . . .*

Kennard's deep voice was harsh:

"Auster, that's enough; I said it before we came here, and I will say it for the last time. The man is not responsible for his parents or their fancied sins. And Cleindori, I remind you, was *my* foster-sister, and *my* Keeper, and if you speak of her again in that tone, you will answer, not to her son, but to *me*!"

Auster hung his head and muttered something; it sounded like an apology. Taniquel came to Kerwin's side and said, "Let's get inside, not stand around on the airfield all day!"

Kerwin felt curious eyes on him as he crossed the field. The air was damp and cold, and it crossed his mind that it would be pleasant to get under a roof, and get warm, and relax, and that he would very much like a bath, and a drink, and some supper—hell—breakfast! Anyhow, he'd been up all night.

"All in good time," Kennard said, and Kerwin jumped, realizing he would have to get used to that trick Kennard had of reading his thoughts. "First, I'm afraid, you'll have to meet the others here; naturally we're anxious to know all about you, especially those of us who haven't had a chance to meet you face to face yet."

Kerwin wiped at the blood still oozing from his lip. He wished they'd let him clean up before thrusting him into the presence of strangers. He had not yet learned that telepaths seldom paid any attention to what a man looked like on the outside. He walked across the bricked-in quadrangle of a building that looked like a barracks, and through a long passage-way barred with a wooden gate. A familiar smell told him that horses were stabled nearby. Only as they neared the Tower did he become aware of the way in which the clean sweep of its architecture was marred by the cluster of low buildings around its foot. They went across two more outer courtyards, and finally reached a carven archway across which shimmered a thin, rainbow mist.

Here Kennard paused momentarily, saying to Kerwin, "No living human, except those of pure and unbroken Comyn blood, has ever crossed this Veil."

Kerwin shrugged. He felt he should be impressed or something, but he was running low on surprise. He was both tired and hungry, he hadn't slept in forty-eight hours, and it made him nervous to realize that they were all, even Auster, watching to see what he would say or do when faced with this. He said irritably, "What is this, a test? My hat's fresh out of rabbits, and anyway, you're writing the script. Do we go this way?"

They kept on waiting, so he braced himself and stepped through the trembling rainbow.

It felt faintly electric, like a thousand pins and needles, as if his whole body were a foot that had gone to sleep, and when he looked back he could not see the others except as the vaguest of shadows. Suddenly he began to shake; had this all been an elaborate build-up to some kind of trap? He stood alone in a tiny windowless cubicle, a cul-de-sac, only the rainbow behind him showing the faintest of lights.

Then Taniquel stepped through the rainbow shimmer, Auster and Kennard following. Kerwin let out a sigh of foolish relief . . . if they'd meant him any harm, they wouldn't have had to bring him this far!

Taniquel made signals with her fingers, not unlike those Auster had used controlling the aircraft, and the cubicle shot upward, with such suddenness that Kerwin swayed and almost fell again. It shivered and stopped and they stepped out through another open archway into a lighted room that opened, in turn, on a broad terrace.

The room was huge, rising to echoing space, yet paradoxically gave an impression of warmth and intimacy. The floor was laid with old tiles worn uneven, as if they had seen many feet walking on them. At the far end of the room was a fire that smelled of fragrant smoke and incense, and something furry and dark and not human crouched there, doing something to the fire with a long, oddly-shaped bellows. As Kerwin came in, it turned large pupilless green eyes on him, fixing him with an intelligent stare of question.

To the right of the fire was a heavy carven table of some glossy wood, a few scattered armchairs, and a big dais or divan covered with heaps of cushions. Tapestries hung on the walls. A middle-aged woman rose out of one of the chairs and came toward them. She stopped a step away from Kerwin, regarding him with cool, intelligent grey eyes.

"The barbarian," she said. "Well, he looks it, with blood on his face. Any more fighting, Auster, and you can go back to the Nevarsin House of Penitence for a full season." She added, considering, "In winter."

Her voice was husky and harsh; there was grey liberally salted in hair that had once been gingery red. Her body was thick and compact beneath the heavy layers of skirts and shawls she wore, but was too sturdy to look fat. Her face was humorous and intelligent, wrinkled around the eyes.

"Well, what name did the *Terranan* give you?"

Kerwin told the woman his name, and she repeated it, her lip curling slightly.

"Jeff Kerwin. I suppose that was to be expected. My name is Mesyr Aillard, and I am your very remote cousin. Don't think I'm proud of the relationship. I'm not."

Among telepaths, polite social lies would be meaningless. Don't judge their manners by Terran standards. Kerwin thought that in spite of her rudeness, there was something about this hearty old lady that he rather liked. He only said courteously, "Perhaps, one day, I can change your mind, Mother." He used the Darkovan word that meant, not precisely *mother,* nor yet *foster-mother,* but a general term for any female relative of a mother's generation.

"Oh, you can call me Mesyr," she snapped. "I'm not *that* old! And close your face, Auster, the hole in it would swallow a banshee! He hasn't the faintest notion that he's being offensive, he doesn't know our customs, how would he?"

"If I have given offense when I intended courtesy—" Kerwin began.

"At that you call me *Mother* if you want to," Mesyr said. "I never go near the screens any more, not since my cub Corus was old enough to work in them; *that* much of a taboo I still observe. My son, Corus; what do we call you, *Jefferson*—" She stumbled a little over the name. "Jeff?"

A long-limbed youngster in his teens came and

gave Kerwin his hand, as if it were a formal act of defiance. He grinned quirkily in a way that reminded Kerwin of Taniquel and said, "Corus Ridenow. Have you been off-world, in space?"

"Four times. Three other planets, including Terra itself."

"Sounds interesting," Corus said, almost wistfully. "I've never been further than Nevarsin, myself."

Mesyr scowled at Corus and said, "This is Rannirl. Our technician."

Rannirl was about Kerwin's own age, a thin, tall competent-looking fellow with a shadow of red beard, and heavy callused muscular hands. He did not offer to shake hands with Jeff, but bowed formally and said, "So they found you. I didn't expect it, and I didn't expect you could make it through the Veil. Kennard, I owe you four bottles of Ravnet wine."

Kennard said with a cordial grin, "We'll drink it together next holiday—all of us. I believe you made a wager with Elorie, too? Your passion for a bet will ruin you some day, my friend. And where is Elorie? She should be on hand to claim the hawk she wagered, if nothing more."

"She will be down in a few minutes," said a tall woman, whom Kerwin decided to be about Mesyr's age. "I am Neyrissa." She was redheaded, too, red glints on rusty-brown hair, tall and angular and plain, but she met Jeff's eyes with a quick, direct stare. She didn't look friendly, but she wasn't hostile, either. "Are you going to be working as monitor here? I don't like to work outside the circle, it's a waste of my time."

"We haven't tested him yet, Rissa," Kennard said,

but the older woman shrugged.

"He has red hair, and he made it through the Veil without being hurt, and that's enough test for me; he's Comyn," she said. "But I suppose you have to find out which *donas* he has. Cassilda grant he's Alton or Ardais, we need the power of that. We're over-balanced on Ridenow gifts—"

"I resent that," said Taniquel gaily. "Are you going to stand there and let her say that, Corus?"

The teenager laughed and said, "In these days we can't afford to be choosy; that's what this is all about, isn't it, that we can't find enough people to work at Arilinn? If he has Cleindori's talents, that's splendid, but don't forget he has Ridenow blood, too."

"We won't know for a while whether he will make monitor or mechanic, or even a technician," Kennard said. "That will be for Elorie to say. Here's Elorie now."

They turned to the door; and then Kerwin realized that the silence in the room was his own imagination, for Mesyr and Rannirl and Neyrissa were still talking, and only in his own mind did a silence move around the girl who stood framed in the doorway. In that instant, as her grey eyes lifted to his, he recognized the face he had seen in the matrix crystal.

She was small and delicately made, and Kerwin realized that she was very young; perhaps even younger than Taniquel. Copper hair, sunrise gold, lay in straight pale strands around her sun-browned cheeks. Her dress was a formal robe of heavy crimson, pinned at the shoulders with clasps of heavy metal; dress and clasps seemed too weighty for her slenderness, as if the slim shoulders drooped under their burden; a child burdened with the robes of a princess or a priestess. She had the long-legged walk of a child, too, and a child's full sulky underlip, and her eyes, framed in long lashes, were grey and dreamy.

She said, "This is my barbarian, I suppose?"

"Yours?" Taniquel lifted her eyebrows at the girl in the crimson robe and giggled, and the grey-eyed girl said in her soft light voice, "Mine."

"Don't fight over me," Kerwin said. He couldn't help feeling a little amused.

"Don't flatter yourself," Auster snarled. Elorie raised her head and gave Auster one sharp, direct look, and to Kerwin's astonishment Auster lowered his head like a whipped dog.

Taniquel looked at Kerwin with that special smile —it was, Kerwin thought, as if they shared some secret—and said, "And this is our Keeper, Elorie of Arilinn. And now that's really all of us, so you can sit down and have something to eat and drink and recover your wits a little. I know this has been a long night, and hard for you."

Kerwin accepted the drink she put into his hand. Kennard lifted his glass to Kerwin and said, with a smile, "Welcome home, my lad." The others joined in, gathering around him, Taniquel with her kittenish grin, Corus with that odd mixture of curiosity and diffidence, Rannirl with a reserved, yet friendly smile, Neyrissa openly studying and appraising him. Only Elorie neither spoke nor smiled, giving Kerwin a grave direct glance over the rim of her goblet, then lowering her eyes. But he felt as if she, too, had said, "Welcome home."

Mesyr set her glass down firmly.

"That's that. And now, since we all stayed up all night to see whether they'd be able to get you back safely, I suggest we all get to bed and have some sleep."

Elorie rubbed her eyes with childish doubled fists and yawned. Auster moved to Elorie's side and said angrily, "You've exhausted yourself again! For *him,*" he added, with a furious glance at Kerwin. He went on speaking, but he had switched to a language Kerwin couldn't understand.

"Come along," Mesyr said, jerking her head at Kerwin. "I'll take you upstairs and find you a room. Explanations can come later, when we've all had some sleep."

One of the nonhumans went before them, bearing a light, as Mesyr led the way through a wide echoing hallway, up a long flight of mosaic stairs.

"One thing we're not short of is houseroom," she said. "So if you don't like this one, look around and find one that's empty and move into it. This place was built to hold twenty or thirty, they used to have three complete circles here, each with its own Keeper, and there are eight of us—nine, with you. Which, of course, is why you're here. One of the *kyrri* will bring you anything you want to eat, and if you need someone to help you dress, or anything like that, ask it for help. I'm sorry we have no human servants, but they can't come through the Veil."

Before he could ask any more questions, Mesyr said, "I'll see you at sunset. I'll send someone to show you the way," and went away. Kerwin stood and looked around the room.

It was huge and luxurious, not just a room but a suite of rooms. The furnishings were old, and the hangings on the walls were faded. In an inner room was a great bed on a dais; the prints of generations of feet had worn depressions in the tiles, but the bedding was fresh and white and smelled faintly of incense. There were some old books and scrolls on shelves, and a couple of musical instruments on a shelf. Kerwin wondered who had last lived in this room, and how long ago. The little furry nonhuman was opening curtains to let in the light in the outer room, closing them to shade the inner room, turning down the bed. Exploring the suite, Kerwin found a bath of almost sybaritic luxury, with a sunken tub deep enough to swim in; and other fixtures to match, alien-looking, but, he discovered, provided with everything a human could want and a few things he wouldn't have thought of for himself. There were a few small, carved ivory-and-silver jars on a shelf; curiously he opened one. It was empty, except for a little dried, resinous paste at the bottom. Cosmetic or perfume, a ghost of some long-dead Comyn *leronis* who had once inhabited these rooms. Was the room filled with ghosts? The perfume stabbed another of those half-memories buried in his mind; he supposed he must have smelled it when he was very young, and he stood very still, fumbling for the memory; but it eluded him . . . he shook his head resolutely, closed the jar. The memory receded, a dream within a dream.

He went back into the sitting-room of the suite. A painting hung there—a slender copper-haired woman struggling in the grip of a demon. Kerwin's childhood memories of Darkovan legend identified the mythical figures, the ravishment of Camilla by the demon Zandru. There were other paintings from

Darkovan legend; he recognized some from the *Ballad of Hastur and Cassilda,* the legendary Cassilda at her golden loom, bending over the unconscious form of the Son of Light on the shores of Hali, Camilla bringing cherries and fruits to him, Cassilda with a starflower in her hand, Alar at his forge, Alar chained in hell with the she-wolf gnawing at his heart, Sharra rising in flames ... Camilla pierced with the shadow-sword. Vaguely he remembered that the Comyn claimed to be descended from the mythical Hastur, Son of Light. He wondered what the God of the legends had to do with the present-day Hasturs of the Comyn. But he was too tired to wonder for long, or ask any more questions. He went and threw off his clothes and crawled into the big bed, and after a time he fell asleep.

When he woke the sun was declining, and one of the soft-footed nonhumans was moving around in the bathroom, drawing water from which came a faint perfume. Remembering what Mesyr had said about a meeting at sunset, Kerwin bathed, shaved, ate some of the food the nonhuman brought him. But when the furry creature gestured toward the bed, where he had laid out some Darkovan clothing, Kerwin shook his head and dressed in the dark uniform of Terran Civil Service. He was sourly amused at himself. Among Terrans he felt a need to emphasize his Darkovan blood, but here he felt a sudden compulsion not to deny his Terran heritage. He wasn't ashamed of being the son of a Terran, whatever Auster said, and if they wanted to call him barbarian, well, let them!

Without a knock, or the slightest word of warning, the girl Elorie came into his room. Kerwin started, taken aback by the intrusion; if she'd come in two minutes earlier, she'd have caught him in his bare skin! Even though he was dressed, except for his boots, it disconcerted him!

"Barbarian," she said with a low laugh. "Of course I knew! I'm a telepath, remember?"

Flushing to the roots of his hair, Kerwin put his foot into his other shoe. Obviously the conventions of life in a group of telepaths wouldn't be what he was accustomed to.

"Kennard was afraid you'd get lost, trying to come down to the big hall; and I told him I'd come and show you the way."

Elorie was no longer wearing the heavy formal robe, but a filmy gown, embroidered with sprays of starflowers and bunches of cherries. She was standing just beneath one of the legendary paintings, and the resemblance was immediately apparent. He looked from the painting to the girl and asked, "Did you sit for your portrait?"

She glanced up indifferently. "No; that was my great-great-grandmother," she said. "The women of the Comyn, a few generations ago, had a passion for being painted as mythological characters. I copied the dress from the painting, though. Come along."

She wasn't being very friendly, or even very polite; but she did seem to take him for granted, as they all had done.

At the end of the hallway, about to lead the way down a flight of long stairs, Elorie paused and went to a window where a deep embrasure in the wall looked over a sunset landscape.

"Look," she said, and pointed. "From here you can see just the tip of the mountain peak at Thendara

—if your eyes are trained to look. There is another Comyn Tower there. Though most of them are empty now."

Kerwin strained his eyes but could see only plains and the faraway foothills dying into bluish haze. He said, "I'm still confused. I don't really know what the Comyn is, or what the Towers are, or what a Keeper is—aside," he added, smiling—"from being a very beautiful woman."

Elorie simply looked at him, and before the direct, leveled stare, Kerwin lowered his own eyes; she made him feel that the compliment had been both rude and intrusive.

Then she said, "It would be easier to explain what we do than what we *are*. What we *are* . . . There are so many legends, old superstitions, and somehow we have to live up to them all . . ." She looked into the distance for a moment, then she said, "A Keeper, basically, works in the central position, centerpolar if you wish, of a circle of matrix technicians. The Keeper—" A faint frown appeared between Elorie's pale eyebrows, as she obviously considered how to put it into words he could understand. "A Keeper is, technically, no more than a specially trained matrix worker who can gather up all of her circle of telepaths into a single unit, act as a kind of central coordinator to make the mental linkages. The Keeper is always a woman. We spend our entire childhood training for it, and sometimes—" She turned to the window, looking out over the mountains—"We lose our powers after only a few years. Or give them up of our own accord."

"Lose them? Give them up? I don't understand," Kerwin said, but Elorie only shrugged slightly and did not answer. Kerwin was not to know until a long time later just how much Elorie overestimated his telepathic abilities. She had never in her life known any man, or for that matter anyone at all, who could not read at such close quarters any thought she chose. Kerwin knew nothing, as yet, of the fantastic seclusion in which the young Keepers lived.

At last she went on. "The Keeper is always a woman—not since the Ages of Chaos have men lawfully worked as Keeper. The others—monitors, mechanics, technicians—can be men or women. Although in these days it is easier to find men for the work. But not very easy, even then. I hope that you will accept me as Keeper and that you will be able to work very closely with me."

"That sounds like nice work," Kerwin said, looking appreciatively at the lovely girl before him. Elorie whirled and stared at him, her mouth wide open in disbelief. Then, her eyes blazing, her cheeks aflame, she said, "Stop it! *Stop it!* There was a day on Darkover, you barbarian, when I could have had you killed for looking at me like that!"

Kerwin, dismayed and amazed, backed away a step. He said, feeling numb, "Take it easy, miss— Miss Elorie! I didn't mean to say anything to offend you. I'm sorry—" he shook his head, not comprehending—"but remember, if I offended you, I haven't the slightest idea how, or why!"

Her hands gripped on the rail, so hard that he could see the white knobs of her knuckles. They looked so frail, those white hands, narrow, with delicate tapered fingers. After a moment of silence, a long moment that stretched, she let go of the rail, tossing her head with a little impatient movement. She said, "I had forgotten. I heard you insulted

Mesyr, too, without the slightest idea that you had done so. If Kennard is to stand as your foster-father here, he had better teach you something of elementary courtesy! Enough of that, then. You said you didn't even know what the Comyn were—"

"A governing body, I thought—"

She shook her head. "Only recently, and not very much; originally, the Comyn were the seven telepath families of Darkover, the Seven Domains, each holding one of the major Gifts of *laran*."

Kerwin blurted, "I thought the whole place was crawling with telepaths!"

She shrugged that off. "Everyone alive has some small degree of *laran*. I'm speaking of special psychokinetic and psi gifts, the Comyn Gifts, bred into our families in the centuries past—in the old days it was believed that perhaps they were inherited, that the Comyn were descended from the seven children— some people say the seven sons, but personally I find that hard to believe—of Hastur and Cassilda; maybe it's because in the old days the Comyn were known as the Hastur-kin, or the Children of Hastur. Specifically, the Gifts of *laran* center upon the ability to use a matrix. You know what a matrix is, I take it."

"Vaguely."

Her pale eyebrows lifted again. "I was told you had the matrix belonging to Cleindori, whose name is written here as Dorilys of Arilinn."

"I do," Jeff said, "but I haven't the faintest idea what it *is*, essentially, and even less notion of what it's good for." He had decided, a long time ago, that the sort of thing Ragan did with his small matrix was essentially irrelevant; and these people were very serious about it.

She shook her head, almost in wonder. "And yet

we found you, guided you with it!" she said. "That proved to us that you had inherited some of the—" She paused and said angrily, "I'm *not* being evasive! I'm trying to put it into words you can understand, that's all! We traced Cleindori's matrix through the monitor banks and relays, which proved to us that you had inherited the mark of our caste. A matrix, essentially, is a crystal that receives, amplifies, and transmits thought. I could talk about space lattices, and neuro-electronic webs, and nerve channels, and kinetic energons, but I'll let Rannirl explain all that; he's our technician. Matrixes can be as simple as this—" she touched a tiny crystal that, in total defiance of gravity, suspended her filmy gown from her throat—"or they can be enormous, synthetically-made screens—the technical term is *lattices*—with immensely complex man-made interior crystalline structures, each crystal of which responds to amplification from a Keeper. A matrix—or rather, the power of thought, of *laran,* controlled by a skilled matrix technician or Keeper's circle—can release pure energy from the magnetic field of a planet, and channel it, either as force or matter. Heat, light, kinetic or potential energy, the synthesis of raw materials into usable form—all those things were once done by matrix. You do know that thought rhythms, brain waves, are electrical in nature?"

Kerwin nodded. "I've seen them measured. We call the instrument an electro-encephalograph—" He spoke the words in Terran Standard, not knowing if the Darkovans had a word for it, and began to explain how it measured and made visible the electrical energies of the brain, but she shrugged impatiently.

"A simple and clumsy instrument. Well, in general, thought waves, even those of a telepath, can't have much effect in the material universe. Most of them can't move a single hair. There are exceptions, special forces—well, you'll learn about that. But in general, the brain waves themselves can't move a single hair. But the matrix crystals somehow act to transform force into form. That's all."

"And the Keepers—"

"Some matrixes are so complex that one person can't handle them; it takes the energy of several minds, linked together and feeding through the crystal, to form a nexus of energy. A Keeper handles and coordinates the forces. That's all I can tell you," she said abruptly, and turned, pointing down the stairs. "Straight down that way." She turned and walked away in a flutter of filmy draperies, and Kerwin watched her go, startled. Had he done something, again, to offend her? Or was this some childish whim? She *looked* childish enough, certainly!

He went down the stairs, finding himself again in the great firelit hall where, this morning at sunrise, they had welcomed him—welcomed him *home*? His home? The room was completely empty, and Kerwin dropped into one of the cushioned chairs, burying his head in his hands. If someone didn't explain things fairly soon, he was going to go crazy with frustration!

Kennard found him there, that way; Kerwin looked up at the older man and said helplessly, "It's too much. I can't take it all in. It's too much, coming all at once. I don't understand it, I don't understand any of it!"

Kennard looked down at him with a curious mixture of compassion and amusement. "I can see how it would be," he said. "I lived a few years on Terra;

I know all about culture shock. Let me get off my feet." He lowered himself, carefully, to the mass of cushions, and leaned back, hands clasped behind his head. "Maybe I can clear it up for you. I owe you that."

Kerwin had heard that the Darkovans, the nobility anyhow, had little to do with the Empire; the news that Kennard had actually lived on Terra amazed him, but no more than anything else that had happened in the last day or so, no more than his own presence here. He was all but immune to further shock. He said, "Start with this. Who am I? Why the devil am I here?"

Kennard ignored the question, staring into space over Kerwin's head. After a while he said, "That night in the Sky Harbor Hotel; do you know what I saw?"

"Sorry. Not in the mood for guessing games." Kerwin wanted to ask straight questions and get straight answers; he definitely didn't want to answer more questions himself.

"Remember, I hadn't the least notion who you were. You looked like one of us, and I knew you weren't. I saw a Terran, but I'm an Alton, I have one of those screwy, out-of-phase time perceptors. So I looked at the Terran and I saw a child, a confused child, one who had never known who or what he was. I wish you had stayed and talked to us, then."

"I do, too," Kerwin said slowly. *A child who had never known who or what he was*. Kennard had put it very precisely. "I grew up, all right. But I left myself somewhere."

"Maybe you'll find yourself here." Kennard got slowly to his feet, and Kerwin rose too; he held out a hand to assist the older man, but Kennard drew away; after a moment, Kennard smiled self-consciously and said, "You're wondering why—"

"No," said Kerwin, suddenly understanding that all of them had deftly avoided touching him. "I hate people jostling me; I've never gotten along with most people at close quarters. And I feel like hell in a crowd. Always have."

Kennard nodded. *"Laran,"* he said. "You have just enough to find physical contact distasteful—"

Kerwin chuckled. "I wouldn't go so far as to say *that*—"

Kennard said, with a sardonic shrug, "Distasteful except in circumstances of deliberate intimacy. Right?"

Kerwin nodded, thinking over the rare personal encounters of his life. He knew he had gravely distressed his Terran grandmother by his violent distaste for demonstrations of affection. And yet he had grown fond of the old lady, had loved her in his own way. His work associates—well, it occurred to him that he had treated them as Auster had treated him on the plane: violently rebuffing the slightest personal contact, shrinking physically from a random touch. It hadn't made him particularly popular.

"You're—how old? Twenty-six, twenty-seven? Of course I know how old you are, Darkovan—I was one of the first ones Cleindori told—but I never can convert that to Terran reckoning. It was too long ago I lived on Terra. Hell of a long time to live outside your proper element!"

"Proper element hell," Kerwin retorted. "Show me where I fit into this mess, will you?"

"I'll try." Kennard went to a table in the corner

and poured himself a drink from an assortment of bottles there; lifted his eyebrows in question at Kerwin.

"We'll have drinks when the others come down; but I'm thirsty. You?"

"I'll wait," Kerwin said. He'd never been that much of a drinker. *Kennard's bad leg must be giving him considerable pain if he'd break custom this way,* the thought flickered through his mind and he wondered impatiently where it had come from, as the older man came cautiously back to his seat.

Kennard drank, set the glass down, locked his fingers meditatively. "Elorie told you; there are seven families of telepaths on Darkover, a ruling family for each of the Seven Domains. The Hasturs, the Ridenow, Ardais, the Elhalyn, the Altons—my family—and the Aillard. Yours."

Kerwin had been counting. "That's six."

"We don't talk about the Aldarans. Although some of us have Aldaran blood, of course, and Aldaran gifts. And there's been some intermarriage —well, we won't talk about that, that's a long story and a shameful one; but the Aldarans were exiled from the Domains a long time ago; I couldn't tell you all about that now, even if I knew it all, and even if we had the time—which I don't and we don't. But, with only six main telepath families—have you any idea how inbred we are?"

"You mean that normally you marry only within your caste? Telepaths?"

"Not entirely. Not—deliberately," Kennard said, "but, being a telepath, and being isolated in the Towers, only with others of our own kind—it's like a drug." His voice was not quite steady. "It completely unfits you for—for contact with outsiders. You, well, you get lost in it, and when you come up for air, as it were, you find you can't breathe ordinary air any more. You find you can't stand having outsiders around, people who aren't tuned to your thoughts, people who—who jostle against your mind. You can't come close to them; they aren't quite real to you. Oh, it wears off, after a while, or you couldn't live outside the Tower at all, but—but it's a temptation. Non-telepaths feel to you like barbarians, or like strange animals, alien, wrong . . ." He was staring into space, over Kerwin's head. "It spoils you for any kind of contact with ordinary people. With women. Even at your level, I should imagine, you've had trouble with women who can't—can't share your feelings and thoughts. After ten years at Arilinn, anything else is like—like bedding with a brute beast . . ."

The silence stretched while Kerwin thought about that, about the curious alienation, the sense of *difference,* which had come between him and every woman he had ever known. As if there had to be something more, deeper than the most intimate contact. . . .

Abruptly with a little shiver, Kennard recalled himself, and his voice sounded harsh.

"Anyway. We're inbred mentally, even more than physically; just because of that inability to tolerate outsiders. And the physical inbreeding is bad enough; some very strange recessives have come up. A few of the old Gifts are bred out altogether; I haven't seen more than one or two catalyst telepaths in my lifetime. That's the old Ardais gift, but Dom Kyril didn't have it, or if he did he never learned to use it, and he's mad as a banshee in a Ghost Wind. In the Aillards, the Gift has become sex-linked; shows up only in the women, and the men don't carry it. And so forth, and so on. . . . If you learn anything about genetics, you'll find out what I mean. A solid outbreeding program might still save us, if we could do it; but most of us can't. So—" he shrugged. "Every generation fewer and fewer of us are born with the old *laran* Gifts. Mesyr told you; once there were three circles here at Arilinn, each with its own Keeper. Once there were over a dozen Towers; and Arilinn was not the largest. Now—well, there are three other Towers working a mechanic's circle; we are the only Tower with a fully qualified Keeper, which means Elorie is virtually the only Keeper on Darkover. And, within the Comyn, and the minor nobility connected to us by blood, there are hardly enough of us, in each generation to keep them alive. So there are two lines of thought within the Comyn." He spoke briskly now, without a trace of the earlier remoteness. "One faction felt we should cling to our old ways while we could, resist every change, until we died out, as we inevitably would in a generation or two, and it didn't matter any more; but at least we would remain what we were. Others felt that, with change inevitable, or at least the only alternative to death, we should make what changes we could tolerate, before intolerable ones were forced upon us. These people felt that matrix science could be taught to anyone with the rudiments of skill at *laran*, developed and trained to work in the same ways that a Comyn telepath could do. There were a few of this faction in power in the Comyn a generation ago, and during those few years, matrix mechanics came into being as a profession. During that time we discovered that most people have some psi power—enough to operate a matrix, anyway—and could be trained in the use of matrix sciences."

"I've met a couple," Kerwin said.

"You've got to remember," Kennard told him, "that this was complicated by a lot of intense, very emotional attitudes. It was virtually a religion, and the Comyn were almost a priesthood at one time. The Keepers, especially, were objects of religious fanaticism that amounted to worship. And now we come to where you fit into the story."

He shifted his weight, uncomfortably, sighed and stared at Jeff Kerwin. Finally he said, "Cleindori Aillard was my foster-sister. She was a *nedestro* of her clan; that means she was not born in a legitimate marriage, but was the daughter of an Aillard woman and one of the Ridenow, a younger son of that clan. She carried the Aillard name because among us a child takes the name of the parent of higher rank, not necessarily the father's name as you do on Terra. She and I were brought up together from the time she was a small girl, and she was handfasted—which is a sort of pledge of marriage, more between the families than the persons concerned—to my older brother Lewis. Then she was chosen to be trained as Keeper at Arilinn."

Kennard was still, his face bitter and remote again. Then he said, "I don't know all the story; and I swore an oath—they forced me to swear, when I came back to Arilinn—there are things I can't tell you. Anyway, during part of it I was away, fostered on Terra; that's a long story, too. My father chose a Terran foster-son, and I went to Terra as what you'd call, I suppose, an exchange student, while Lerrys was fostered here. And so I did not see Cleindori for six or seven years, and when I came back she was Dorilys of Arilinn. Keeper. Cleindori was—in some ways—the most powerful person in the Comyn, the most powerful woman on Darkover. Lady of Arilinn. She was a *leronis* of surpassing skill; and, like all Keepers, she was pledged virgin, living in seclusion and a rigid isolation . . . she was the last. Even Elorie was not trained as Cleindori had been trained, in the old ways; Cleindori accomplished that much, at least." He slid away for a moment into the bitter remoteness again. Then, sitting upright on his cushions, his voice dry and emotionless, he said:

"Cleindori was a fighter; a rebel. She was a reformer at heart; and, as Lady of Arilinn, and one of the last surviving Aillard women in the direct line, she had considerable power and Council status in her own right. So she tried to change the laws of Arilinn. She fought bitterly against the new Council, and the conviction they held, that the Comyn Towers should maintain their secrecy and their old, protected, semi-religious status. She tried to bring in outsiders to the Towers—she succeeded in that, a little. Neskaya Tower, for example, will take anyone with telepathic power—Comyn, commoner, or beggar born in a ditch. But then, they have not had a real Keeper for half a hundred years. But then she began to attack the taboos around her own special status. And that was too much, that kind of heresy raised up rebellion . . . Cleindori broke the taboos again and again, insisting that she could break them with impunity because, as Keeper, she was responsible only to her own conscience. And at last she ran away from Arilinn."

Kerwin had begun to suspect that it would end there, but even so it was a shock. He said, very low, "With an Earthman. With my father."

"I am not sure whether she left the Tower with him, or whether he came later," Kennard evaded. "But yes, this is why Auster hates you, why there are many, many people who think your very existence is a sacrilege. It was not unheard of that a Keeper should lay down her powers and marry. Many have done so. But that a Keeper should leave the Towers and give up her ritual virginity and remain a Keeper . . . no, that they would not tolerate." The bitterness in his voice deepened. "After all, a Keeper is not so unusual; it was discovered, or rediscovered, in my father's time, that any halfway competent technician can do a Keeper's work. Including some men. I can, if I must, do it myself, though I am not especially skillful at it. But the Keeper of Arilinn—well, she is a symbol. Cleindori said once to me that what the Comyn really needed was a child's waxen doll on a stick, to wear the crimson robe and speak the right words at the proper time, and there would be no need for Keepers at Arilinn; and since the doll could remain virgin forever without fuss or pain or sacrifice, all the troubles of Arilinn would be forever solved. I don't suppose you can imagine just how shocking that was to the more conservative men and women of the Council. They were very bitter against Cleindori's—sacrilege."

He scowled at the floor. "Auster too has a special reason to hate you. He too was born among the *Terranan,* although he does not remember; for a time he too was in the Spacemen's Orphanage, although we got him back from them before he had even learned their language. I have not heard him speak a word of

Terran, or *cahuenga,* since he was thirteen years old; but that's neither here or there. That's a strange story." Kennard raised his head and looked at Kerwin, saying, "It's fortunate for you that the Terrans sent you to the Kerwins on Terra. There were plenty of fanatics who would have considered that they had done a virtuous deed—to avenge the dishonor of a *vai leronis* by killing the child she had borne to her lover."

Kerwin found that he was shivering, although the room was warm. "If that's the case," he said, "what in the hell am I doing here at Arilinn?"

"Times have changed," Kennard said. "As I told you, we're dying out. There just aren't enough of us any more. Here at Arilinn, we have a Keeper, but there are not more than two or three Keepers in all of the Domains, and a couple of little girls growing up who might grow *into* Keepers. The fanatics have died off or mellowed into old age; and even if there are still a few around, the ones who are left have learned to listen to the voice of expediency. I ought to say, of stark necessity; we cannot afford to waste anyone who might be carrying Aillard or Ardais gifts, or . . . others. You have Ridenow blood, and Hastur blood not too many generations back, and Alton. For a variety of reasons—" He checked himself. He said, "Different people are ruling the Council. When you came back to Thendara . . . well, it didn't take me long to guess who you must be. Elorie saw you in the monitor screens—saw Cleindori's matrix, rather—and confirmed it. That night in the Sky Harbor Hotel, half a dozen of us from the few remaining Towers gathered there—outside Comyn Castle, so that we could talk freely about it—and the reason we met was to try and reach some agreement about standards for admission to the Towers, so that we could keep more than one or two of them working. When you walked in—well, you remember what happened; we thought you were one of us, and it wasn't just that you had red hair. We could *sense* what you were. So we called you. And you came. And here you are."

"Here I am. An outsider—"

"Not really, or you could never have passed the Veil. You have guessed that we don't like having non-telepaths around; that's why we have no human servants, and why Mesyr stays and keeps house for us even though she's past working in the screens. You passed the Veil, which means you have Comyn blood. And I feel at ease with you. That's a good sign."

Kerwin felt his eyebrows lift. Kennard might feel at ease with him, but it sure as hell wasn't mutual, not yet. He was inclined to like the older man, but that was a good long way from feeling at home with him.

"He's wishing he felt the same way about you," said Taniquel, popping her head into the room. "You will, Jeff. You've just lived among barbarians too long."

"Don't tease, *chiya,*" Kennard said, in indulgent reproof. "He's not used to you either, which doesn't necessarily mean he's a barbarian. Get us a drink and stop making mischief, why don't you? We're going to have trouble enough."

"No drinks yet," said Rannirl, pausing beneath the arch into the room. "Elorie will be down in a minute. We'll wait."

"That means she's going to test him," Taniquel

said. She came over to the cushions and dropped gracefully, catlike, her head leaning against Kennard's knee. She flung out her arms, one of them striking Kerwin; she yawned, crooked her arm carelessly round his foot, giving it a little, absent-minded pat with her hand. She let her hand rest on his ankle, her eyes glinting up at him in a mischievous smile. He was uncomfortably conscious of the touch. He had always disliked being touched, and he felt Taniquel knew it.

Neyrissa and Corus drifted into the room, found places on the cushions; they shifted, making room for Kennard's lame leg, and Taniquel moved restlessly until she was between Kerwin and Kennard, snuggled into the cushions like a kitten, an arm across the lap of each. Kennard patted her curly head affectionately, but Kerwin drew uneasily away. Damn it, was the girl just an outrageous tease? Or was she simply naive, relaxing, childlike, among men she found as neutral as if they were brothers or close relatives? Certainly she treated Kennard—and he, her—as if he were a favorite uncle, and there was nothing provocative in the way she touched him, but somehow it was subtly different with Kerwin, and he was conscious of the difference, and wondered if *she* was. Was he just imagining things? Once again, as when Elorie had walked unannounced into his room before he had finished dressing, Kerwin felt troubled. Damn it, the etiquette of a telepath group was still a mystery to him.

Elorie, Mesyr and Auster came together into the room. Auster's glare instantly sought out Kerwin, and Taniquel straightened herself and drew just a little away from Kerwin. Corus went to a cabinet, evidently from long habit. "What will you drink? Your usual, Kennard, Mesyr? Neyrissa, what will you have? Elorie, I know you never drink anything stronger than *shallan* . . ."

"She will tonight," Kennard said. "We'll have *kirian*."

Corus turned, startled, for confirmation. Elorie nodded. Taniquel rose and went to help Corus, filling low goblets from a curiously shaped flask. She brought a glass to Kerwin, not asking if he wanted it.

The liquid in the glass was pale and aromatic; Kerwin glanced at it and felt that they were all watching him. Damn it, he was getting tired of that performance! He set the goblet, untasted, on the floor.

Kennard laughed. Auster said something Kerwin didn't catch, and Rannirl frowned, murmuring a reproving reply. Elorie watched them, smiling faintly, raising her own goblet to her lips and barely tasting the liquid within. Taniquel giggled, and Kennard exploded:

"Zandru's hells! This is too serious for a joke! I know you like your fun, Tani, but just the same—" He accepted the glass Corus brought him, staring into it with a frown. "I seem to be cast in the role of schoolmaster too much of the time!" He sighed, lifted the goblet and said to Kerwin, "This stuff—it isn't pure *kirian*, in case you know what that is, but *kirian* liqueur—it's not exactly a drug or a stimulant, but it does lower the threshold of resistance against telepathic reception. You don't have to drink it unless you want it, but it helps. Which is why we're all sharing it." He sipped his own briefly and went on: "Now that you're here, and you've had a chance to rest a bit, it's fairly important that we test you for *laran,* find out how much of a telepath you are, what *donas* you may be carrying, how much training you'll need before you can work with the rest of us—or the other way round. We're going to test you half a dozen ways; it's more efficient in a group. Hence—" he drank another sip—*"kirian."*

Kerwin shrugged and picked up the glass. The liquid had a sting and a curious volatile smell; it seemed to evaporate on his tongue even before he could taste it. It wasn't his idea of a good way to get drunk. It was more like inhaling perfume than drinking anything. The flavor was vaguely lemony. Four or five sips finished the glass, but you had to take it slowly; the fumes were simply too strong to drink it like an ordinary drink. He noticed that Corus made a face over his, as if he violently disliked the taste. The others were apparently accustomed to it; Neyrissa swirled it in her glass and inhaled the fumes as if it were a fragrant brandy. Kerwin decided the stuff was very much of an acquired taste.

He finished the goblet and set it down.

"Now what happens?" To his surprise, the words, on his tongue, sounded curiously thick; he had some trouble framing them, and when he had finished speaking, he was not sure what language he had been speaking. Rannirl turned toward him and with a grin that Kerwin knew was meant to reassure him said, "Nothing to worry about."

"I don't know why this is necessary," Taniquel said. "He's already been tested for *laran.* They saved us that much trouble with the monitor screens." As she spoke, a picture flickered, unbidden, in Kerwin's mind, the brother and sister who had studied his matrix, arrogantly told him he was not welcome in their house or on their world.

"They had the damned insolence!" Corus said angrily. "I didn't know that!"

Taniquel said, "As for the rest—"

Kerwin looked down at the girl curled up close to his knee, her face upturned to him, her eyes, meeting his, bright and sympathetic. She was very close to him. Kerwin could have bent down and kissed her.

He did.

Taniquel leaned against him, smiling, her cheek resting against his. She said, "Mark him positive for empathy, Kennard."

Kerwin started, startled, at his own arms around Taniquel; then laughed and relaxed, suddenly not worrying about it. If the girl intended to object, she would have done it already; but he sensed that she was pleased, nestling within his arm as if she was quite content to be there. Auster exploded into a mouthful of unintelligible syllables, and Neyrissa shook her head reprovingly at Taniquel.

"Chiya, this is a serious matter!"

"And I was perfectly serious," said Taniquel, smiling, "even if my methods strike you as unorthodox." She laid her cheek against Kerwin's; suddenly, surprisingly, Kerwin felt a lump in his throat, and for the first time in years he felt tears gathering and blurring his eyes. Taniquel was not smiling now; she moved away from Kerwin a little, but left her hand cradling his cheek, like a promise.

She said softly, "Can you think of a better test for an empath? If he didn't belong, no harm would be done, for he wouldn't receive from me; and if he did —then he deserves it." Kerwin felt her soft lips touch his hand, and felt an almost overwhelming emotion.

The gentleness and intimacy of that small gesture was somehow more meaningful to him than anything any woman had ever done in his whole life. He felt that it had been an absolute acceptance of him, as a man and as a human being, that somehow, here before them all, Taniquel and he had suddenly become more intimate than lovers.

The others had suddenly ceased to exist. His arm was round her; he drew her head to his shoulder, and she leaned against him, tenderly, comfortingly, a gesture of reassurance and warmth unlike anything he had ever felt. He raised blurred eyes, and blinked, embarrassed at this display of emotion; but he saw only understanding and kindliness.

Kennard's grim face looked a little less craggy than usual. "Taniquel's the expert on empathy. We could have expected that—he has Ridenow blood. Though it's damned unusual for a man to have it to this degree."

Taniquel said, still clinging to Kerwin, "How lonely you must have been." The words were barely audible.

All my life. Not belonging, never belonging anywhere.

But you belong here now.

All the looks were not benevolent. Auster met Kerwin's eyes, and Kerwin had the definite feeling that if looks could burn, he would be lying in a sizzled cinder on the floor. Auster said, "Much as I dislike to interrupt this touching display . . ."

Taniquel, with a resigned shrug, dropped Kerwin's hand. Auster was still speaking, but he had dropped back into that language Kerwin did not understand. Kerwin said, "I'm sorry, I don't understand you," and Auster repeated it, but in the same language Kerwin didn't know. Auster turned to Kennard and said something, raising his eyebrows with a sardonic grin.

Kennard said, "Aren't you getting it at all, Jeff?"

"No, and it's damned funny, because I understand you and Taniquel just fine."

Rannirl said, "Jeff, you've understood most of what I said, haven't you?"

Kerwin nodded. "All but a few words now and then."

"And Mesyr?"

"Yes, perfectly."

"You *should* understand Auster," Rannirl said. "He has Ridenow blood and is the closest kinsman you have here, except perhaps—" He frowned. "Jeff, answer me quickly. What language am I speaking?"

Kerwin started to say, the language I learned as a child, the Thendara dialect, then stopped, confused. He didn't know. Kennard nodded, slowly. "That's right," he said. "That's what I noticed about you first of all. I've spoken to you in three different languages tonight and you never hesitated about answering me in any of them. Taniquel spoke a fourth. Yet Auster tried you in two languages that you had understood when Rannirl and I spoke, and you didn't understand a word. But even when Auster is speaking Cahuenga, you only understand him part of the time. You're a telepath, all right. Haven't you always been an exceptionally good linguist?" He nodded, not waiting for Kerwin's answer. "I thought so. You catch the thought without waiting for the words. But you and Auster simply don't resonate enough to one another for you to pick up what he says."

"It may come in time," Elorie said diffidently, "as they know one another better. Don't jump to conclusions too quickly, Uncle." She used the word that was slightly more intimate than, simply, *kinsman;* it was a catch-all term for any close relative of a father's generation. "So we have verified that he has basic *laran,* telepathy, and a high degree of empathy; Ridenow gift, full measure. He's probably carrying an assortment of minor talents—we'll have to sort them out one by one, perhaps in rapport. Jeff—" She seemed somehow to turn to him, even though she was looking off into the distance and, though he tried to catch her eye, she did not glance in his direction. "You have a matrix. Do you know how to use it?"

"I haven't the faintest idea."

She said, "Rannirl. You're the technician."

Rannirl said, "Jeff, can you let me see your matrix?"

Kerwin said, "Of course," and pulled it out, slipped the chain over his head and handed it to Rannirl. Shielding his hand with a silk kerchief, the tall man took it from him; but to his surprise, as the man took it between his fingers, Kerwin felt a vague, crawling discomfort. Automatically, without conscious thought, he reached out and snatched it back into his own hands. The discomfort faded. He stared, amazed, at his own hands.

"I thought so." Rannirl nodded. "He's managed to key himself to it, roughly."

Kerwin said, "That never happened before!" He was still staring at the matrix within his hands, shocked at the way he had acted without thought to protect himself against the touch.

"Probably it happened while we were guiding you

to us," Elorie said. "You were in rapport with the crystal for a long time; it's how we reached you." She extended her slender fingers and said, "Give it to me, if you can."

Bracing himself, Kerwin let Elorie take the crystal. He felt the touch as if her delicate hands were actually touching his nerves; it was not acutely painful, but he was excruciatingly aware of it, as if the indefinable touch might become agony at a moment's notice . . . or unendurable pleasure.

"I'm a Keeper," she said. "One of the skills I must have is to handle matrixes that are not keyed to me. Taniquel?"

Kerwin felt the hypersensitive awareness ebb away as Taniquel took the matrix from Elorie; she smiled and said, "That's no fair test; Jeff and I are close in rapport just now. It feels as if you were handling it yourself, doesn't it?"

He nodded.

"Corus?" Taniquel handed it on.

Kerwin flinched uncontrollably at the rough prickling sensation all over his body as Corus touched the matrix; Corus shuddered as if the touch hurt him, and quickly handed the crystal to Kennard.

Kennard's touch was not acutely painful, although Kerwin was extremely conscious of it, unpleasantly so. The discomfort lessened somewhat, as Kennard held the crystal in his hand, to a sense of not-unpleasant warmth; but it was still intrusive, an unwelcome intimacy, and Kerwin was relieved when Kennard passed it on to Neyrissa.

Again the excruciatingly close, almost painful sensitivity that lessened, somewhat, as Neyrissa held it;

he could feel her warm breath on the crystal, which made no sense because she was halfway across the room from him. She said quietly, "I'm accustomed to monitor work; I can do what Tani does, resonate to your body's magnetic field, although not so well because we're not so closely in rapport. So far, so good. That leaves only Auster."

Auster gasped and dropped the matrix as if it were a live coal. Kerwin felt the pain like a shock all along his nerves, felt Taniquel shiver under his hand as if she, too, felt the pain. Neyrissa glanced at the dropped crystal without venturing to touch it and said, "Tani? Will you—"

The pain stopped as Taniquel cradled the matrix in her hand; Kerwin drew a deep, shaking breath. Auster, too, was white and shaking.

"Zandru's hells!" His look at Kerwin was not so much malevolence, now, as fear. He spoke Cahuenga —Kerwin got the feeling that he wanted to be clearly understood, this time. "I'm sorry, Kerwin, I swear I didn't do that deliberately."

"He knows that, he knows that," Taniquel soothed; she dropped Jeff's hand and went to Auster, laying an arm around his waist, gently caressing his hand. Kerwin watched, in surprise and sudden, jealous amazement. How could she pull out of such close, emotional contact with him, and go straight to that— that so-and-so, Auster—and start making a fuss over *him*? Jealously intent, he watched Taniquel draw Auster down, watched the lines in Auster's lean face smoothing out and calming.

Elorie met Kerwin's eyes as he tucked away the matrix. She said, "It's evidently been keyed to you. First lesson in proper handling of a matrix—even under *kirian*, like this, never again let anyone handle it except in your own circle, and only when you are very sure they are in rapport with you. We were all trying for maximum attunement, even Auster; and it seems, except for him, to have worked well enough. But from an outsider, you could have had a *really* painful shock."

Kerwin wondered what a really painful shock would be like, if Elorie didn't think that one from Auster was very important. He glowered at Taniquel and Auster, feeling wrathful and deserted.

Rannirl grinned his lean sardonic grin and said, "All that, just to find out what we could have guessed this morning when we saw Kerwin with blood on his face; they aren't sympathetic and they can't attune."

"They'll have to," Elorie said tensely. "We need them both, and we can't have that kind of friction here!"

Auster said, his eyes closed, "I said I would abide by the majority decision. You know my feelings in the matter, but I promised, and I said I would do my best. I meant it."

"That's all anyone could expect of you," Taniquel soothed, and Kennard said, "Fair enough. What next?"

Rannirl said, "He can key into the circle when we help him; but can he *use* his matrix? Try a pattern test."

Kerwin grew suddenly apprehensive again; for Kennard looked tense and drawn, and Taniquel came and held his hand again. She said, "If he managed to key his own matrix, maybe he can get the pattern spontaneously."

"Maybe pigs can fly," Kennard said shortly.

"We'll test for the possibility, but I think it would be forcing our luck to take it for granted. Let me have your goblet, Tani." He up-ended the glass on a low table. "Jeff, take the crystal—no, don't give it to me," he said, as Kerwin would have handed it over. "Just a test." He pointed at the goblet. "Crystallize it."

Kerwin looked at him, uncomprehending.

"Make a clear picture in your mind of that glass going to pieces. Careful, don't let it shatter or explode; nobody wants to be hit by flying glass. Use the matrix to see into its crystalline structure."

Suddenly Kerwin remembered the man Ragan doing something like that, in the spaceport cafe. It couldn't be so difficult, if Ragan could do it. He stared intently at the glass, then at the crystal, as if intense concentration could *force* the process into his mind, and felt a curious stirring. . . .

"No," Kennard said harshly, "don't help him, Tani. I know how you feel, but we have to be sure."

Kerwin stared into the crystal; his eyes began to ache and blur. "Sorry," he muttered. "I can't figure out how."

"Try," Taniquel insisted. "Jeff, it's so simple. Terrans, children, anyone can be taught to do it, it's nothing more than a trick!"

"We're wasting time," Neyrissa said. "You'll have to give him the pattern, Ken. He can't do it spontaneously."

Kerwin stared at them suspiciously, for Kennard was looking grim. "What now?"

"I'll have to show you how it's done, and the technique's nonverbal; I'll have to go straight in. I'm an Alton; that's our special technique, forced rapport." He hesitated; and it seemed to Kerwin that they were all watching him apprehensively. He wondered what was going to happen now.

Kennard said, "Watch my finger." He put it close to Kerwin's nose; Kerwin watched, startled, wondering if it would disappear or something, and what kind of demonstration of psi power *this* could possibly be, watched as Kennard very slowly drew it back. Then he felt the older man's hands, touching his temples, then . . .

He remembered no more.

He moved his head, groggily. He was lying back on the cushions, his head pillowed on Taniquel's lap. Kennard was looking down at him with friendly concern. Elorie's face, over Kennard's shoulder, was aloof, curious. Kerwin's head felt strange, as if he had a hangover.

"What the hell did you do to me?" he demanded.

Kennard shrugged. "Nothing, really. Next time you won't consciously remember this, but it will be easier." He handed Kerwin the goblet. "Here. Crystallize it."

"I just *tried* . . ."

Under Kennard's eyes he stared rebelliously at the matrix. Suddenly the goblet before him blurred, took on a strangeness. It was no longer a flat piece of glass; he seemed to be seeing it differently. It wasn't glass at all, glass was amorphous; the goblet was crystal, and within it he could see curious tensions and movements. He was conscious of a strange throb from the matrix crystal in his hand, an emotional tension, an equilibrium. . . . *The crystals lie in a plane,* he thought, suddenly perceiving the plane, and even as it became clear in his mind, he heard a faint *crack*;

the new kind of sight blurred and vanished, and he stared down, unbelieving, at the goblet lying on the cushions before him in two halves, split evenly down the center as if by a sharp knife. *Surrealistic,* he thought. A few drops of the pale *kirian* lay soaking into the cushions. He shut his eyes. When he opened them, it was still there.

Kennard nodded in satisfaction. "Not bad, for a first attempt. Not quite even, but pretty good. Your molecular perception will sharpen with practice. Zandru's hells—you've got strong barriers, though! Head ache?"

Kerwin started to shake his head no, realized it should be yes instead. He touched his temples gingerly. Elorie's grey eyes met his for a moment, cool and aloof.

"Mental defense," she said, "against intolerable stress. Typical psychosomatic reaction; you say to yourself, *if I'm in pain they'll stop hurting me and let me alone.* And Kennard's squeamish about hurting people; he stopped, to avoid hurting you more. Pain is the best defense against mental invasion. For instance, if anybody tries to pick your mind, and there's no damper, the best defense is simply to bite your lip until it bleeds. Damned few telepaths can get through that. I could give you a technical explanation about sympathetic vibrations and nerve cells, but why bother? I'll leave that to the technicians." She went to the cabinet where the drinks were kept, shook three flat green tablets from a small vial and put them into his hand, deftly, without touching him.

"Take these. In an hour or two it will be better. When you've had more practice, you won't need them because you can work on the channels directly, but for the meantime—"

Kerwin obediently swallowed the pills, looking again, without belief, at the goblet lying in neat halves, sundered along a clean line of cleavage. "Did I really do that?"

"Well, none of us did," Rannirl said dryly. "And I imagine you can estimate the probabilities of all the molecules losing their tension along a line like that by chance. Putting them at one in a hundred trillion would be *very* good odds."

Kerwin picked up the two halves, feeling the sharp fracture edge with his fingertips. He was trying to formulate some explanation that would satisfy the Terran half of his mind, playing with phrases like *subliminal perception of atomic structure*—Hell, for a minute he'd *seen* the way the crystals were held together by a pattern of living tensions and forces! During his schooling, he remembered, he had learned that atoms were just whirling aggregates of electrons, that every solid object really consisted of empty space occupied by infinitesimal forces in stasis. It made him feel dizzy.

"You'll learn," counseled Rannirl, "or you can always do like Tani does—think of it as magic. Concentrate, wave your hand, and there you are—*Poof!* All done by magic!"

"It's easier that way," Taniquel protested. "It *works*, even if I haven't figured out the exact forces involved in the molecular stresses. . . ."

"And that's just playing into the hands of the people who enjoy being superstitious about us!" Elorie said angrily. "I think you like it when they call you *sorceress* and *witch*—"

"They're going to do it anyway, no matter what I

call myself," Taniquel said with equanimity. "They said it of Mesyr, and she was one of the top technicians in her day. What does it matter what they think, Lori? We know what we are. Or what's that proverb Kennard's so fond of, about going to learn logic from the barkings of your dog?"

Elorie didn't answer. Kerwin took up the broken glass and fitted the edges together, staring at it fiercely. Once again the new kind of perception came, the insight as if seeing beneath the surface, all the forces and tensions in the *structure* of the crystal . . .

The glass lay whole in his hand, joined neatly, but a little out of true, a notch in the rim showing where the split had been.

Kennard smiled, as if relieved. He said, "That leaves only one test."

Kerwin was still staring at the slightly off-center goblet. He asked, "Can I keep this?"

Kennard nodded. "Bring it along."

Again Kerwin felt Taniquel's small fingers folding through his own, and he could sense that she was frightened, feel her fear like a pain somewhere inside him. "Is that really necessary, Kennard?" she appealed. "Can't you put him in the outer circle and see if he can be shocked open that way?"

Elorie gave her a pitying glance. "That almost never works, Tani. Not even in a mechanic's circle."

Kerwin began to be afraid again. He had come so well through the other tests, had begun to be proud of what he was accomplishing. "What is it? What now, Taniquel?"

But it was Elorie who answered, gently. "What Kennard means is only this; now we have to try you in a circle and see how you can fit into the relays—

the nexus of power. We know you're a high-level empath, and you've passed the basic tests—you have enough PK for a good mechanic, when you learn how. But this is the real test—to see how you'll mesh with the rest of us." She turned to Kennard. "You tested him in rapport, you know how he works on pattern. How are his barriers?"

"Hellish," Kennard said. "How would you expect them to be, coming of age among the head-blind?" He explained to Kerwin, "She means that I forced rapport on you, to give you the pattern there—" He pointed to the broken-and-joined goblet, slightly out of line. "And so I had a chance to test how strong your defenses are. Everyone has some natural defense against telepathic invasion—the technical term we use is *barrier;* protective shielding among telepaths, to keep you from broadcasting your private thoughts all over the locality, and to protect you from picking up a lot of random telepathic static—after all, you don't need to hear the groom deciding which horse he'll curry first, or the cook wondering what to have for dinner. Everybody has it; it's a conditioned reflex, and the stronger the telepath, in general, the stronger the barrier. Well, when we work in a circle, we have to learn to lower that barrier, work without the protective reflex. Most of us started work when we were in our teens, and we learn how to keep the barriers up, or lower them, consciously. Growing up on a world of non-telepaths, you probably learned to keep them locked in place all the time. Sometimes the barrier won't drop at all, and has to be forced, or shocked, open. We have to know how hard it's going to be to work with you, and how much resistance you have."

"But why tonight?" Mesyr asked, speaking for the first time—Kerwin had a vague notion that she considered herself apart from the others, no longer a part of their inner circle. "He's doing so well; why hurry things? Can't you give him time?"

"Time is the one thing we don't have to give him," Rannirl said. "Remember, we're working against a deadline."

"Rannirl's right," Kennard said, looking at Kerwin almost in apology. "We brought Kerwin here because we were desperately short-handed here at Arilinn, and if we can't use him, you know as well as I do what's going to happen to us all." He looked around bleakly. "We need to get him in shape to work with us, damned fast, or else!"

"We're wasting time," said Elorie, and rose, her pale draperies floating like some intangible drift of air around her. "But we'd better do it up in the matrix chamber."

One by one they rose; at Taniquel's tug on his hand, Kerwin stood up, too. Kennard looked pityingly at Taniquel and said, "I'm sorry, Tani; you know as well as I do why you can't be part of it. The link's already too strong. Neyrissa will monitor." To Kerwin he explained, "Taniquel is our empath, and in rapport with you. If she was part of this, she'd help you too much; she couldn't stand it otherwise. Later, the rapport between you will make the link stronger and help the circle, but not while we're testing you. Tani, you have to stay here."

Reluctantly, she let go of his hand. Kerwin felt cold and alone; evidently the sense of warmth, of confidence, had been part of what Taniquel was radiating and pouring into him. He felt, quite suddenly, scared.

Rannirl said, "Cheer up," and put his own arm lightly through Jeff's. The gesture was reassuring, but the tone wasn't; it sounded too much like an apology.

Kennard motioned and they went in a close group through the long hall, up a flight of stairs and through a corridor; and finally up another flight of stairs to a closed-in room Kerwin had not seen before. It was small, eight-sided. Along the walls were glass and mirrory surfaces that reflected random images, distorting their shapes out of recognition, and Kerwin saw himself, a lean streak of black uniform topped with a brief crimson flame of hair. At the center of the room was a sunken circle lined with padded seats, and Kerwin saw them moving into the circle in an order that seemed familiar, predetermined. At the central part of the circle there was a small flat table or stand, with a woven cradle like the one he had seen in the house of the *leronis*, giving Kerwin a brief painful flash of *déjà vu* again. In it lay a crystal, larger than any he had seen before. Rannirl murmured in his ear, "It's the relay lattice," which seemed to make no sense at all to Kerwin. Trying to explain himself, Rannirl added, "It's a synthetic lattice, not a natural matrix," but that explained nothing at all to Kerwin.

"Take us out of the relays, Neyrissa, just for tonight," Elorie murmured. "There's no reason those people at Neskaya should know what we're doing here, and I don't think Hali wants to know!"

Neyrissa went to the central seat, insulating her hands with a length of the silk as the *leronis* in Thendara had done. She leaned over the crystal, and Kerwin covered his eyes with his hands, the *déjà vu* was so strong, as he watched her graceful gestures.

What was wrong with him? He'd never been in a matrix chamber before, never seen a circle form . . . an illusion, a false perception of the two halves of the brain, he told himself fiercely; nothing more than that . . ..

He heard the drift of thought, the random flickers around him, then clearly, though Neyrissa did not speak. *We are testing at Arilinn, we will be out of the relays for twenty-eight hours . . .*

Carefully, shielding her hand, Neyrissa removed the enormous crystal from the cradle. "We're shielded," she said, "and out of the screens." She put the crystal away in the cabinet, wrapping it carefully in its heavy silks, but she did not return to the central seat. She said to Elorie, with a curious formality, "The circle is in your hands, *tenerésteis*." Kerwin recognized the archaic term for Keeper, without quite knowing how.

Elorie laid her own crystal in the cradle, taking it from around her neck. She looked questioningly at the circle, at the others. Kennard nodded; Neyrissa and Rannirl followed suit. Auster looked briefly doubtful, but finally said, "I defer to your judgment, Elorie. I said all along I'll go with the majority decision."

Young Corus pursed his lips, looked skeptically at Kerwin. He said, "I think Mesyr was right, we ought to have waited. But I can manage, if you think *he* can."

Elorie was looking at Auster; he said something unintelligible to Kerwin, and Elorie nodded in agreement. Kennard leaned toward Kerwin and said, "As long as you and Auster can't resonate, we'll have to keep you on separate levels."

Elorie said, "I'll take Auster first, and bring Kerwin in last." She glanced from Rannirl to Kennard, finally said, "Kennard, you bring him in." She glanced quickly round the circle, shifted slightly in her seat, and Kerwin saw a slight, almost imperceptible communication run round the circle, nods, glances, a kind of mutual settling-down, small agreements needing no words. Elorie lowered her head, glanced for a moment into the matrix, then pointed a slender finger at Auster.

Kerwin, watching, apprehensive, sensitized to these currents, felt something like a palpable line of force connecting the delicate girl with Auster; felt a small electrical shock in the air as they dropped into rapport.

An overtone of emotion in the room like a sullen flame, a covered flame burning against the ice . . .

Rannirl . . .

Forces in tension, aligning, a strong bridge across an empty abyss . . .

"Corus," Elorie whispered aloud, and Kerwin knew, without knowing how, picking it up like flickers of thought, that Corus was young enough, and inexperienced enough, that he could not pick up the circle without the verbal cue. Grinning nervously, the youngster covered his face with his hands, his forehead screwed up into intense concentration. He looked very young. Kerwin, still tentatively feeling out the atmosphere in the room, sensed his curious visualization of hands and wrists interlocking, like the meshing grip of acrobats in midair, a tightening grip . . .

Neyrissa, came the silent command, and suddenly the room was filled with small electrical sparkles, a web of little shimmers interconnecting. For a moment Kerwin felt them all melt together, a blend of eyes, circling faces, and as he felt Kennard slip away from him and into the rapport, he sensed the flight of birds, wheeling as one, swooping, faces, waiting eyes . . .

"Easy," Kennard whispered to him. "I'll bring you in." Then Kennard's voice thinned, dimmed, seemed to hum in Kerwin's ears from an enormous distance. He could see them all now, not with his eyes, but like a circle of faces, waiting eyes . . . He knew he was hovering on the edge of the telepathic rapport; it looked to him like a web, delicately waving its strands . . .

Elorie whispered, "Jeff," but the soft word was like a shriek.

Just let go and slide into contact, it's easy. It was like the instructions he had been given about finding his way to them, random walking through the streets of Thendara. He could tell where they were, he could *feel* the circle waiting for him, somehow visualized them as a ring holding hands, a space left empty for him . . . but how to move toward it? He stood helpless, as if hanging back from their stretched hands, and suddenly felt as if he were swinging in midair over an immense gulf, awaiting a signal to jump for some moving target . . . He knew he was picking up a mental image from Corus, and didn't know why, but he felt the same nerve-twitching fear of the great height, paralyzing terror of the great gulf, the fall, the plunge down and down . . . what was he supposed to do? They seemed to think he knew.

You can do it, Jeff. You have the Gift. It was Kennard's voice, pleading.

No use, Ken. He can't quite make it.

The barrier's a conditioned reflex. After twenty years with the Terrans, he'd have gone mad without it. Kennard's face wavered in the curious light in the room, reflecting from Elorie's crystal, flashing prismatic flares of color all around them. He could see Kennard's lips move but he could not hear him speak. *It's going to be rough. Twenty years. It was hard enough for Auster after five, and he was pure Comyn.*

He moved blurrily through the light in the room; he seemed to be swimming underwater.

Try not to fight it, Jeff.

Abruptly, like a knife-stab, he felt the touch—indescribable, unbelievable, so alien and indefinable that it could be interpreted only as pain . . . in a fractional second, he knew that this was what Kennard had done before, that this was what could not be borne or remembered, this intolerable touch, intrusion, violation . . . It was like having his skull bored open with a dentist's drill. He stood it for about five seconds, then felt himself twitch convulsively all over, and heard someone scream from a million miles away as he slid into the darkness.

When he came out of it this time he was lying on the floor of the octagonal matrix chamber, and Kennard and Neyrissa and Auster were standing and looking down at him. Somewhere he heard muffled sobbing and saw, with the fringes of his mind, young Corus hunched over, his face buried in his hands. Rannirl was standing with his arm around Corus, holding the boy against him. Kerwin's head was a giant balloon filled with red-hot seething pain. It was so awful he couldn't breathe for a second; then he felt his lungs expand and a hoarse sound coming from him, without volition.

Kennard knelt beside him and said, "Can you sit up?"

Somehow he managed it. Auster put out a hand to help him, looking sick. He said, with an unusual friendliness in his voice, "Jeff, we've all been through it, one way or the other. Here, lean on me." Detached, surprised at himself, Kerwin accepted the other man's hand. Kennard asked, "Corus, are you all right?"

Corus raised a blotched, tear-stained face. He looked sick, but he said, "I'll live."

Neyrissa said with gentle detachment, "You're doing it to yourself, you know. You have a choice."

Elorie said, in a taut voice, "Let's get through it quickly. None of us can take much more." She was shaking, but she stretched a hand to Corus, and Kerwin felt, like a faint snap and jolt of electricity, felt it somewhere inside his mind, the re-building of the mesh. Auster, then Rannirl, Neyrissa, dropped into place; Kennard, still holding Kerwin, dropped away and was gone. Elorie did not speak, but suddenly her grey eyes filled up all the space in the room and Jeff heard her commanding whisper:

"Come."

With a jolt, the breath crashing from his body, he felt the impact of their meshed minds as if he had dropped into one facet of the carven crystal. A pattern flamed like a giant star of fire in his mind, and he felt himself run all around the circle, flowing like water, swirling in and out of contact; Elorie, cool, aloof, *holding him at the end of a lifeline* . . . Kennard's gentle sureness; a feather-touch of rapport, shaky, frightened, from Corus; a sullen flare from Auster, sparks meshing, jolting apart ... Neyrissa, a soft searching touch ...

"Enough," said Kennard sharply, and suddenly Kerwin was himself again, and the others were not intangible energy-swirls in the room around him, but separate people again, standing grouped around him.

Rannirl whistled. "Zandru's hells, what a barrier! If we ever get it all the way down, Jeff, you'll be one hell of a technician, but we've got to get rid of that barrier first!"

Corus said, "It wasn't quite as bad the second time. He did make it, part way."

Kerwin's head was still one seething mass of fire. He said, "I thought, whatever it was you did to me—"

"We got rid of part of it," Kennard said, and he went on speaking, but suddenly the words had no meaning. Elorie glanced sharply at Kerwin; she said something, but the words were just noise, static in Kerwin's brain. He shook his head, not understanding.

Kennard said in Cahuenga, "Headache any better?"

"Yeah, sure," Kerwin muttered; it wasn't, if anything it was worse, but he didn't have the energy to say so. Kennard didn't argue. He took Kerwin firmly by the shoulders, led him into the next room and put him into a cushiony chair. Neyrissa said, "Here, this is my business," came and put her light hands on Kerwin's head.

Kerwin didn't say anything. He was past that now. He was rocking in a giant swing, faster and faster, on a pendulum of dizzy pain. Elorie said something. Neyrissa spoke to him in a tone of urgent question, but none of it made any sense to Kerwin. Even Kennard's voice was only a blur of meaningless syllables, verbal hash, word salad. He heard Neyrissa say, "I'm not getting through to him. Get Taniquel up here, fast. Maybe she can . . ."

Words rose and fell around him like a song sung in a strange language. The world blurred into grey fog and he was swinging on a giant pendulum, further and further out, into darkness and pale lights, nothingness . . .

Then Taniquel was there, blurring before his eyes; she fell to her knees beside him with a cry of distress.

"Jeff! Oh, Jeff, can you hear me?"

How could he help it, Kerwin thought with the unreason of pain, when she was shouting right in his ear?

"Jeff, please look at me, let me help—"

"No more," he muttered. "No more of this. I've had enough for one night, haven't I?"

"Please, Jeff, I can't help you unless you let me—" Taniquel begged, and he felt her hand, hot and painful on his throbbing head. He twitched restlessly, trying to throw it off. It felt like hot iron. He wished they would all go away and let him alone.

Then slowly, slowly, as if some tense, full vein had been tapped, he felt the pain drain away. Moment by moment it receded until at last he could see the girl clearly again. He sat up, the pain just a dim throb at the base of his brain.

"Good enough," Kennard said briskly. "I think you'll work out, eventually."

Auster muttered, "It's not worth the trouble!"

Kerwin said, "I heard that," and Kennard gave a

slow, grimly triumphant nod.

"You see," he said. "I told you so. I told you it was worth the risk." He drew a long, weary sigh.

Kerwin lurched to his feet and stood there, gripping the chair back. He felt as if he had been dragged through a wringer, but he was painfully at peace. Taniquel was slumped beside his chair, grey and exhausted, Neyrissa beside her, holding her head. She said, weakly, raising her eyes, "Don't worry about it, Jeff. I was just—just glad I could do something for you."

Kennard looked tired, too, but triumphant. Corus looked up and smiled at him, shakily, and it struck Kerwin, with a curious wrench, that the boy had been crying over *his* pain. Even Auster, biting his lip, said, "I've got to give you this. You're one of us. You can't blame me for doubting, but—well, don't hold it against me."

Elorie came and stood on tiptoe; close enough to embrace him, though she didn't. She raised one hand and touched his cheek, just a feather-touch with the tips of her fingers. She said, "Welcome, Jeff-the-barbarian," and smiled into his eyes.

Rannirl linked arms with him as they went down the stairs to the hall where they had met earlier that night. "At least, this time, we can decide for ourselves what we want to drink," he said, laughing, and Kerwin realized that he had come through the final ordeal. Taniquel had accepted him from the beginning, but now they all accepted him with the same completeness. He, who had never belonged anywhere, was now overwhelmed with the knowledge of how deeply he belonged. Taniquel came and sat on the arm of his chair. Mesyr came and asked if he wanted something to eat or drink. Rannirl poured him a glass of a cool, fragrant wine that tasted faintly of apples, and said, "I think you'll like this; it comes from our estates." It was incongruously like a birth-day party.

Sometime later that evening he found himself next to Kennard. Sensitized to the man's mood, he heard himself say, "You look happy about this. Auster isn't pleased, but you are. Why?"

"Why isn't Auster, or why am I?" Kennard asked with a twist of droll laughter.

"Both."

"Because you're part Terran," Kennard replied somberly. "If you *do* become a working part of a matrix circle—actually inside a Tower—and the Council accepts it, then there's a chance the Council will accept *my* sons."

He frowned, looking over Kerwin's head into a sad distance.

"You see," he said at last, "I did what Cleindori did. I married outside Comyn—married a woman who was part Terran. And I have two sons. And it sets a precedent. I would like to think that one day, my sons could come here . . ." He fell silent. Kerwin could have asked a dozen more questions, but he sensed that this wasn't the time. It didn't seem to matter. He belonged.

Chapter Eight: The World Outside

The days slipped by in Arilinn and Kerwin soon began to feel as if he had been there all his life. And yet, in a curious way, he was like a man lost in an enchanted dream, as if all his old dreams and desires had come to life and he had stepped into them and closed a wall behind him. It was as if the Terran Zone and the Trade City had never existed. Never, in any world, had he felt so much at home. Never had he belonged anywhere as he belonged here. It made him almost uneasy to be so happy; he wasn't used to it.

Under Rannirl's guidance, he studied matrix mechanics. He didn't get too far with the theory; he felt that maybe Tani had the right idea when she called it magic. Spacemen didn't understand the mathematics of an interstellar drive, either, but it worked. He was quicker in learning the simpler psychokinetic feats with the small matrix crystals; and Neyrissa, the monitor, taught him to go into his own body, searching out the patterns of his blood flowing in his veins, to regulate, quicken or slow his heartbeats, raise or lower his blood pressure, watch over the flows of what she called the channels, and what Kerwin suspected would have been called, by Terran medics, the autonomic nervous system. It was considerably more sophisticated than any biofeedback technique he had ever known in the Terran Zone.

He made less progress in the rapport circle. He had learned to take his turn—with Corus or Neyrissa at his side—in the relays, the communication network of telepaths between the Towers, which sent messages and news of what was happening, between Neskaya and Arilinn and Hali and faraway Dalereuth; messages that still meant little to Jeff, about a forest fire in the Kilghard Hills, an outbreak of bandit raids far away on the fringes of the Hellers, an outbreak of a contagious fever in Dalereuth, the birth of triplets near the Lake Country; citizens, too, came to the Stranger's Room of the Tower and asked that messages be sent through the relays, matters of business or news of births and deaths and the arrangement of marriages.

But in the working of the circle he was less successful. He knew they were all anxiously watching his progress, now that they had accepted him; it seemed sometimes that they watched over him like hawks. Taniquel insisted they were pushing him too fast, while Auster glowered and accused Kennard and Elorie of coddling him. But as yet he could endure only a few minutes at a time in the matrix circle. It wasn't, evidently, a process that could be hurried; but he gained a few seconds a day, holding out longer each time under the stresses of contact before he collapsed.

The headaches continued, and if anything they got worse, but for some reason it didn't discourage any of them. Neyrissa taught him to control them, a little, by regulating the inner pressure of the blood vessels around the eye sockets and inside the skull. But there were still plenty of times when he found himself unable to endure anything but a darkened room and silence, with his head splitting. Corus made up rude jokes about him, and Rannirl predicted pessimistically that he'd get worse before he got better, but they were all patient with him; once, even, when he was shut up with one of the blinding headaches, he heard Mesyr—whom he had thought disliked him—remonstrating with Elorie, whom she obviously adored, for making noise in a hallway outside the corridor of his room.

Once or twice, when it got too bad, Taniquel came unasked to his room and did the trick she had done the first night, touching his temples with light fingers and draining the pain away as if she had tapped a valve. She didn't like doing it, Kerwin knew; it exhausted her, and it scared Kerwin—and made him ashamed, too—seeing her so grey and haggard afterward. And it infuriated Neyrissa.

"He has got to learn to do it for himself, Tani. It is not good for you, or for him either, if you do for him what he can and must learn to do for himself! And now look at you," she scolded, "you have incapacitated yourself, too!"

Taniquel said faintly, "I can't endure his pain. And since I have to feel it anyway, I may as well help him."

"Then learn to barrier yourself," Neyrissa admonished. "A monitor must never become so deeply involved, you know that! If you go on like this, Tani, you know very well what will happen!"

Taniquel looked at her with a mischievous smile. "Are you jealous, Neyrissa?" But the older woman only frowned at Kerwin angrily, and went out of the room.

"What was all that about, Tani?" Kerwin asked, but Taniquel did not answer. Kerwin wondered if he would ever understand the small interactions among the people here, the courtesies and the things left unsaid in a telepathic society.

And yet he had begun to relax. Strange as the Arilinn Tower was, it wasn't a magical fairy-tale castle, just a big stone building where people lived. The gliding, silent, nonhuman servants still made him a little uneasy, but he didn't have to see much of them, and he was getting used to their silent ways and learning to ignore them as the others did, unless he wanted something. The place wasn't all wizard and hobgoblin. The enchanted tower wasn't enchanted at all. For some curious reason he felt pleased when he discovered a leak in the roof, right over his room, and since no workman or outsider could come inside the Veil, he and Rannirl had to climb up on the dizzily sloping roof and fix it themselves. Somehow that prosaic incident made the place more real to him, less dreamlike.

He began to learn the language they spoke among themselves—they called it *casta*—for, while he could understand and telepathically, he knew that sooner or later he would have to deal with local non-telepaths. He read some history of Darkover from the Darkovan, not the Terran point of view; there weren't many books, but Kennard was something of a scholar, and had an extensive history of the days of the Hundred Kingdoms—which seemed, to Jeff, somewhat more complicated than that of medieval Europe—and another of the Hastur Wars which, at the end of the Ages of Chaos, had united most of the countryside under the Seven Domains and the Comyn Council. Kennard warned him that accurate history was all but unknown; these had been compiled from tradition, legend, old ballads, and stories, since for almost a thousand years writing had been left to the brothers of Saint Valentine at Nevarsin Monastery, and literacy had been all but lost. But from all this Jeff gathered that at one time, Darkover had had a highly developed technology of the matrix stones, and that its misuse had reduced the Seven Domains to a chaotic anarchy, after which the Hasturs had formed the system of Towers under the Keepers, pledged to chastity to avoid dynastic squabbles, and bound by vows and severe ethical principles.

He had begun to lose track of time, but he thought he had been at Arilinn for three or four tendays when Neyrissa, at the end of a training session, said unexpectedly, "I think you could function as monitor in a circle now, without too much difficulty. I'll certify you as monitor, and give you the oath, if you want me to."

Jeff regarded her in astonishment and dismay. She mistook his surprise and said, "If you would rather take the oath at Elorie's hands, it is your lawful right, but I assure you, in practice we don't trouble the Keeper with such things; I am fully qualified to receive your first oath."

Kerwin shook his head. He said, "I'm not sure I want to take any kind of oath! I wasn't told—I don't understand!"

"But you cannot work in the circle without the monitor's oath," Neyrissa said with a faint frown. "No one trained at Arilinn would ever consider it. Nor would anyone from another Tower be willing to work with you, unsworn—why don't you want to take the oath?" She regarded him with dismay and the suspicion that had vanished from all their eyes except Auster's. "Are you proposing to betray us?"

It was a minute or two before Kerwin realized she had not spoken that last sentence aloud.

She was, he realized, old enough to be his mother; he wondered, suddenly, if she had known Cleindori, but would not ask. *Cleindori had betrayed Arilinn.* And Kerwin knew her son would never be free of that stigma, unless he earned the freedom.

He said slowly, "I wasn't told I would have to take oaths. It's not, in general, a Terran custom. I don't know what I would have to swear to." He added, on an impulse, "Would you take an oath you didn't know, without knowing to what it bound you?"

Slowly the suspicion and anger left her face. She said, "I hadn't thought of that, Kerwin. The monitor's oath is taken even of children when they are tested here. Other oaths may be asked of you later, but this one binds you only to basic principles; you swear never to use your starstone to force the will or conscience of any living thing, never to invade the mind of any other unwilling, and to use your powers only for helping or healing, and never to make war. The oath is very old; it goes back to the days before the Ages of Chaos, and there are those who say it was devised by the first Hastur when he gave a matrix to his first paxman; but that's a legend, of course. We *do* know it has been formally given in Arilinn since the days of Varzil the Good, and perhaps before." She added, with a scornful twist of her thin mouth, "Certainly there is nothing in a monitor's oath that could offend the conscience of Hastur himself, let alone a *Terranan!*"

Kerwin thought about that a moment. It had been a long time since anyone had called him that; not since his first night here. Finally he shrugged. What had he to lose? Sooner or later he would have to put

aside his Terran standards, choose Darkovan principles and ethics, and why not now? He shrugged.
"I'll take your oath," he said.

As he repeated the archaic words—*to force no living
thing against will or conscience, to meddle unasked with no
mind nor body save to help or heal, never to use the powers of
the starstone to force the mind or conscience*—he thought
almost for the first time of the truly frightening
powers of the matrix in the hands of a skilled opera-
tor. The power to interfere with people's thoughts, to
slow or speed their heartbeats, check the flow of
blood, withdraw oxygen from the brain . . . a truly
terrifying responsibility, and he suspected that the
monitor's oath had much the same force as the Hip-
pocratic oath in Terran medicine.

Neyrissa had insisted that the oath be taken in
rapport—it was customary, she said, and he suspected that the reason was to monitor any mental
reservations, a rudimentary form of lie-detector,
which was so normal between telepaths that he realized it did not imply lack of trust. As he spoke the
words—understanding, now, why they were being
exacted, and realizing that he genuinely meant them
—he was aware of Neyrissa's closeness; somehow it
felt as if they were physically very close together, although actually the woman was sitting at the far end
of the room, her head lowered and her eyes bent on
her matrix, not even looking at him. As soon as
Kerwin had finished, Neyrissa rose quickly and said,
"I'm tired of being shut up indoors; let's go out into
the air. Would you care for a ride? It's still early, and
there's nothing much to do today, neither of us is
listed for the relays. What would you say to hawking? I'd like some birds for supper, wouldn't you?"

He tucked away his matrix and followed her. He

had learned to enjoy riding—on Terra it was an exotic luxury for rich eccentrics, but here on the Plains of Arilinn it was a commonplace means of getting around, since the air-cars, matrix-powered, were very rare and used only by the Comyn; and those only under very special circumstances.

He followed her to the stables without demur; but halfway down the stairs she said, "Perhaps we should ask one or two of the others to come?"

"Just as you like," he replied, slightly surprised. She hadn't been particularly friendly before and he hadn't expected that she had much interest in his company. But Mesyr was busy about some domestic affairs somewhere in the Tower, Rannirl had some unspecified business in the matrix laboratory—he tried to explain it, but Kerwin couldn't understand more than one word in five, he didn't have the technical background—Corus was in the relays, Kennard's bad leg was bothering him, and Taniquel was resting for her shift in the relays later that night. So in the end they went out alone, Auster having curtly refused an offer to join them.

Kennard had placed a horse at Kerwin's disposal, a tall rangy black mare from his own estates; Kerwin understood that the Armida horses were famous throughout the Domains. Neyrissa had a silvery-grey pony with gold-colored mane and tail, which she said came from the Hellers. She took her hawk on the saddle-block before her; she wore a grey-and-crimson cape and a long full skirt that Kerwin finally realized was a divided skirt cut like very full trousers. As she took the bird from the hawkmaster, she glanced at him and said, "There is a well-trained sentry-hawk that Kennard has given you leave to use; I heard him."

"I don't know anything of hawking," Kerwin said, shaking his head. He had learned to ride acceptably, but he didn't know how to handle hunting-birds and wasn't going to pretend he did.

There were a few curious stares and murmurs, which Neyrissa ignored, as they rode through the fringes of the town. He realized he had seen almost nothing of the city of Arilinn—which, he had heard, was the third or fourth largest city in the Seven Domains—and decided he would go exploring some day. Neyrissa's cape was flung back, revealing her greying copper hair coiled in braids around her head. Because it was cold, Kerwin had put his leather ceremonial cape over his Terran clothing, and, hearing the murmurs, seeing the awed faces, he realized that they took him for any other member of the Tower circle. Was this what the people in Thendara had thought, his first night on Darkover?

Outside the gates of Arilinn the plains stretched wide, with clumps of bushes here and there, a few tracks and an old cart road, now deserted. They rode for an hour or so beneath the lowering sky, in the pale-purple light of the high sun. At last Neyrissa drew her horse to a walk, saying, "There is good hunting here. We should get some birds, or a rabbithorn or two . . . Elorie hasn't been eating much lately. I'd like to tempt her with something good."

Kerwin had been thinking of hawking, actually, as an exotic sport, an alien thing done for excitement; for the first time he realized that in a culture like this one, it was a very utilitarian way to keep meat on the table. Perhaps, he thought, he ought to learn it. It seemed to be one of the practical skills of a gentleman —or for that matter, he thought, watching Neyrissa's small sturdy hands as she unhooded her hawk, of a

lady. One didn't think of noblewomen hunting for
the pot. But of course that was how hawking had
begun, as a way of pot-hunting for the kitchen! And
while a lady might not be able to do much with large
meat animals, there was no reason a woman
shouldn't equal or surpass a man at this skill. Kerwin
suddenly felt very useless.

"Never mind," said Neyrissa, glancing up at him,
and he realized they were still touched by the fringes
of rapport. "You'll learn. Next time I'll find you a
verrin hawk. You're tall enough and strong enough to
carry one."

She tossed the hawk high into the air; it took off,
winging higher and higher, and Neyrissa watched
the flight, her hands shading her eyes. "There," she
said in a whisper, "he has sighted his prey . . ."

Kerwin looked, but could see no trace of the bird.
"Surely you can't see that far, Neyrissa?"

She looked up impatiently. *Of course not, rapport with
hawk and sentry-bird is one of our family gifts.* The
thought was careless, with the very surface of her
mind, and Kerwin realized that there was a strong
rapport still between them, as with a part of his mind
he *felt* flight, long pinions beating, the all-encompassing excitement of the chase, seeing the world wheeling below, stooping, striking a rush of ecstasy
through his whole body . . . Shaking his head in wonder, Kerwin brought himself back to earth, following
Neyrissa as she rode swiftly toward the spot where
the hawk had brought his kill to the ground. She
gestured to the falconer, following them at a distance, to take up the small dead bird and carry it on
his saddle; the hawk stood on her glove, and Neyrissa
took the head of the dead bird and fed it, still warm,
to the hawk. Her eyes were closed, her face flushed;

Kerwin wondered if she, too, had shared the excitement of that kill; he watched the hawk tearing at the blood and sinews with a sense of excitement combined with revulsion.

Neyrissa looked up at him and said, "She feeds only from my glove; no well-trained bird will taste her own kill until it is given her. Enough—" She wrenched the bloody tidbit away from the cruel beak, explaining, "I want another bird or so." Again she flung the hawk into the air and again Kerwin, sensing the thread of rapport between woman and hawk, followed it in his mind, knowing he was not prying, that she had somehow opened to him to share the ecstasy of flight, the long strong soaring, the strike, the gushing blood. . . .

As the falconer brought the head of the second bird to Neyrissa, through the excitement and revulsion, he became abruptly aware of how deeply he was sharing this with Neyrissa, of arousal, almost sexual, deep in his body. Angrily, Kerwin turned away from the thought, troubled and shamed lest Neyrissa should be aware of it. He wasn't trying to seduce her . . . he didn't even *like* her! And the last thing he wanted, here, was to complicate his life with any women!

Yet as the sun lowered, and the hawk climbed the sky again and again, striking and killing, Kerwin was drawn once more into the ecstatic rapport of woman and falcon, blood and terror and excitement. At last Neyrissa turned to the falconer, said, "No more, take the birds back," and drew her horse up, breathing in long, slow breaths as she watched him ride away. Kerwin was sure she had forgotten him. Without a word she turned her horse back toward the distant gates of Arilinn.

Kerwin rode after her, curiously subdued. A wind was rising, and he drew his cloak carefully around his head. Riding after Neyrissa's shrouded figure, with the dim red sun low in the sky and a crescent of violet moon low over a distant hill, pale and shadowy, he had the curious sense that he was alone on the face of this world with the woman, her head turned away, riding after her as the falcon had pursued the fleeing bird . . . He dug his heels into the flanks of his horse and rode after her, racing as if on the wings of the flying wind, lost in the excitement of the chase . . . clinging to his horse with his knees, by instinct, his whole mind caught up in the excitement of the chase, awareness surging in him. As he rode, he was faintly aware of the still-lingering rapport with the woman, the excitement in her own body, her awareness of the pursuing hoofs, the long chase, a strange hunger not unmixed with fear. . . . Images flooded his mind, overtaking her, snatching her from her horse, flinging her to the ground . . . it was a flooding, cresting sexual excitement, sharing it with her, so that unconsciously he speeded his mount, till he was at her very heels at the gate of the city. . . .

Realization flooded over him. What was he doing? He was an invited guest here, a co-worker, now sworn to them; a civilized man, not a bandit or a hawk! The blood pounded in his temples, and he avoided Neyrissa's eyes as grooms came to take their horses. They dismounted; yet he sensed that she too was weak with excitement, that she could hardly stand. He felt ashamed and troubled by the prevalence of the sexual fantasy, aghast at the thought that she had shared it. In the small dimensions of the stable she moved past him, their bodies not quite touching, yet he was very aware of the woman under the folded cloak, and he ducked his head to conceal the color that flooded through his face.

Just beyond the Veil, on the inner staircase, she suddenly stopped and raised her eyes to him. She said quietly, "I am sorry. I had forgotten—please believe me, I did not do that willingly. I had forgotten that you would not—not yet be able to barricade, if it was unwelcome to you."

He looked at her, a little shamefaced, hardly taking it in that she had formed and shared that curious fantasy. Trying to be polite, he said, "It doesn't matter."

"But it does," she said angrily. "You don't understand. I had forgotten what it would mean to you, and it is not what it would mean to one of us." Abruptly her mind was open to him and he was shockingly aware of the taut excitement in her, nakedly sexual, now unmasked by the symbolism of the falcon-hunt. He felt troubled, embarrassed. She said, in a low, vicious voice, "I told you; you do not understand; I should not have done that to you unless your barriers were adequate to block it, and they were not. In a man—in one of our own—the fact that you accepted it and—and shared it—would mean something more than it does to you. It is my fault; it happens sometimes, after rapport. It is my failure. Not yours, Kerwin; you are not bound by anything. Don't trouble yourself; I know you don't want—" She drew a long breath, looking straight at him, and he could feel her anger and frustration.

Kerwin said, troubled, still only half understanding, "Neyrissa, I'm sorry, I didn't mean to—to do anything to offend or hurt you—"

"I know that, damn you," she said in a rage. "I tell you: It happens sometimes. I have been a monitor for enough years that I know I am responsible for it. I misjudged the level of your barriers, that is all! Stop making a thing of it, and get control of yourself before we spread this all through Arilinn! I can handle it; you can't, and Elorie is young. I won't have *her* disturbed with this nonsense!"

It was like a sudden flooding with ice water, drowning it all, drenching his awareness of the woman, in shock and awareness, that the other telepaths here might pick up his fantasies, his needs . . . He felt naked and exposed, and Neyrissa's rage was like crimson lightning through the flooding shock. He felt stripped, shamed to the ultimate. Stammering a sickened apology, he fled up the stairs and took refuge in his own room. He was still not entirely aware what had happened, but it troubled him.

Long introspection told him that concealment of emotions was impossible in a telepath group; and when they met again, though he was worried for fear his shameful inability to block his own thoughts should have spoilt the ease with which he was accepted, no one spoke of it or even seemed to think about it. He was beginning to understand a little what it meant to be open, even to your innermost thoughts, to a group of outsiders. He felt flayed, embarrassed, as if he had been stripped nude and displayed; but he supposed none of them had gone through life without an embarrassing thought, and he'd simply have to get used to it.

And at least he knew, now, that there was no use trying to pretend with Neyrissa. She knew him, she had gone, as a monitor, deep into his body, and now into his mind too, even those bare spots he would rather she hadn't seen. And she still accepted him. It was a good feeling. Paradoxically he didn't like her any better than he had before, but now he knew that didn't matter; they had shared something, and accepted it.

He had been at Arilinn about forty days when it occurred again to him that he had seen nothing of the city, and one morning he asked Kennard—he was not sure of his status here—if he could go and explore. Kennard stared briefly, and said, "Why not?" Then, breaking out of reverie, said, "Zandru's hells, youngster, you don't have to ask permission to do anything you please. Go alone, or one of us will come and show you about, or take one of the *kyrri* to keep you from getting lost. Suit yourself!"

Auster turned from the fireplace—they were all in the big hall—and said sourly, "Don't disgrace us by going in those clothes, will you?"

Anything Auster said always roused Kerwin's determination to do exactly that. Rannirl said, "You'll be stared at in those things, Jeff."

"He'll be stared at anyway," Mesyr said.

"Nevertheless. Come along, I'll find you some of my things—we're just about the same height, I think —for the time being. And we ought to do something about getting you a proper outfit, too."

Kerwin felt ridiculous when he got into the short laced jerkin, the long blouse with loose sleeves, the full breeches coming down only to the top of his boots. Rannirl's notions of color were not his, either; if he had to wear Darkovan clothing—and he supposed he *did* look pretty silly in Terran uniform—he needn't go about in a magenta doublet with orange insets! At least, he hoped not!

He was surprised, though, to discover, glancing into a mirror, how the flamboyant outfit suited him. It showed to advantage the unusual height and coloring that had always made him feel awkward in Terran clothing. Mesyr cautioned him against wearing any headgear; Arilinn Tower telepaths showed their red heads proudly, and this protected them against accidental injury or insult. On a world of daily violence like Darkover, where street riots were a favorite form of showing high spirits, Jeff Kerwin conceded that this probably made good sense.

As he walked in the streets of the city—he had chosen to go alone—he was conscious of stares and whispers, and nobody jostled him. It was a strange city to him; he had grown up in Thendara, and the dialect here was different, and the cut of the clothing the women wore, longer skirts, fewer of the imported Terran climbing jackets and more of the long hooded capes, on men and women both. The footgear of a Terran did not suit the Darkovan clothing he was wearing—Rannirl, taller than Kerwin, had surprisingly small feet for a man, and his boots had not fitted—so on an impulse, passing a street-shop where boots and sandals were displayed, Kerwin went inside and asked to see a pair of boots.

The proprietor seemed so awed and respectful that Kerwin began to wonder if he had committed some social error—evidently the Comyn rarely went into ordinary shops—until the bargaining began. Then the man kept trying so hard to shift Kerwin from the modestly-priced boots he had chosen to the most expensive and well-crafted pairs in the shop, that Kerwin grew angry and began to bargain hotly. The shopkeeper kept insisting with a beautifully-genuine distress that these poor things were not worthy of the *vai dom*. Finally Kerwin settled on two pairs, one of riding boots, and one set of the soft low-cut suede boots that all the men of Arilinn seemed to wear all the time indoors. Taking out his wallet, he asked, "What do I owe you?"

The man looked shocked and offended. "What have I done to merit this insult, *vai dom?* You have lent grace to me and to my shop; I cannot accept payment!"

"Oh, look here," Kerwin protested. "You mustn't do that—"

"I have told you these poor things are not worthy of your attention, *vai dom,* but if the High-lord would venture to accept from me a pair truly worthy of his notice—"

"Hells's bells," muttered Kerwin, wondering what was going on and what Darkovan taboo he'd blundered into, unknowing, this time.

The man gave Kerwin a sharp look, then said, "Forgive my presumption, *vai dom,* but you are the high-lord Comyn Kerwin-Aillard, are you not?"

Recalling the custom that gave a Darkovan child the name and rank of the highest-ranking parent, Kerwin admitted it, and the man said, firmly and respectfully, but rather as if he were instructing a retarded child in suitable manners, "It is not the custom to accept payment for anything that a Comyn high-Lord condescends to accept, sir."

Kerwin gave in gracefully, not wanting to make a scene, but he felt embarrassed. How the devil could he get the other things he wanted? Just go and ask for them? The Comyn seemed to have a nice little racket going, but he wasn't larcenous enough to enjoy it. He was used to working for what he wanted, and paying for it.

He tucked the package under his arm, and walked along the street. It felt curiously different and pleasant, to walk through a Darkovan city as a citizen, not an outsider, not an interloper. He thought briefly of Johnny Ellers, but that was another life, and the years he had spent with the Terran Empire were like a dream.

"Kerwin?"

He looked up to see Auster, clad in green and scarlet, standing before him. Auster said, pleasantly for him, "It occurred to me that you might get lost. I had business in the city and I thought perhaps I might find you in the marketplace."

"Thanks," Kerwin said. "I wasn't lost yet, but the streets are a little confusing. Good of you to come after me." He was startled at the friendly gesture; Auster alone, of all the circle, had been persistently unfriendly.

Auster shrugged, and suddenly, as clearly as if Auster had spoken, Kerwin sensed it, clear patterned:

He's lying. He said that so I wouldn't ask his business down here. He didn't come to meet me and he's sore about it. But he shrugged the thought aside. What the hell, he wasn't Auster's keeper. Maybe the man had a girl down here, or a friend, or something. His affairs were none of Kerwin's business.

But why did he think he had to explain to me why he was in the city?

They had fallen into step together, turning their steps back in the direction of the Tower, which lay like a long arm of shadow over the marketplace. Auster paused.

"Care to stop somewhere and have a drink before we get back?"

Although he appreciated the friendly offer, Kerwin shook his head. "Thanks. I've been stared at enough for one day. I'm not that much of a drinker, anyhow.

Thanks all the same. Another time, maybe."

Auster gave him a quick look, not friendly, but understanding. He said, "You'll get used to being stared at—on one level. On another, it keeps getting worse. The more you're isolated with—with your own kind—the less you're able to tolerate outsiders."

They walked for a moment, shoulder to shoulder. Behind him, then, Kerwin heard a sudden yell. Auster whirled, giving Kerwin a hard, violent shove; Kerwin lost his footing, taken off balance, slipped and fell sprawling as something hurtled past and struck the wall behind him. A flake of stone ricocheted off, striking Kerwin's cheek, and laid it open to the bone.

Auster had slid off balance and fallen to his knees; he hauled himself to his feet, looking warily around, picked up the heavy paving-stone someone had hurled with what could have been a deadly accuracy.

Kerwin said, "What the hell!" He picked himself up, staring at Auster.

Auster said stiffly, "I apologize—"

Kerwin cut him short. "Forget it. You saved me a nasty bruise. If that thing had hit me amidships, I could have been killed." He touched his cheek with careful fingers. "Who threw that damn thing?"

"Some malcontent," Auster said, and looked round, unquiet. "Strange things are abroad in Arilinn these days. Kerwin, do me a favor?"

"I guess I owe you one at that."

"Don't mention this to the women—or to Kennard. We have enough to worry about now."

Kerwin frowned; but finally nodded. Silently, side by side, they walked up toward the Tower. It was surprising how much at ease he felt with Auster, in spite of the fact that Auster obviously disliked him. It was as if they'd known each other all their lives. *Being isolated with your own kind,* Auster had said, Was Auster his own kind?

He had two facts to chew on. One, Auster, who didn't like him, had moved—automatically, by instinct—to shield him from a thrown rock; by standing still, he could have let Kerwin be hurt and saved himself some aggravation and trouble. But even more than Auster's strange behavior, was the surprising event of the rock. Despite all the deference shown the Comyn by the people of Arilinn, there was *somebody* in Arilinn who would like to see one of them dead.

Or was it the half-Terran interloper who was supposed to be killed? Kerwin suddenly wished he had not given Auster his promise. He'd have liked to talk it over with Kennard.

When the joined the others in the hall that night, Kennard looked strangely at his bandaged cheek, and if Kennard had then asked a point-blank question, Kerwin might have answered—he had not promised Auster to lie about it—but Kennard said nothing, and so Kerwin only told him about the shopkeeper and the boots, mentioning his own disquiet at the custom. The older man threw back his head and guffawed.

"My dear boy, you've given the man prestige—I suppose a *Terranan* would say, free publicity—that will last for years! The fact that a Comyn of Arilinn, even one who's not very important, came into his shop and actually bargained with him—"

"Nice racket," said Kerwin sourly. He wasn't amused.

"Actually, Jeff, it makes excellent good sense. We give a good slice of our lives to the people, we can do things nobody else can do. They wouldn't think of letting us have a good excuse to do anything else. I spent some time as an officer in the Guards; my father is the hereditary Commander, it's an Alton post; and when he dies, I shall have to command it. I should be at his side, learning; but Arilinn was short-handed, so I came back. If my brother Lewis had lived—but he died, leaving me Heir to Alton, and with that, the command of the Guards." Kennard sighed. His eyes strayed into the distance. Then he said, abruptly recalling what he had been saying to Kerwin:

"In a sense, it's a way of keeping us prisoner here; a bribe. Anything we happen to want—any of us— we're given, so we have no shadow of excuse to leave the Tower on the grounds that there could be more for us elsewhere." He looked at the boots and frowned: "—and poor enough merchandise he gave you! The man should be ashamed; it speaks ill of him and his shop!"

Kerwin laughed. No wonder the man had tried so hard to steer him to a better pair! He said so, and Kennard nodded.

"Seriously, it would please the man if you went back when you next visit the town, and accepted the best pair in his shop. Or better yet, commission him to make a pair for you specially, from some design you happen to fancy! And while you're at it, let some clothingmaker fit you out with proper clothing for this climate, why don't you? The Terrans believe in heating their houses, not their bodies; I nearly suffocated when I was there. . . ."

Kerwin accepted the change of subject, but he still did not wholly understand what the Towers *did* that was so important. Messages, yes. He supposed the relays were simpler and less troublesome than a system of telephones or wireless radio communication.

But if that was all they wanted, a radio system would be simpler. As for the other things, he hadn't yet connected the simpler tricks with crystal to the overwhelming importance that the Comyn telepaths seemed to have on Darkover.

And now there was another piece of the puzzle that did not fit; a rock, thrown in broad daylight, at two of the revered Tower telepaths. Not accident. Not mistaken aim on the fringes of a riot somewhere. A rock thrown deliberately, to disable or kill—and it had come near enough to doing it. It didn't fit, and he cursed having given his promise to Auster.

He got the answer to one of his questions a couple of tendays later. In one of the insulated rooms, supervised by Rannirl, Kerwin was working on elementary mechanics, practicing simple force-emission techniques, not unlike the glass-melting tricks Ragan had shown him. They had been at it for over an hour, and Jeff's head was beginning to throb, when Rannirl said abruptly, "Enough for now; something's going on."

They came out on the landing just as Taniquel darted up the stairs; she almost ran into them, and Rannirl reached out and steadied her.

"Careful, *chiya!* What's happening?"

"I'm not sure," she said. "But Neyrissa has had a message from Thendara; the Lord Hastur is coming to Arilinn."

"So soon," Rannirl murmured. "I'd hoped we'd have more time!" He looked at Kerwin and frowned. "You're not ready."

Kennard limped up the steps toward them, holding heavily to the rail. Kerwin asked, "Has this something to do with me?"

"We're not sure yet," Kennard said. "It might be.

It was Hastur who gave his consent to bringing you here, you know—though we accepted responsibility."

Kerwin felt sudden fear constricting his throat. Had he been traced here? Were the Terrans going to enforce their deportation order? He did not want to leave Darkover, felt he could not bear, not now, to leave Arilinn. He belonged here; these were his people. . . .

Kennard followed his thoughts and smiled kindly to him.

"They have no authority to deport you, Jeff. By Darkovan law, citizenship follows the parent of higher rank; which means you are Darkovan by blood-right, and Comyn *Aillard*. No doubt, when Council season comes again, Lord Hastur will confirm you as Heir to Aillard, since there is no female heir to that line; Cleindori had no daughters, and she was herself *nedestro*." But he still looked troubled, and as he went up toward his room he looked over his shoulder, edgily, saying, "But, damn it, wear Darkovan clothes!"

Kerwin had had himself outfitted in the city; as he got into the somber blue-and-grey outfit he had chosen from the best tailor he could find, he thought, looking at himself in the mirror, that at least he *looked* Darkovan. He felt like one—most of the time, anyway. But he still had the sense of being on trial. Did Arilinn, or for that matter Comyn Council, really have the power to defy the Terran Empire?

That, Jeff decided, was a damn good question. The only problem was that he didn't know the answer, and couldn't even guess.

They gathered, not in the big hall they used evenings, but in a smaller, more formally arranged chamber high in the Tower, which Kerwin had heard called the Keeper's audience-chamber. The room was brightly lit with prisms suspended from silver chains; the seats were old, carved from some dark wood, and in their midst was a low table inlaid with patterns in pearl and nacre, a many-pointed star at the center. Neither Kennard nor Elorie was in the room; Kennard, he knew, had gone to the airfield to welcome the distinguished guest. Kerwin, taking one of the low seats around the table, noticed that one chair was higher and more imposing than the rest; he supposed that this was reserved for the Lord Hastur.

A curtain was drawn back by one of the non-humans; Kennard hobbled in and took his seat. Behind him came a tall, dark, commanding man, slightly built, but with a soldierly air of presence. He said ceremoniously, "Danvan Hastur of Hastur, Warden of Hastur, Regent of the Seven Domains, Lord of Thendara and Carcosa—"

"And so forth and so forth," said a gentle, resonant voice. "You lend me grace, Valdir, but I beg of you, spare me all these ceremonies." And the Lord Hastur came into the room.

Danvan Hastur of Hastur was not a tall man. Simply clad in grey, with a blue cloak lined in silvery fur, he seemed at first just a scholarly, quiet man, edging past middle age; his hair was fair, silvering at the temples, and his manner was courteous and unassuming. But something—the stately straightness of his slim body, the firm line of his mouth, the swift, incisive look with which he summed up the room of people—made Kerwin aware that this was no elderly nonentity; this was a man of tremendous presence, a man accustomed to command and to be obeyed; a man absolutely secure in his own position and power, so secure that he did not even need arrogance.

Somehow, he seemed to take up more space in the room than he physically occupied. His voice filled it to the corners, without being loud.

"You lend me grace, children. I am glad to return to Arilinn."

The clear blue eyes fixed on Kerwin, and the man moved toward him. So compelling was that presence that Kerwin rose to his feet in automatic deference.

"*Vai dom*," he said. "I am here at your service."

"You are Cleindori's child, then, the one they sent to Terra," Danvan Hastur said. He spoke the Thendara dialect of Kerwin's own childhood. Somehow, not knowing precisely how he sensed it, Kerwin knew Hastur was not a telepath. "What name did they give you then, son of Aillard?"

Kerwin told the man his name; Hastur nodded thoughtfully.

"Well enough; although *Jeff* has an unnecessarily barbarian sound. You might well consider adopting one of the names of your clan; your mother would certainly have given you one of the family names, Arnad or Damon or Valentine. Had you thought about it? When you are presented before Council, surely, you should wear a name befitting an Aillard noble."

Kerwin said tightly, resisting the man's charm, "I'm not ashamed of wearing my father's name, sir."

"Well, please yourself," Hastur said. "I assure you I meant no offense, kinsman; and I had no intention of suggesting that you deny your Terran heritage. But you look Comyn. I wanted to see you myself and be sure of you."

Kennard said dryly, "You did not trust my word,

Lord Danvan? Or—" He glanced at the dark sallow
man he had called Valdir. "Or was it you who could
not accept my word, my father?" A look half hostile,
half affectionate passed between them, before he said
formally to Kerwin, "My father, Valdir-Lewis
Lanart of Alton, Lord of Armida."

Kerwin bowed, startled; Kennard's father?

Valdir said, "It did not occur to us that you would
attempt to deceive us, Kennard, even if you could.
But Lord Hastur wished to be certain that the Terrans had not duped you all into accepting an im-
poster." His sharp eyes studied Kerwin briefly, then
he sighed and said, "But I can see that it is true." He
added, directly to Kerwin, "You have your mother's
eyes, my boy; you are very like her. I was her foster-
father; will you embrace me as a kinsman, nephew?"
He stepped forward, embracing Jeff formally, pressing his cheeks to each of Kerwin's in turn. Kerwin,
sensing—correctly—that this was a very meaningful
act of personal recognition, bowed his head.

Hastur said, frowning a little, "These are strange
days. I never thought I would welcome the son of a
Terran to the Council. Yet if we must, we must." He
sighed and said to Kerwin, "Be it so then; I recognize
you." His smile was wry. "And since we have accepted the son of a Terran father, we must, I suppose, accept the son of a Terran mother. Bring
Lewis-Kennard to Council, then, if you must, Kennard. How old is he now—eleven?"

"Ten, sir," Kennard said and Hastur nodded. "I
cannot speak for what the Council will do. If the boy
has *laran*—but then, he is too young to tell, and the
Council may refuse to recognize him; but I, at least,
will not fight you any further, Ken."

"*Vai dom*, you are too kind," said Kennard, in a voice heavily overlaid with sarcasm. Valdir said sharply, "Enough. We will fly that falcon when her pinions are grown. For the moment—well, Hastur, young Kerwin here would not be the first of Terran blood to stand before Comyn Council by marriage-right. Nor even the first to build a bridge between our two worlds, to the betterment of both."

Hastur sighed. "I know your views on that, Valdir; my father shared them, and it was by his will that Kennard was sent to Terra when he was no more than a boy. I do not know if he was right or wrong; only time will tell. For the moment, we are confronted with the consequences of that choice, and we must deal with them, will we nil we."

"Strange words for the Regent of Comyn," Auster said from his place, and Hastur gave him a fierce hawk-blue stare, saying, "I deal in realities, Auster. You live here isolated with your brothers and sisters of Comyn blood; I, at the very edge of the Terran Zone. I cannot pretend that the ancient days of Arilinn are still with us, or that the Forbidden Tower has never cast a shadow over every Tower in the Domains. If King Stephen—but he is dead, sound may he sleep, and I rule as Regent for a child of nine, and not a very clever or sound one; one day, if we are all fortunate, Prince Derek will rule, but until that day comes, I do what I must in his place." He turned with a gesture of finality that silenced Auster, and took his seat—not, Kerwin noticed with astonishment, the high seat, but one of the ordinary seats around the table. Valdir did not seat himself but remained standing by the door. Although he wore no weapon, Kerwin somehow thought of a man with a hand on the hilt of his sword.

"Now tell me, my children, how does it go with you in Arilinn?"

Kerwin, watching Lord Hastur, thought: *I wish I could tell that old fellow about the heaved rock! There's no nonsense to Lord Hastur; he'd know what to make of it, and no mistake!*

The curtains at the entrance moved. Valdir said ceremoniously, "The Lady Elorie, Keeper of Arilinn."

Once again her small stately body seemed weighted with the cruelly heavy ceremonial robes. The golden chains at her waist and fastening her cloak seemed almost fetterlike with their weight; they clasped at her shoulders, heavy, a burden. In silence, not looking at any of them, she moved to the thronelike chair at the head of the table. Valdir's deep bow startled Kerwin no less than the Lord Hastur, who rose in his place and bowed the knee deeply to Elorie.

Kerwin watched, paralyzed; this was the same girl who played with her pet birds in the great hall, and quarreled with Taniquel and made silly bets with Rannirl and rode like a hoyden with her hawks; he had not seen her before in the full regalia of the Keeper, and it was a shock and a revelation. He felt as if he too should bow, but Taniquel touched his wrist and he heard the unspoken thought:

The Tower Circle at Arilinn, alone in the Domains, need not rise for their Keeper. The Keeper of Arilinn is sacrosanct; but we are her own, her chosen. There was pride in Taniquel's thought, and Kerwin felt a flicker of it, too; even Hastur could not refuse deference to the Keeper of Arilinn. *So in a sense we are more powerful than the Regent of the Seven Domains. . . .*

"Welcome, in the name of Evanda and Avarra," Elorie said in her soft throaty voice. "How may Arilinn serve the son of the Hasturs, *vai dom?*"

"Your words brighten the sky, *vai leronis,*" Hastur replied, and Elorie motioned him to resume his seat.

Kennard said, "It's a long time since you honored us with a visit to Arilinn, Lord Hastur. And we are honored indeed, but if you'll forgive me, we know you didn't come to do us honor, or to have a look at Jeff Kerwin, or to bring me messages about the Council, or even to let me visit my father and ask about the health of my sons. Nor, I venture to say, even for the pleasure of our company. What do you want with us, Lord Hastur?"

The Regent's face crinkled up in a pleasant grin.

"I should have known you'd see through me, Ken," he said. "When Arilinn can spare you, we need someone like you in Council; Valdir is too diplomatic. You're right, of course; I came from Thendara because we have a delegation waiting—with the big question."

All of them, except Kerwin, seemed to know what he meant. Rannirl muttered, "So soon?"

"You haven't given us much time, Lord Hastur," Elorie said. "Jeff's making good progress, but it's slow."

Kerwin leaned forward, gripping at the chair arm.

"What's this all about, why are you looking at me?"

Hastur said, solemnly, "Because, Jeff Kerwin-Aillard, you have given us, for the first time in many years, a Tower Circle with a full complement of power, under a Keeper. If you do not fail us, we may be in a position to save the power and prestige of the Comyn—if you do not fail us. Otherwise—" He spread his hands. "The Terrans will have their entering wedge. The rest will follow and there won't be any way to stop it. I want you—all of you—to come and talk to the delegation. What about it, Elorie? Do you trust your Terran barbarian as much as that?"

In the silence that followed, Kerwin felt Elorie's glance, calm, childlike, resting on him.

Barbarian. Elorie's barbarian. I'm still that, to all of them.

Elorie turned to Kennard and said quietly, "What about it, Ken? You know him best."

By now Kerwin was used to being discussed before his face. In a telepath society there was no way to avoid it anyway. Even if they had tactfully sent him out of the room, he would have been aware of what was being said. He tried to keep his face impassive.

Kennard sighed and said, "As far as trusting goes, we can trust him, Elorie," he said. "But the risk is yours and so the decision has to be yours. Whatever you decide, we'll stand by you."

"I speak against it," Auster said passionately. "You know how I feel—you too, Lord Hastur!"

Hastur turned to the younger man and said, "Is it blind prejudice against Terrans, Auster?" His calm manner contrasted curiously with Auster's tense, knotted face and angry voice. "Or have you some reason?"

"Prejudice," Taniquel said angrily, "and jealousy!"

"Prejudice, yes," Auster admitted, "but not, I think, blind. It was entirely too easy to get him from the Terrans. How do we know that the whole thing wasn't concocted for our benefit?"

Valdir said, in his deep voice, "With Cleindori's face written in his own? He has Comyn blood."

"I think, by your leave," Auster said, "that you, too, are prejudiced, Lord Valdir. You, with your Terran foster-son and half-caste grandson—"

Kennard leaped to his feet. "Now, damn it, Auster—"

"And you speak of Cleindori!" As he spoke it, the word was an epithet, a foulness. "She who was Dorilys of Arilinn—renegade, heretic—"

Elorie rose, angry and white. "Cleindori is dead. Let her lie in peace! And Zandru send scorpion whips to those who murdered her!"

"And to her seducer—*and all his blood!*" Auster flung back. "We all know Cleindori was not alone when she fled from Arilinn—"

New, unaccustomed emotions were battling in Jeff Kerwin. This was his father, his unknown mother, that they were cursing! For the first time in his life he felt a surge of sympathy for his Terran grandparents. Unloving and cold they had seemed; and yet they had taken him in as a son and never once had they reproached him with his unknown, alien mother or his mixed blood. He longed to rise, fling challenge at Auster; he half rose to his feet, but Kennard's angry look fixed him in his seat; and Hastur's ringing voice commanded, "Enough!"

"Lord Hastur—"

"Not a word!" Hastur's angry, emphatic voice silenced even Auster. "We are not here to rake up the deeds and misdeeds of men and women a generation dead!"

"Then, under favor, Lord Hastur, why are we here?" asked Neyrissa. "I have given Kerwin the monitor's oath; he will do for a mechanic's circle."

"But a Keeper's circle?" Hastur asked. "Are you all ready to risk him for that? To do again what

Arilinn could do in Leonie's time and has not done since? Are you ready for that?"

There was silence, a deep silence, and Kerwin sensed that there was fear in it. Even Kennard was silent. At last Hastur added, urgently, "Only the Keeper of Arilinn can make that decision, Elorie. And the delegation awaits the word of Arilinn's Keeper."

"I don't think we ought to risk it," Auster said. "What is the delegation to us? The Keeper should choose in her own good time!"

"The risk is *mine*—to accept or refuse!" Two spots of angry color burned in Elorie's cheek. "I have never before used my authority; I am not a witch, not a sorceress, I will not let men place on me the supernatural power. . . ." She spread her hands in a little, helpless gesture. "Yet, for good or ill, I am Arilinn; authority rests by law in me, Elorie of Arilinn. We will hear the delegation. There is no more to be said; Elorie has spoken."

There were bent heads, murmurs of assent, and Kerwin, watching, was shocked. Among themselves, they quarreled with Elorie and argued points with her without hesitation; this public assent had the feel of ritual.

Elorie turned to the door, stately and unbending. Kerwin watched her, and suddenly felt at one with her disquiet. He *knew*, not quite knowing how the knowledge had come to him, how Elorie hated to invoke her supreme and ritual authority; how much she disliked the superstitious awe surrounding her high office. Suddenly this pale, childish girl seemed *real* to him, her calmness merely a mask for passionate convictions, for emotions so severely controlled that they were like the eye of the hurricane.

And I thought her calm, emotionless? A mask she wears, no more, only a mask no one can remove, not even she herself. . . .

He felt Elorie's emotions as if they were his own.

So I've done what I swore I would never do. I've used their conditioned reverence for a Keeper, just to force them to do what I want! But I had to, oh, I had to, or we'd have another hundred years of this superstitious rubbish. . . . And then a thought that, Kerwin knew, shocked Elorie as much as it shocked him, a flaring, frightening question: *Was Cleindori right?* And he felt Elorie's thoughts flare into silence, knowing she had frightened herself with that last question.

Chapter Nine:
Challenge to Arilinn

Riding down in the shaft, between Taniquel and Elorie, Kerwin was still shaken by the backlash of that contact with Elorie. What had Kennard called his gift? *Empath*—gifted with the power of sensing the emotions of others. He had accepted, intellectually, that this was true; had tested it a little under laboratory conditions and among the circle. Now, for the first time, it had hit him deep, on the level of his guts, and he *felt* it and knew it.

He didn't know where they were going. He followed the others. But they went down through the Veil and outside, and into a building near the Tower, that Jeff had never seen before. It was a long, narrow, silk-hung hall, and somewhere a ceremonial gong rang out as they filed into the room. There were a few spectators in the seats, and before them, at a long table, were half a dozen men.

They were prosperous looking men, most of them middle aged and more, wearing Darkovan dress in the fashion of the cities. They waited silently while Elorie was announced and took the central chair. The Tower circle seated themselves quietly around Elorie, not speaking.

It was Danvan of Hastur who spoke, at last.

"You are the men who call yourselves the Pan-Darkovan Syndicate?"

One of the men, a heavy-set and swarthy man with fierce eyes, bowed.

"Valdrin of Carthon, *z'par servu*, my lords and ladies," he confirmed. "By your leave I will speak for all."

"Let me review the situation," said Hastur. "You have formed a league—"

"To encourage the growth of manufacturing and trade on Darkover, in the Domains and beyond," Valdrin said. "I hardly need to tell you the political situation—the Terrans and their foothold on our world. The Comyn and the Council, saving your presence, Lord Hastur, have tried to ignore the Terran presence here and its implications for trade—"

Hastur said quietly, "That is not precisely the situation."

"I won't bandy words with you, *vai dom*," said Valdrin, respectfully but impatiently too. "The facts are these: In view of our agreements with the Terrans, we have an opportunity we've never had before, to bring the Domains out of our Dark Ages. Times change. Like it or not, the Terrans are here to stay. Darkover is being swept into the Empire. We can pretend they're not there, refuse to trade with them, ignore their offers of trade, and keep them locked up inside their Trade Cities, but the barriers we put up will come tumbling down in another generation, maybe two at most. I've seen it happening on other worlds."

Kerwin remembered what the Legate had said, that they left governments alone, but that the people saw what the Terran Empire had to give, and started demanding to come into it. *It's almost a mathematical formula—you can predict the thing.*

Valdrin of Carthon was saying the same thing, quite passionately.

"In short, Lord Hastur, we protest the decision of Comyn Council; we want some of the advantages that come with being a part of the Empire!"

Hastur said quietly, "Do you understand the decision of the Council, to retain the integrity of the Darkovan way of life, rather than becoming just another Empire satellite state?"

"With all respect, Lord Hastur, when you talk about the Darkovan way of life, you're talking about letting us stay a barbarian culture forever? Some of us want civilization and technology—"

Hastur said quietly, "I have seen the Terran civilization more closely than you. I tell you, Darkover wants none of it."

"Speak for yourselves, *vai dom,* not for us! Perhaps in the old days there was some justification for the rule of the Seven Domains; in those days, Comyn gave us something to compensate for what we gave them in the way of allegiance and support!"

Valdir Alton said, "Man, am I listening to treason against the Council and Hastur?"

Valdrin of Carthon said heavily, "Treason? Not that, sir. God forbid. And we don't want to be part of the Empire any more than you do. We're talking about trade, technological advances. There was a day when Darkover had its own science and technology. But those days are gone, and we've got to have something to replace them, or else sink into a second Ages of Chaos. It's time to admit that they're gone, and find something to replace them. And if the Terrans want to be here, they can offer us something—

trade, metals, tools, technological consultants. Because it's for certain that the old sciences of the Towers are gone forever."

Kerwin was beginning to see it clearly. By virtue of their inborn psi powers, once, the Comyn had been rulers—and, in a certain sense, slaves—of Darkover and the Domains. Through the tremendous energy of the matrixes, not the small individual ones, but the great ones demanding linked circles of Tower-trained telepaths linked under a Keeper, they had given Darkover her own science and her own technology. This explained the vast ruins of a forgotten technology, the traditions of ancient sciences. . . .

But what had the cost been, in human terms? The men and women possessed of these powers had lived, perforce, lives constrained and circumscribed, guarding their precious powers carefully, spoilt for ordinary human contacts.

Kerwin wondered if the natural drift of evolution, in nature, toward the norm and away from extremes, had been responsible for the waning of these powers. For they had waned. Arilinn, Mesyr had told him, had once held three circles, each with its own Keeper; and Arilinn had been only one of many Towers. Fewer and fewer were born in these days with a full measure of the precious *laran*. The science of Darkover had become a forgotten myth and a few psi tricks. . . . And this was not enough to keep Darkover independent of the lure of Terran trade and Terran technology.

"We have dealt with the Terrans," Valdrin of Carthon said, "and I think, also, that we have won most of the people to our side."

Valdir said, "In Thendara, the people are loyal to Comyn Council!"

"But, under favor, *vai dom,* Thendara is only a very small part of the Domains," Valdrin said, "and the Domains are not all of Darkover. The Terrans have pledged that they will lend us technicians, engineers, industrial developers and experts—everything necessary to begin extensive mining and manufacturing operations here. Metals and ores are the key, my lord. Before we have technology we must have machinery, and before we have machinery we must have—"

Hastur raised a hand. He said, "I know it all like an old song. Before you have mines you must have machinery, and someone must make the machinery, and someone must mine the materials to make the machinery. We are not a mechanized civilization, Valdrin—"

"True, more's the pity!"

"Is it such a pity? The people of Darkover are content on their farms and lands and cities. We have what industries we need; dairy farming, cheesemaking, the milling of grains, and weaving of cloth. There are papermills and felting-mills, the processing of nuts and cereals—"

"Transported at horseback pace!"

"And," Hastur said, "no men to slave at the building of roads to keep them in condition for monstrous robot vehicles to whiz over at breakneck speed and make our clean air rotten with their chemical fuels!"

"We have a right to industries and wealth—"

"And to factories? To wealth gained by forcing men to labor in inhuman conditions, to build things that men do not really need or want? To work done by automatic machinery, leaving men with nothing to do but drug their senses with cheap amusements, and work at repairing the machinery? To mines, and people herded together in cities to build and repair these machines, so they have no time to grow and prepare the food they need? So that the raising of food becomes another monster factory enterprise, and a man's children become a liability instead of an asset?"

Valdrin's voice was calm, tinged with contempt. "You are a romantic, my lord, but your biased picture will not convince those men who want something better than starving on their land from year to year and dying in a bad year. You cannot hold us back forever to a primitive culture, my lord."

"Do you really want to become a replica of the Terran Empire, then?"

"Not that," Valdrin said, "not what you think. We can take what we need from the Terran system without being corrupted by it."

Hastur smiled faintly and said, "That is a delusion that has seduced many peoples and worlds, my good man. Do you think we can fight the Terrans on their own ground? No, my friend; the world that accepts the good things that come from the Terran Empire— and I am not deceived, there are many—must also accept the evil that comes with it. And yet perhaps you are right; we cannot bar the way forever, and keep our people poor and simple, an agricultural society in an interstellar age. It may be that your accusation is just. Once we were more powerful than now; it is true that we are just emerging from a Dark Ages. But it is not true that we must go Terra's way. What if the old powers were to return? What if the Comyn could do again all the things that legend said they could do? What if energy sources were available

again, without the endless search for fuels, without
the evils that blasted our land in the years before the
Compact?"

"What if Durraman's donkey could fly?" asked
Valdrin. "It's a good dream, but there hasn't been a
competent Keeper, let alone a fully qualified circle,
for years."

"There is now." Hastur turned with a gesture. "A
Comyn circle complete and ready to demonstrate
their powers. I ask only this; that you keep free of the
Terrans, and their ruinous, dehumanizing methods.
Don't accept their technicians and their engineers, to
destroy our lands! And if you must trade with Terra,
do it as equals, not as poor protégés, being helped up
from barbarian status! Our world is old, older than
Terra dreams, and prouder. Don't shame us this
way!"

He had caught them on their pride and their patri-
otism, and Kerwin saw it catch fire in the eyes of
each of the delegation, although Valdrin still seemed
skeptical.

"Can the Tower circle do this?"

"We can," Rannirl said. "I'm the technician; we
have the skill and we know how to use it. What do
you need?"

"We've been dealing with a group of Terran engineers, to make a survey of the natural resources in
the Domains for us," Valdrin said. "Our major
needs are for metals: tin, copper, silver, iron,
tungsten. Then for fuels, for sulfur, hydrocarbons,
chemicals—they promised us a complete inventory,
to locate with their surveying equipment all the major accessible deposits of natural resources for mining—"

Rannirl held up a hand. "At the same time finding

out where they are," he drawled, "and spreading all over Darkover with their infernal machines instead of staying decently shut up in their Trade Cities!"

Valdrin said hotly, "I deplore that as much as you do! I have no love for the Empire, but if the alternative is to slip backward into primitivism . . ."

"There is an alternative," Rannirl said. "We can make your survey for you—and do the mining, too, if you like. And we can do it quicker than the Terrans."

Kerwin drew a deep breath. He should have guessed. If a matrix crystal could power an aircraft, what were the limits of that power?

God, what a concept! And to keep the Terran engineers out of the Domains . . .

Kerwin had not realized until this moment how deeply he felt on this subject; his years on Terra came back to his mind, dirty industrialized cities, men living for machinery, his dismay when he came back to Thendara and found the Trade City only a little corner of the Empire. With the passionate love of an exile for his home, he understood Hastur's dream; to keep Darkover what it was, keep it out of the Empire.

Valdrin said, "It sounds good, my lords, but the Comyn haven't been that strong, not for centuries— maybe never. My great-granfer used to tell stories of buildings raised by matrix power, and roads built, and such-like things, but in my time it's been all a man can do to get enough iron to shoe his horses!"

"It sounds good, yes," said another of the men, "but I think it more likely the Comyn are just trying to delay us until the Terrans lose interest and go elsewhere. I think we ought to deal with the Terrans."

Valdrin said, "Lord Hastur, we need more than vague talk about the old Comyn powers and the Tower circles. How long would it take you to make this survey for us?"

Rannirl glanced at Hastur, as if asking permission to speak. He asked, "How long would the Terrans need to do it?"

"They've promised it to us in half a year."

Rannirl glanced at Elorie, at Kennard, and Kerwin felt that they shared an exchange from which he was excluded. Then he said, "Half a year, eh? What would you say to forty days?"

"On one condition," Auster broke in passionately. "That if we do it for you, you'll abandon all ideas of dealing with the Terran engineers!"

"That seems only fair," said Elorie, speaking for the first time, and Kerwin noticed how a silence dropped in the room as the Keeper spoke. "If we prove to you that we can do more for you than your Terran engineers, will you be content to be guided by the Council? Our only desire is that Darkover shall continue to be Darkover, not a replica of the Terran Empire . . . or a third-rate imitation! If we succeed, you will allow yourselves to be guided by Comyn Council and Arilinn in all things."

"That seems fair enough, my lady," Valdrin said. "But it's only fair it should go both ways. If you can't deliver what you say, will Comyn Council pledge itself to withdraw all objections, and let us deal with the Terrans without interference?"

Elorie said, "I can only speak for Arilinn, not for Comyn Council," but Hastur rose. In the quiet, resonant voice that filled the Council chamber without being loud, he said, "On the word of a Hastur, it shall be so."

Kerwin met Taniquel's eyes, seeing the shock in them. The word of Hastur was proverbial. And now it was all in their hands—if they could indeed do what Rannirl had said they could do, what Hastur had pledged they could do. The whole future direction of Darkover hung on their success or failure. And that success or failure hung on him, on Jeff Kerwin, on "Elorie's barbarian"—the newest member of the circle, the weak link in the chain! It was a paralyzing responsibility, and Kerwin was terrified by the implications.

The formalities of leavetaking were endless, and halfway through them Kerwin slipped away unseen, back through the courtyards and through the shimmering haze of the Veil.

It was too heavy a weight to be borne, that their success or failure should hang on him alone . . . and he had thought he would have more time to learn! He remembered the agony of the first rapports, and was horribly afraid. He turned into his room and flung himself down on his bed in silent despair. It wasn't fair to demand so much of him, so soon! It was too much, to insist that the whole fate of Darkover, the Darkover he knew and loved, should depend on his untried powers!

The ghostly scent in the room felt strong to him; in a flash of remote recognition, it penetrated a closed place in his memory.

Cleindori. My mother, who broke her vows to the Comyn, for an Earthman . . . must I pay for her betrayal?

A flash of something, recognition, memory, hovered at the edge of his senses, a voice that said *it was not betrayal.* . . . He could not identify the dark, closing door of memory, standing half-ajar, a voice . . .

Blinding pain struck through his head; it was

gone. He stood in his room, crying out in despair. "It's too much! It's not fair, that it should all depend on me. . ." And heard the words echoing in his mind, as if from the walls, as if someone else had stood here, crying these words in the same despair.

A soft step in the room, a voice that whispered his name, and Taniquel was at his side, the web of rapport meshing between them. The girl's face, now solemn and free of mischief, was drawn and grieved with his trouble.

"But it's not like that, Jeff," she whispered at last. "We trust you, we all trust you. If we fail, it's not your doing alone. Don't you know that?" Her voice broke and she clung to him, holding him in her arms. Kerwin, shaken with a new, violent emotion, crushed the girl to him. Their lips met; and Kerwin knew that he had been wanting this since he first saw her, through the rain and sleet of a Darkovan night, through the smoke of a Terran room. The woman of his own people, the first to accept him as one of themselves.

"Jeff, we love you; if we fail, it's not your failure, it's ours. You won't be the one to blame. But you won't fail, Jeff. I know you won't . . . ."

Her arms sheltered him, their thoughts blended, and the upsurge of love and desire in him was something he had never known, never guessed.

Here was no easy conquest, no cheap girl from the spacemen's bars, to give his body a moment's ease but leave his heart untouched. Here was no encounter to leave the aftertaste of lust in his memory, and the sickening of loneliness when he sensed, as he had sensed so often, the woman's emptiness as deep as his own disillusion.

Taniquel. Taniquel, who had been closer than any

previous lover from that first instant of rapport between them, from her first accepting kiss. How was it that he had never known? He shut his eyes, the better to taste this closeness, the closeness that was more intense than the touch of lips or arms.

Taniquel whispered, "I've sensed . . . your loneliness and your need, Jeff. But I was afraid to let myself share them until now. Jeff, Jeff—I've taken your pain to myself, let me share this too."

"But," Kerwin said hoarsely, "I'm not afraid now. I was afraid only because I felt alone."

"And now," she spoke his thoughts, sinking into his arms with a surrender so absolute that he seemed never to have known a woman before, "you'll never be alone again."

Chapter Ten:
The Way of Arilinn

If Kerwin had visualized the planetary survey as something to be done by magic, concentration into the matrixes, a quick mental process, he was quickly shown how wrong he was. The actual rapport work, Kennard told him, would come later; meanwhile there were preparations to be made, and only the Tower telepaths themselves could make them.

It was almost impossible to focus telepathic rapport, so they explained to him, unless the object or substance had first been brought into rapport with the telepath who would be using it. Kerwin had imagined that the gathering of the materials would be done by outsiders or menials; instead, he himself, as the least skilled in actual telepathic matrix work, was put to several small technical jobs in the preliminary stages. He had learned something of metallurgy on Terra; assisted by Corus, they located samples of various metals, and, working in a laboratory that reminded Jeff of an Earth-history conception of an alchemist's study, smelted them down and with primitive but surprisingly effective techniques, reduced them to pure form. He wondered what on earth they were going to do with those miniature samples of iron, tin, copper, lead, zinc, and silver. He was even more confused when Corus started making molecular models of these metals, kindergarten af-

fairs with little clay balls on sticks, pausing at times
to concentrate on the metals and "sound" the atomic
structure with his matrix. Kerwin quickly picked up
the trick of this—it was not unlike his early experiments with glass and crystal structure.

Meanwhile Taniquel was out daily in the airlaunch with Auster and Kennard, examining great
maps, carefully coordinating them with photographs
(made on excellent Terran cameras) of the terrain.
Sometimes they were away for two or three days at a
time.

Taniquel had explained to Kerwin why they
needed the maps and pictures of the countryside.
"You see," she explained, "the picture—and the
map—becomes a symbol of that piece of ground, and
we can establish rapport with it through the picture.
There was a time when a good psychic could find
water, or minerals in the ground, but he had to be
walking over it at the time."

Kerwin nodded; even on Earth, where psi powers
were still not much regarded, there were water-find-
ers and dowsers. But on a *map*?

"We don't find them on the map, silly," Taniquel
said. "The map is a device to establish contact with
that piece of land, the territory *represented* by the map.
We could find it by pure psychism, but it's easier if
we have something that directly represents it; like a
photograph. We use the map to establish the contact,
and to mark what we find there."

Kerwin supposed the principle was the same as the
folk-tale of the man who killed his enemy by sticking
pins in his image; but as the memory came into his
mind, Taniquel blanched and said, "No one trained
at Arilinn would ever, *ever* do such a wicked thing!"

"But the principle is the same," Kerwin said, "us-

ing an object as a focus for the powers of the mind."
But Taniquel still would not admit it. "It isn't the
same at all! That's meddling with the mind, and it's
unlawful and—*dirty*," she said vehemently, then
looked at him with suspicion. "You took the
monitor's oath, didn't you?" she demanded, as if
wondering how anyone sworn that way could even
have such thoughts. And Kerwin sighed, knowing he
would never understand Taniquel. They shared so
much, they had been so often in rapport, he felt that
she was utterly known to him: And yet there were
times when, as now, she became alien, wholly a
stranger.

While they were making the maps and checking
their accuracy with the Terran photographs
(Kerwin, who knew something of cameras from his
years on Terra, was pressed into service developing,
printing, and enlarging the enormous aerial views),
Corus finished the work of making the metal
samples; then Elorie brought them in on the work of
constructing the matrix lattices, or "screens."

This was hard, demanding work, both mentally
and physically; they worked with molten glass,
whose amorphous structure was nevertheless solid
enough to hold the matrix crystals in the desired
structure, a solid network encased in glass. Corus,
whose PK potential was enormously high, had the
task of holding the glassy stuff in a state of liquid
pliancy without heat. Kerwin attempted this several
times, but it frightened him to see Elorie plunge her
frail white hands into the apparently boiling mass.
Rannirl said dryly that if Kerwin lost his nerve and
his control they could all be badly hurt, and refused
to let him have control of the glass while they were
working inside it. Layer after layer of the glass was

poured, Elorie activating, with her own matrix, the tiny sensitized crystals suspended inside each layer; Rannirl, standing by to take control when hers faltered; and meanwhile following the whole process on a monitor screen not unlike the one Kerwin had seen in the house of the two matrix mechanics in Thendara, monitoring the complex interior crystalline structures being built up in the layers of glass, by a process analogous to the monitoring process that Taniquel, or Neyrissa, could do with the body of one of them.

Rannirl said once, at the end of a long stint working with the lattices, "I shouldn't say this; but Elorie is wasted as a Keeper. She has the talent to be a technician; and she never will be, because we need Keepers too badly. If there were more women willing to work as Keepers—a Keeper doesn't need that kind of talent, a Keeper doesn't even have to learn to monitor; she simply has to hold the energon flows. Zandru's hells, we could use a damned *machine* for that. I could build an amplifier that would do it, one that any good mechanic could handle! But it's traditional, using a Keeper's polarities and energy flows. And I can't even teach Elorie as much as she wants to know about mechanics; she needs all her energy for the work she does in the circle! Damn it—" He lowered his voice and said, as if he expected to be overheard and blasted, "Keepers are an anachronism in this day and age. Cleindori was right, if they could only see it!" But when Kerwin stared and asked him what he had meant, Rannirl shook his head, tightened his mouth and said, "Forget I said it. It's a dangerous point of view." He would say no more, but Kerwin caught a fragment of thought about fanatics who thought that a Keeper's ritual virginity was more important than her efficiency at the matrixes, and that this point of view was going to destroy the Towers sooner or later, if it hadn't already.

Working with them, he felt his own sensitivity growing, day by day. He had no trouble now in visualizing almost any atomic structure; the work he had done with Neyrissa, in learning to monitor his own internal organs and processes, was beginning to carry over to seeing energy fields and atomic processes, and he had no trouble in maintaining the stasis in any crystalline structure. He was beginning to sense the internal structure of other substances now; once he found himself aware of oxidation of the iron in a slowly-rusting doorhinge; in his first unsupervised effort, he pulled out his matrix and with a fierce mental effort reversed the process.

He still got the splitting headaches when he was actually working with the screens—though now he could handle a shift in the relay nets unassisted—and the effort was tremendous, racking, each expenditure of psychic energy leaving him spent and drained, his body demanding enormous quantities of food and sleep.

He understood, now, the gargantuan appetites they all had—Elorie, for instance; he had been amused at her childlike greediness for sweets, and had been astonished at seeing so frail and dainty a little girl put away quantities of food that would have satiated a horse-drover. But now he realized that he was hungry all the time; his body, drained of energy, demanded replacements with ravenous hunger. And when the day's work was completed—or called to a halt because Elorie could not endure any more of the strain—and Kerwin could rest, or when Taniquel had a little leisure to spend with him, he found that he could only fling himself down beside her and sleep.

"I'm afraid I'm not a very ardent lover," he apologized once, half sick with chagrin; Taniquel close to him, loving and willing, but the only desire in his body was an exhausted hunger for sleep. Taniquel laughed softly, bending to kiss him.

"I know; I've been around matrix workers all my life, remember? It's always that way when there's work in hand—you have only so much energy, and it all goes into the work, and there's nothing left. Don't worry about it." She laughed, a small mischievous chuckle. "When I was training at Neskaya, we used to test ourselves, sometimes, one of the men and I; we'd lie down together—and if either of us could even *think* of anything but sleep, we'd know we'd been cheating, not giving all we had to the matrix work!"

He felt a sudden inner storm of jealousy for the men she had known that way; but he was really too tired to care.

She stroked his hair. "Sleep, *bredu*—we'll have time together when this is over, if you still want me."

"*If* I still want you?" Kerwin sat upright, staring at the girl. She lay back on the pillow, her eyes closed, the freckles pale on her pixie face, her hair loosened, sunbright on the sheets. "What do you mean, Tani?"

"Oh, people change," she said vaguely. "Never mind that now. Here—" She pulled him gently down, her light hands caressing his forehead. "Sleep, love; you're worn out."

Weary as he was, the words had driven sleep from his mind. How could Taniquel doubt—or was the girl in the grip of some premonition? Since they had been lovers, he had been happy; now, for the first time, disquiet moved in him, and he had a sudden mental flash of Taniquel, hand in hand with Auster, walking along the battlements of the tower. What had been between Taniquel and Auster?

He *knew* Taniquel cared for him in a way he had never guessed possible with any woman. They were in total harmony. He knew, now, why his casual affairs with women had never gone beneath the surface; the unrecognized telepathic sensitivity in him had picked up the fundamental shallowness of the kind of women he had known; he had chided himself for being an idealist, wanting more than any woman could give. Now he knew it was possible; his relationship with Taniquel had brought a whole dimension into focus; his first taste of shared passion and emotion, real intimacy. He *knew* Taniquel cared for him; could she possibly care for him so deeply, if she cared for someone else that way?

Many disquiets began to come into focus as he lay awake, his head throbbing, of course. Now it was clear to him; everyone in the Arilinn Tower knew they were lovers. Small things he had not noticed at the time, a smile from Kennard, a meaningful glance from Mesyr, even the small interchange with Neyrissa—*Are you jealous?*—now took on significance.

And I never realized; in a telepath culture they would take it for granted, there would be no such thing as privacy and I never understood. . . . Suddenly the thought was violent, embarrassing: Telepaths all, were they reading his thoughts, his emotions, spying on what he had shared with Taniquel? Scalding embarrassment flooded him, as if he had had some shameful dream of walking naked in the public square and waked to find that it was true. . . .

Taniquel drowsily holding his hand, curled against him, jerked awake as if touched by a live wire. Indignation flamed in her face.

"You—you *are* a barbarian," she raged. "You—you *Terranan!*" She scrambled out of bed and caught up her dressing-gown; quickly she was gone, her light footsteps dying away with an angry pattering on the uneven floor. Kerwin, baffled at her sudden rage, lay with his head throbbing. He told himself that this would not do, he had work to do the next day, and lay down, trying hard to apply the techniques Neyrissa had taught him, relaxing his body, slowing his breathing to normal, trying to calm the tensions in his body by controlling his breath, to ease the blood pounding in his temples. But he was too confused and dismayed for much success.

But when they met again, she was gentle and affectionate as ever, greeting him with her spontaneous embrace. "Forgive me, Jeff, I shouldn't have been angry. It was unfair of me. It's not for me to blame you, that you've lived among the *Terranan* and picked up some of their—their strange ways. You'll come to understand us better, in time."

And with the reassurance of her arms around him, her emotions meshing with his, he could not doubt the sincerity of her feelings.

Thirteen days after Hastur's visit to Arilinn, the matrixes were prepared; and later that same day, in the great hall, Elorie told them, "We can begin the first surveying operation tonight."

Kerwin felt last-minute panic. This would be his first experience in the prolonged rapport of a matrix circle.

"Why at night?" he asked.

It was Kennard who answered. "Most people sleep during the dark hours; we get less telepathic interference—in radio you'd call it static. There's telepathic static, too."

"I want all of you to get some sleep during the day," Neyrissa said. "I want you all fresh and rested for tonight."

Corus winked at Kerwin and said, "Better give Jeff a sedative; otherwise he'll lie awake fretting." But there was no malice in his words. Mesyr looked at him, questioningly.

"If you want something—"

He shook his head, feeling foolish. They talked a few minutes longer, then Elorie, yawning, said she was going to take her own advice, and went upstairs. One by one, they began to drift away from the fireside. Kerwin, not sleepy in spite of his weariness, waited, hoping Taniquel would join him. Perhaps, if she were with him, he might be able to forget the impending ordeal and relax.

"Neyrissa meant it, youngster," said Kennard, pausing beside him. "The monitor's word is law, in cases like this. Better get some rest, or tonight will be too much for you."

A moment of silence; then Kennard's heavy brows went into his hairline. "Oh," he said, "it's like that, is it?"

Kerwin exploded. "Damn it, is there no privacy at all here?"

Kennard looked at him with a wry, apologetic smile. "I'm sorry," he said. "I'm an Alton; we're the strongest telepaths in the Comyn. And—well, I've lived on Terra; I married a Terran woman. So perhaps I understand more than some of the younger ones would. Don't be offended, but—may I say something, as I would to—to a younger brother or a nephew?"

Touched against his will, Kerwin said, "Yes, of course."

Kennard thought for a minute, then said, "Don't blame Taniquel for leaving you alone just now, just when you feel that you need her most. I know how you feel—Zandru's hells, how well I know!" He chuckled as if at some private joke. "But Tani knows, too. And when a matrix operation is in train, a big one like this especially, celibacy is the rule, and necessary. She knows better than to play around with that. For that matter, one of us should have talked to you about it before."

"I don't think I understand," Kerwin said slowly, rebelling. "Why should it make any difference?"

Kennard answered with another question. "Why do you think the Keepers are required to be virgins?"

Kerwin hadn't the faintest idea, but it suddenly struck him that it explained Elorie. On the surface, she was a lovely young woman, certainly as beautiful as Taniquel, but as sexless as a child of seven or eight. Rannirl had said something about ritual virginity—and Elorie was certainly as unconscious of her own beauty and desirability as the youngest, most unaware of children. Or more so; most little girls, by eight or nine, were quite aware of their own femininity and one could see in them the seeds of desirability. Elorie, somehow, seemed entirely unaware of her own womanhood.

"In the ancient days it was regarded as a ritual thing," Kennard said. "I think that's drivel. The fact remains that it's terribly dangerous for a woman to work in the centerpolar position in a matrix circle, holding the energon flows, unless she's a virgin; it has something to do with nerve currents. Even on the edges of the circle, the women observe strict chastity for a considerable time beforehand. As for you—well, you are going to need every scrap of your nervous energy and strength tonight, and Taniquel knows that. Hence, you get some sleep. Alone. And I might as well warn you, if you haven't already found it out, that you won't be much good to a woman for some days afterward. Don't let it worry you; it's just a side effect of the energy drains." He laid a kindly, almost fatherly hand on Kerwin's wrist. "The trouble is, Jeff, you've become so much a part of us that we forget you haven't always been here; we take it for granted that you'll know all these things without being told."

Jeff said in a low voice, touched by Kennard's warmth, "Thank you—kinsman." He used the word without selfconsciousness, for the first time. If he had been foster-brother to Cleindori, Jeff's mother— Kerwin already knew that fosterage, on Darkover, created family ties that were, in many cases, stronger than those of blood.

He asked on an impulse, "Did you know my father, Kennard?"

Kennard hesitated. Then he said, slowly, "Yes. I suppose you could say I knew him quite well. Not— not as well as I could have wished, or things might have been different. It didn't help me to change anything."

"What was my father like?" Kerwin asked.

Kennard sighed. He said, "Jeff Kerwin? Not much like you; you look like my sister. Kerwin was big and dark and practical; a no-nonsense kind of man. But he had imagination, too. Lewis—my brother—knew him better than I did. He introduced him to Cleindori." Kennard frowned suddenly and said, "Look, this is no time for this. Go and rest." He sensed that Kennard was troubled. Abruptly, whether because he sensed something, picked up an image from Kennard's mind, Kerwin asked:

"Kennard, how did my mother die?"

Kennard's jaw set in a tight line. He said, "Don't ask me, Jeff. Before they consented to let you come here—" He stopped, obviously considering what to say, and Kerwin sensed that the older man was holding himself tightly blocked against Kerwin picking up even a fragment of thought. He said, "I was at Arilinn, too, then. And they asked me to come back because they were so short-handed, after—after what happened. But before they consented to let you come here, they made me—made me swear I wouldn't answer certain questions, and that's one of them. Jeff, the past is *past*. Think of today. Everybody at Arilinn, everybody in the Domains, has to put the past behind us and think of what we're doing for Darkover and for our people." There was a hint of old pain in his face, but he was still tightly barriered.

"Jeff, when you came here, we were all very doubtful about you. But now, win or lose, you're one of us. True Darkovan—and true Comyn. That thought may not be as reassuring as it would be to have Tani with you," he added, with an attempt at flippancy, "but it should help, just a little. Now go and sleep—kinsman."

They sent for him at moonrise. The Arilinn Tower felt strange and still in the deep night, and the matrix chamber was filled with the strange resonating quiet. They gathered, speaking in hushed voices, feeling the stillness as a living thing around them, a very real presence they hated to disturb. Kerwin felt slack, empty, exhausted. He noticed that Kennard was limping more than usual; Elorie looked sleepy and cross, and Neyrissa spoke sharply when Rannirl made some jocular remark.

Taniquel touched Kerwin's forehead, and he felt the faint feather-touch of her thoughts, the swift sure rapport. He did not flinch away from it now. "He's all right, Elorie."

Elorie glanced from Taniquel to Neyrissa. "You monitor, Tani. We need Neyrissa in the circle," she explained, at Neyrissa's injured glance. "She's stronger; and she's been working longer." To Kerwin, she explained, "When we're working in a circle like this, we need a monitor outside the circle, and Taniquel's the best empath we have; she'll stay in rapport with all of us, so if one of us forgets to breathe, or gets a muscle cramp, she'll know it before we do, and keep us from being too depleted or damaged. Auster, you hold the barriers," she directed, adding, for the benefit of the newcomer, "we all drop our individual barriers, and he puts up a group barrier which keeps out telepathic eavesdropping; and he'll sense it if anyone tries to interfere with us. In the old days there were alien forces on Darkover; perhaps, for all we know, there still are. The barrier around the gestalt formed by our minds will protect us."

Kennard was holding a smaller matrix lattice—one of the glass-surfaced screens like the one they had constructed. He was turning it this way and that, toward each of them, frowning and making some small adjustments on a calibrated dial. Lights glowed here and there in its depth. He said, absentmindedly, "Auster's barrier should hold, but just for safety's sake I'll put a damper on, and focus it around the Tower. Second level, Rannirl?"

"Third, I think," Elorie said.

Kennard raised his eyebrows. "Everyone in the Domains will know that something's going on in Arilinn tonight!"

"Let them," Elorie said indifferently. "I already asked them to take Arilinn out of the relay net tonight. It's our affair."

Kennard finished what he was doing with the damper, and began to lay the maps out on the table in front of them; and with them a large number of colored crayons. He asked, "Do you want me to mark the maps? Or shall we have Kerwin do it?"

"You mark them," Elorie said. "I want Corus and Jeff in the outer circle. Corus has enough PK that sooner or later we'll be able to do mining with him, and Jeff has a fabulous sense of structural perception. Jeff—" She placed him just beyond Rannirl. "And Corus here."

The great matrix lattice lay in its cradle before her. Auster said, "Ready here."

To Kerwin the moonlit silence in the room seemed to deepen; in the quiet air, it seemed that they were somehow insulated, their very breathing deepening, echoing around them. A faint picture floated through his mind, and he knew that Corus had touched him with a fragment of rapport, *a strong glass wall surrounding us, clearly seen through, but impenetrable* . . . He could sense the very walls of the Arilinn Tower, not the real Tower somehow but a mental picture of it, like but unlike, an archetypal Tower, and he heard someone in the circle thinking, *It has stood here like this for hundred and hundreds of years* . . .

Elorie's hands were folded before her; he had been

cautioned again and again, *never touch a Keeper, even accidentally, within the circle,* and indeed none of them ever touched Elorie, though sometimes Rannirl, who was the technician, would support her briefly with a light hand on her shoulder; and Elorie never touched anyone. Kerwin had noticed that; she could come very close to them, could hand him pills, stand close to him, but she never actually *touched* anyone; it was simply part of the taboo that surrounded a Keeper, banning even the most fragmentary physical touch. And yet, even though he could see her slender hands folded on the table, he *felt* her reach out her hands to them, and all round the circle it seemed that they linked hands, meshing into a tight grip all round; and yet to Kerwin it seemed, and he knew that each of them shared the sensation, that Elorie held one hand, and Taniquel, the monitor, the other. Kerwin swallowed, his mouth suddenly dry, as Elorie's grey eyes met his; they glimmered, like the molten shimmer of the matrix, and he felt her pick them up like a meshed web drawn between her strong hands, a net of sparkling threads in which they were embedded like jewels, each its own flashing color; the warm rose-grey of Taniquel's watchfulness, the diamond-hard brilliance of Auster, Corus with a bright colorless luster, each of them with his or her own individual sound and color in the moonglow net that was Elorie. . . .

Through Kennard's eyes they saw the map spread on the table. Kerwin floated toward it, and somehow felt himself soaring out, as if he flew, bodiless, wingless, over a great expanse of countryside, with the magnet strength of the pure metallic sample that lay in the cradle beside the matrix lattice. He seemed to stretch out, infinitely extended, unaware of the limits of his body; then Rannirl projected a swift, whirling pattern, and Kerwin, without surprise, found himself tracing, with all of his mind and consciousness, a molecular model as once his fingers had traced the clay balls and sticks of the kindergarten model. Through Corus's sensitive fingertips he felt the whirling electrons, the strange amalgam of nucleus, protons, the atomic structure of the metal they sought.

Copper. Its structure seemed to glow and swirl from the map, attuned as it was to the terrain which the map had suddenly become, he could *feel* the metal there. It was not, quite, like sinking into the crystal structure of the glass. It was curiously different, as if, through map and photographs that had, somehow, the texture of soil and rock and grass and trees, he traced the palpable magnetic currents and brushed aside all irrelevant atomic patterns. He was hundreds of times as sensitive to the terrain under his —hands? Surely not! Under his mind, his thoughts, but still, somehow, he was sifting the very soil in search of the glowing and complex structure of copper atoms, to where they clustered . . . rich deposits of ore . . .

Dull, throbbing pain knifed him; he twisted *through* the copper atoms, he had *become* copper, hiding within the ground, entangled with other unfamiliar electrons, other structures, so thickly entangled that it was impossible to breathe, atoms whirling and meshing and colliding. He was *in* the energy currents; he wandered in them and flowed in them. For a moment, disembodied sentience, he looked out through Rannirl's eyes at the complex patterns, looked down on a strange flat-squeezed countryside, which he knew intellectually was the map, but which was still somehow the great aerial perspective of the

Kilghard Hills spread out below him, hilltop eyries
and crags and chasms, rocks and trees—and through
it all he traced the sequences of copper atoms. . . . He
saw and felt through Kennard's eyes, moved on the
tip of an orange crayon down to the surface of the
map, a mark that meant nothing, absorbed as he was
in the whirl of structures and patterns, pure copper
atoms entangled painfully into the complex
molecules of rich ores . . . Kennard, he knew, followed him, measuring distances and transmuted
them into measurements and marks on the maps . . .
he moved on, interwoven with the meshing, sparkling
layers of the matrix lattice, which had, somehow, become the map and the very surface of the planet. . . .

He never knew, for time ceased entirely to have
meaning, how long he whirled and probed and
flashed, soil, rock, lava, riding magnetic currents,
how many times Rannirl's perceptions picked him
up and he rode down on the tip of Kennard's crayon,
for his whole substance to be transmuted into mark-
ings on the map. . . . But at last the whirling slowed
and stilled. He felt Corus (a liquid crystallizing, cooling into crystal) drop out of the mesh with a sensation like a shattering crash; heard Rannirl slide out
of some invisible gap; felt Elorie gently open her
hand and drop Kennard (invisible fingers set a doll
on a table) out of the web; then pain, like the agony
of breathing water, racked Kerwin as he felt himself
drop in free-fall into nowhere; Auster (a glass shattering, freeing a prisoner) made a thick sound of exhaustion, sliding forward with his head on the table.
An invisible rope broke and Neyrissa fell, crumpled,
as if from a great height. The first thing Kerwin saw
was Taniquel, sighing wearily, straightening her
cramped body. Kennard's knotted fingers, swollen

and tight with pain, released a stump of crayon, and he grimaced, holding one hand with the other. Kerwin could see the swelling in the fingers, the tension in them, and for the first time was aware of the joint-disease that had crippled Kennard and would some day paralyze him if he lived so long. The map was covered with cryptic symbols. Elorie put her hands over her face with a sound like a sob of exhaustion, and Taniquel rose and went to her, bending over her with a look of concern and dismay, running her hands over her in the monitor's touch, an inch away from her forehead.

Taniquel said, "No more. Corus's heart nearly stopped; and Kennard is in pain."

Elorie came on unsteady tiptoe to stand behind Rannirl and Kennard, looking at the maps. She touched Kennard's swollen hand with the lightest of fingertip-touches, more a symbolic gesture than a real one. She said, with a swift sidelong glance at Kerwin, "Jeff did all the structural work; did you notice?"

Kennard raised his head to grin unsteadily at Kerwin. He was still absentmindedly rubbing his hands, as if they hurt him, and Taniquel came and took them gently into her own, holding them cradled softly between her soft fingers. Kerwin saw the taut lines of pain leaving the older man's face. Kennard said, "He was there all the time, holding all the structures; it was easy with him in the net. He's going to be as good a technician as you are, Rannirl."

"That wouldn't take much doing," Rannirl said. "I'm a mechanic, not a technician; I can do a technician's work, but I look pretty bad when there's a real technician around. Kerwin can have my place any time he wants it; *you* could, Ken, if you were strong enough."

"Thanks. I'll leave it to Jeff, *bredu*," Kennard said, with an affectionate smile at Rannirl. He leaned forward, resting his head for a minute on Taniquel's shoulder, and Kerwin caught a fragment of her thought, *he's too old for this work,* and a furious surge of resentment, *we're so damned short-handed.* . . .

"But we did it," said Corus, looking at the map, and Elorie touched the surface of the map with a light finger. "Look, Kennard has measured every copper deposit in the Kilghard Hills, and all the places where the ores are richest, as well as those places where they are so mixed with other ores as to be practically useless. Even the depth is marked, and the richness, and the chemical composition of the ores so they will know what equipment they will need for assaying and refining." Suddenly, through her heavy-eyed weariness, her eyes were exultant. "Show me the Terrans who could do so much, for all their technology!"

She stretched, catlike. "Do you realize what we've *done?*" she demanded. "It worked, all of you—it worked! Now are you glad you listened to me? Who's a barbarian *now?*" She went to Jeff, stretched her hands to him, and her delicate fingertips just touched his; a gesture, he sensed, as meaningful to Elorie, behind the structure of taboo and untouchability, as another girl's spontaneous hug would have been. "Oh, Jeff, I knew we could do it with you, you're so strong, so powerful, you helped us so much!"

Impulsively, his hands tightened on hers; but she drew away, her face suddenly white, and her eyes met his; he could see the flash of panic in them. She clasped her hands together in a terrified gesture, and there was sudden appeal in her eyes; but it was only a moment. Then she slumped, and Neyrissa caught the girl in her arms.

"Lean on me, Elorie," she said gently. "You're exhausted, and no wonder, after all that."

Elorie swayed tiredly and covered her eyes, childishly, with her clenched fists. Neyrissa lifted her into strong arms, and said, "I'll take her to her room and see that she eats something."

Kerwin was aware again of his own agonizingly cramped muscles; he stretched and turned to the window, where the sun was flooding in, already high in the sky. He had not been aware of its rising. They had been within the matrix, and in rapport, for more than an entire night!

Rannirl folded the map carefully. "We'll try again in a few days with iron samples," he said. "Then tin, lead, aluminum—it will be easier next time, now that we know what Jeff can do in the network." He grinned at Jeff and said, "Do you know this is the first time there's been a full circle at Arilinn in twelve years or more?" He looked past Auster, frowning. "Auster, what's the matter with you, kinsman? This is a time for rejoicing!"

Auster's eyes were fixed on Kerwin with steady, unblinking malevolence. And Kerwin knew: *He's not happy that I did it.*

He wanted me—us—to fail. But why?

Chapter Eleven:
Shadows on the Sun

The depression lingered even after Kerwin had slept away the fatigue. As he dressed himself to join the others, near sunset, he told himself that he should not let Auster's malice spoil this for him. He had come through the acid test of full rapport within the Tower Circle, and it was his triumph. Auster had never liked him; it might even be that he was jealous of the fuss they were making over Kerwin. Probably there was no more to it than that.

And now, he knew, there would be a free interval, and he looked forward to spending some of it with Taniquel. Despite Kennard's warning, he felt fresh and rested, eager to join her. He wondered if she would consent, as she had done often, to spend the night with him, and there was a pleasant anticipation in his thoughts as he went downstairs. But there was no hurry; if not tonight, then later.

The others had all wakened before him and were gathered in the hall. The very casualness of their greetings warmed him; he belonged, he was family. He accepted a glass of wine and sank down in his accustomed seat. Neyrissa came over to him, trailing an armful of some kind of needlework, and settled down near him. He felt a little impatient, but there was time. He looked around for Taniquel, but she was near the fireplace, talking to Auster, her back to him, and he could not catch her eye.

"What are you making, Neyrissa?"

"A coverlet for my bed," she said. "You do not know how cold it is here in the winter; and besides, it keeps my hands busy." She turned it to show him. It was a white quilt, with cherries in three shades of red stitched on in clusters, with green leaves, and bands of the same three shades of red at the edges; and the whole now being quilted with delicate stitches in a pattern of loops and curls. He was astonished at the amount of work and thought that must have gone into the design; it had never occurred to him that Neyrissa, monitor of Arilinn and a Comyn lady, would occupy herself with such tedious stitchery.

She shrugged. "As I say, it keeps my hands busy when there is nothing else to do," she said. "And I am proud of my handiwork."

"It is certainly very beautiful," he said. "A piece of handiwork like this would be priceless on most of the planets I have visited, for most people now have their bedding made easily and quickly by machine."

She chuckled. "I do not think I would care to sleep under anything that had been made by machinery," she said. "It would be like lying down with a mechanical man. I understand they have such things on other worlds, too, but I do not suppose women are very pleased with them. I prefer genuine handiwork on my bed as well as in it."

It took Jeff a moment to understand the double entendre—which was somewhat more suggestive in *casta* than in the language he spoke—but no one with a scrap of telepathic force could misunderstand her meaning, and he chuckled, a little embarrassed. But she met his eyes so forthrightly that he could not retain his embarrassment and laughed heartily. "I suppose you're right, some things are better when they're the work of nature," he agreed with her.

"Tell me something about your work for the Empire, Jeff. If I had been a man, I sometimes think, I would like to have gone offworld. There is not a great deal of adventure in the Kilghard Hills, and certainly not for a woman. Have you lived on many worlds?"

"Two or three," he conceded, "but in the Civil Service you don't see much of them; it's mostly working with communications equipment."

"And you do the same thing with your communications machinery that we can do with the relay-nets?" she said, curiously. "Tell me a little of how they work, if you can. I have been working in the relays since I was fourteen years old; it would seem strange to do this with machinery. Are there truly no telepaths in the Terran Empire?"

"If there are," Kerwin said, "they're not telling anyone."

He told Neyrissa about the CommTerra communications network that linked planet with planet by interstellar relay systems, explaining the difference between radio, wireless, and interstellar hypercomm. He found that she had a quick mechanical intelligence and swiftly picked up the theory involved, although she found the thought of communicating by machinery somewhat distasteful.

"I would like to experiment with some of them," she said. "But only as a toy. I think the Tower relays are more reliable and swifter, and they do not get out of order so easily, I suppose."

"And you have been doing this all your life?" Kerwin asked, wondering again how old she was.

"What made you want to go into a Tower, Neyrissa? Have you never married?"

She shook her head. "I never had any wish to marry," she said, "and for a woman in the Domains, it is marriage or the Tower—unless," she laughed— "I wished to crop my hair and take up the sword and the oath of a Renunciate! And I had seen my sisters marry, and spend their lives catering to the whims of some man and bearing babe after babe till at twenty-nine they were thick and ugly, their bodies worn with childbearing, and their minds worn as narrowly into the track of nursery and laundry and hen-yard! Such a life, I thought, would not suit me; so when I was tested for *laran*, I came here as a monitor; and the work suits me, and the life."

It occurred to Kerwin that when she was a young woman she must have been a beauty; the materials of beauty were there still, the aristocratic bones of her face, the rich color of her hair, only a little tinged with grey, and her body was as slim and erect as Elorie's own. He said, gallantly, "I am sure there were many to protest that decision."

Her eyes met his, just a flicker. She said, "You are not naive enough to think I took Keeper's vows as well? I bore Rannirl a child ten years ago, hoping it would inherit my *laran;* my sister has fostered her, but I had no wish to drag a babe round at my heels. I would have given Kennard one as well, for he had no heirs and the Council was wroth with him, but he chose instead to marry. They did not like the woman he married, but she bore him two sons, and they have accepted the oldest son as his Heir—though it was hard enough to get them to do it. And I am well-enough pleased, for I am very much needed here, though not quite so much, now that Taniquel has been discovered to have enough *laran* for a monitor. Still, Tani is young. It is likely that she may decide to leave the Tower and marry; many of the younger women do so. I was surprised when Elorie came here; but she is the daughter of old Kyril Ardais, and he has spread the tale of his lecheries from Dalereuth to the Hellers; after seeing what her own mother suffered, I am sure Elorie had no wish to marry, and began with a fear and dread of all men. She is my half-sister, you know; I am one of old Dom Kyril's bastards." She spoke with dispassionate calm. "I was responsible for bringing her here, you know. The old man would have had her to sing and entertain his drinking companions, and once, when she was still very small, one of them laid rough hands on her—our brother came near to killing him. And after that, he complained to the Council, and Elorie was brought to Arilinn, and Dyan petitioned them to set Father aside and name him Regent of the Domain, so when Father's wits are not with him, the Domain will not be brought into disrepute because of his indecencies and debaucheries. It cost Dyan something to do this; he is a gifted musician, and a healer; he wished to study all the healing arts at Nevarsin, and now he has the weight of the Domain on his shoulders. But I am gossiping," she added with a faint smile. "At my age, I think I can be excused for it. I brought Lori here, as I say, and I had hoped she would make a monitor, perhaps even a technician; she has a good mind. Instead, they chose to try and teach her the Keeper's way, and so we are the only Tower on Darkover with a Keeper qualified in the old way. I suppose we should be proud of it; but I am sorry for Elorie. It is a hard life; and since she is the only Keeper we have—although there is a little girl at

Neskaya who is being taught—she will not feel free to leave the Tower, as most Keepers in past ages have felt free to do when the weight of their work grows too heavy. It is a dreadful burden," she added, meeting his eyes, "and despite the fact that the Lady of Arilinn stands higher than the queen, I would not want it for myself; nor for any child of mine."

Her glass was empty; she leaned forward and asked him to refill it. Rising, Kerwin went to the table where the drinks were kept. Corus and Elorie were playing some sort of game with cut-crystal dice. Rannirl had a scrap of leather in his hands and was stitching it into a falcon's hood.

Taniquel was near the fireplace, deep in conversation with Auster; Kerwin tried to catch her eye, to make an unobtrusive signal that she should join him; a signal she knew well. He fully expected her to make some light-hearted excuse to Auster and join him.

But she only gave him a little eye-blink of a smile, and lightly shook her head. Startled, rebuffed, he looked at her hand lying in Auster's, their heads close together. They seemed quite absorbed. Kerwin filled Neyrissa's glass and took it to her, his puzzlement growing. The girl had never seemed half so desirable as now, when her laughter, her impish smile were all for Auster. He went back and sat down by Neyrissa, giving her the glass, but from irritation he proceeded to bewilderment, and then to resentment. How could she do this to him? Was she nothing, then, but a heartless tease?

As the evening passed, he sank deeper and deeper into depression. He listened to Neyrissa's gossip with half an ear, the attempts of Kennard and Rannirl to engage him in conversation fell flat; after a time they assumed he was still weary and left him to himself.

Corus and Elorie finished their game and started another; Neyrissa went to show Mesyr her needlework
and ask for advice, the two women sorting a lapful of
threads and comparing the colors of dyes. It was a
perfectly comfortable domestic scene except for
Kerwin's knifelike awareness of Taniquel, her head
resting on Auster's shoulder. A dozen times Kerwin
told himself that he was a fool to sit and watch it, but
bewilderment and resentful anger strove in him.
Why was she doing this, why?

Later Auster rose to refill their glasses, and
Kerwin rose abruptly; Kennard looked up, troubled,
as Kerwin crossed the room and bent to touch Taniquel on the arm.

"Come with me," he said. "I want to talk to you."

She looked up, startled and not pleased, but with
a quick glance around—he could almost feel her ex-
asperation, mingled with her resolve not to make a
scene—she said, "Let's go out on the terrace."

The last remnants of the sunset had long vanished;
the mist was condensing into heavy splatters of rain
that would, before long, be a downpour. Taniquel
shivered, dragging her yellow knitted shawl close
around her shoulders. She said, "It's too cold to
stand out here very long. What's the matter, Jeff?
Why have you been staring at me like that, all evening?"

"You don't know?" he flung at her. "Haven't you
any heart? We've had to wait—"

"Are you *jealous?*" she asked, good-naturedly. Jeff
drew her into his arms and kissed her violently,
crushing her mouth under his; she sighed, smiled
and returned the kiss, but with tolerance rather than
passion. He seized her by the elbows, saying hoarsely, "I should have known you were just deviling me,

but I couldn't stand it—watching you with Auster, right under my very eyes—"

She held herself away from him, puzzled and, he sensed, angry.

"Jeff, don't be so dense! Can't you see that Auster needs me now? Can't you understand that? Have you *no* feelings, no kindness at all? This is your triumph—and his defeat, can't you see?"

"Are you trying to say you've turned against me?"

"Jeff, I simply don't understand you," she said, frowning in the half-light from the window behind them. "Why should I have turned against you? All I'm saying is that Auster needs me—now, tonight— more than you do." She raised herself on tiptoe, kissing him coaxingly, but he held her roughly at arm's length, some hint of her meaning beginning to reach him.

"Are you saying what I think you're saying?"

"What is the *matter* with you, Jeff? I can't seem to get through to you at all tonight!"

He said, his throat tight, "I love you. I—I want you; is that so hard to understand?"

"I love you, Jeff," she said, with a faint undertone of impatience in her words. "But what has that to do with it? I think you're overtired, or you wouldn't talk this way. What is it to do with you, if for this one night Auster needs me more than you do, and I choose to comfort him in the way he needs most?"

He asked flatly, "Are you trying to tell me you're going to sleep with him tonight?"

"Why, yes, certainly!"

His mouth felt dry. "You little bitch!"

Taniquel stepped back as if he had struck her. Her face, in the dim light, was dead white, the freckles standing out like dark blotches.

"And you are a selfish brute," she retorted. "Barbarian as Elorie called you, and worse! You—you Terrans think women are *property!* I love you, yes; but not when you act like this!"

He felt his mouth twitch, painfully. "*That* kind of love I can buy in the spaceport bars!"

Taniquel's hand went up, hard and stinging, flat across his cheekbones. "You—" she stammered, speechless. "I belong to *myself*, do you hear? You take what I give and think it right; but if I give it to another, you are ready to name me whore? Damn you, you filthy-minded *Terranan!* Auster was right about you all along!"

She moved swiftly past him, and he heard her steps receding, swift and final; somewhere a door slammed inside the Tower.

His face burning, Kerwin did not follow. The rain was heavy now, blowing around the cornice of the Tower, and there were traces of ice in the heavy drops; he brushed it from his smarting cheek. What had he done now? On a numb, shamed impulse to hide himself—they must all have seen Taniquel's rejection of him, the way she had turned to Auster, they must all have known what it meant—he went swiftly along the passageway and up the stairs to his own room; but before he reached it, he heard an uneven footfall and Kennard stood behind him in the doorway.

"Jeff, what's the matter?"

He did not want to face the older man's craggy, knowing face just now. He went on into his room, muttering, "Still tired—guess I'll go to bed, get some more sleep."

Kennard came behind him, put his hands on the younger man's shoulders and, with surprising strength, physically turned him around to face him. He said, "Look, Jeff, you can't keep it from us like that. If you'll talk about it—"

"Damn it," Jeff said, his voice cracking, "is there no privacy in this place at all?"

Kennard slumped and sighed. He said, "My leg's giving me hell; can I sit down?"

Kerwin could not refuse; Kennard dropped into an armchair. He said, "Look, son, among us, things have to be—well, they have to be faced; they can't be hidden away to fester. For better or for worse, you're a member of our circle—"

Jeff tightened his mouth again. He said, "Keep out of this. It's between me and Taniquel, and none of your business."

"But it's not between you and Taniquel at all," Kennard said. "It's between you and Auster. Look, everything that happens in Arilinn affects us all. Tani is an empath; can't you understand how she feels when she senses—when she has to *share*—that kind of need, and hunger, and loneliness? You were broadcasting it everywhere; we all picked it up. But Tani is an empath, and vulnerable. And she answered that need, because she's a woman, and kind, and an empath, and she couldn't endure your unhappiness. She gave you what you needed most, and what it was natural for her to give."

Kerwin muttered, "She said she loved me. And I believed her."

Kennard put out his hand, and Kerwin sensed the sympathy in him. He said, "Zandru's hells, Jeff— words, words, words! And the way people use them, and what they mean by them!" It was almost like an imprecation. He touched Jeff lightly on the wrist, the accepting, telepath's touch, which somehow meant more than a handclasp or an embrace. He said gently, "She loves you, Jeff. We all do, every one of us. You are one of us. But Tani—is what she is. Can't you understand what that means? And Auster—try and imagine what it means to be a woman, and an empath, and feel the kind of despair and need that was in Auster tonight? How can she feel that, and not—not respond to it? Damn it," he said, despairingly, "if you and Auster understood each other, if you had empathy with him, you'd feel his pain, too, and you'd understand what Taniquel was feeling!"

Against his will, Jeff began to grasp the concept; in a close-knit circle of telepaths, emotions, needs, hungers, did not affect only the one who felt them, but everyone who was near him. He had been disrupting them all with his loneliness and his hunger for acceptance, and Taniquel had responded to it, as naturally as a mother quiets a crying child. But now, when Jeff was happy and triumphant, and Auster apparently defeated, it was Auster's pain she desired to soothe. . . .

Human flesh and blood couldn't endure it, he thought savagely. Taniquel, whom he loved, Taniquel, the first woman who had ever meant anything to him, Taniquel in the arms of a man he hated. . . . He closed his eyes, trying to barricade away the thought, the pain of it.

Kennard looked at him, and Kerwin, uncomfortably, recognized his expression as pity.

"It must be very difficult for you. You spent so much time among the Terrans, you've taken their neurotic codes to yourself. The laws of the Tower are not the same as the laws of the Domains; among telepaths they can't be. Marriage is a fairly recent development on Darkover; what you call monogamy is more recent yet. And it's never been really accepted. I'm not blaming you, Jeff. You are what you are, just as Tani is what she is. I only wish you weren't so unhappy about it." He hauled himself wearily out of his chair and went away, and Kerwin caught the trail and overflow of his thought. Kennard, too, had married a Terran, known the pain of a man caught between two worlds and belonging to neither, seen his two sons rejected because he could not father a son on the suitable wife the Council had given him, but whom, too sensitive to unspoken emotions, he could not love. . . .

Lying awake, aflame with jealous rage, Kerwin fought a solitary battle, and toward morning came to grim equilibrium. The woman wasn't worth it. He wasn't going to let Auster wreck things for him. They had to work together, somehow or other. It was galling to lose out to Auster, but after all, it was only his pride that was involved. If Taniquel wanted Auster, she was welcome to him. She'd made her choice, and she could just stick to it.

It wasn't ideal, but it worked, after a fashion. Taniquel was polite and icily remote, and he took his tone from her. Once again they began the work of building matrix screens, keying them into maps and aerial photographs; again they gathered for the circle, searching out iron deposits, and a few days later, silver and zinc. They day before they were to go into a fourth rapport search, Jeff came in from a solitary ride in the foothills to find Corus waiting for him, pale and excited.

"Jeff! Elorie wants us all in the matrix chamber, quickly!"

He followed the kid, wondering what had happened. The others were already gathered there, Rannirl with the maps in hand.

"Trouble," he said. "I had word from our clients, just after I passed this map to them. In three separate places, here, here, and here—" he indicated on the marked maps, "the people from across the Hellers, the damned Aldarans and their men, have moved in and filed claims on the lands we marked as being the richest deposits of copper; you know as well as I do that the Aldarans are pawns of the Terrans, with their Trade City at Caer Donn; they're fronting for the Empire, claiming that land to set up a Terran industrial colony there. It's empty land in the Hellers, not good for agriculture, and I don't think anyone's ever guessed it was good for mining; it's too inaccessible. How did they know?"

"Coincidence," Neyrissa said. "You know the people from Aldaran are close to the forge-folk. They're always prospecting for metals, and they use fire-talismans in the hills the way we use matrix circles."

Auster said angrily, "I can't believe it's coincidence! That this should happen the very first time Jeff is part of the circle! The front men for Terra move in on the richest claims, leaving us nothing to offer our clients but some weak ores, almost impossible to smelt! Not one, not two, but *three* of the claims!" He swung around angrily to face Kerwin. "How much did the Terrans pay you to betray us?"

"If you believe that, damn you, you're more of a fool than I ever thought!"

Taniquel said angrily, "I know you don't like Jeff, Auster, but this is outrageous! If you believe that, you'd believe anything!"

"It's bad luck," Kennard said, "but that's all it is; sheer bad luck."

Auster raged, "Once, I would believe coincidence; twice, coincidence and bad luck. But three times? *Three?* It's coincidence like work for the midwife after a Ghost Wind is coincidence!"

Elorie frowned. She said, "Hush, hush! I won't have this brawling! There is one way to settle it, Kennard. You're an Alton. He can't lie to you, Uncle."

Kerwin knew immediately what she meant, even before she turned to him and said, "Will you consent to telepathic examination, Jeff?"

Rage surged through him. "Consent to it? I *demand* it," he said. "And then, damn it, I'll make you eat those words, Auster, I'll cram them down your throat with my fist!" He faced Kennard, rage making him oblivious to the fear of facing that nightmarish probe. "Go ahead! Find out for yourself!"

Kennard hesitated. "I don't really think—"

"It's the only way," said Neyrissa briskly. "And Jeff is willing."

Kerwin closed his eyes, bracing himself for the painful shock of forced rapport. No matter how often it was done, it never became easier. He endured it for a moment, incredible intrusion, nightmarish violation, before the grey and merciful haze blotted out the pain. When he came to he was standing before them, gripping the edges of the table to keep from falling over. He heard his own breathing loud in the silent room.

Kennard was looking back and forth from him to Auster.

"Well?" Jeff demanded, his voice angry and defensive.

"I have always said that we could trust you, Jeff," Kennard said quietly, "but there is something here.

Something I do not understand. There is some blocking of your memory, Jeff."

Auster said, "Could the Terrans have given him some kind of post-hypnotic conditioning? Planted him on us—a time bomb?"

"I assure you," Kennard said, "you overestimate their knowledge of the mind. And I can assure you, Auster, that Jeff is not feeding them information. There's no guilt in him."

But a cold bleak horror had suddenly gripped Jeff by the throat.

Ever since arriving on Darkover he had been pushed around by some mysterious force. It had certainly not been the Comyn who destroyed his birth records, and the records of Jeff Kerwin who had claimed him, and gotten Empire citizenship for him, in the Terran computers. It had not been the Comyn who kept pushing him around until he had no place to go, and he had escaped; escaped to the Comyn.

Had he been planted on them, an unconscious spy within the Arilinn Tower?

"I never heard anything so damnably foolish," Kennard said angrily. "I'd as soon believe it of you, Auster; or of Elorie herself! But if there's this kind of suspicion among us, no one will benefit but the Terrans!" He took up the map. "More likely it's one of the Aldarans; they have some telepaths there, and they work with unmonitored matrixes, outside the Tower relays. Your barrier may have slipped, Auster; that's all. Call it bad luck and we'll try again."

Chapter Twelve: The Trap

He tried to dismiss the idea from his mind. After all, Kennard had warranted him guiltless after telepathic examination. That was, he knew, legal defense anywhere. But once roused, the idea persisted like pain in a nagging tooth.

Would I even have to know it, if the Terrans had planted me here?

I was so damned glad to be free of the Terran Zone that I didn't even ask questions. Like, why did the computer at the Spaceman's Orphanage have no records of me? They said that Auster, too, was born among the Terrans. I wonder if there's a record of him there? Is there any reason why a telepath with a matrix, as Ragan suggested, couldn't wipe the memory bank of a computer—clear it of one specific record? Everything he knew of computers, and everything he knew of matrixes, suggested that that wouldn't be a difficult trick at all.

He went through the days silent and morose, lying on his bed for hours and trying to think of nothing, riding alone in the hills. He was conscious of Taniquel's eyes watching him whenever he was with the others, feeling her sympathy (*damned bitch, I don't want her pity!*) and the pain of her awareness. He avoided her when he could, but the memory of their little time as lovers cut like a knife. Because it had gone so much deeper with him than any casual relationship, it could not be casually dismissed; it stayed with him, painful.

263

He was vaguely aware that she was trying to encounter him, alone; he took perverse pleasure in evading her. One morning, however, he met her face to face on the stairs.

"Jeff," she said, reaching out her hand to him. "Don't run away—please, don't keep running away. I want to talk to you."

He shrugged, looking over her head. "What's there to say?"

Her eyes filled with tears, and spilled over. "I can't stand this," she said, brokenly. "The two of us like enemies, and the Tower filled with—with spearpoints of hate and suspicion! And jealousy—"

He said, the ice of his resentment giving way before the genuineness of her pain, "I don't like it either, Tani. But it wasn't my doing, remember."

"Why must you—" She controlled her temper, biting her lip. She said, "I'm sorry you're so unhappy, Jeff. Kennard explained to me, a little, how you felt about it, and I'm sorry, I didn't understand—"

He said, knifing the words with heavy sarcasm, "If I'm unhappy enough, would you come back to me?" He took her, not gently, by the shoulders. "I suppose Auster's got you to thinking the worst of me, that I'm a spy for the Terrans, or something like that?"

She was quiet between his hands, making no effort to break away. She said, "Auster isn't lying, Jeff. He's only saying what he believes. And if you think he is happy about it, then you are very much mistaken."

"I suppose his heart would be broken if he managed to drive me away?"

"I don't know, but he doesn't hate you the way you feel that he does. Look at me, Jeff, can't you tell I'm telling you the truth?"

"I suppose you ought to know just what Auster's feeling," he said, but Taniquel's shoulders were trembling, and somehow the sight of Taniquel, the mischievous, the carefree, in tears, hurt worse than the suspicions of all the others. That was the hell of it, he thought wearily. If Auster had been lying out of malice, if Taniquel had left him for Auster in order to hurt him to make him jealous, he could at least have *understood* that kind of motivation. As it was, it was a complete mystery to him. Taniquel neither attacked nor defended, even in thought; she simply shared his pain. She fell against him, sobbing, clinging help-lessly.

"Oh, Jeff, we were so happy when you came, and it meant so much to us to have you here, and now it's all spoilt! Oh, if we could only know, if we could only be sure!"

He faced them down that night in the hall, waiting until they had gathered for their evening drinks before rising aggressively, hands clenched behind his back. Defiantly he had put on Terran clothes; de-fiantly, he spoke Cahuenga.

"Auster, you made an accusation; I submitted to telepathic examination, which should have settled it, but you didn't accept my word or Kennard's. What proof would you demand? What would you accept?"

Auster rose to his feet, slender, graceful, cat-lean; he said, "What do you want from me, Kerwin? I can-not call challenge on your Comyn immunity—"

"Comyn immunity be—" Kerwin used a word straight from the spaceport gutters. "I spent ten years on Terra, and they have an expression there which can be roughly translated as put up or shut up. Tell me, right here and now, what proof you *will* accept, and give me a chance here and now to prove it to your satisfaction. Or shut your mouth on the subject once and forever, and believe me, brother, if I hear one damned syllable, or pick up one single telepathic insinuation, I'll beat the stuffing out of you!" He stood, fists clenched, and when Auster stepped to one side Jeff moved too, keeping straight in front of him. "I'm saying it again. Put up, or shut up and stay shut forever."

There was a shocked silence in the room, and Jeff heard it with satisfaction. Mesyr made a small, re-monstrating noise, almost an admonitory cluck: *Now, children. . . .*

"Jeff's right," Rannirl said. "You can't keep this up, Auster. Prove what you're insinuating, or apologize to Jeff and keep your mouth buttoned about it afterward. Not just for Jeff's sake; you owe it to all of us. We can't live this way; we're a circle. I don't insist that you swear the oath of *bredin*, but you must somehow manage to live together in harmony. We can't live like this, divided into two factions, with each group snarling at the other half. Elorie has enough to cope with, as it is."

Auster looked at Kerwin. If looks could kill, Kerwin thought, Auster wouldn't have any problem. But when he spoke, his voice was calm, considerate. "You're right. We owe it to all of you to find out the truth once and for all. And Jeff himself has pledged to abide by the result. Elorie, can you build a trap matrix?"

"I can," she flared. "But I won't! Do your own dirty work!"

"Kennard can," Neyrissa said, and Auster frowned. "Yes. But he's prejudiced—in Jeff's favor. He's standing foster-father to him here!"

Kennard's voice was quiet and dangerous. "If you

dare assume that I, who have been mechanic at Arilinn since before the Changes, would falsify my oath—"

Rannirl raised his hand to stop them both. "I'll build it," he said. "Not because I'm on your side, Auster, but because we have to settle this one way or the other. Jeff—" He turned to Kerwin. "Do you trust me?"

Kerwin nodded. He wasn't sure what a trap matrix was; but with Rannirl in charge of it, he was sure the trap wouldn't be set for *him*.

"All right, then," Rannirl said. "That's settled. So until we can set the trap matrix for the next circle, can't you two declare a truce?"

Jeff felt like saying, *the hell I can*, and he knew, looking at Auster's sullen face, that the other man was equally unwilling. How could telepaths pretend? But Taniquel was on the edge of tears; and Jeff suddenly shrugged. What the hell, it wouldn't hurt him to be civil; Auster only wanted to know the truth, and that was one thing they were agreed on anyhow. He said with a shrug, "I'll let him alone if he lets me alone. Agreed?"

Auster's taut face relaxed. He said, "Agreed."

With the decision made, the tension relaxed and the next phase of the work began with an atmosphere that was, by contrast, almost friendly. This time they had to build a matrix lattice for the work known as "clearing"—which had not been done on this scale since the great days of the Comyn, when Towers dotted the land, giving power and technology to all the Domains.

They had located mineral and ore deposits and marked them for richness and accessibility. In the next step they would separate the deposits from the other minerals that contaminated them, so that the copper and other metals could be mined in a pure form without need for refining. Drop by drop, atom by atom, deep within the earth, by tiny shiftings of energy and force, the pure metals would be separated from the ores and the rock. Corus spent more time with his molecular models, fussing over precise weights and proportions. And this time, Elorie, with Rannirl, specially asked for Kerwin's help in placing the crystals within their lattices. He was required to hold complex molecular patterns clearly visualized on a monitor screen, so that Elorie and Rannirl could place the blank crystals precisely inside the amorphous layers of glass. He learned things about atomic structure that even the Terran scientists did not know—his education in physics, for instance, had told him nothing about the nature of *energons*. It was wearying work, monotonous and nerve-racking rather than physically taxing, and always at the back of his mind was the knowledge of the test that would come with the trap matrix, whatever that was.

I want to know the truth, whatever it is.

Whatever it is?

Yes. Whatever it is.

One day they were working in one of the matrix laboratories, Jeff holding the complex internal crystal structure visualized for the monitor screen, when suddenly he saw the lattice structure blur together; melt into a blue flare and streak. Pain knifed through him; hardly knowing what he did, Jeff acted on pure instinct. He swiftly cut the rapport between Rannirl and Elorie, blanked the screens, and caught Elorie's fainting body as she fell. For a panicked moment he thought she was not breathing; then her eyelashes moved and she sighed.

"Working too hard, as usual," said Rannirl, staring down at the lattice. "She *will* keep on, even when I beg her to rest. Good thing you caught her, Jeff, just when you did; otherwise we'd have the whole lattice to rebuild, and that would cost us a tenday. Well, Elorie?"

Elorie was crying weakly in exhaustion, lying limp in Jeff's arms. Her face was deathly white, and her sobs shallow as if she no longer had the strength to breathe. Rannirl took her from Jeff's arms, lifting her like a small child, and carried her out of the lab. He flung back over his shoulder, "Get Tani up here, and hurry!"

"Taniquel went with Kennard in the airlaunch," Kerwin said.

"Then I'd better go up and try to get them in the relays," Rannirl said, kicked the nearest door open with his foot. It was one of the unused rooms; it looked as if no one had set foot in it for decades. He laid the girl down on a couch covered with dusty tapestry, while Kerwin stood helplessly in the door. "Anything I can do?" he asked.

"You're an empath," Rannirl said, "and qualified as a monitor; I haven't done it in years. I'll go up and try to get Neyrissa, but you'd better monitor her and see if her heart's all right."

And suddenly Kerwin remembered what Taniquel had done for him on that first night of testing, taking his pain into herself, when he collapsed with the breaking of his barriers.

"I'll do what I can," he said, and came closer to her. Elorie moved her head from side to side, like a fractious child. "No," she said irritably. "No, let me be, I'm all right." But she had to breathe twice while she said it and her face was like scraped bone.

"She's always like this," Rannirl said. "Do what you can, Jeff, I'll go and find Neyrissa."

Jeff came and bent over Elorie.

"I don't suppose I'm as good at it as Tani or Neyrissa," he said, "but I'll do what I can." Quickly, heightening his sensitivity, he ran his fingertips along her body, an inch or two away, feeling deep into the cells. Her heart was beating, but thin, irregular, threadlike; the pulse was faint, almost unreadable. Her breathing was so faint he could hardly feel it. Cautiously, he reached for rapport, seeking, with that heightened awareness, the limits of her weakness, trying to take her exhaustion upon himself as Taniquel had taken his pain. She stirred and made a faint movement, reaching with her hands for his, and he remembered how Taniquel had taken his hands in her own. The searching movement of her hands went on, and after a moment Jeff put his own between them, feeling the faint effort she made to close hers over them. She was almost unconscious. But gradually, as he knelt there with her hands in his, he could feel her breathing steady, sensed that her heart had begun to beat smoothly again, and saw the deathly white of her face beginning to transmute into a healthy color again. He did not realize how frightened he had been until he heard her breathing, calm and steady; she opened her eyes and looked at him. She was still a little pale, her soft lips still colorless.

"Thank you, Jeff," she whispered weakly, and her hands tightened on his; then, to his astonishment, she put out her arms, reaching up to him in appeal. Quickly responding, he gathered her close to him, sensing that she wanted the reassurance of contact; he held her for a moment, feeling her close to him, soft and limp, still weak. And then, without surprise, Kerwin felt the soft and exquisite blending of perceptions as their lips met.

He felt it with an intensely heightened dual consciousness, Elorie's limp slight body in his arms, sensing the fragility mingled with steely strength, the childlike quality blended with the calm, ageless wisdom of her caste and her training. (*And dimly through all these things he felt what Elorie felt, her weakness and lassitude, the terror she had known when her heart faltered and she felt herself near to death, the need for the reassurance of contact, the strength of his own arms around her; he felt the lassitude and the eagerness with which she accepted his kiss, a strange and half-understood wakening in her senses; he shared with the woman her own wonder and surprise at this touch, the first touch she had ever known that was not fatherly and impersonal; shared her shy and shameless surprise at the strength of his man's body, at the sudden rising heat in him; felt her reach out to him, unmistakably, for a deeper contact, and answered it. . .*)

"Elorie," he whispered, but it was like a triumphant shout. "Oh, Elorie—" And only to himself he whispered, *my love,* and for a moment he felt everything in the woman move toward him, felt her sudden warmth and flooding longing for his kiss. . . .

Then there was a spasmodic moment of shattering, convulsive fear, clawing with anguish at every nerve in him; the rapport between them smashed like a breaking crystal, and Elorie, white and terrified, was straining away from him, fighting like a cat in his arms.

"No, no," she gasped. "Jeff, let me go, let me go— don't—"

Dazed, numb with shock, Kerwin released her; she scrambled quickly up and away from him, her hands crossed in terror over her breasts, which rose and fell with soundless, anguished sobs. Her eyes were wide with horror, but she was barriered tightly against him again. Her childish mouth moved silently, her face screwed up in a little girl's grimace against tears.

"No," she whispered, again, at last. "Have you forgotten—forgotten what I am? Oh, Avarra pity me," she said in a broken gasp, covered her face with her hands and fled blindly from the room, half tripping over a stool, evading Jeff's automatic reach to steady her, slipping through the door and running, running away down the hall. Far away, far up in the Tower, he heard the closing of a door.

He did not see Elorie again for three days.

For the first time, that night, she did not join them for the evening ritual of drinks in the great hall. Jeff, from the moment Elorie fled from him, felt cut off and alone, a stranger among them in a world suddenly cold and strange.

The others seemed to take Elorie's seclusion for granted; Kennard said with a shrug that all Keepers did that now and then, it was part of being what they were. Jeff, holding his barriers firm against involuntary betrayal (of himself? Of Elorie?) said nothing. But Elorie's eyes, luminous and haunted with dismay and that shocking, sudden fear, as well as the memory of her warmth in his arms, seemed to swim before his eyes in the darkness every night before he slept; he felt, with an almost tactile memory, her kiss on his mouth, her frail and frightened body in his arms, and the shock after she had broken away and run from him. At first he had been half angry: *She* had initiated the contact. Why now should she break away as if he had attempted rape?

Then, slowly and painfully, understanding came.

He had broken the strictest law of the Comyn. A Keeper was a pledged virgin, trained lengthily for her work, body and brain given lengthy conditioning for the most difficult task on Darkover. To every man in the Domains, Elorie was inviolate. A Keeper, *tener-êsteis*, never to be touched by lust or even by the purest love.

He had heard what they said—and worse, felt what they felt—about Cleindori, who had broken this vow. (And she, too, with one of the despised Terrans.)

In his old life Kerwin might have defended himself, saying that Elorie had invited his advances. She had first touched him, first raised her lips to his. But after a time of training in the unsparing self-honesty of Arilinn, there were no such easy evasions. He had been aware of the taboo, and of Elorie's ignorance; he was aware of the forthright way with which she showed affection to the others of her circle, completely confident in the taboo that protected her; to all of them, she was sexless and sacrosanct. She had accepted Jeff in the same way—and he had betrayed her trust!

He loved her. He knew now that he had loved her from the first time he laid eyes on her; or perhaps before, when their minds touched through the matrix and he had heard her soft *I recognize you*. And now he saw nothing ahead of him but pain and renunciation.

Taniquel—his infatuation with Taniquel now seemed like a dream. He knew now that it had been gratitude for her acceptance, for her kindness and warmth; he was still fond of her, but what had been between them, for a time, could not survive any interruption of the sexual tie between them. It had never been anything like this overwhelming thing that swallowed up his whole consciousness; he knew that he would love Elorie for the rest of his life, even if he could never again touch her and she never showed the slightest sign of returning his love.

(But she had, she had. . . .)

But worse than this was a terrible fear, knifing at his consciousness. Kennard had warned him of the dangers of nervous exhaustion, counseling him to remain apart from Taniquel during the days immediately before a heavy load of matrix work, to avoid depleting his energies. The Keepers, he knew, keyed themselves completely, body and mind, into the matrixes they operated; this was why they must never be touched by a hint of emotion, and far less by sexuality. His memory went back to his first night in Arilinn; Elorie's dismay at the mildest flirtatious or gallant remark, her comment that Keepers trained lifelong for their work and sometimes lost the ability for it after a very short time. Neyrissa had underlined that there were no other Keepers, so that Elorie, unlike Keepers in the past, was not free to set aside her high office for marriage—or for love.

And now, when perhaps the very fate of Darkover rested upon the strength of the Arilinn Tower—and perhaps upon Elorie alone, when the strength of Arilinn rested upon the fortitude of their cherished Keeper—he, Jeff Kerwin, the stranger in their midst, the outsider they had taken to their hearts, had betrayed them and struck through the defenses of their Keeper.

And at this point in his thoughts Kerwin sat up and buried his head in his hands. He tried to blank out his thoughts completely. This was worse than Auster's accusation that he was a spy, feeding information to the Empire.

Alone in the night he fought his way to the end of a hard-won battle. He loved Elorie; but his love for her could destroy her as a Keeper. And without a Keeper, they would fail in the work they were doing for the Pan-Darkovan Syndicate, and the Syndicate would take that as permission to bring in the Terrans, experts in the remodeling of Darkover into the image of the Empire.

A traitor part of himself asked: *Would that be so bad?* Sooner or later, Darkover would fall into line. Every planet did.

And even for Elorie, he told himself, it would be better. No young woman should have to live like this, in seclusion, avoiding everything that made life worthwhile. No woman should have to know that her body is no more than a machine to transform the energies of matrix work! Even Rannirl had rebelled, and Rannirl was the chief technician of Arilinn. Rannirl had said that Keepers like Elorie were an anachronism in this day and age. If the Arilinn Tower and matrix technology could not survive except by the sacrifice of the lives of young women like Elorie, perhaps it did not deserve to survive at all. If their work for the Pan-Darkovan Syndicate failed, then Elorie need not be Keeper, and she was free.

Traitor! he accused himself bitterly. The people of Arilinn had taken him in, a stranger, homeless, exile of two worlds, and accepted him as one of themselves, given him kindness and love and acceptance. And he was ready to strike at their weakest point; he was willing to destroy them!

Lying there in the night, he willed himself to give up Elorie. She was the one that mattered; and her choice was to be Keeper, and remain Keeper. At whatever cost to himself in renunciation and agony, her peace of mind must never be endangered.

On the morning of the fourth day he heard her voice on the stairs. He had fought himself to acceptance, but at the sound of her soft voice it all surged up; he went back and flung himself down blindly, willing himself to calm through the blind ache and rebellion in him. *Oh, Elorie, Elorie . . .* He could not face her yet.

Later he heard Rannirl's voice at his door.

"Jeff? Will you come down?"

"Give me just a minute," Jeff said, and Rannirl went away. Left alone, Kerwin fought to apply all the techniques of control that he had been taught, steadying his breathing, forcing himself to relax; and when he knew that he could face them all without revealing his pain or his guilt, he went downstairs.

The circle of Arilinn was gathered before the fire, but Kerwin had eyes only for Elorie. She had put on again the filmy gown embroidered with cherries, anchored at her throat with a single crystal; her copper hair was twisted up in an elaborate coiffure of looped braids, caught with a blue flower dusted with gold; the *kireseth* flower, colloquially called the golden bell —*cleindori*. Was she testing his control? Or, he wondered suddenly, her own?

She raised her eyes, and he remembered how to breathe. For her smile was gentle, aloof, indifferent.

Had she felt nothing, then. Had he imagined it all? Had her reaction to him been no more than fear, then, as if he had reawakened the old fear—he remembered Neyrissa's story; one of her mad father's drinking-companions had laid rude hands on the girl, and her brother had brought her here for safety and refuge.

Kennard laid his hand gently on Jeff's shoulder; somehow, through the touch, an unspoken awareness passed through them both. *The Keepers are trained, in ways you could hardly guess at, to keep themselves free of all emotion.* Somehow, in those three days of seclusion, Elorie had managed to bring herself back to remote calm, untouched peace. Her smile was almost exactly as it had always been. *Almost.* Kerwin sensed that it was brittle, wary, a thin skin of control over panic; and with a surge of compassion and pain, he thought, *I must do nothing, nothing to trouble her. She wants it this way. I must not infringe on her control even with a thought.*

She said quietly, "We have arranged the separating operation for tonight; and Rannirl tells me that the trap matrix is ready for you, Auster."

"I'm ready," Auster said. "Unless Jeff wants to back out."

"I said I'd abide any test you gave me. But what the hell is a trap matrix?"

Elorie made one of her childish faces. "It's a filthy perversion of an honest science," she said.

"Not necessarily," Kennard protested. "There are valid ones. The Veil outside Arilinn is one kind of trap matrix; it keeps out everyone not accepted as Comyn and blood-related. And there are others in the *rhu fead,* the holy place of Comyn. What kind is yours, Auster?"

"Trap set on the barrier," Auster said. "When we put up the group barrier around our circle, I'll set the trap matrix in synch with it. Then, if anyone is picking a mind within the circle, it will hold him and immobilize him, and we can get a look at him afterward in the monitor."

"Believe me," said Kerwin, "if anyone's spying through *my* mind, I'm as anxious to find it out as you are!"

"We'll start then." She hesitated, bit her lip and moved to the cupboard where the drinks were kept. "I want some *kirian.*" At Kennard's disapproving look she brushed past him, poured it for herself. "Anyone else who doesn't trust himself tonight? Auster? Jeff? Stop looking at me like that, Neyrissa, I know what I'm doing, and you're not my mother!"

Rannirl said roughly, "Lori, if you're not feeling ready for the clearing operation, we could delay it a few days—"

"We've already delayed three days, and I am as ready as I shall ever be," she said, and lifted the *kirian* to her lips. But she glanced at Jeff when she thought he did not see her, and her eyes struck Kerwin to the heart.

So it was that way for her, too. He had thought himself hurt that she could set it all aside, that she had been able to forget or ignore what had been between them. Now, seeing the hurt in her eyes, Kerwin wished with all his heart that Elorie had been truly untouched by what had happened. He could endure the suffering, if he must. But he did not know if he could endure what it had done to Elorie.

He could, because he must. He watched her finish the *kirian* liqueur, and went, with the others, upstairs to the matrix chamber.

They were placed as before, Taniquel monitoring, Neyrissa within the circle, Auster holding the group barrier, Elorie at the center, holding in her slender hands the forces that could tap the magnetic field of a planet, gathering up all their joined minds and directing their mingled forces into the matrix lattice designed for this operation.

Kerwin felt the waiting like a pain, bracing himself for control against the moment when Elorie's grey eyes, turned on him, would pull him into the rapport of the circle. He felt it taking shape around him; Auster, strong and protective; the intangible strength that was Kennard, so at odds with the man's crippled body; Neyrissa, kindly and detached; Corus a flood of tumbling images.

Elorie.

He felt her firm, directing presence guiding him into the layers of the crystal lattice that somehow, was also the map lying before Kennard and the countryside of the Domains, extending his awareness beyond time and space, sending him out to travel, deep in the core of the world. . . .

He came out of it hours later, coming slowly up to consciousness to see dawn light in the room and the faces of the Tower circle around him. And Auster; drawn, hostile—triumphant. Wordless, he gestured them around him.

Kerwin had never seen a trap matrix before. It looked like a bit of strangely shiny metal, studded with crystals here and there, the glassy surface enlaced with little ribbons of gleaming light deep inside. Auster said, "Tired, Elorie? Take the monitor screen for a minute, Corus, let's see what we have in here." He pointed a finger at the beautiful, deadly thing in his lap. "I set it for anyone who tried to work through the group barrier; and I felt the trap sprung. Whoever it was, he's immobilized here, and we can get a good look at him."

Fastidiously, as if he touched something dirty, Corus picked up the trap matrix. He moved a calibration on the big monitor screen, and lights began to blink inside it. Then, in the glassy surface, a picture slowly formed. It hovered over the city of Arilinn; passed landmark after landmark. Then, gradually, it centered upon a small, mean room, almost bare, and the figure of a man, bent in soundless concentration, motionless as death.

"Whoever he is, we've got him in stasis," Auster said. "Can you get his face, Corus?"

The picture focused; and Jeff cried out as he recognized the face.

"Ragan!"

Of course. The little bitter man from the spaceport gutters, who had all but admitted being a Terran spy, who had dogged Jeff's footsteps and taught him to use a matrix and pushed him at every step.

Who else could it have been?

Suddenly he was swept by a great, calm, icy rage. Some atavistic thing in him, all Darkovan, shook loose everything but his wrath and injured pride at having been manipulated like this, his mind picked. Ancient words sprang without thought to his mind.

"Com'ii, *this man's life is mine!* When, how, and as I can, I claim his life, one to one, and who takes it before I do, answers to me!"

Auster—braced, Kerwin knew, to fling new challenges and charges, stopped cold, his eyes wide and shocked.

Kennard met his eyes. He said "*Comyn* Kerwin-Aillard, as your nearest kinsman and Warden here, I hear your claim and allot this life to you; to claim or spare as you will. Seek it, take it, or give your own."

Jeff heard the ritual words almost without understanding. His hands literally ached to tear Ragan limb from limb. He said tersely, gesturing the picture off the screen, "Can that thing hold him long enough for me to get to him, Auster?"

Auster nodded, the trap matrix still held between his hands. Taniquel broke into the silence, her voice shrill.

"You can't let him do this! It's murder; Jeff has no idea how to use a sword, and do you think that—that *sharug,* that cat-spawn, will even fight fair?"

"I may not be able to handle a sword," Jeff said tautly, "but I'm damn good with a knife. Kinsman, give me a dagger, and I can take him," he added, turning to Kennard, who had acknowledged him.

But it was Rannirl who unbuckled the knife he wore at his waist. He said slowly, "Brother, I'm with you. Your foes are mine; let there never be a knife drawn between us." He held the knife out, hilt first, to Kerwin. Kerwin took it in a daze. From somewhere he remembered that on Darkover this had a very serious meaning. He didn't know the ritual words, but he remembered that this exchange had the ritual force of an oath of brotherhood, and even through his all-encompassing rage he was warmed by it. He caught Rannirl into a quick embrace. All he could think of to say was, "Thank you—brother. Against my foes—and yours." It must have been the right thing to say, or something near to it, for Rannirl turned his head and, somewhat to Jeff's embarrassment, kissed him on the cheek.

"Come on," he said, "I'll see fair play done in your name, Kennard. If you doubt it, Auster, come along."

Kerwin took the knife, balancing it in his hands. He had no doubt in his ability to handle himself. There had been a couple of fights on other worlds; he had found that inside himself there was a roughneck buried, and he was glad, now, to know it. The code of his childhood, the code of blood-feud, seemed to fill him to the roots of his whole being.

Ragan was going to get a damned big surprise.

And then he was going to get very, very dead.

Chapter Thirteen: Exile

They came out of the Tower, through the Veil, into dim red sunlight, the Bloody Sun rising over the foothills far away to the east. Jeff walked with his hand on his knife, feeling strange and cold. At this hour the streets of Arilinn were deserted; only a few startled onlookers in the street saw the three redheads, moving shoulder to shoulder, armed and ready for a fight; and those who did, suddenly discovered that they had urgent business in a couple of other directions.

They went through the outlying district, through the market where in a happier day Jeff had chosen a pair of boots, and into a crowded and dirty suburb. Auster, his hands still on the trap matrix, said in a low voice, "This won't hold him much longer."

Kerwin's grin stretched his mouth, mirthless. "Hold him long enough for me to *find* him, and then let him go any damn time you please."

They went through a narrow alley, a filthy courtyard cluttered with rubbish, a stable with a couple of ill-kept animals. A half-witted stableman in rags, his mouth hanging open, watched them briefly, then turned and fled. Auster pointed up a steep, crazy flight of stairs to an outside gallery with a couple of rooms opening off it. As they climbed the stairs, a girl in a torn skirt and scarf came out on the gallery, her mouth a wide O of astonishment. Rannirl made an angry, abrupt gesture, and she bolted back into one of the rooms and slammed the door.

Auster stopped outside the other door. He said, "Now," and his bony hands did something to the trap matrix that Jeff didn't see. From inside the room came a long cry of rage and despair as Kerwin, leaping forward, kicked the door open and burst in.

Ragan, still in the held-fast posture of the trap matrix, suddenly broke free and whirled on them like a trapped cat, knife flashing from his boot. He backed off and faced them, naked steel between them, baring his teeth with a snarl. "Three against one, *vai dom'yn?*"

"Just one!" Kerwin rasped, and with his free arm, motioned Rannirl and Auster to stand back. In the next moment he reeled under the impact of Ragan's body crashing into his. He felt the slash of the point along his arm as he whipped his knife up, but it had only torn his sleeve. He countered with a fast thrust, shoving Ragan off balance; then they were locked into a deadly clinch, and he was struggling to keep Ragan's knife from his ribs. He felt his own knife rip leather; it came away red. Ragan grunted, struggled, made a sudden swift feint—

Auster, watching like a cat at a mousehole, suddenly flung himself against them. He knocked Jeff off balance, and Kerwin, hardly believing that this was really happening—*he should have known he couldn't trust Auster!*—felt Ragan's knife rip along his arm and go in a few inches below the armpit. Numbness, then burning pain, spread in him; the knife dropped from his left hand and he snatched it up with the other, fighting Auster's deathgrip, dragging his arm down. Kerwin swore, brutally, kicking out with booted feet.

"Get away, damn you—is this your notion of a fair fight?" And Rannirl ran to fling his arms around

Auster from behind, grab him and drag him away, taking a slash from Ragan's knife that tore along his forearm and down the back of his hand. He was swearing.

"Man, are you crazy?" he panted.

Ragan wrenched loose. There was a crash, the sound of running feet on the staircase, the clatter of rubbish kicked loose on the staircase. Auster and Rannirl fell, still struggling, to the ground. Auster, somehow, had Ragan's knife. Rannirl panted, "Jeff! Get the knife!"

Kerwin dropped his own knife, flung himself on the struggling bodies, and forced Auster's hand back. Auster struggled briefly, then his hand relaxed and he dropped it, sanity coming slowly back to his eyes. There was a long slash on his cheek—Kerwin didn't know from which knife—and his eye was darkening, blood streaming from his nose, where Jeff's elbow had smashed at him.

Rannirl picked himself up, wiping the blood from his forearm. The knife had not gone into him at all; it was a cut less than skin deep. He stared down at Auster in shock and horror. Auster started to get up and Kerwin made a menacing gesture. For two cents he'd have kicked Auster's ribs right in. "Stay right where you are, damn you."

Auster wiped blood from his nose and mouth, and stayed where he was. Kerwin went to the window and looked into the dirty courtyard. Ragan, of course, was gone. There wasn't a chance they'd find him again.

He walked back to Auster and said, "Give me one good reason I shouldn't kick your brains out!"

Auster sat up, bloody, but not beaten. "Go ahead, *Terranan*," he said. "Pretend we owe you the protection of our codes of honor!"

Rannirl stood over him, menacing. "Do you dare call *me* traitor?" he said. "Kennard accepted the challenge; you did not speak to it then. And I have given this man my knife; he is my brother. By rights, Auster, I could kill you!" He looked ready to do it, too.

"Kennard gave him the right—"

"To murder his accomplice, so that we'd never know the truth! Didn't you see he was set to kill the man before we could question him? Didn't you see that he recognized him? Oh, yes, he put on a good show for us," Auster said. "Damned clever; kill him before any of us could get at the truth. I wanted to take him alive, and if you'd have the sense of a rabbithorn, we'd have him, now, for questioning and telepathic interrogation!"

He's lying, lying, Kerwin thought hopelessly, but doubt had begun to cloud even Rannirl's face. As usual, Auster had managed to confuse the issue, to put him on the defensive.

"Come on," he said wearily, "we might as well get back." He felt weary and anticlimactic; his arm was beginning to ache where Ragan had stabbed him. "Help me get this shirt off and stop the bleeding, will you, Rannirl? I'm bleeding like a summer slaughterhouse!"

There were more people in the streets now, and more to stare at the three Comyn, one with his face smeared from a bloody nose, and one with his arm pinned up in an improvised sling from Rannirl's undertunic. Kerwin felt all the weariness of a night spent at matrix work descending on him; he felt as if every step was his last effort. Auster, too, was staggering with weariness. They passed a cookshop where workmen were clustered, eating and drinking,

and the smell of food reminded Kerwin that after a
night in the matrix screens they had eaten nothing
and that he was starving. He glanced at Rannirl and
with one unspoken movement they went into the
shop. The proprietor was awed and voluble, pouring
out promises to set his finest before them, but Rannirl shook his head, caught up a couple of long loaves
of fresh hot bread and a pan of cooked sausages,
flung some coins at the cook and jerked his head at
his companions. Outside he broke the bread, handed
a portion to Kerwin and, glaring, one to Auster; they
strode on through the streets of Arilinn, munching at
the coarse food with wolfish hunger. It felt like the
tiniest of between-meal snacks, a dainty morsel for a
small and finicky child, but it did restore his strength
somewhat. When they reached the Tower, and
passed through the Veil, the faint stinging seemed to
drain the last of Kerwin's strength.

"Jeff," said Rannirl, "I'll come and bandage that
for you."

Kerwin shook his head. Rannirl looked exhausted,
too, and it hadn't even been his fight. "Go and rest—"
awkwardly, he added—"brother. I'll manage."

Rannirl hesitated, but he went, and Kerwin, relieved to be alone, went into his own room and flung
the door shut. In the luxurious bath he ripped off
sling and shirt, awkwardly raising his arm with a
grimace of pain. Rannirl had crudely stanched the
bleeding with a heavy pad from his torn shirt; he
worked it loose and examined the wound. A flap of
skin had been sliced away, skin and flesh hanging
down like a bloody rag, but as far as he could tell the
wound was simply a flesh one. He stuck his head into
the fountain; raised it, dripping but clear-headed.

The furry nonhuman who served him glided into
the room and stood dismayed, green pupilless eyes

wide in consternation; he went quickly and came back with bandages, some thick yellow stuff he smeared on the wound; and deftly, with his odd thumbless paws, bound it up. That done, he looked at Kerwin in question.

"Get me something to eat," Kerwin said, "I'm starving." The bread and sausages they had shared on the way back had only begun to fill the vast crater of emptiness inside him.

He had eaten enough for three hungry horse-breakers after a fall round-up when the door opened, and Auster came, unannounced, into the room. He had bathed and changed his clothes, but, Kerwin was gratified to see, he had a splendidly black eye that would take a good while to heal. Kerwin wiped his mouth, shoved his plate away, and gestured at Rannirl's knife on the table.

"If you've had another brainstorm, there's a knife," he said. "If not, get the hell out of my room."

Auster looked pale. He touched his eye as if it hurt. Jeff hoped it did. "I don't blame you for hating me, Jeff," he said, "but I have something to say to you."

Kerwin started to shrug, found that it hurt, and didn't. Auster watched him and flinched as if the pain had been his own. "Are you badly hurt? Did the *kyrri* make sure there was no poison on the knife?"

"A hell of a lot you care," Kerwin said, "but that's a Darkovan trick; Terrans don't fight that way. And what the hell are you worrying about, when you did your level damnedest to make sure I got knifed in the first place?"

Auster said, "I deserve that, maybe. Believe anything you want to. I only care about one thing—two things, and you're destroying them both. Maybe you don't realize—but, damn it, it's worse than if you did!"

"Get to the point, Auster, or get out."

"Kennard said there was a block in your memory. Look, I'm not accusing you of betraying us on purpose—"

"That's damn good of you," Kerwin said with heavy sarcasm.

"You don't want to betray us," Auster said, his face suddenly cracking and going to pieces, "and you still don't realize what this *means*! It means that *the Terrans planted you on us*! They put that block in your memory, probably before you ever left the Spacemen's Orphanage, before you ever went to Terra. And when you came back here, they set it up, hoping that just this would happen—that we'd come to accept you, think of you as one of us, depend on you—*need* you! Because it was so obvious that you were one of us—" His voice broke; in shock, Kerwin realized that Auster was fighting back tears, shaking from head to foot. "So we fell for it, Kerwin, and for you—and how can we even hate you for it— brother?"

Kerwin shut his eyes. This was the very thought he had been pushing away.

He had been maneuvered every step of the way, from the first moment when Ragan had met them in the shops. Perhaps Johnny Ellers had been set up to introduce him to Ragan; he would never know. Who but the Terrans could have done it? Maneuvered into his experiments with the matrix. Maneuvered into confrontation with the Comyn. And at last threatened with deportation, to force the Comyn to move and reclaim him.

He was an elaborate booby trap! Arilinn had taken him in—and at any moment, he might explode in their faces!

Auster took Jeff gently by the arm, careful not to

injure his wounded shoulder. "I wish we'd liked each other better. Now you must think I'm saying this because we haven't been friends."

Kerwin shook his head. Auster's pain and sincerity were obvious to anyone with a scrap of *laran*. "I don't think that. Not now. But what could they hope to achieve?"

"I'm not sure. Perhaps they thought the Tower Circle would disintegrate with you in it; perhaps they wanted information, leaked to them through the break in the barrier. I know they're curious about how matrix science operates, and they haven't been able to find out very much. Not even from Cleindori, when she ran away with your damned father. I don't know. How the hell would *I* know what the Terrans want? You should; you're one of them. You've lived with them. You tell me what they want!"

Kerwin shook his head. "Not now. I left them, didn't I? I never was one of them, except on the surface," he said slowly. "But now that we have the spy, now that we know what they're doing—can't we guard against it?"

"If it were only that, Jeff," Auster said earnestly. "But there's something else; the thing I've been trying not to see." His face was set and white. "What have you done to Elorie, my brother?"

Elorie. What have you done to Elorie.

And if Auster knew, they all knew.

He could not speak. His guilt, Auster's fear, was like a miasma in the room. Auster let him go and said earnestly, "Go away, Jeff. For the love of any Gods you know about on Terra, go away before it's too late. I know it's not your fault. You didn't grow up with the taboo. It isn't deep in your blood and bone. But if you care about Elorie, if you care about any of us, go away before you destroy us all."

He turned and went out, and Kerwin went and threw himself face down on his bed, seeing it clearly for the first time.

Auster was right. He heard, like a grim echo, the words of the matrix mechanic who had paid with her own life for showing him a scrap of his own past. *You are the one who was sent, a trap that missed its firing.* But she had said something else too. *You will find the thing you love, and you will destroy it; but you will save it, too.*

True, her prophecy, that old and unlovely and doomed woman whose name or history he was never to know. He had found what he loved, and already he had come close to destroying it. Could he save it, if he went away now, or was it already too late?

Oh, Elorie, Elorie! But he must not even whisper her name. Even a thought could disturb her hard-won peace. Kerwin rose, grim-faced, knowing what he must do.

Slowly he stripped off the suede-leather breeches and laced boots, the bright jerkin; he dressed himself again in the Terran uniform he had laid aside—forever, he thought—when he came here.

He hesitated over the matrix stone, cursing, torn, wanting to fling it from the highest window of the Tower and shatter it on the stones; but at last he put it into his pocket. He was under enough stress now, and he had always felt uneasy when it was, physically, out of his reach.

It was my mother's. It went with her into exile. It can go with me, too.

He hesitated, too, over the embroidered ceremonial cloak lined with fur that had begun this chain of events; but at last he put it round his shoulders. It was his, honestly bought with money earned on another world; and, sentiment aside, it was a bulwark against the bitter cold of the Darkovan night. He was still wearing the slash of Ragan's knife (was this all the Comyn could give him, knife wounds in his body, keener wounds in his soul?) and he couldn't afford to get chilled. And—another immensely practical consideration—on the streets of Arilinn, a man in Terran uniform would show up like a starflower on the bare glaciers of the Hellers. The cloak would keep him decently anonymous until he was a good long way away from here.

He went to the door of his room. There was a good smell of hot food somewhere; knife fights, blood feuds, endless telepathic operations within the matrix chamber could come and go, but practical Mesyr would plan their dinners, persuade the *kyrri* to cook them as she wished, chide Rannirl for spoiling his appetite with wine before dinner, search out new ribbons for Elorie's filmy dresses, scold the men for flinging muddy boots in the great hall after riding or hunting. He heard her cheery calm voice with a wrench of nostalgia. This was the only home he had ever known.

I always wanted my grandmother Kerwin to be just like her.

He passed an open door. The drift of Taniquel's delicate, flowery perfume wafted out, and he heard her singing somewhere in the suite. A brief vision caught at him, of her slim, pretty body half-submerged in greenish water, her curls piled atop her head as she scrubbed. Tenderness overwhelmed him; she had slept away the weariness of the night's work, and did not yet know of the aftermath of the knife fight . . . nor did Kennard.

The thought froze him. Soon now, if not already, the touch of rapport would begin to drift among them as they gathered for the evening, and then they would all know what he planned. He must go quickly, or he would not be able to go at all.

He flung the hood over his head, slipped down the stairs unseen, and out through the Veil. Now he was safe; the Veil insulated thought, too. Moving resolutely, holding his weariness at bay, he went through the cluster of buildings near the Tower, across the airstrip, and toward the city of Arilinn.

His plans were vague. Where could he go? The Terrans had not wanted him. Now there was no place for him on Darkover either, no safety; wherever he hid, from Dalereuth to Aldaran, there was no refuge so remote that the Comyn could not find him; certainly not while he bore the matrix of the renegade Cleindori.

Back to the Terrans, then. Let them deport him, stop fighting his fate. They might simply deport him. But if they had actually planted him on the Comyn, a giant booby trap, what would they do when they discovered that he had sabotaged their plan, a carefully-laid plan that had taken two generations to bring to fruition?

Did it matter? They could do their worst.

Did anything matter now?

He raised his eyes, looked directly into the great red bloodshot eye of what some romantic Terran, a few generations ago, had dubbed the Bloody Sun. It was sinking behind the Arilinn Tower; he watched it vanish, and with it came the swiftly lowering darkness, the chill and silence. The last gleam of the bloody sun went out; the Tower lingered a minute, a pale afterimage on Jeff's eyelids, then dissolved in stinging rain. A single blue light shone from near the tip of the Tower, battling valiantly to pierce the mist and rain; then vanished as if it had never been. Kerwin wiped the rain from his eyes (was the rain salt and warm, stinging his face?) turned his back resolutely on the Tower and walked into the city.

He found a place where they did not recognize him either as Terran or Comyn, but looked only at the color of his money, and gave him a bed, and privacy, and enough to drink—he hoped—to blot out thought and memory, blur the vain, unavoidable reliving of those brief weeks in Arilinn.

It was a monumental drunk. He never knew how many days it lasted, or how many times he staggered into the streets of Arilinn for more to drink and back to his hole like a wounded animal. When he slept, the darkness was blurred with faces and voices and memories he could not endure; he came at last up to consciousness from a long forgetfulness, more sleep than stupor, and found them all around his bed.

For a moment he thought it was the aftermath of bad whiskey, or that his overloaded mind had cracked. Then Taniquel made an uncontrollable sound of dismay and pity and flung herself down on her knees beside the filthy pallet where he was lying. And then he knew they were really there.

He rubbed a hand over his unshaven chin, wet his cracked lips with his tongue. His voice wouldn't obey him.

Rannirl said, "Did you really think we would let you go like this, *bredu?*" He used the inflection that made the word mean, *beloved brother*.

Kerwin said thickly, "Auster—"

"Doesn't know everything," Kennard said. "Jeff, can you listen to us sensibly now, or are you still too drunk?"

He sat up. The squalor of the hideout room, the empty bottle at the foot of the tangled blanket, the ache, still sharp, in the neglected knife wound, seemed all part of the same thing, his own misery and defeat. Taniquel was holding his hand, but it was the monitor's touch of Neyrissa that he felt on his mind.

"He's sober enough," she said.

He looked around at them. Taniquel, her firm little fingers pressing his; Corus, looking troubled, almost tearful; Rannirl, troubled and friendly; Kennard, sad and concerned; Auster, bitterly aloof.

Elorie, her face a white mask, the eyes red and swollen; Elorie, in tears!

Kerwin sat up, gently letting Taniquel's hand go. He said, "Oh, God, why must we go through all this again? Didn't Auster tell you?"

"He told us a lot of things," Kennard said, "all rooted in his own fears and prejudices."

"I don't even deny that," Auster said. "I ask if the fears and prejudices weren't justified. That spy— what did Jeff say his name was? Ragan. He's another of them. It's fairly obvious—damn it, I *recognize* the man. I'd swear he's a *nedestro* of Comyn, maybe Ardais or even Aldaran! With Terran blood. Just right to spy on us. And Jeff—He could even come through the Veil! And fool Kennard on telepathic interrogation!"

Rannirl said angrily, "I think you see Terran spies under every pillow, Auster!"

Taniquel reached for Kerwin's hand again. She said, "We can't let you go, Jeff. You're one of us, you're a part of ourselves. Where will you go? What will you do?"

Kennard said, "Wait, Tani. Jeff, bringing you to Arilinn was a calculated risk; we knew that before we called you through the matrix, and we all agreed on the risk. And it was more than that. We wanted to strike a blow against dark magic and taboo, take a first step toward making matrix mechanics a science, not a—a thing of sorcery. To prove it could be learned by anyone, not by a sacrosanct—priesthood."

"I don't know that I agree with Kennard on that," Neyrissa said. "I want no shadow of the Forbidden Tower, with their dirty ways and their forsworn Keepers, to touch Arilinn. But we've reclaimed Arilinn; and Jeff, Tani is right, you're one of us. We all agreed on the risk."

"But can't you understand?" Kerwin's voice broke. "I'm *not* willing to take the risk. Not when I'm not sure that I'm—I'm a free agent, not a planted spy; when I don't know what they might make me do. When they might make me destroy you."

"Maybe *this* was how you were meant to destroy us," Corus said, and his voice was bitter. "To make us trust you—and then, when we can't work without you, to walk out on us."

"That's a damnably unfair way of putting it, Corus," Jeff said hoarsely. "I'm trying to save you; I can't be the one to destroy you!"

Taniquel bent her head and put her cheek against his hand. She was crying without a sound. Auster's face was hard. "Kerwin is right, Kennard, and you know it. He's got guts enough to want to do the right thing, anyway. And you're only hurting us all by prolonging this."

Kennard stood leaning heavily on his stick, looking down at them all with contempt, with lip-biting repressed anger.

"Cowards, all of you! Now that we have a chance to *fight* this damned nonsense! Rannirl, you know what's right! You've said it yourself—"

Rannirl clenched his teeth. He said, "My private beliefs are one thing; the will of the Council is another. I refuse to make a political statement about my career in Arilinn. I'm a technician, not a diplomat.

Jeff is my friend. I gave him my knife. I call him brother, and I will defend him against his enemies. He doesn't have to go back to the Terrans. Jeff—" He turned to the man on the bed and said, "When you leave here, you don't need to go back to the Terrans; go to my family home in the Kilghard Hills. Ask anyone where to find Lake Mirion. Tell anyone there that you are my sworn brother; show them the knife I gave you. When this is settled, perhaps you can come back to Arilinn."

"I didn't think you were such a coward, Rannirl," Kennard said. "Defend him here, why don't you? If he needs a home, Armida is his; or, as Cleindori's child, Mariposa Lake. But isn't there anyone with the guts to stand up for him at Arilinn? He's not the first Terran—"

"You're too damn transparent, Kennard," Auster said. "All you care about is getting that half-caste boy of yours into Arilinn some day, and you'll even put up with a Terran spy to create a precedent! Can't your damned son make it into Arilinn on his own merits, if he has any? I don't wish Jeff any harm now; Zandru seize this hand—" he laid it briefly on the hilt of his dagger—"if I wish him any harm. But he must not return to Arilinn; we cannot risk a Terran spy actually within a matrix circle. If he returns to Arilinn, I will go."

"And I," said Neyrissa. Rannirl, looking bitterly ashamed, said, "I am sorry. So will I."

"Cowards," Corus flung at them fiercely. "The Terrans have broken our circle after all, haven't they? They didn't need to make Jeff their spy. They just had to make us suspect him!"

Kennard shook his head in disbelieving disgust. He said, "Are you really going to do this, all of you?"

Kerwin wanted to cry out: *I love you all, stop torturing*

me this way! He said thickly, "Now that you know it can be done, you'll find someone to take my place."

"Who?" Elorie asked bitterly. "Kennard's half-caste son? He's not ten years old yet! Old Leominda from Neskaya? The Heir to Hastur, who's only four years old, or the Heir to Elhalyn, who's nine years old and not much better than a half-wit? My madman of a father, perhaps? Little Callina Lindir from Neskaya?"

Kennard said, "We went all over this when we decided to bring Jeff here. In all the Seven Domains we could find no other candidates. And now, when we have a fully qualified and functioning Keeper's Circle at Arilinn, you are going to throw that away and let Jeff go? After all we went through to get him here?"

"No!" Elorie startled them all with her cry. She flung herself forward; afraid she would fall, Kerwin put out a hand to catch her. He would have let her go at once, respectfully, but she clung to him, her arms tightening around him. Her face was whiter than when she had collapsed in the matrix chamber.

"No," she whispered. "No, Jeff, no, don't go! Stay with us, Jeff, whatever happens—I beg you, I can't bear to see you go—"

For an instant Kerwin held her tight, his own face like death. He whispered, under his breath, "Oh, Elorie, Elorie . . ." But then, steeling himself, he put her gently away.

"Now do you see why I must go?" he said, almost in a whisper, speaking to her alone. "I *must* go, Elorie, and you know it as well as I. Don't make it harder for me."

He saw shock, anger, compassion, accusation dawning in the faces all around him. Neyrissa came to take Elorie away, murmuring to her, but Elorie flung off her hand. Her voice was high and shrill.

"No. If this is what Jeff has decided, or what you force on him, then I have decided too, and it is over. I—I can't give up my life for it this way anymore!" She faced them all, her eyes enormous, looking like bruises in her pale face.

"But Elorie, Lori," Neyrissa pleaded. "You know why you cannot withdraw, you know how much you are needed—"

"And what am I, then? A doll, a machine to serve the Comyn and the Tower?" she cried, her voice high and hysterical. "No. No. It's too much! I cannot stand it, I renounce it—"

"Elorie—*breda*," Taniquel pleaded. "Don't say that—not like this, not now, not here! I know how you feel, but—"

"You say you know how I feel! You dare to say that to me, you who have lain in his arms and known his love! Oh, no, you have not denied yourself, but you are all too ready to tell me what I must do—"

"Elorie," Kennard's voice was tender. "You don't know what you are saying. I beg of you, remember who you are—"

"I know who I am supposed to be!" she cried, sounding frantic, beside herself. "A Keeper, a *leronis*, a sacred virgin without mind or heart or soul or life of my own, a machine for the relays—"

Kennard closed his eyes in agony, and Kerwin, looking at the old man's face, seemed to hear words spoken like this, years before, and saw, mirrored in Kennard's mind and memory, the face of his mother. *Cleindori. Oh, my poor sister!* But aloud Kennard only said, very gently, "Lori, my darling. Everything you suffer, others have suffered before you. When you came to Arilinn, you knew it would not be easy. We cannot allow you to renounce us, not now. Another Keeper is being trained, and when that day comes you can be freed. But not now, *chiya*, or you throw away all we have done."

"I cannot! I cannot live like this!" Elorie cried. "Not now, when at last I know what it is I swore to renounce!"

"Lori, my child—" Neyrissa said softly, but Elorie turned on her like a fury. "You have lived as you saw fit, you found freedom, not slavery in the Tower! For you it was a refuge; for me it has never been anything but a prison! You and Tani both, you are quick to urge me to give up forever what you have known, love and shared joy and children—" her voice broke. "I didn't know, I didn't know, and now—" She flung herself into Jeff's arms again; he could not put her away.

Auster said in a low voice, staring at Elorie in horror, "This is worse treachery than the Terrans could ever compass. And to think, Jeff, that I believed you had done this innocently!"

Rannirl shook his head, staring at them in dismay. He said in a low, vicious voice, "I gave you my knife. I called you brother. And you have done this to us, done this to *her*!" He spat. "There was a day when the man who seduced a Keeper would be torn on hooks, and the Keeper who violated her oath—" He could not continue. He was too angry. "And so history repeats itself—Cleindori and this filth of a Terran!"

"You said it yourself," Elorie cried out in torment. "You said that any mechanic could do a Keeper's work, that a Keeper was an anachronism, that Cleindori was right!"

"What I believe, and what we can do at Arilinn, are two different things," he spat at her, contemptuously. "I had not believed you were such a fool! Nor did I think you weak enough to go whoring after this handsome Terran who has seduced us all with his charming ways! Yes, I too was charmed by him—and he used this, damn him, he used it to break the Tower!" Rannirl swore, turned his back on them.

"Dirty bitch," Neyrissa said, and raised her hand to slap Elorie. "No better than that dirty old man, our father, whose filthy lecheries—"

Kennard moved swiftly to grab Neyrissa's hand in midair. "What? Lay a hand on your Keeper?"

"She has forfeited that," said Neyrissa, curling up her lip in contempt.

Auster said, staring somberly at them, "In days past, it would have been death for you, Elorie—and death by torture for *him*."

In shock and dismay Kerwin realized the mistake they were all making; for Elorie was clinging to him, white and terrified, her face hidden against his breast. He stepped forward quickly, to deny the accusation, to reaffirm Elorie's innocence. The words were already on his lips: *I swear that she has been sacred to me, that her chastity is untouched—*

But Elorie flung back her head, white and defiant. "Call me what you will, Neyrissa," she said. "All of you; it's no use. I have renounced Arilinn; I proclaim myself unfit to be Keeper by Arilinn's laws—"

She turned then to Kerwin, sobbing bitterly, and flung her arms around him again, hiding her face on his breast. The words still unspoken—*This is only an innocent girl's fantasy. I have not betrayed her, or you*—died forever on his lips. He could not rebuff or repudiate her now; not as he saw the shock and disbelief on their faces changing to revulsion and disgust. She was clinging helplessly, holding herself to him with desperate force, her whole body shaken with her weeping.

Deliberately, accepting, he bowed his head and faced them, his arms sheltering Elorie.

"They should die for this!" Auster cried.

Rannirl shrugged. "What's the use? They've sabotaged everything we tried to do, everything we've accomplished. Nothing we could do now would make any difference. Wish them joy of it!" He turned his back on them and walked out.

Auster and Corus followed; Kennard lingered a moment, his face lined and miserable with despair. "Oh, Elorie, Elorie," he said in a whisper, "if you had only come to me, warned me in time—" and Kerwin knew that he was not speaking to Elorie, but to a memory. But she did not raise her head from Jeff's breast and after a time Kennard sighed, shaking his head, and went away.

Stunned, still shaken by the force of her lie, Kerwin heard the door closing behind them. Elorie had quieted a little; now she began to weep again, brokenly, like a child; Kerwin held her in his arms, not understanding.

"Elorie, Elorie," he entreated. "Why did you do it? Why did you lie to them?"

Sobbing and laughing at once, hysterical, Elorie leaned back to look at him. "But it wasn't a lie," she sobbed. "I couldn't have lied to them again! It was my being Keeper that had become a lie, ever since I touched you—oh, I know you would never have touched me, because of the law, because of the taboo, and yet when I spoke to them they knew I was telling the truth! Because I had come to want you so, to love you so, I couldn't have endured it, to turn myself into a robot again, a machine, a dead-alive automation as I did before—" Her sobbing almost drowned out the words. "I knew I could never endure it again, to go on being Keeper—and when you went away, I thought at first without you there I could perhaps go back to being what I was, but there was nothing, nothing any more in my world, and I knew that if I never saw you again, I would be more dead than alive—"

"Oh, Elorie! Oh, God, Elorie!" he whispered, overwhelmed.

"So now you have lost everything—and you're not even free," she said wildly. "But I have nothing, no one else, if you do not want me, I have nothing, nothing—"

Kerwin picked her up in his arms like a child, cradling her close to him. He was awed at the immensity of her trust; shaken and dismayed at what she had given up for him. He kissed her wet face; laid her down on the tumbled bed and knelt at her side.

"Elorie," he said, and the words were a prayer and a pledge, "I don't care if I have lost everything else, now that I have you. My only regret in leaving Arilinn was because I thought I was leaving you."

The words were not true and he knew as he spoke them that they were not true, and he knew that Elorie knew. Yet the only thing that mattered now was to reassure Elorie with a deeper truth. "I love you, Elorie," he whispered, and that at least was true. "I will never let you go." He leaned forward, kissing her on the lips, and gathered her childish body again into his arms.

Chapter Fourteen: Doorway to the Past

Thendara, in the dying light, was a mass of black towers and shapes; the Terran HQ below them was a single brightly lighted spike against the sky. Jeff pointed it out to Elorie through the window of the Terran airliner.

"It may not be very beautiful to you now, my darling. But somewhere I'll find a world to give you."

She leaned against his shoulder. "I have all the world I want."

The seat-belt sign flashed, and he helped her to buckle her straps; she put her hands over her ears, hating the noise, and he put his arm around her, holding her tight.

The last three days had been days of joy and discovery for both of them, even through their shared sense of being outcaste, driven from the only home either of them had ever wanted. Neither spoke of this; they had too much else to share with one another.

He had never known a woman like Elorie. Once he had thought her aloof, passionless; then he had come to see that calm as a deep-seated control, not as absence of passion.

She had come to him, frightened, desolate, innocent almost to ignorance, and terrified. And she had given him her fear as she had given the rest of herself, without pretense and without shame. That utter trust frightened Kerwin, too—how could he ever be worthy of it? But it was typical of Elorie that she could do nothing by halves or meanly; as Keeper she had kept herself clear even from the fringes of passion; even in imagination, she had never thought of love. And having discarded that place, she had given herself over to Jeff with all of her long-controlled passion and dedication.

Once he had said something of this to her; his surprise, his fear that she would be frightened or frigid, his overwhelming surprise and delight at her response to his passion. Somehow he had believed that a woman who could live the life of a Keeper would be cold at the core, without passion or desire.

She had laughed aloud, shaking her head. "No," she said. "Kennard explained this once to me; outsiders would think that a passionless woman, who would not suffer in living alone and loveless, would be right for a Keeper. But anyone who knew anything of *laran* would know better. *Laran* and sexuality arise from the same place within, and are closely akin, and a woman who could be keeper without suffering would not have enough *laran* to be a Keeper, or anything else!"

Now, as they landed, she drew her cloak over her bright hair; he held her arm on the hard and unfamiliar metal steps. He must seem resolute for her sake, even if he was not. "I know it is strange to you, darling. But it won't be strange for long."

"No place will be strange to me where you are," she said valiantly. "But—but will they allow this? They won't—won't separate us?"

On that he could reassure her. "I may be Darkovan under your laws," he said, "but I have Terran citizenship and they cannot deny me that. And any woman who legally marries a citizen of the Empire is

automatically given citizenship." He remembered
the bored, incurious clerk in the Trade City at Port
Chicago who had married them three days ago. Port
Chicago was beyond the Domains; the clerk had
glanced briefly at Jeff's identity disk, heard Elorie
give her name as "Elorie Ardais" without a ripple of
interest; probably he had never heard of the Comyn,
or of the Arilinn Tower. He brought in a woman in
his office to witness the marriage; she had been
chirpy and friendly, saying to Elorie that with their
two red heads they should have quite a crop of
redheaded children. Elorie had blushed, and Kerwin
had felt a great and unexpected tenderness. The
thought of a child of Elorie's touched him in a way he
had not thought he could be moved.

"You are my wife in Empire law, wherever we go,"
he repeated. He added, gently, "We may have to
leave Darkover, though."

She nodded, biting her lip. The Comyn might be
as anxious, now, to have Jeff deported as, before,
they had been anxious to prevent it.

Kerwin secretly felt it would be better that way.
Darkover could never be, for either of them, more
than a reminder of what they had lost. And there
were worlds enough, out there.

Nervously, he approached the barrier. He might,
just possibly, be taken into custody as a man under
sentence of deportation. There were certain legal formalities he could invoke, appeal, delays to which he
was legitimately entitled. It hadn't seemed worth it,
for himself. For Elorie, he would do all he could to
evade the summary judgment, turn it in his favor.

The tall Spaceforce man in black leather stared at
Kerwin's shabby Terran clothing, at the shrinking,
veiled girl on his arm. He glanced at Jeff's identity
certification.

"And the woman?"

"My wife. We were married in Port Chicago three days ago."

"I see," said the Spaceforce man, slowly. "In that case there are certain formalities."

"Just as you like."

"If you'll come inside the HQ, please."

He led them inside, Jeff squeezing Elorie's arm reassuringly. He tried to hide the apprehension he felt. The marriage would have to be recorded through Records, and once Jeff surrendered his identification, the computer would immediately come up with the information that he was under sentence of deportation and suspension.

He had considered returning to the Terran Zone anonymously, at least for a day or two. But the peculiarity of Empire law concerning native women and marriage made that unthinkable. She had insisted, when he explained, that she did not care. But Jeff said firmly, asserting himself over her protest for the first time, "*I* care," and had left her no room for argument.

The Empire Civil Service consists largely of single men; few Terran women care to accompany their men halfway across the Galaxy. This means that on every planet liaisons with native women, both formal and informal, are taken for granted. To avoid endless complications with various planetary governments, the Empire makes a very clear distinction.

An Empire citizen may marry any woman, on any planet, by the laws of her own world and her own customs; it is a matter between the individual Terran, the woman, her family, and the laws under which she lives. The Empire has no part in it. Whether the marriage is formal or informal, temporary or permanent, or no marriage at all, is a matter for the private ethical and moral standards of the parties involved. And that man is carried as single on the Records of the Empire, making such provision for his wife as he privately chooses; although he may, if he wishes, file for citizenship for any child of the marriage, and obtain certain privileges for him. As the elder Jeff Kerwin had done for his son.

But if he chooses to register the marriage through Terran records, or signs any Empire document speaking of any native woman on any world, legally, as his wife, she is so in fact. From the moment their marriage contract was signed, and went through the Records, Elorie was entitled legally to all the privileges of a citizen; and if Jeff had died in the next breath after signing, she would still have been entitled to all the privileges of a citizen's widow. Kerwin was uncertain as to what the future would hold; but he had wanted to protect Elorie and provide for her in this way. Words spoken in bitterness still rang in his ears and turned up in his nightmares.

In the old days it would have been death for you, Elorie— and death by torture for him! And an old terror was upon him. There were those who might feel compelled to avenge the honor of a Keeper.

Kennard had said—what had Kennard said? Nothing. But still, Jeff was afraid without knowing why. So he watched with relief as a registry clerk took his thumbprint, and Elorie's, and tapped out information for Records. Now there was no way for the long arm of the Comyn to reach out and snatch Elorie from him.

He hoped.

Watching the details disappear into the computer, he was sure he had set trouble in motion for himself. Within a few hours he would have questions to answer, he might have to face deportation. He had a blot on his record, but he was a civilian, after all, and leaving his job without formal permission was only a minor offense against his seniority, not a crime. Somehow, he had to arrange to make a living. He had to decide whether to go to Terra or take a chance on another world—he was fairly sure his Terran grandparents wouldn't really welcome Elorie—but all those details could wait.

Most of his knowledge of Thendara was of bars and similar places, where he couldn't take Elorie. He could have claimed quarters in the HQ, putting in a requisition for married personnel, but he wouldn't do that until he had to. Equally unwise would be to find quarters in the Old Town—he had had a taste in Arilinn of how the Comyn were treated when recognized. A hotel in the Trade City was the obvious temporary solution.

He pointed out to her, as they passed, the Spaceman's Orphanage. "That's where I lived until I was twelve years old," he said, and let the silent puzzlement strike him again: *Or did I? Why, then, did the place have no records of me?*

"Elorie," he asked, when they were alone in their hotel, "did the Comyn have anything to do with destroying my records in the Orphanage?" A matrix, he supposed, could easily wipe out the data on a computer. At least, with what he knew of computers and matrixes, he could easily have devised a way to do it.

"I don't know," she said. "I do know we got Auster back from them when he was a small child, and *his* records were destroyed."

Kennard had referred to that as a curious story, and had implied that he would tell Jeff about it sometime. But he hadn't.

Long after Elorie slept, he lay awake at her side,

thinking about the false leads and blind alleys that had obscured his search for his own background. When the Comyn found him, he had abandoned the search—after all, he had found out the main thing he wanted to know; where he belonged. But there were still mysteries to be solved, and before he left Dark-over forever—and he supposed, now, that was only a matter of time—he was going to have a last try at solving them.

He told Elorie a little, the next day.

"There was no record of me there; I saw what the machine gave out. But if I could get into the place and check—there might even be someone there, one of the matrons or teachers, who remembered me."

"Would it be dangerous—to try and get in?"

"Not dangerous to life or limb, no. But I could be arrested for trespassing, or for breaking and entering. I wish to hell I knew a way a matrix could make me invisible."

Her smile was faint. "I could barricade you— throw what they call a *glamour* over you, so you could pass in among them unseen." She sighed. "It is un-lawful for a Keeper who has given back her oath to use her powers. But I have broken so many laws al-ready. And certain powers—I have lost."

She looked pale and wretched, and Kerwin felt his heart turn over at the thought of what she had given up for him. But why should it make so much dif-ference? He would not ask, but she picked the ques-tion up directly from his mind, and said, "I do not know. I—I have always been told that a Keeper must be—must be virgin, and resigns her powers if she gives back her oath and takes a lover, or a husband."

Kerwin was startled by her acceptance of this; she had defied so many superstitions, had refused to ac-cept her ritual authority, had hated the word *sorceress* when applied to her. But this one, perhaps, was so deeply ingrained in her that she could not resist it.

Kennard had called it superstitious rubbish. But whether she had really lost her powers, or only believed she had, the effect would be much the same. And perhaps there was some truth it, too. He knew the terrible exhaustion and nervous drain of matrix work, even on his newcomer level. Kennard had counseled him to avoid sex for some time before serious work in the screens. It made sense that the Keepers must remain always at the peak of strength, guarding their powers in seclusion, sparing no energies for any other ties or concerns.

He remembered the day she had collapsed in the matrix screens; how he had thought her heart had stopped. Kerwin took her in his arms, holding her tight, thinking: *At least she is safe from that, now!*

But he had touched her, that day; had lent her strength. Had that contact destroyed her as Keeper?

"No," she said quietly, knowing his thoughts as she so often did. "From the first moment I touched you through the matrix, I knew that you would be— someone special, someone who would trouble my peace; but I was proud. I thought I could keep my control. And there was Taniquel; I envied her, but I knew you would not be too much alone." Her eyes suddenly brimmed over.

"I shall miss Tani," she said softly. "I wish it could have been different, that we could have—could have left in a way that would not leave them hating us. Tani is so dear to me."

"You aren't jealous? Because she and I—"

She laughed a little. "Oh, you Terrans! No, darling. If things were different, if we could have lived among our own people, I would willingly have called her *bredhis,* it would have been Tani that I chose for your bed if I were ill or pregnant—does that seem so shocking to you?"

He kissed her, without speaking. Darkovan customs were idealistic, but they took some getting used to. And he was just as glad to have Elorie to himself.

But that made him think of something else.

"Taniquel was no virgin, certainly. And yet she worked in the matrix circle—"

"Taniquel was not a Keeper," Elorie said soberly, "and she was never required to do a Keeper's work, never required to gather the energons of the circle and direct them. Such vows, and such—such abstinence—were not required of her, nor of Neyrissa, no more than of any of the men. And a few generations ago—in the time of the Forbidden Tower —there was a Keeper who left Arilinn to marry, and continued to use her powers; it was a great scandal; I do not know all the story, it was such a tale as they did not tell to children. And I do not know how she did it." Quickly, as if she feared he would question further, she said, "Some things, I am sure, I can still do with my own matrix. Let me try."

But when she had taken it from the tiny leather case in which she kept it, wrapped in its insulating silks, she hesitated.

"I feel so strange. Not like myself. I don't seem to —to belong to myself any more."

"You belong to me," Kerwin said firmly, and she smiled.

"Are your Terran wives property? No, I think not, love; I belong to myself; but I will willingly share every moment of my life with you," she said.

"Is there a difference?" Kerwin asked.

Her soft laugh always delighted him. "To you, perhaps not. To me, it is very important. If I had wished to be some man's property, I could have wedded someone before I was out of childhood, and would never have gone to the Tower." She took the matrix in her hand; but Kerwin saw the tentative way in which she touched it, contrasting her hesitation with the sureness she had shown in the matrix chamber. She was frightened! He wanted to tell her he didn't give a damn, put it away, he didn't want her to touch the accursed thing—she was too precious to risk—and then he saw her eyes.

Elorie loved him. She had given up her whole world for him, all she was and all she could have been. Even now, Kerwin knew, he had only the dimmest, outsider's perception of what it meant to be a Keeper. If she needed this, he had to let her try. Even if it killed her, he had to let her try.

"But promise me, Elorie," he said, taking her shoulders in his hands and tipping her head back to look into her eyes, "no risks. If it doesn't feel right, don't try."

He felt that she hardly heard him. Her slight fingers curved around the matrix; her face was distant and abstracted. She said, not to him, "The shape of the air here is different, we are among the mountains; I must be careful not to interfere with his breathing." She moved her head, an imperious small signal, and he felt her drop into rapport; intangibly, like a caress.

I don't know how long I can hold it, when there are Terrans around, but I will try. There. Jeff, look in the mirror.

He rose and looked into the mirror. He could see Elorie perfectly well, in her thin grey dress, her bright hair bent over the matrix in her hand; but he could not see himself. He looked down; he could see himself perfectly well, but he did not reflect in the mirror.

"But, but, I can see myself—"

"Oh, yes, and if anyone bumps into you, they will know perfectly well that you are there," she said with a sting of a smile. "You have not become a ghost, my love of a barbarian, I have only changed the look of the air around you, for a little while. But I think it will hold long enough for you to get into the orphanage unseen."

Her face held the triumph of a gleeful child. Jeff bent down to kiss her and saw the strangeness in the mirror, Elorie evidently lifted up and resting on nothing. He smiled. It was not a difficult matrix operation; he could probably have done it himself. But it had proved to her . . .

"That I'm not blind and deaf to it," she said, picking up his thought, and her voice sounded tight, though she was still smiling the childish smile. "Go, darling, I'm not sure how long I can hold it, and you shouldn't waste any time."

He left her there in the Terran hotel room, passing silently and unseen down the corridors. In the lobby people passed him, unseeing. He had a curious, lunatic sense of power. No wonder the Comyn were all but invincible—

But at what cost? Girls like Elorie, giving up their lives. . .

The Spacemen's Orphanage looked just as it had looked a few scant months ago. A few of the boys were doing something to the grounds, kneeling around a patch of flowers, supervised by an older boy with a badge on his arm. Silent as a ghost, Kerwin hesitated before walking up the white steps. What should he do first? Go unseen into the office, check files and records? Quickly he dismissed that notion; he might be invisible, but if he started handling books or punching buttons, the people in the office would see *something* even if it was only books and papers moving of their own accord; and sooner or later they'd start investigating.

And sooner or later someone would bump into him.

He stopped and considered. In the third-floor dormitory where he had slept with five other boys, he had carved his initials, at the age of nine, into a window-frame. The frame might have been repaired or replaced; but if it hadn't, and he could find the carving, it would prove something, to his own satisfaction; at least he wouldn't have to carry around the sneaking suspicion that he never *had* been there, that he had imagined the whole thing, that all his memories were hallucinations.

And after all, the dormitory was an old one and many of the boys had done the same thing. The Darkovan nurses and the children's counselors had left them a good deal of freedom in some areas. In his day the dormitory had been battered, orderly and clean enough, but bearing the imprint of many childish pranks and experiments with tools.

He went up through the halls, passing an open classroom door, trying to tread lightly, but two or three heads turned as he passed. *So they heard someone walking in the halls, so what?* Nevertheless, he rose on tiptoe and tried to make as little noise as possible.

A Darkovan woman, hair coiled low on her neck and fastened with a leather butterfly-clasp, her long tartan skirt and shawl faintly scented with incense, went along the hall, singing softly to herself. She went into one of the rooms and came out with a sleepy toddler cradled in her arms. Kerwin froze automatically, even though he knew himself invisible, and the woman seemed unconscious of him, still humming her mountain song.

"Laszlo, Laszlo, dors di ma main . . ."

Kerwin had heard the song of his own childhood, a silly rhyme about a little boy whose foster-mother stuffed him with cakes and sweets until he cried for bread and milk; he remembered, once, being told that the song went back to the historical period called the time of the Hundred Kingdoms, and the Hastur Wars that had ended them, and that the verses were a political satire about over-benevolent governments.

Kerwin drew aside as the woman passed him, feeling the rustle of her garments; but as they passed each other, she frowned curiously, and broke off her song; had she heard his breathing, smelled some unfamiliar scent from his clothing?

"Laszlo, Laszlo . . ." she began to croon her little song again, but the child in her arms twisted, turning his face over the woman's shoulder, looking straight at Kerwin. He said something in baby-talk, thrusting one chubby fist at Kerwin, and the nurse frowned, turning.

"What man? There's nobody there, *chiy'llu*," she scolded softly, and Kerwin turned and tiptoed down the hallway, his heart suddenly pounding. Could a child's eyes penetrate Elorie's illusion?

He paused at the top of the stairs, trying to get his bearings. Finally he turned toward what he thought was the right room.

It was quiet and sunlit, eight small, neatly-made cots in little cubicles around the edges of the room, and in the open play space between, a group of toy figures, men and buildings and spaceships, was arranged on a small table. Carefully stepping around the toys, he saw that a tall white skyscraper had been built at the center of the toy group, and sighed; the children had built the Terran HQ that loomed so large in their thoughts.

He was wasting time. He moved to the windows and moved his fingers along the molding at eye-level. No, there were no carvings . . . suddenly he realized what he was doing. Yes, he had carved his initials at eye-level, but the eye-level of a nine-year-old boy, not his present two meters and more!

He stooped and felt again at mid-level. Yes, there were carvings in the soft wood; rough crosses, hearts, tick-tack-toe crosses. And then, at the left, in the squarish letters of Terran Standard alphabet, he saw the childish work of his first pocketknife.

J. A. K. JR

Not until he saw the initials did he realize that he was shaking. His fists were clenched so hard that his nails hurt his palms. He did not realize, until now, that he had ever doubted finding them; but now, as he touched the childish, rude gouges in the wood, he knew that he had doubted his own sanity and that the doubt had gone deep.

"They lied, they lied," he said aloud.

"Who lied?" asked a quiet voice. "And why?"

Kerwin turned quickly toward the door. A short, sturdy, grey-haired man was standing there, looking straight at him. So Elorie's illusion had worn off; he had been seen, and heard—and found.

Now what?

Chapter Fifteen:
Through the Barrier

The man's eyes, intelligent and kindly, rested on Kerwin without anger. "We never allow visitors in the dormitories," he said. "If you wanted to see a particular child, you should have asked to see him in the playroom." His eyes narrowed suddenly. "But I know your face," he said. "Your name is Jeff, isn't it? Kerradine, Kermit—"

"Kerwin," he said, and the man nodded.

"Yes, of course; we called you *Tallo*. What are you doing here, young Kerwin?"

Abruptly, Kerwin decided to tell the truth. "Looking for my initials, carved here," he said.

"Now why would you want to do that? Sentiment? Old times sake?"

"Not a bit of it. A few months ago I came here," Kerwin said, "and they told me in the office that there were no records of my ever having been here, no records of my parentage—that I was lying when I claimed to remember being brought up here. I don't blame the matron—she evidently was since my time —but when the computer showed no records of my fingerprints—well, I started doubting my own sanity." He pointed to the carved initials. "I'm sane, anyhow. I cut those initials here when I was a kid."

"Now why would that happen?" the man demanded. "Oh, I forgot—I don't suppose you remember my name; I'm Jon Harley. I used to teach mathematics to the older boys. Still do, as far as that goes."

Jeff clasped the hand the man held out to him. "I remember you, sir. You stopped a fight I got into once, and bandaged up my chin afterward, didn't you?"

Harley chuckled. "I remember that, all right. You were a young rowdy, right enough. I remember when your father brought you to us. You were about five, I think."

Had his father lived so long? I ought to remember him, then, thought Kerwin, but try as he might there was only the elusive blank space in his memory, fragmentary memories of dreams.

"Did you know my father, sir?"

The man said, regretfully, "I saw him only that once, you know, when he brought you here. But, for goodness sake, young Kerwin, come downstairs and have a drink or something. Computers do get out of order, sometimes, I suppose; perhaps we should check the written files and school records."

Kerwin realized that he should have waited, demanded, tried to see someone who would actually *remember* him. Like Mr. Harley. "Is there anyone else still here who could remember me?"

Harley thought it over. "I don't think so," he said. "It's been a long time, and there's a considerable turnover. Some of the maids, perhaps, but I think I'm the only teacher who would remember you. Most of the nurses and teachers are young; we try to keep them young, children need young people about them. I go on and on, old fellow that I am, because it's hard to get good teachers to come out from Terra, and they want someone who speaks the language without accent." He said, with a deprecating shrug,

"Come down to my office, young Jeff. Tell me what you're doing these days. I remember you were sent to Terra. Tell me how you happened to come back to Darkover."

In the old man's austere office, filled with the open-window noises of children playing outside, Jeff accepted a drink he didn't want, fighting unspoken questions to which, he supposed, old Harley wouldn't have the answer.

"You say you remember my father bringing me here. My mother—was she with him?"

Harley shook his head. "He said nothing about having a wife," he said, almost prissily.

But, Kerwin thought, he had acknowledged his son, and that wasn't easy under Terran Empire laws. "What was my father like?"

"As I say, I saw him only once, and it wasn't easy to tell what he looked like. His nose had been broken, and he'd been in some kind of fight; there was a lot of rioting in Thendara about then; some political upheaval. I never knew the details. He was wearing Darkovan clothing; but he had his Terran identifications. We asked you questions about your mother, but you couldn't talk."

"At *five years old*?"

"You didn't talk for another year or so," Harley said, frankly. "To be truthful, we thought you were mentally deficient. That's one reason I remember you so well; because we all spent a lot of time trying to teach you to talk; we had a speech therapist come from Thendara HQ to work with you. You didn't speak a word, either in Terran *or* Darkovan."

Kerwin listened in amazement as the old man talked on.

"Kerwin—your father—finished up all the formalities for having you admitted here that night," he

said. "Then he went away and we never saw him
again. We were fairly curious, because you didn't
look at all like him, and of course you had red hair;
and that same week we had taken in another little
red-headed fellow, a year or so younger than you."

Kerwin said, with sudden curiosity, "Was his
name—Auster?"

Harley frowned. "I don't know; he was in the
younger division and I never saw much of him,
though I know he had a Darkovan name. He was
only here for a year or so, and that's very odd too. He
was kidnapped and all his records stolen at the same
time . . . well, I'm talking too much. I'm an old man
and it's nothing to do with you. Why do you ask?"

"Because," Kerwin said slowly, "I think perhaps I
know him."

"His records aren't here; as I said, they were stolen, but there's the record of the kidnapping,"
Harley said. "Shall I look it up?"

"No, don't bother." Auster was nothing to do with
him now; whatever the curious story, and both Kennard and Harley had called it odd, he would never
know. It was unlikely that he would have been listed
here as *Auster Ridenow*, in any case. Perhaps Auster
too was born of two of the Comyn traitors, who had
fled with the renegade Cleindori and her Terran lover. Did it matter? He had been brought up among
the Comyn and he had inherited all their powers and
he had gone to Arilinn at the appointed time. And
he, Kerwin, brought up on Terra, had gone to
Arilinn and he had betrayed them. . . .

But he wouldn't think of that now. He thanked
Harley, refused another drink, submitted to being
shown around the new playground and dormitory
buildings, and finally took his leave, filled with new

questions to replace the old ones.

Where and how had Cleindori died?

How and why had the elder Jeff Kerwin, his nose broken, bruised and battered after a terrible fight, brought their son to the Spaceman's Orphanage?

And where had he gone after that, and where and how had he died? For surely he had died; if he had lived, surely, surely, he would have reclaimed his son.

And why had Jeff Kerwin's son, at five years old, been unable to speak a word in either of his parents' languages, for more than a year?

And why had Jeff Kerwin, grown, no memory of mother or father, no memory at all except the curious half-memories of dreams—walls, arches, doors, a man who strode proudly, cloaked, through a castle corridor, a woman bending over a matrix, taking it up with a gesture that remained when all the rest of his memory had blurred . . . a child's scream . . .

Shuddering, he cut off the half-formed memory. He had found out a part of what he wanted to know, and Elorie would be waiting to know what had happened.

When he got back, she was asleep, flung across the bed in exhaustion, grey smudges under her long-lashed eyes; but she sat up as he came in, and put up her face to be kissed.

"Jeff, I'm sorry, I held it as long as I could . . ."

"It's all right."

"What did you find out?"

He hesitated, not sure he should tell her. Would the questions surging in him raise disquiet in her? What did she know of Cleindori, except that she had been taught to despise the "renegade"?

Her hand closed over his. "What would really hurt

me," she said, "would be if you refused to share these things with me. As for Cleindori . . . how can I look down on her? She did only what I have done; and now I know why." Her smile made Kerwin feel that his heart would break. "Don't you know that *Elorie of Arilinn* will be written beside Ysabet of Dalereuth and Dorilys of Arilinn as renegade Keepers, who fled without giving back their oath or asking leave?" He had forgotten that Cleindori had been only his mother's nickname, not her real name; at Arilinn she was written as *Dorilys*.

He sat down close beside her, then, and told her everything; all that had happened since his first moment on Darkover, when he had encountered Ragan and learned what his matrix was, the frustration of his first visit to the orphanage, the matrix mechanics who had refused to help him and the old woman who had died trying to help; and then all the rest, including what Harley had told him.

"And time's running out," he concluded. "I ought to face facts; it's not likely that I'll ever find out any more. As soon as the report I put in at the spaceport HQ goes through, I'll probably have to face charges and perhaps a civil inquiry. But there it is; the story of my life, for what it's worth, Elorie. You've married a man without a country, darling."

As if in answer, the communicator in the corner of the room sounded and when he picked it up, a metallic mechanical voice said, "Jefferson Andrew Kerwin?"

"Speaking."

"Coordination and Personnel," said the mechanical recorded voice. "We are informed that you are within the Terran Zone, where a civil charge has been placed against you of unlawful flight to avoid deportation. You are hereby notified that the City

Council of Thendara, acting in the name and with
the authority of Comyn Council on a warrant signed
by Danvan, Lord Hastur, Regent for Derek of
Elhalyn, has declared you persona non grata. You
are officially forbidden to leave the Terran Zone; and
since proceedings have been instituted to declare
your wife, Elorie Ardais Kerwin, a citizen of the Empire, this prohibition applies also to Mrs. Kerwin.
This is an official order; you are forbidden to travel
more than two Universal Kilometers from your present accommodations, or to leave them for more than
two hours; and within fifty-two hours you are ordered to surrender yourself to the appropriate authorities, which may be accomplished by presenting
yourself, with identification, to any member of
Spaceforce in uniform, or to any employee of Coordination and Personnel. Do you understand the communication? Please acknowledge."

Jeff muttered, "Damn!"

The mechanical voice repeated patiently, "Please
acknowledge," and waited.

Elorie whispered, "Do your Terran officials all
talk like that?"

"Please acknowledge," the mechanical voice repeated a third time, and Jeff muttered, "Acknowledged." Turning from the communicator, he
murmured, "Do we want to fight this, darling?"

"Jeff, how would I know? I'll abide by your decision. Do what you think best, love."

The mechanical voice was proceeding steadily.
"Kindly indicate whether you will accept the sum-
mons and surrender within the time indicated, or
whether you elect to file a legal request for an appeal."

Jeff's mind was racing. It went against the grain to
accept the deportation order calmly. An appeal

would give him a tenday's automatic delay, and perhaps in that time he might discover something further. He was resigned to leaving Darkover; but if he acted as if he might make trouble, they might offer him a better post when he was finally forced to transfer.

"I request an appeal," he said at last, and the silence from the communicator made him think of computers racing, selecting the appropriate loop for communicating further.

"Kindly indicate the nature of your appeal and the legal grounds on which you attempt to file the appeal," the voice said, and Kerwin thought quickly. He was not a legal expert. "I claim Darkovan citizenship," he said at last, "and I appeal their right to declare me *persona non grata*."

It probably wouldn't do any good, he thought while the communicator's patient taped voice repeated his words. But he wasn't sure whether this was the old declaration of *persona non grata* after which he had fled from the HQ, or a new one, filed against him since he had left Arilinn. He didn't think the Arilinn Tower could have reached Hastur yet and persuaded him to issue a new order so quickly. Anyhow, this would gain time. But if they had, not a soul on Darkover would stand between him and legal deportation.

Kennard might help . . . if he could reach Kennard. But Kennard was in Arilinn, a long way from here. And however he might sympathize with them, he was bound by his oath to Arilinn.

And none of the questions would ever be answered. He would never know who Cleindori had been, or why she had died, or why she had left Arilinn. He would never know the secrets of his own childhood.

Elorie rose and came to him. She said, "I could—perhaps—get through the barrier in your memory with this, Jeff. Kennard said you had a fantastic degree of barrier; that was why he didn't spot the block in your mind at first. Only—Jeff, why do you want to know? We're done with the Comyn, and probably leaving Darkover forever. What does it matter, then? The past is past."

For a moment he was not sure how to answer. Then he said, "Elorie, all my life I've had this—this fantastic compulsion to get back to Darkover. It was an obsession, a hunger; I could have made a life for myself on other worlds, but Darkover was always at the back of my mind. Calling me. Now I begin to wonder if it was really me—or if the pushing-around really started way back during the time I can't remember anything."

He did not go on, but he knew Elorie followed his thoughts. If his hunger for Darkover was not real, but a compulsion implanted from outside, then what was he? A hollow man, a tool, a mindless booby trap, a programmed thing no more real than the mechanical taped voice of the communicator. What was reality? Who and what was he?

She nodded gravely, understanding. "I'll try, then," she promised. "Later. Not now. I'm still tired from the illusion. And—" she smiled faintly—"hungry. Can we get anything to eat in this hotel or near it, Jeff?"

Remembering the dreadful drain of matrix work, he took her to one of the spaceport cafés, where she ate one of her enormous meals. They walked about the Terran Zone for a little, and Jeff made a gesture at showing her some of the sights of the Zone, but he knew that she cared no more than he did.

Neither of them spoke of Arilinn, but Jeff knew

that her thoughts, like his, kept returning there. What would this failure mean to Darkover, to the Comyn?

They had located and clarified the mineral deposits in the contract; but the actual work of mining was still to be done, the major operation of lifting them to the surface of the planet.

Elorie said once, as if at random, "They can work it with a mechanic's circle. Rannirl can do most of the work with the energons. Any halfway good technician can do most of a Keeper's work. They don't need me." And at another time, apropos of nothing at all, she said, "They still have all the molecular models we made, and the lattice is still workable. They ought to be able to handle it."

Jeff pulled her to him. "Regretting?"

"Never." Her eyes met his honestly. "But—oh, wishing it could have happened another way."

He had destroyed them. He had come back to the world he loved, and he had destroyed its last chance to remain as it was.

Later, when she took the matrix between her hands, he was filled with sudden misgiving. He recalled the matrix mechanic who had died in trying to read his memory. "Elorie, I'd rather never know, than risk harming you!"

She shook her head. "I was trained at Arilinn; I risk nothing," she said with unconscious arrogance. She cupped the matrix between her two hands, brightening the moving points of light. Her ruddy hair fell like a soft curtain along either cheek.

Kerwin was feeling frightened. The breaking of a telepathic barrier—he remembered Kennard's attempt—was not an easy process, and the first attempt had been painful.

The light in the crystal brightened, seemed to pour in a thick flood over Elorie's face. Kerwin shaded his eyes from the light, but he was caught in the brilliant, reflecting patterns. And suddenly, as if printed plain before his eyes, the light thickened and darkened into moving shadows that suddenly cleared into color and form. . . .

Two men and two women, all of them in Darkovan clothing, seated around a table. One of the women, very frail, very fair, bending over a matrix . . . *he had seen this before!* He froze, terror clawing at him, as the door opened, slowly, slowly . . . on horror . . .

He heard his own cry, shrill and terrified, the shriek of a frightened child from the full throat of a man, just in the moment before the world blurred and went dark.

. . . He was standing, swaying, both hands gripping at his temples. Elorie, very white, was staring up at him, the crystal fallen into the lap of her skirt.

"Jeff, what did you see?" she whispered. "Avarra and Evanda guard you, I never dreamed of such a shock!" She breathed deeply. "I know now why the woman died! She . . ." Elorie swayed suddenly, fell back against the wall. Jeff moved to steady her, but she went on, not noticing. "Whatever she saw—and I'm not an empath, but whatever it was that struck you dumb as a child, that poor woman evidently caught the full backlash of it. If she had a weak heart, it probably stopped, literally frightened to death by something you saw more than a quarter of a century ago!"

Jeff took her hands. He said, "Let's forget it. It's too dangerous, Elorie, it's killed one woman already. I can live without knowing whatever it is."

"No," she said. "I think we have to know. There

have been too many mysteries. No one knows how Cleindori died, and Kennard knows but has been sworn not to tell. I don't think he killed her," she went on, and Kerwin stared at her in shock; *that* had never occurred to him.

"No. I'd stake my life on Kennard's honesty." And, Kerwin thought, his very genuine affection for them both.

"I'm a trained Keeper, Jeff, there's no danger for me. And I'm as eager to know as you are. But wait, give me *your* matrix," she added. "It was Cleindori's. And let's start with something else. You said that you had only a very few memories before the orphanage; let's try and go back to them."

She looked into Kerwin's matrix; as always when it was in a Keeper's hands, Jeff felt only the faint threading of Elorie's consciousness through his own. He shut his eyes, remembering.

The light in the matrix brightened. There were colors, swirls like mist; there was a blue beacon shining somewhere, a low building gleaming white on the shores of a strange lake that was not water, a ghost of perfume; a low and musical voice singing an old song, and Kerwin knew, with a thrill of excitement, that the voice was the voice of his mother, Cleindori, Dorilys of Arilinn, renegade Keeper, singing a lullaby to the child who should never have been born.

Wrapped in a cloak of fur, he was carried through long corridors in the arms of a man with blazing red hair. It was not the face of Jefferson Kerwin, familiar to him from pictures on Terra; but Kerwin knew, in the strange alienated corner of his mind that was his adult self, that he looked on the face of his father. *But whose son am I, then?* He saw, briefly and in a glimpse, the face of Kennard, younger, unlined, a gay and light-hearted face. Other pictures came and went; he saw himself playing games in a tiled courtyard among flowering plants and bushes, with two smaller children, as alike as twins, except that one had the red hair of their caste, like his own, and the other was small and dark and swarthy. And there was a big burly man in strange dark clothing, who spoke to them in a strangely accented voice, and treated them all with rough kindness, and the twins called him father, and Jeff called him by a word very like it, which meant, in the mountain tongue, foster-father or Uncle; as he called Kennard; and the grown-up Jeff Kerwin felt the hair rising on his head as he knew that he looked on the face of the man whose name he bore; he was not like his pictures in the household of his grandparents, but this was the elder Jeff Kerwin. More hazy were the memories of the fair-haired woman, more blonde than copper-haired, and of another woman whose hair was dark with red glints in the sunlight, and of the hills behind the castle, sharp-toothed mountains, and an old high tower . . .

But that is Castle Ardais, that is my home . . . How did you come to be there, Jeff? Kennard and my half-brother Dyan were bredin, *they were much together in childhood. . . . And you were brought up in the Hellers, then? And that is the wall of Castle Storn. . . .*

How did you come to be reared in the Hellers, beyond the Seven Domains, then? Did Cleindori take refuge there, then, when she fled the Tower? What does my brother Dyan know of this, I wonder? Or was it only that my father was mad, and could not betray them all?

The memories moved on. Kerwin realized that his breath choked in his throat, that he was approaching the point of peril; he felt his own blood pounding in his ears. Suddenly there was a blaze of blue light, and a woman stood before him; a tall woman, slender and youthful, but no longer young; and he

knew he looked on his mother. Why had he never
been able to remember her face before this moment?
She was wearing a curiously-cut crimson robe, the
robe Elorie had cast aside forever, the ceremonial
robe of a Keeper of Arilinn; but even as he looked on
her it shredded and disappeared, to leave her standing before him in the old, workaday tartan skirt and
white embroidered tunic embroidered in a pattern of
butterflies that she wore every day; he could remember the very texture of the cloth.

Why did not Elorie see her? "Mother," he said in
a whisper, "I thought you were dead." And he knew
his voice as a child's voice. And then he knew she was
not there, that it was her image he saw; the image of
a woman many, many years dead; and he felt the
tears coming into his throat and choking him, tears
he knew he had never been able to shed before.

*My mother. And she died, horribly, murdered by
fanatics. . . .*

But he heard her voice, distracted, desperate, sor-
rowing.

*How can I do this to my child? My son, my little one, he
is too young to bear such a weight, too young for the matrix,
and yet . . . twice now I have so narrowly escaped death, and
soon or late, they will have me and kill me, those fanatics who
believe a Keeper's virginity is more important than her
powers! Even when I have shown them what I can do. . . .*

And another voice, a man's voice deep and gentle,
sounded in his mind: *Did you expect anything else of
Arilinn, my Cleindori?* And somehow through his
mother's memory and perceptions, Kerwin saw, as a
child and as a man, with a strange double vision, the
face of the speaker—an old man, stooped with age,
with a remote, scholarly face, his hair silver-grey, his
eyes remarkably kind—but bitter. *They cast Callista
forth, though I showed them what you tried to show them.*

Father, are all the folk of Arilinn such fools? It was a cry of despair. *Look, here is my son, your namesake, Damon Aillard; and they will not stop at killing me, and Lewis, and Cassilde; they will kill Jeff and Andres and Kennard and all the rest of us, down to Cassilde's little boys and the daughter she will bear to Jeff this summer! Father, father, what can I do? Have I brought death upon them all? I never meant any harm, I would have given them new laws, I would have cast down the cruel old laws of Arilinn, so that the women there might live in happiness, that the men and women of Arilinn might not give themselves up to a living death; and they would not listen, even though the Keeper of Arilinn spoke! The Law of Arilinn is that the Keeper's word is law; and yet when I would have given them this new dispensation, they would not hear me, and persecuted me, and Lewis, until we fled. . . . Father, father, how could I have been so wrong? And now they have killed my son's father and I know they will not stop until they have killed every last child of the Forbidden Tower! Is there no way I can save them?*

Kerwin shared, for a searing moment, the thoughts of Damon Ridenow; all of them, everyone who had worked within the walls of what they still called, defiantly, the Forbidden Tower, had drawn a death sentence, which sooner or later would fall upon them all.

He felt the despair with which Damon spoke.

There is no way to use reason with fanatics, Cleindori. Reason and justice tell you that a Keeper is responsible to her own conscience; but they are immune to reason and justice. You are not the matrix worker; it is not as a matrix worker that they want you in Arilinn for Keeper, but what they want in Arilinn is a sacred virgin, a sacrifice to their own guilts and fears. I do not think the forces of reason have any weight against fanatics and blind superstition, Cleindori.

Father, you reared me to believe in reason!

I was wrong. Oh, my darling, I was wrong.

And then he heard the resolution.

I could hide here forever, and be safe, or hide among the Terrans. But if I must die, and I know now that soon or late I must die, I will go to Thendara, and I will teach others the work I have learned can be done. You have taught many matrix workers. I will teach others. They can kill me, then, but they cannot forever hide what I have learned, and what I have taught. There will be matrix workers outside the Tower; and when the Arilinn Tower comes crashing down in the ruins of its hatred and the living death of the souls of the men and women who live there, blind to justice and right and truth, then there will be others, so that the old matrix sciences of Darkover will never die. Bid me farewell, Father, and bless my son. For I know now that we will never meet again.

They will kill you, Cleindori. Oh, my daughter, my golden bell, must I lose you too?

Soon or late, all men and women born of this earth must die. Bless me, father, and bless my son.

Kerwin, through his strange divided double consciousness, felt Damon's hand on his head. *Take my blessing, darling. And you, too, little one in whom my own name and my own childhood are reborn.* And then consciousness was swamped in the awareness of anguish, as father and daughter parted for the last time.

Kerwin, caught up in the memory, knew that tears were flooding down his face; but he was caught up in the matrix, caught up in the memory Cleindori had imprinted into her child; unwilling, for he was too young, but still knowing that some record must be kept, lest the knowledge of her death be forever hidden. . . .

Time had come and gone; he did not know how many days and nights he had lived in the hidden room, how many people had come and gone secretly to the house in Thendara where the work of teaching went on, led by Cleindori and the gentle woman he called foster-mother, whose name was Cassilde, the mother of Auster and Ragan, who were his playmates. She was, he knew vaguely as a child knows, soon to give them all a little sister. Already they called the unborn child Dorilys, which he knew was his own mother's name, for Cassilde said that was a fine name for a rebel. "And may she raise a storm over the Hellers as her namesake did in years gone by! For she will one day be our Keeper," Cassilde had promised. They had to play quietly, for no one must know that folk lived there, his mother said; and Jeff and Andres, coming and going from the spaceport, brought them food and clothing and whatever else they needed. Once he had asked why his foster-father Kennard was not with them.

"Because there are too many who could find him, Damon; he is trying to gain amnesty for us in Council, but it is long work, and he has not the ear of Hastur," his mother had replied, and he did not know what an amnesty was, but he knew it was very important, for his foster-father Arnad talked of nothing else. He never asked about his father; he knew vaguely that his father had gone away to fight, and that he would not come back. Valdir, Lord Alton, and Damon Ridenow, the old Regent of Alton, were fighting with the Council, and Jeff's child-mind wondered if they were fighting duels with swords and knives in the Council room and how many people they would have to fight before he and his mother and all of them could all go home again.

And then . . .

Jeff felt his heart pounding, the breath coming hard in his veins, and knew that the hour he could never remember, the terror that had blotted out mind and memory, was upon him. And suddenly, fighting the memory in terror, feeling Elorie's relentless will driving through the matrix, he *was* his own childish self, he was five years old, playing on the rug in the small, dark, cramped room, a little toy spaceship in his hands. . . .

. . . The tall man in Terran clothing stood up, letting the toy ship fall from his hands. The three of them began to squabble over it, but Jeff Kerwin silenced them with a gesture.

"Boys, boys—hush, hush, you must not make so much noise. . . You know better than that," he admonished in a whisper.

"It is hard to keep them so quiet," Cassilde said in a low voice. She was heavy, now, and clumsy, and Jeff Kerwin went and put her into a chair before he said, "I know. They ought not to be here; we should send them to safety."

"There is no safety for them!" Cassilde said, and sighed. The twins were playing, now, with the toy ship, but the child Damon, who was one day to be called Jeff Kerwin, knelt a little apart from them, his eyes fixed on his mother, standing behind the matrix in its cradle.

"Cleindori, I have told you what you should do," Kerwin said, and there was tenderness in his eyes. "I have offered to find safety for all of you with the Empire. You need not tell them more than you think they should know; but even for that much they will be more than grateful; they will send you and the children to safety on any world you choose."

"Am I to go into exile because fools and fanatics yell and shout slogans in the streets of Thendara?"

Cassilde said, cradling her hands over her pregnant body as if to protect the child that sheltered there, "Fools and fanatics can be more dangerous than the wise men. I am not afraid of Hastur, nor of the Council. And the people of Arilinn itself—they may despise us, but they will not harm us; no more than Leonie harmed Damon, after the duel that won him the right to keep the Forbidden Tower. But I am afraid of the fanatics, the conservatives who want everything, including Arilinn and Hali, to go as they were in the times of our grandsires. I cannot go to Terra, not until after my child is born; and the children are too young for star-travel. But I think you should go, Cleindori. Leave your child in the care of the Terrans, and go. I will ask shelter of the Council; and I am sure they will have me at Neskaya."

"Oh, Evanda and Avarra guard you," Cleindori said despairingly, looking at her half-sister. "I endanger you simply by remaining, do I not? You are not a Keeper, Cassie, and you can go where you will and live as you will, but it is I, I that am the renegade and under sentence of death, from the moment I stood before them and proclaimed that I had made fools of them all, that Lewis and I had been lovers for more than a year and yet I continued to work as Keeper in their precious Arilinn! Lewis—" her voice broke. "I loved him . . . and he died for my love! Kennard should hate me for it. And yet he continues to fight for me in the Council—"

Jeff said cynically, "The death of Lewis Lanart-Alton has made Kennard Heir to Alton, Cleindori."

"And yet you want me to beg for the protection of the Council, from Lord Hastur who has called me abominable things? Yet I will do it if you all ask me. Jeff? Cassie? Arnad?"

The tall man in the green-and-golden cloak came up behind Cleindori and put his arms around her, laughing. He said, "If any of us had any such thoughts we would be ashamed to show it before you, Golden Bell! But I think we must be realistic."

"Believe me," the Terran said, "I would rather defy them all, at least until the Council has made its decision. But I think Cassilde should go to Neskaya, or at least to Comyn Castle, until her child is born; no assassin can touch her there. The Council may disapprove of her, but they will protect her physically; she is under no sentence of death."

"Except," Cassilde said, "that I have borne children to the despised Terrans." Her mouth was wry.

Arnad said, "You are not the first; nor will you be the last. There have been intermarriages enough. No one, I think, cares, except the fanatics. And you, Cleindori, must go; leave your child with the Terrans, who will protect him—even in Comyn Castle, the child of a forsworn Keeper might not be safe from an assassin's knife, but the Terrans will protect him."

Cleindori's mouth quirked up in a smile. "And what would induce the Terrans to give refuge to the child of a renegade Keeper and the late Heir to Alton? What is he to them?"

"How are they to know he is not *my* son?" Kerwin asked. "The Terrans have none of your elaborate monitoring methods; the child calls me *foster-father*, and there are not enough language experts on Darkover to know the difference between the words. I am legally entitled to have my son reared in the Spacemen's Orphanage; even if I thought my child's mother unfit to rear him as befits the son of a Terran, they would accept him there." He came and touched Cleindori's shoulder, a gesture of great tenderness. "I beg you, *breda;* let me do this, and send you to Terra for a year or two on another world, until this fanaticism dies down, and then you can come back and teach, openly, what you teach secretly now. Already, Valdir and Damon managed to persuade the

City Elders to license matrix mechanics as a profession; and they are working in Thendara and Neskaya, and one day they will work in Arilinn too. The Council does not like it, but how runs the proverb . . . *the will of Hastur is the will of Hastur, but it is not the law of the land.* Let me do this for you, *breda.* Let me send you to Terra."

Cleindori lowered her head. "As you will, if you all think it best. You will go to Neskaya, then, Cassie? What of you, Arnad?"

"I'm tempted to go with you to Terra," the red-haired man in green and gold said defiantly, "but if you're going under Jeff's protection, it wouldn't be wise; I suppose he'll have to call you his wife?"

Cleindori shrugged. "What do I care what it says on the Terran records? They live in computers and believe that because their record says a thing it is true; what do I care?"

"I'll go now, to make the arrangements," Jeff said, "but are you all safe here? I'm not sure. . ."

Arnad said, with an arrogant gesture, dropping his hand to his sword, "I have this; I'll protect them!"

Time seemed to spin out and drag endlessly when he had gone. Cassilde put the twins to bed behind a curtained alcove; Arnad paced the floor restlessly, his hand straying now and then to his sword hilt. The child Damon knelt forgotten on the rug, motionless, waiting, filled with the apprehension of the adults around him. At last Cleindori said, "Jeff should be back by now—"

"Hush," Cassilde said urgently. "Did you hear— quiet; there is someone in the street?"

"I heard nothing," Cleindori said impatiently. "But I am afraid of what has happened to Jeff! Help me, Arnad."

She drew the matrix from her breast and laid it on

the table. The child tiptoed closer, staring in fascination. His mother had made him look into it so often, lately; she didn't know why, and Arnad said he was too young, that it could hurt him, but he knew that for some reason his mother wanted him able to handle and touch the matrix that no one else, not even his father, could ever touch, or any of his foster-fathers.

He moved closer, now, to the center of the glowing circle, reflected on the faces bending over the matrix; some slight sound distracted him; he turned to look, in growing terror, at the turning handle of the door. . . .

He shrieked and Arnad turned a moment too late; the door burst open and the room was full of hooded and masked forms; a deadly, thrown knife took him in the back and he fell with a gurgling cry. He heard Cassilde scream aloud and saw her fall. Cleindori bent and snatched up Arnad's knife, fighting and struggling with one of the masked men. The child ran, shrieking, struggling, pounding at the dark forms with small fists; biting, kicking, clawing like a small, enraged wild animal. Scratching and kicking, he ran right up the back of one of the men, sobbing wild threats.

"You let my mother alone—! Let her go, fight like a man, you coward—"

Cleindori shrieked and burst away from the man who held her. She caught up Damon to her breast, holding him tight, and he felt her terror like a physical agony reflected in a great blue glow like the glow of the matrix. . . . *There was one instant of blinding, blazing rapport, and the child knew, in agony, exactly what they had done, knew every instant of Cleindori's life, as her whole life flashed before her eyes. . . .*

The rough hands seized him; he was flung through the air and struck his head, hard, on the stone flooring. Pain exploded in him and he lay still, hearing a voice crying out as he went down into darkness:

"Say to the barbarian that he shall come no more to the plains of Arilinn! The Forbidden Tower is broken, and the last of its children lie dead, even to the unborn, and so shall we deal with all renegades until the last of days!"

Unbelievable, unbearable agony thrust a knife into his heart; then, mercifully, the rapport burned out, and the room went dark, and the world vanished into darkness. . . .

There was a pounding at the door. The child who lay unconscious on the floor stirred and moaned, probing, wondering if it was his foster-father, but felt only strangeness, seeing only darkness and strange men bursting again into the room. *They came back to kill me!* Memory flooded over him like a trapped rabbit and he clutched his small fingers over his mouth, squirming painfully under the table and cowering there. The pounding on the door increased; it broke open, and the terrified child, cowering under the table, heard heavy boots on the floor and felt shock in the minds of the men who stood holding a lamp high and looking at the carnage in the room.

"Avarra be merciful," a man's voice muttered, "we were too late, after all. Those murdering fanatics!"

"I told you we should have appealed directly to Lord Hastur before this, Cadet Ardais," said another voice, vaguely familiar to the child under the table, but he was afraid to move or cry out. "I was afraid it would come to this! Naotalba twist my feet, but I never guessed it would be murder!" A fist struck the table in impotent wrath.

"I should have known," the first voice said, a harsh, somehow musical voice, "when we heard that old Lord Damon was dead, and Dom Ann'dra, and the rest. A fire, they said . . . I wonder whose hand set that fire?" Before the despairing wrath in that voice the concealed child cowered, clasped his fingers harder over his mouth to stifle his cries.

"Lord Arnad," the voice said, "and the lady Cassilde, and she so heavy with child that you would think even one of those murdering fanatics would have had pity on her! And—" his voice fell—"my kinswoman Cleindori. Well, I knew she was under sentence of death, even from Arilinn; but I had hoped the Hasturs would protect her." A long, deep sigh. The child heard him moving around, heard the curtain drawn from the alcove. "In Zandru's name— children!"

"But where's the Terran?" one of the men asked. "Dragged away alive for torture, most likely. Those must be Cassilde's children by Arnad; look, one of them has red hair. At least those fanatic bastards had decency enough not to harm the poor brats."

"Most likely, they didn't see them," retorted the first man. "And if they find out they left them alive— well, you know what will happen as well as I do, Lord Dyan."

"You're right—the more shame to us all," said the man he had called Lord Dyan, frowning. "Gods! If we could only reach Kennard! But he isn't even in the city, is he?"

"No, he went to appeal to Hali," the first man said, and there was a long silence. Finally Lord Dyan said, "Kennard has a town house here in Thendara. If the Lady Caitlin is there—would she shelter them until Kennard returns and can appeal to Hastur on their behalf? You're Kennard's sworn man; you know the Lady Caitlin better than I do, Andres."

"I wouldn't ask any favors of the Lady Caitlin, Lord Dyan," Andres said slowly. "She grows more bitter as the years go by and she is more certain of her barrenness; she knows well that Kennard must one day put her aside and father sons somewhere, and any child we asked her to shelter for Kennard's sake—well, she would certainly think them bastards of Kennard's fathering, and lift no one of her fingers to protect them. Besides, if assassins broke into Kennard's town house, they might well slaughter the Lady Caitlin too—"

"Which would be no grief to Kennard, I think," said Lord Dyan, but Andres drew a breath of horror.

"Still, as Kennard's sworn man, Lord Dyan, I am pledged to safeguard her too; he may not love his wife, but he honors her as he must by law; and I dare not endanger her by the presence of these children. No, by your leave, Lord Dyan, I will take them to the Terrans and find shelter for them there. Then, when the memory of these riots has died down, Kennard can appeal to Hastur for amnesty for them. . . ."

"Quick," said Lord Dyan. "Someone's coming. Bring the children and keep them quiet. Here, wrap the little one in this blanket—there, now, little copper-hair, keep still." Damon crept to the edge of the table, hiding in shadow, and saw the two men, one in Terran clothing, the other in the green-and-black uniform of the City Guard, wrapping his playmates in blankets and carrying them away. The room went dark around him. . . .

Then there was a terrible cry of anguish and Jeff Kerwin stood in the room. He was swaying on his feet; his clothes were torn and cut, his face covered in blood. The child hiding under the table felt something break inside him, some terrible pain, he wanted to scream and scream, but he could only gasp, he thrust aside the tablecloth, staggered out into the room, and heard Kerwin's cry of dismay as he was caught up into his foster-father's strong arms.

He was wrapped warmly in a blanket; snow was falling on his face. He was wet through and in pain, and he could feel the pain of his foster-father's broken nose. He tried to speak and he could not make his voice obey him. After a long time of cold and jolting pain he was in a warm room, and gentle hands were spooning warm milk into his mouth. He opened his eyes and whimpered, looking into his foster-father's face.

"There, there, little one," said the woman who was feeding him. "Another spoonful, now, just a little one, there's my brave fellow—I don't think it's a skull fracture, Jeff; there's no bleeding within the skull; I monitored him. He's just bruised and battered, those lunatics must have thought him dead! Murdering devils, to try and kill a child of five!"

"They killed my little ones, and dragged their bodies away somewhere, probably flung them in the river," said his foster-father, and his eyes were terrible. "They'd have killed this one too, Magda, only they must have thought he was dead already. They killed Cassilde, and her unborn babe with her . . . fiends, fiends!"

The woman asked gently, "Did you see your mother die, Damon?" But although he knew she was speaking to him, he could not speak; he struggled to speak, in terror, but not a single word would come through the fear and dread. It felt as if a tight fist was holding his throat.

"Frightened out of his wits, I shouldn't wonder, if he saw them all die," Kerwin said bitterly. "God knows if he'll ever have all his wits again! He hasn't spoken a word, and he wet and soiled himself, big boy that he is, when I found him. My children dead, and Cleindori's son an idiot, and this is the harvest we reap for seven years' work!"

"It may not be as bad as that," the woman Magda said gently. "What will you do now, Jeff?"

"God knows. I wanted to keep away from the Terran authorities until we could make our own terms— Kennard and Andres and young Montray and I. You know what we were working for—to carry on what Damon and the rest had started."

"I know." The woman cradled him in her lap. "Little Damon here is all that's left of it; Cleindori's mother and I were *bredini,* sworn sisters, when we were girls . . . and now they are all gone. Why should I stay here?" Her eyes were bitter. "I know you tried, Jeff. I tried, too, to help Cleindori, but she wouldn't come to me. But she had agreed to go offworld—"

"And it was just a day too late," Kerwin said bitterly. "If only I had persuaded her a single day sooner!"

"There is no use in regretting," Magda said. "I would keep the child myself; but I could be transferred away from Darkover at any moment, and he is too young to travel on the Big Ships, even if drugged—"

"I'll take him to the Spacemen's Orphanage," Kerwin said. "I owe that to Cleindori, at least. And when I can manage to find Kennard—I think Andres is in the city, somewhere; I'll look for him and find out from him where Kennard has gone—then, perhaps, something can be done for him. But he will be safe with the Terrans."

The woman nodded, gently smoothed down Damon's aching head, drawing him against her for a final caress. Her hand tangled in the chain about his neck and she gave a cry of consternation.

"The matrix! Cleindori's matrix! Why didn't it die when she died, Jeff?"

"I don't know," Kerwin said. "But it was still alive. And though the boy didn't speak, he knew enough to grab for it. My guess is that she had let him play with it, touch it; it had keyed roughly into his consciousness and if he felt her die, through the matrix—well, it would account for the kid's state," he said bitterly. "It's safe enough where it is, round the neck of an idiot child. They won't be able to get it away without killing him. But they'll be kind to him. Maybe they can teach him something, sooner or later."

And then he was cold again, and he was held in his foster-father's arms, each step jolting his broken ribs, as he was carried through heavy rain and blowing sleet through the streets of Thendara. . . .

And then he was gone, he was nowhere, nothing. . . .

He was standing, white and shaken, tears on his face, in his room in the hotel in Thendara, still shaking with a child's terror. Elorie was staring up at him. She was crying, too. Jeff struggled to speak, but his voice would not obey him. Of course not, he could not speak a word . . . *he would never speak again.* . . .

"Jeff," Elorie said quickly. "You are here. Jeff—Jeff, come up to present time! *Come up to present time!* That was twenty-five years ago!"

Jeff put a hand to his throat. His voice was thick, but he could speak. "So that was it," he whispered. "I saw them all killed. Murdered. And—and I am not Jeff Kerwin. My name is Damon, and Kerwin was not my father; he was my father's friend. He befriended their child . . . but I am not Jeff Kerwin. *I'm not a Terran at all*!"

"No," Elorie said in a whisper. "Your father was Kennard's elder brother! By right you, not Kennard, are Heir to Alton—*and Kennard knows it!* You could displace Kennard's half-caste sons. Was that why he didn't speak up for you, at the last? He loves you. But he loves the sons of his second wife, his Terran wife, more than anything in the world. More than Arilinn. More, I think, than his own honor. . . ."

Jeff gave a short, hard laugh. "I'm a bastard," he said, "and the son of a renegade Keeper. I doubt if they'd want me as Heir to Alton, or anything else. Kennard can stop worrying. If he ever did."

"And then the final complication in this farrago of mistaken identity," Elorie said. "Cassilde's children were taken to the Spacemen's Orphanage—I know Kennard's man, Andres. But Lord Dyan—he is my half-brother, Jeff. I didn't know he knew Auster at all. But he must have known, and that is why he insisted on getting Auster from the orphanage; he must have thought he was Cassilde's child by Arnad Ridenow, because of his red hair."

"God help us all," Jeff said. "No wonder Auster thought he recognized Ragan! They're twin brothers! They don't look all that much alike, but they are twins—"

"And the Terrans used Ragan to spy upon the Comyn," Elorie said. "For the telepath bond between the twin-born is the strongest known! It was

Auster, not you, who was the time-bomb planted by the Terrans! They knew about the telepath link between twins. So they let them have Auster back—and kept Ragan, linked to him in mind, to spy on Auster. Even after he went to Arilinn!"

"And Jeff Kerwin took me to the Spacemen's Orphanage, and registered me there as his son," Jeff said. "And then—God knows; he must have been killed, too."

"Strange," Elorie said, "and sad, that when children were in danger, both factions should have realized that they'd be safer with the Terrans. Our laws of blood-feud are relentless; and the fanatics felt they must exterminate the Forbidden Tower even to the unborn children and the babies."

"I lived on Terra," Jeff said. "Most of them are good people. And it's true that they're a little less likely to drag children into adult affairs, or blame the sins of the fathers on the heads of the children."

He fell silent. Always, the knowledge that he was a Terran, an exile, had become part of his existence. And now, legally, he *was Terran;* and under sentence of deportation by the Terran Empire!

"But I'm not Terran," he said. "I'm no relation to Jeff Kerwin, I haven't any Terran blood at all. My name isn't even Kerwin; it's—what would it be?"

"Damon," she said. "Damon Aillard, since the child takes the name of the parent of higher rank, and the Aillard rank higher in the Comyn than the Altons; just as our children, if we ever had any, would be Ardais instead of Aillard. . . . Only if you married a Ridenow, or a commoner, would your children be Altons. But by Terran custom, you'd call yourself Damon Lanart-Alton, wouldn't you? They take the father's name, and you were brought up to that."

Her face suddenly whitened. "Jeff! We have to warn them at Arilinn!"

"I don't understand, Elorie."

"They may try the mining operation—though I think they'd be mad to try it without a Keeper—and Auster is still in mental link with Ragan, the spy— and doesn't know it!"

Cold struck at Jeff's heart. But he said, "My love, how can we warn them? Even if we owed them anything—and they cast us out, calling you filthy names —that's *there*, and we're *here*. Even if we could get out of the Terran Zone—and I'm under house arrest, remember—I doubt if we could *reach* Arilinn. Except, perhaps, telepathically; you can try that, if you want to."

She shook her head. "Reach Arilinn from Thendara, unaided? Not without one of the special relay screens," she said. "Not with my matrix alone. Not —" she hesitated, colored, and said—"not now. At one time—as Keeper of Arilinn—I might have done so. But not now."

"Then don't worry about them! Let them take their own risks!"

Elorie shook her head.

"Arilinn trained me; Arilinn made me what I am; I cannot stop caring what will happen to my circle," she said. "And there is a relay screen in Comyn Castle in Thendara. I could reach them through *that*."

"Fine," said Kerwin, with a sardonic smile. "I can just see it. You, the Keeper who was cast out of Arilinn, and I, the Terran under sentence of deportation, walking up to Comyn Castle and asking politely for the use of the relay screen there."

Elorie bent her head. "Don't be cruel, Jeff," she said. "I know, well enough, that we are under the ban. But Council will not meet till summer. No one will be resident in Comyn Castle at this season except the Regent, Lord Hastur. Lady Cassilda was my mother's friend. And my half-brother, Lord Dyan, is an officer in the City Guard. I think—I think he will help me to gain audience with Lord Hastur."

"If he's that good a friend to Kennard," Jeff said, "he'd probably be glad to see me dead."

"He loves Kennard, yes. But he does not approve of his second marriage, nor of his Terran wife nor his half-Terran sons; and you are pure Darkovan," Elorie said. "Dyan wanted to serve at Arilinn; the Comyn means much to him. He would have gone there with Kennard when they were lads, I heard, but he was tested, and found—unsuitable. I think— I hope I can prevail upon him for audience with Hastur." She added, her mouth tight, "If all else I will appeal to Lord Alton; Valdir Alton loved his older son, too, and you are, after all, his elder son's only son."

Jeff still could not take it in. Lord Alton, the old man who had embraced him as a kinsman, was actually his grandfather.

But it went against the grain for Elorie to go begging on his account. "Arilinn has turned against us. Forget them, Elorie!"

"Oh, Jeff, no," she begged. "Do you want the Pan-Darkovan Syndicate to turn to Terra, and Darkover to become no more than a second-rate Terran colony?"

And that touched him. Darkover had been his home, even when he thought himself a son of Terra and a citizen of the Empire. Now he knew himself *really* Darkovan; he had not a scrap of legal right to call himself Terran. He was Comyn through and through, a true son of the Domains.

"Can't you see? Oh, I know failure is almost certain, especially if they try it with a mechanic's circle with Rannirl in charge, or if they're mad enough to try it with a half-trained Keeper," she said. "And I'm afraid that's what they'll do. They'll bring little Callina from Neskaya, and make *her* try to hold the matrix ring; and she's only twelve years old or so. I've spoken to her in the relays. She's gifted, but she's not Arilinn-trained, and Neskaya doesn't have the tradition of great Keepers anyway; the best ones were always from Arilinn. But," she added, "now that they know you're not Terran, *you* could go back, and the circle would be that much stronger!" Her face was pale and eager. "Oh, Jeff, it means so much to our world!"

"Darling," he said, wrung, "I'd try anything. I'd even go back into the matrix circle, if they'd have me; but that notice I got says we're prisoners! If we try to go more than a kilometer from the hotel, they'll arrest us. Just because we're not behind bars doesn't mean I'm not under arrest. I can appeal against the deportation, and if I can prove I'm not Kerwin's son by blood I may be able to stay here, but for the moment we're as much prisoners as if we were in the brig!"

"What right have they—" The arrogance of the princess, the sheltered, pampered, worshipped Lady of Arilinn, was in her voice now. She caught up her hooded cape—Jeff had bought it for her in Port Chicago to conceal her red hair, which marked her out as Comyn—and flung it over her shoulders. "If you will not come with me, Jeff, I will go alone!"

"Elorie—you're serious about this?" Her eyes answered for her, and he made up his mind. "Then I'll come with you."

In the streets of Thendara she moved so swiftly he

could hardly keep up with her. It was late afternoon; the light lay blood-red along the streets and shadows crept, long and purple, between the houses. As they neared the edge of the Terran Zone, Kerwin wondered if this was insanity; they'd certainly be stopped at the gates. But Elorie moved so quickly that all he could do was to follow at her heels.

The great square was empty, and the gates of the Terran Zone were guarded desultorily by a single uniformed Spaceforce man. Across the square he could see little clusters of Darkovan restaurants and shops, including the one where he had bought his cloak. As they approached the gate, the Spaceforce man barred their way briefly.

"Sorry. I have to see your identification."

Kerwin started to speak, but Elorie prevented him; swiftly she flung back the grey hood over her red hair, and the light of the Bloody Sun, setting, turned it to fire, as Elorie sent a high, clear cry ringing across the square.

And all through the square Darkovans turned round, startled and shocked at what Kerwin knew, somehow, was an ancient rallying-cry; someone shouted "Hai! A Comyn *vai leronis,* and in the hands of the Terrans!"

Elorie seized Jeff's arm; the guard stepped forward, threatening, but a crowd was already materialized, as if by magic, all through the square; the sheer weight of it rolled over the Terran guard—Jeff knew they had orders not to fire on unarmed people—and Elorie and Jeff were borne along on it, a way opening for them through the crowd, with deferential cries and murmurs following them. Breathless, startled, Jeff found himself in the mouth of a street opening on the square; Elorie caught his hand and dragged him away down the street, the sounds of riot dying away behind them.

"Quick, Jeff! This way or they'll be all around us wanting to know what it's all about!"

He was startled, and a little shocked. There could be repercussions; the Terrans would not be happy about a riot right on their doorstep. But, after all, no one had been hurt. He would trust Elorie, as she had trusted him with her life.

"Where are we going?"

She pointed. High above the city, Comyn Castle rose, vast, alien and indifferent. Except for a few of the highest dignitaries, no Terran had ever set foot there; and then only by invitation.

Only he wasn't a Terran, and he would have to remember it.

Funny. Ten days ago that would have made me very happy. Now I'm not so sure.

He followed her through the darkening streets, the steep climb to Comyn Castle, wondering what would happen when they got there, and if Elorie had any specific plan. The Castle looked both big and well-guarded, and he didn't suppose that two strangers could walk in and ask to speak to Lord Hastur without any formalities or so much as an appointment!

But he had reckoned without the enormous personal prestige of the Comyn themselves. There were guards, in the green and black of the Altons who had, so Kerwin had heard from Kennard, founded the Guard and commanded it from time out of mind. But at the sight of Elorie, even afoot and humbly clad, the Guard fell back in reverence.

"*Comynara*—" The guard looked at Jeff's red head, then at his Terran clothes, but decided to play it safe and amended, "*Vai Comynari,* you lend us grace. How many we best serve the *vai domna?*"

"Is Commander Alton within the castle?"

"I regret, *vai domna,* the Lord Valdir is away at Armida these ten days."

Elorie frowned, but hesitated only a moment. "Then say to Captain Ardais that his sister, Elorie of Arilinn, would speak with him at once."

"At once, *vai domna.*" The guard still looked askance at Jeff's Terran clothes; but he did not question. He went.

Chapter Sixteen:
The Broken Tower

It was not more than a few minutes before the guard came back; and with him was a tall, spare man in dark clothing—Kerwin supposed he was somewhere in his forties, though he looked younger —with a keen, hawklike face.

"Elorie, *chiya*," he said, lifting his eyebrows, and Kerwin flinched. He had heard before that harsh, musical, and melancholy voice; heard it as a frightened child, battered and left to die, crouching unseen under a table. But after all, Dyan Ardais had meant him no harm; would have certainly, if he had been appealed to, taken him under his protection as he had taken those other children, overlooked by the assassins. He knew Elorie's brother for a harsh man, but kindly, even soft-hearted toward young children, cruel as he could be to his peers.

"I heard you had fled from Arilinn," he said, looking at her humble garments and coarse cloak with distaste, "and with a Terran. Sorrow upon Arilinn, that twice within forty years this must happen to them. Is this the Terran?"

"He is no Terran, my brother," she said, "but the true son of Lewis-Arnad Lanart-Alton, elder son of Valdir, Lord Alton, by Cleindori; who laid down her office, though unpermitted, by the laws of Arilinn, to take a consort of her own rank and station; and this is her son. A Keeper, Dyan, is responsible only to her own conscience. Cleindori did only what the law would have permitted; she is not responsible for those who denied the right of the Lady of Arilinn to declare just laws for her circle."

He looked at her, frowning. His eyes, Kerwin thought, were colorless as cold metal, grey steel. He said, "Some of this I had from Kennard, who tried to tell me of Cleindori's innocence; though I called it folly. Lewis, too, was a foolish idealist. But he was Kennard's brother; and I owe to his son a kinsman's dues." His thin lips moved into a sarcastic grin. "So we have here a rabbithorn in the fur of a catman; Comyn in Terran garb, which is a change after the ranks of spies and imposters we have had to face from time to time. Well, what did they name you, then, Cleindori's son? Lewis, for your father, and with a better right to that name than Kennard's bastard?"

Kerwin had the uncomfortable feeling that Dyan was amused—no, that he took a positive pleasure—in his discomfiture. In years to come, knowing Dyan better, he knew that Dyan seldom missed an opportunity to twist a knife of malice. He said sharply, "I am not ashamed of bearing the name of my Terran foster-father; it would hardly be honorable to disown him at this stage of my life; but my mother called me Damon."

Dyan threw back his head and laughed, a long shrill laugh like the screaming of a falcon. "The name of one renegade for another! I had never suspected that Cleindori had such a sense of the right thing," he said, when he had done laughing. "Well, what do you want from me. Elorie? I don't suppose you want to take your husband—" actually the word he used was *freemate;* if he had shaded the word to

make it mean *paramour,* Jeff would have struck him—
"to our mad father at Ardais?"

"I need to see Lord Hastur, Dyan. You can arrange it, as *seconde* for Valdir!"

"In the name of all nine of Zandru's hells, Lori!
Doesn't the Lord Danvan have enough troubles?
Will you bring down the shadow of the Forbidden
Tower on him again, after a quarter of a century?"

"I must see him," Elorie insisted, and her face
crumpled. "Dyan, I beg you. You were always kind
to me when I was a child; and my mother loved you.
You saved me from Father's drunken friends. I swear
to you—"

Dyan's mouth twisted and he said cruelly, "The
standard oath is, Elorie, *I swear it by the virginity of the
Keeper of Arilinn.* I doubt even you would have the insolence to take that oath now."

Elorie flared at him: "That is the kind of stupid
madness and fanaticism that has kept the Keepers of
Arilinn as ritual dolls, priestesses, sorceresses. I
thought better of you than to think you would throw
it at me! Do you want the Tower of Arilinn to be the
laughingstock of all our people, because they are
more concerned with a Keeper's virginity than her
powers as Keeper? You have a good mind, Dyan,
and you are not a fool or a fanatic! Dyan, I beg of
you," she said, her anger suddenly vanishing into seriousness. "I swear to you, by the memory of my
mother, who loved you when you were a motherless
boy, that I will not abuse the Lord Hastur's kindness, and that it is not a trivial or a frivolous request.
Won't you take me to him?"

His face softened. "As you will, *breda,*" he said
with unusual gentleness. "A Keeper of Arilinn is responsible only to her own conscience. I will show re-

spect to yours until I learn otherwise, little sister. Come with me. Hastur is in his presence-chamber, and he should be finished now with the last delegation for today."

He led them into the Castle, through broad corridors and into a long pillared passageway; Jeff stiffened, shaking, again a child, carried through this long corridor. *One of the strange and colorful dreams that had haunted him in the Spacemen's Orphanage. . . .*

Dyan ushered them into a small anteroom; gestured to them to wait. After a little while he came back, saying, "He'll see you. But Avarra protect you if you waste his time or try his patience, Lori, for I won't." He motioned them into a small presence-chamber, where Danvan Hastur sat on his high seat; bowed and went away.

Lord Hastur bowed to Elorie; his brows ridged briefly in displeasure as he saw Kerwin, but immediately the frown vanished; he was reserving judgment. He gave Kerwin the briefest possible polite nod of acknowledgment, and said, "Well, Elorie?"

"It is kind of you to see me, kinsman," Elorie said. Then, and Jeff could hear her voice shake, she said, "Or—don't you know—"

Danvan Hastur's voice was courteous and grave.

"Many, many years ago," he said, "I refused to listen when a kinsman begged for my understanding. And as result, Damon Ridenow and all his household were burned by a fire whose origin I refused to question, telling myself that it was the hand of the Gods that burned their household to cinders. And I stood by and raised no hand to help, and I have never felt guiltless of Cleindori's death. At the time I thought it the just vengeance of the Gods, even though I did not sanction, and I knew nothing of the fanatical assassins who had actually compassed her death. I thought, may all the Gods forgive me, that the breaking of the Forbidden Tower, cruel as the deaths were, would restore our land and our Towers to the old, righteous ways. Oh, I had no hand in any of the deaths, and if the murderers had come into my hands I would have delivered them into the hands of vengeance; but I did not stretch out my hand to prevent the murders, either, or to discredit the fanatics who were responsible for the death of so many of the Comyn whom we could spare so ill. I told myself, when she appealed to me, that Cleindori had forfeited all right to my protection. I don't intend to make that mistake twice; if I can prevent it, there will be no more deaths in Comyn. Nor will I visit the sins of men long dead on the heads of their descendants. What do you want from me, Elorie Ardais?"

"Now just a minute here," said Kerwin, before Elorie could open her mouth, "let's get one thing straight. I didn't come here to ask for anybody's protection. The Arilinn Tower threw me out, and when Elorie stuck by me, they threw her out too. But coming here wasn't my idea, and we don't need any favors."

Hastur blinked; then, over his stern and austere face, an unmistakable smile spread. "I stand reproved, son. Tell it your way."

"To start with," Elorie said, "he isn't a Terran. He isn't Jeff Kerwin's son." She explained what she had found out.

Hastur looked startled. He said softly, "Yes. Yes, I should have known. You have a look of the Altons; but Cleindori's father had Alton blood, and so I never thought anything of it." Gravely, he bowed to

Elorie. "I have done you a grave injustice," he said.
"Any Keeper may, at the promptings of her own conscience, lay down her holy office and take a consort of
her own rank and station. We wronged Cleindori;
and now we have wronged you. The status of your
Comyn husband shall be regularized, kinswoman;
may all your sons and daughters be gifted with
laran. . . ."

"Oh, the hell with that," Jeff said, in a sudden
rage. "I haven't changed one damn bit from what I
was four days ago, when they thought I wasn't good
enough for Elorie to spit on! So if I marry her while
they think I'm Jeff Kerwin, Junior, she's a bitch and
a whore, but if I marry her after I find my father was
one of your high-and-mighty Comyn, who couldn't
even be bothered to notify his family that I existed,
all of a sudden it's all right again—"

"Jeff, Jeff, *please*—" Elorie begged, and he heard
her frightened thoughts, *nobody dares speak like this to
the Lord Hastur*—

"I dare," he said curtly. "Tell him what you came
to tell him, Elorie, and then let's get the hell out of
this place! You married me thinking I was a Terran,
remember? I'm not ashamed of my name or the man
who gave it to me when my own father wasn't around
to protect me!"

He broke off, suddenly abashed before the old
man's steady blue eyes. Hastur smiled at him.

"There speaks the Alton pride—and the pride of
the Terrans, which is different, but very real," he
said. "Take pride in your Terran fostering as well as
your heritage of blood, my son; my words were to
ease Elorie's heart, not to cast disparagement on
your Terran foster-father. By all accounts he was a
good and brave man, and I would have saved his life

if I could. But now tell me, both of you, why you came here."

His face grew graver as he listened.

"I knew Auster had been in the hands of the Terrans," he said, "but it never occurred to me that they could use him in any way; he was so very young. Nor did I know that Cassilde had borne twins. We did the other child a grave injustice; and you say, Kerwin—" he stumbled a little over the name, making it nearer to the Darkovan name *Kieran*, "that he is embittered, and a Terran spy. Something must be done for him. Why, I wonder, did not Dyan tell me?"

Elorie said, shaking her head, "Dyan knew from Kennard something of the ways of the Forbidden Tower. The children were unlike; perhaps he thought one of them, being dark-haired and dark-eyed, was the son of the Terran; and he helped you only to reclaim the one he believed to be Arnad Ridenow's son."

"It is true that we acknowledged Auster as son to Arnad Ridenow," Hastur said. "He had the Ridenow gift; but he could have had it through Cassilde, who was Callista Lanart-Carr's daughter by Damon Ridenow." He shook his head with a sigh.

"The thing is, Lord Hastur," Jeff said, "that I thought *I* was the time-bomb the Terrans had planted; and it's Auster. *And he is still in the matrix circle at Arilinn!*"

"But he has *laran!* He grew up among us! He is Comyn!" Hastur said in dismay, and Kerwin shook his head.

"No. He is Jeff Kerwin's son," Kerwin said, "and I'm not." Auster, then, had been his foster-brother; they had played together as children. He did not like Auster; but he owed him loyalty. Yes, and love—for

Auster was the son of the man who had given him
name and place in the Terran Empire. Auster was
his brother, and more, his friend within the matrix
circle. He did not want Auster used to break the
Arilinn Tower.

"But—a Terran? In Arilinn?"

"He thought he was Comyn," Kerwin said, a
curious yeasting excitement boiling within him as he
began to understand. "He *believed* he was Comyn, he
expected to have *laran*—and so he had it, he never developed any mental block against believing in his
own psi powers!"

"But don't you see," Elorie interrupted. "We have
to warn them at Arilinn! They may try the mining
operation—and Auster is still linked to Ragan—and
it will fail!"

Hastur looked pale. "Yes," he said. "They sent
the little Keeper from Neskaya there—and they were
going to try it tonight."

"Tonight," Elorie gasped. "We've got to warn
them! It's their only chance!"

Kerwin's thoughts were bitter as they flew through
the night. Rain beat and battered at the little airship;
a strange young Comyn knelt in the front of the machine, controlling it, but Kerwin had neither eyes nor
thought for him.

They had tried to warn Arilinn through the relay
screen high in Comyn Castle; but Arilinn had already been taken out of the relay net. Neskaya Tower
had told them that they had closed the relays to
Arilinn three days ago, when they had sent for
Callina Lindir.

So he was going back to Arilinn. Going, after all,
to warn them, perhaps to save them—for there was

no question that this, the greatest of the Tower operations, was the primary target of the Terrans who wanted Arilinn to fail; fail, so that the Domains would fall into the hands of the Terran advisers, engineers, industrialists.

The young Comyn flying the ship had looked with reverence at Elorie when the name of Arilinn was spoken. It seemed that they all knew about the tremendous experiment at Arilinn, which might keep Darkover and the Domains out of the hands of the Terran Empire.

But it would fail. They were racing through the night to stop it before it started; but if they didn't do it at all, it would be default, and default would have the same weight as failure, which was why they were trying this desperate experiment with a half-trained Keeper. Either way, it meant the end of the Darkover they knew.

If only I had never come back to Darkover!

"Don't, Jeff," she said softly. "It's not fair to blame yourself."

But he did. If he had not come back, they might have found someone else to take the vacant place at Arilinn. And Auster, without Jeff to antagonize him, would perhaps have discovered the truth about the Terran spy. But now they were all bound to abide by the success or failure of this experiment; and if it failed—and it would fail—then they were all pledged, on the word of Hastur, to offer no more resistance to Terran industrialization, Terran trade, the Terran culture, the Terran way.

Without Kerwin to lend them this false confidence, the Terran's spying would have yielded only minor information.

Elorie's hand felt cold as ice in his. Without asking, Kerwin wrapped his fur-lined cloak around her, remembering against his will one of Johnny Eller's stories. He could shelter Elorie against physical cold in his Darkovan cloak; but now that he knew he had no more right to his Terran citizenship than to Arilinn, where could he take her?

She pointed through the window of the plane. "Arilinn," she said, "and there is the Tower." Then she drew a deep breath of consternation and despair; for, faintly around the Tower, he could see a bluish, flickering iridescence.

"We're too late," she whispered. "They've already started!

Chapter Seventeen:
The Conscience of a Keeper

Kerwin felt as if he were sleepwalking as they hurried across the airfield, Elorie moving dreamlike at his side. They had failed, then, and it was too late. He caught at her, saying, "It's too late! Accept it!" But she kept moving, and he would not let her go alone. They passed through the sparkling Veil, and Kerwin caught his breath at the impact of the tremendous, charged force that seemed to suffuse the entire Tower, radiating from that high room where the circle had formed. Incomplete, yes, but still holding incredible power. It beat in Kerwin like an extra heartbeat, and he felt Elorie, at his side, trembling.

Was this dangerous for her, now?

Swept on, dominated by her will and that mysterious force, Kerwin climbed the Tower. He stood outside the matrix chamber, sensing what lay within.

Auster's barrier was no more than a wall of mist to him. His body remained outside the room, but he was inside, too, and with senses beyond his physical eyes he touched them all: Taniquel, in the monitor's seat, Rannirl firmly holding the technician's visualization; Kennard bent over the maps; Corus in his own, Kerwin's place; and holding them together, on frail spiderweb strands, an unfamiliar touch, like pain. . . .

She was slight and frail, not yet out of childhood, yet she wore the robe of a Keeper, crimson, not the ceremonial robe but the loose hooded robe they all wore within the matrix chamber, her robe crimson, so that no one would touch her even by accident when she was carrying the load of the energons. She had dark hair like spun black glass, still braided like a child's along her face, and a small, triangular, plain face, pale and thin and trembling with effort.

She sensed his touch and looked puzzled, yet somehow she knew it was not intrusion, that he *belonged* here. Quickly Kerwin made the rounds of the circle again, Rannirl, Corus, Taniquel, Neyrissa, Kennard—Auster. . .

Auster. He sensed something, from outside the circle as he was, like a sticky, palpable black cord, extending outside the barrier; the line that chained them, kept the matrix circle from closing their ring of power. *The bond, the psychic bond between the twin-born, that bound Auster's twin without his knowledge to the fringes of the circle. . .*

Spy! Terran, spy! Auster had sensed his presence, turned viciously in his direction . . . though his body, immobile in the rapport, did not move . . . but the tension rippled the calm of the circle, came near to breaking.

"Spy and Terran. But not I, my brother!" Kerwin moved into the circle, fell into full rapport and projected into Auster's mind the full memory of that room where Cleindori, Arnad, Cassilde had been murdered, Cassilde struck down still bearing Auster's sister, who was never born . . .

Auster screamed noiselessly in anguish. But as the barrier around the circle dropped, Kerwin caught it up in his own telepathic touch; flashed round the

circle in a swift round, locking himself into it; and
with one swift, deliberate thrust, cut through the
black cord . . . (*sizzling, scorching, a bond severed*) and
broke the bond forever.

(Miles away, a swart little man who called himself
Ragan collapsed with a scream of agony, to lie senseless for hours, and wake with no knowledge of what
had happened. Days later, they found him and took
him to Neskaya, where, in the Tower, the psychic
wound was healed and Auster was ready, again, to
greet his unknown twin; but that came later.)

Auster's mind was reeling; Kerwin supported him
with a strong telepathic touch, dropping into deep
rapport.

Bring me into the circle!

There was a brief moment of dizzy timelessness as
he fell into the old rapport. A facet of the crystal, a
bodiless speck floating in a ring of light . . . then he
was one of them.

*Far down beneath the surface of the world lie those strange
substances, those atoms, molecules, ions known as minerals.
His touch had searched them out, through the crystal structure
in the matrix screen; now, atom by atom and molecule by
molecule, he had sifted them from impurities so that they lay
pure and molten in their rocky beds, and now the welded ring
of power was to lift them, through psychokinesis, molding the
circle into a great Hand that would bring them in streams to
the place prepared for them.*

They were poised, waiting, as the frail spiderweb
touch of the child-Keeper faltered, trying to grasp
them. Kerwin, deeply in rapport with Taniquel, felt
the monitor's despair as she felt the girl's wavering
touch.

No! It will kill her!

And then, as the welded circle faltered, ready to

dissolve, Kerwin felt again a familiar, secure, beloved touch.

Elorie! No! You cannot!

I am a Keeper, and responsible only to my own conscience. What matters? my ritual status, an old taboo that lost its meaning generations ago? Or my power to wield the energons, my skill as Keeper? Two women died so that I could be free to do this work I was born and trained to do. Cleindori proved it, even before she left Arilinn, she would have freed the Keepers from laws she had found to be pious frauds, meaningless and superstitious lies! They would not hear her; they drove her out to die! Now, with the Terrans waiting for us to fail, will you sacrifice the success of Arilinn for an old taboo? If you will, let Arilinn be broken, and let Darkover fall to the Terrans; but the blame is upon you, not me, my brothers and my sisters!

Then, with infinite gentleness (a steadying arm slipped around childish shoulders, a faltering and spilling cup held firmly in place), Elorie slid into the rapport, gently displacing the spiderweb-threads of the child-Keeper's touch with her own strong linkage, so gently that there was neither shock nor hurt.

Little sister, this weight is too strong for you. . . .

And the rapport locked suddenly into a closed ring within the crystal screen; the power flared, flowed . . . Kerwin was no longer a single person, he was not human at all, he was one with the circle, part of a tremendous, glowing, burning river of molten metal that surged upward, impelled by great throbbing power; it burst, spilled, flamed, engulfed them. . . .

Slowly, slowly, it cooled and hardened and lay inert again, awaiting the touch of those who had need of it, awaiting the tools and hands that would shape it into tools, energy, power, the life of a world.

One by one, the circle loosened and dissolved. Kerwin felt himself drop from the circle. Taniquel raised eyes, blazing with love and triumph, to welcome him back. Kennard, Rannirl, Corus, Neyrissa, they were all round him; Auster, deep shock in his cat's eyes, but burnt clean of hatred, came to welcome him with a quick, hard embrace, a brother's touch.

The little girl, the Keeper from Neskaya, lay fallen in a heap; she had physically fallen from the Keeper's seat to the floor, and Taniquel was bending over her, hands to her temples. The child looked boneless, exhausted, fainting. Taniquel said, troubled, "Rannirl, come and carry her. . . ."

Elorie! Kerwin's heart sucked and turned over. He leaped over the chairs to throw open the door of the room. He had no memory of how he had gotten into the room, but Elorie had not managed, however it was, to follow him. Her mind had come into the matrix ring . . . but her body lay outside the shielded room, unguarded.

She was lying on the floor in the hall, sprawled there white and lifeless at his feet. Kerwin dropped to his knees at her side, all his triumph, all his exaltation, melting into hatred and curses, as he laid his hand to her unmoving breast.

Elorie, Elorie! Driven by the conscience of a Keeper, she had returned to save the Tower . . . but had she paid with her life? She had gone unprepared, unguarded, into a tremendous matrix operation. He knew how this work drained vitality, exhausting her nearly to the point of death; and even when she was carefully guarded and isolated, this work taxed her to the breaking point! Even guarding her vitality and nervous forces with chastity and sacrosanct isolation, she could hardly endure it! No, she had not lost her powers . . . but was this the price she must pay for daring to use them now?

I have killed her!

Despairing, he knelt beside her, hardly knowing it when Neyrissa moved him aside.

Kennard shook him roughly.

"Jeff! Jeff, she's not dead, not yet, there's a chance! But you've got to let the monitors get to her, let us see how bad it is!"

"Damn you, don't touch her! Haven't you devils done enough—"

"He's hysterical," Kennard said briefly. "Get him loose, Rannirl." Kerwin felt Rannirl's strong arms holding him, restraining him; he fought to reach Elorie, and Rannirl said compassionately, "I'm sorry, *bredu*. You have to let us—damn it, brother, hold still or I'll have to knock you senseless!"

He felt Elorie taken by force from his arms, cried out with his rage and despair . . . then slowly, sensing their warm touch on his mind, he subsided. Elorie wasn't dead. They were only trying to help. He subsided, standing quiet between Rannirl and Auster, seeing with half an eye that Rannirl's mouth was bleeding and that there was a scratch on Auster's face.

"I know," Auster said in a low voice, "but easy, foster-brother, they'll do everything that can be done. Tani and Neyrissa are with her now." He raised his eyes. "I failed. I failed, *bredu*. I would have broken, if you hadn't been here. I never had any right to be here at all, I'm Terran, outsider, you have more right here than I. . . ."

Unexpectedly, to Kerwin's horror, Auster dropped to his knees. His voice was just audible.

"All that I said of you was true of myself, *vai dom*; I must have known it, hating myself and pretending it was you I hated. All I deserve at the hands of the Comyn is death. There is a life between us, Damon Aillard; claim it as you will." He bowed his head and waited there, broken, resigned to death.

And suddenly Jeff was furious.

"Get up, you damned fool," he said, roughly hauling Auster to his feet. "All it means is that some of you half-wits—" and he looked around at all of them, "are going to have to change some of your stupid notions about the Comyn, that's all. So Auster was born of a Terran father—so what? He has the Ridenow Gift—*because he was brought up believing he had it!* I went through all kinds of hell in my training . . . *because all of you believed that with my Terran blood I'd find it difficult, and made me believe it!* Yes, *laran* is inherited, but it's not nearly to the extent you believed. It means that Cleindori was right; matrix mechanics is just a science anyone can learn, and there's no need to surround it with all kinds of ritual and taboo! A Keeper doesn't need to be a virgin . . ." He broke off.

Elorie believed it. And her belief could kill her!

And yet . . . she knew, she had been part of his link, with Cleindori; this was why Cleindori had given him the matrix, although his child's mind had almost broken under the burden: so that one day another Keeper could read what Cleindori had discovered, and deliver to Arilinn the message they would not hear from her, read the mind and heart and conscience of the martyred Keeper, who had died to free other young women from the prison the Arilinn Tower would build around their minds and their hearts.

"But we've won," Rannirl said, and Jeff knew they had all followed his thought.

"A period of grace," said Kennard somberly. "Not a final victory!"

And Jeff knew Kennard was right. This experiment might have succeeded, and the Pan-Darkovan Syndicate was now bound in honor to be guided by the will of Hastur in accepting Terran ways. But there had been a failure, too.

Kennard put it into words.

"The Tower circles can never be brought back as they were in the old days. Life can only go forward, not back. It's even better to ask help from the Terrans—in our own way and on our own terms—than to let all this weight rest on the shoulders of a few gifted men and women. Better that the people of Darkover should learn to share the effort with one another, Comyn and Commoner, and even with the people of Terra." He sighed.

"I deserted them," he said. "If I had fought all the way beside them—things might have gone differently. But this was what they were working for; Cleindori and Cassilde, Jeff and Lewis, Arnad, old Damon —all of us. To make an even exchange; Darkover to share the matrix powers with Terra, for those few things where they could be safely used, and Terra to give such things as she had. But as equals; not the Terran masters and the Darkovan suppliants. A fair exchange between equal worlds; each world with its own pride, and its own power. And I let you be sent to Terra," he added, looking straight at Jeff, "because I felt you a threat to my own sons. Can you forgive me, Damon Aillard?"

Jeff said, "I'll never get used to that name. I don't want it, Kennard. I wasn't brought up to it. I don't even believe in your kind of government, or inherited power of that kind. If your sons do, they're welcome to it; you've brought them up to take those kinds of responsibility. Just—" He grinned. "Use what influence you have to see that I'm not deported, day after tomorrow."

Kennard said gently, "There is no such person as Jeff Kerwin, Junior. They cannot possibly deport the grandson of Valdir Alton to Terra. Whatever he chooses to call himself."

There was a feather-light touch on Jeff's arm. He looked down into the pale, childish face of the child-Keeper; and remembered her name, Callina of Neskaya.

She whispered, "Elorie—she is conscious; she wants you."

Jeff said gravely, "Thank you, *vai leronis*," and watched the child blushing. What Elorie had done had freed this girl, too; but she did not know it yet.

They had taken Elorie into the nearest room and laid her on a couch there; pale, white, strengthless, she stretched her hands to Jeff. He reached for her, not caring that the rest of the circle had crowded into the room behind him. He knew, when he touched her, how deep the shock had been, going unguarded, unprepared into the matrix circle; in days to come, Keepers would learn ways to guard themselves against the energy drains of massive work like this; without the tremendous dedication of lifelong ritual chastity, but with strong safeguards nevertheless. Elorie had indeed been injured; she had come closer to death than any of them would ever want to remember, and many suns would rise and set over Arilinn before her old merry laughter would be heard again in the Tower; but her glowing eyes blazed out in love and triumph.

"We've won," she whispered, "and we're here!"

And Kerwin, holding her in his arms, knew that they had won indeed. The days that were coming, for

Darkover and the Comyn, would change them all; both worlds would struggle with the changes that the years would bring. But a world that remains always the same can only die. They had fought to keep Darkover as it was; but what they had won was only the victory of determining what changes would come, and how quickly.

He had found what he loved, indeed; and he had destroyed it, for the world he loved would never be the same, and he had been the instrument of change. But in destroying it, he had saved it from ultimate and final destruction.

His brothers and sisters were all around him. Taniquel, so white and worn that he realized how ruthlessly she had spent herself to bring Elorie back to herself. Auster, with the mold of his life broken, but with a new strength from which it could be forged anew. Kennard, his kinsman, and all the others . . .

"Now, now," said the sensible voice of Mesyr, calm and level. "What's the sense of standing here like this, when your night's work is done, and well done? Downstairs, all of you, for some breakfast . . . yes, you too, Jeff, let Elorie get some rest." With brisk hands she drew up the covers beneath Elorie's chin and made shooing gestures at all of them.

Jeff met Elorie's eyes again, and, weak as she was, she began to laugh; and then they all joined in, so that the corridors and stairways of the Tower rang with shared mirth. Some things, at least, never changed at all.

Life in Arilinn, for now, was back to normal.

They were home again. And this time they would stay.

To Keep The Oath

The red light lingered on the hills; two of the four small moons were in the sky, green Idriel near to setting, and the tiny crescent of Mormallor, ivory-pale, near the zenith. The night would be dark. Kindra n'ha Mhari did not, at first, see anything strange about the little town. She was too grateful to have reached it before sunset—shelter against the rainswept chill of a Darkovan night, a bed to sleep in after four days of traveling, a cup of wine before she slept.

But slowly she began to realize that there was something wrong. Normally, at this hour, the women would be going back and forth in the streets, gossiping with neighbors, marketing for the evening meal, while their children played and squabbled in the street. But tonight there was not a single woman in the street, nor a single child.

What was wrong? Frowning, she rode along the main street toward the inn. She was hungry and weary.

She had left Dalereuth many days before with a companion, bound for Neskaya Guild-house. But unknown to either of them, her companion had been pregnant; she had fallen sick of a fever, and in Thendara Guild-house she had miscarried and still lay there, very ill. Kindra had gone alone to Neskaya; but she had turned aside three days' ride to carry a

message to the sick woman's oath-mother. She had
found her in a village in the hills, working to help a
group of women set up a small dairy.

Kindra was not afraid of traveling alone; she had
journeyed in these hills at all seasons and in all
weathers. But her provisions were beginning to run
low. Fortunately, the innkeeper was an old acquaintance; she had little money with her, because her
journey had been so unexpectedly prolonged, but old
Jorik would feed her and her horse, give her a bed for
the night, and trust her to send money to pay for it—
knowing that if she did not, or could not, her Guild-
house would pay, for the honor of the Guild.

The man who took her horse in the stable had
known her for many years, too. He scowled as she
alighted. "I don't know where we shall stable your
horse, and that's certain, *mestra,* with all these
strange horses here . . . will she share a box stall
without kicking, do you suppose? Or shall I tie her
loose at the end?" Kindra noticed that the stable was
crammed with horses, two dozen of them and more.
Instead of a lonely village inn, it looked like Neskaya
on market-day!

"Did you meet with any riders on the road,
mestra?"

"No, none," Kindra said, frowning a little. "All
the horses in the Kilghard Hills seem to be here in
your stable—what is it, a royal visit? What is the
matter with you? You keep looking over your shoulder as if you expect to find your master there with a
stick to beat you—where is old Jorik, why is he not
here to greet his guests?"

"Why, *mestra,* old Jorik's dead," the old man said,
"and Dame Janella trying to manage the inn alone
with young Annelys and Marga."

"Dead? Gods preserve us," Kindra said. "What happened?"

"It was those bandits, *mestra,* Scarface's gang; they came here and cut Jorik down with his apron still on," said the old groom. "Made havoc in the town, broke all the ale-pots, and when the menfolk drove 'em off with pitchforks, they swore they'd be back and fire the town! So Dame Janella and the elders put the cap round and raised copper to hire Brydar of Fen Hills and all his men to come and defend us when they come back; and here Brydar's men have been ever since, *mestra,* quarreling and drinking and casting eyes on the women until the townfolk are ready to say the remedy's worse than the sickness! But go in, go in, *mestra,* Janella's ready to welcome you."

Plump Janella looked paler and thinner than Kindra had ever seen her. She greeted Kindra with unaccustomed warmth. Under ordinary conditions, she was cold to Kindra, as befitted a respectable wife in the presence of a member of the Amazon Guild; now, Kindra supposed, she was learning that an innkeeper could not afford to alienate a customer. Jorik, Kindra knew, had not approved of the Free Amazons either; but he had learned from experience that they were quiet guests who kept to themselves, caused no trouble, did not get drunk and break bar-stools and ale-pots, and paid their reckoning promptly. *A guest's reputation,* Kindar thought wryly, *does not tarnish the color of his money.*

"You have heard, good *mestra?* Those wicked men, Scarface's fellows, they cut my good man down, and for nothing—just because he flung an ale-pot at one of them who laid rough hands on my little girl, and Annelys not fifteen yet! Monsters!"

"And they killed him? Shocking!" Kindra murmured, but her pity was for the girl. All her life, young Annelys must remember that her father had been killed in defending her, because she could not defend herself. Like all the women of the Guild, Kindra was sworn to defend herself, to turn to no man for protection. She had been a member of the Guild for half her lifetime; it seemed shocking to her that a man should die defending a girl from advances she should have known how to ward off herself.

"Ah, you don't know what it's like, *mestra*, being alone without the goodman. Living alone as you do, you can't imagine!"

"Well, you have daughters to help you," Kindra said, and Janella shook her head and mourned. "But they can't come out among all those rough men, they are only little girls!"

"It will do them good to learn something of the world and its ways," Kindra said, but the woman sighed. "I wouldn't like them to learn too much of that."

"Then, I suppose, you must get you another husband," Kindra said, knowing that there was simply no way she and Janella could communicate. "But indeed I am sorry for your grief. Jorik was a good man."

"You can't imagine how good, *mestra*," Janella said plaintively. "You women of the Guild, you call yourselves free women, only it seems to me I have always been free, until now, when I must watch myself night and day, lest someone get the wrong idea about a woman alone. Only the other day, one of Brydar's men said to me—and that's another thing, these men of Brydar's. Eating us out of house and home, and just look, *mestra*, no room in the stable for the horses of our paying customers, with half the village keeping their horses here against bandits, and those hired swords drinking up my good old man's beer day after day—" Abruptly she recalled her duties as landlord. "But come into the common-room, *mestra*, warm yourself, and I'll bring you some supper; we have a roast haunch of *chervine*. Or would you fancy something lighter, rabbithorn stewed with mushrooms, perhaps? We're crowded, yes, but there's the little room at the head of the stairs, you can have that to yourself, a room fit for a fine lady, indeed Lady Hastur slept here in that very bed, a few years gone. Lilla! Lilla! Where's that simpleminded wench gone? When I took her in, her mother told me she was lack-witted, but she has wits enough to hang about talking to that young hired sword, Zandru scratch them all! Lilla! Hurry now, show the good woman her room, fetch her wash-water, see to her saddlebags!"

Later, Kindra went down to the common-room. Like all Guild-women, she had learned to be discreet when traveling alone; a solitary woman was prey to questions, at least, so they usually journeyed in pairs. This subjected them to raised eyebrows and occasional dirty speculations, but warded off the less palatable approaches to which a lone woman traveling on Darkover was subject. Of course, any woman of the Guild could protect herself if it went past rude words, but that could cause trouble for all the Guild. It was better to conduct oneself in a way that minimized the possibility of trouble. So Kindra sat alone in a tiny corner near the fireplace, kept her hood drawn around her face—she was neither young nor particularly pretty—sipped her wine and warmed her feet, and did nothing to attract anyone's attention. It occurred to her that at this moment she, who called herself a Free Amazon, was considerably less constrained than Janella's young daughters, going back and forth, protected by their family's roof and their mother's presence.

She finished her meal—she had chosen the stewed rabbithorn—and called for a second glass of wine, too weary to climb the stairs to her chamber and too tired to sleep if she did.

Some of Brydar's hired swords were sitting around a long table at the other end end of the room, drinking and playing dice. They were a mixed crew; Kindra knew none of them, but she had met Brydar himself a few times, and had even hired out with him, once, to guard a merchant caravan across the desert to the Dry Towns. She nodded courteously to him, and he saluted her, but paid her no further attention; he knew her well enough to know that she would not welcome even polite conversation when she was in a roomful of strangers.

One of the younger mercenaries, a young man, tall, beardless and weedy, ginger hair cut close to his head, rose and came toward her. Kindra braced herself for the inevitable. If she had been with two or three other Guild-women, she would have welcomed harmless companionship, a drink together and talk about the chances of the road, but a lone Amazon simply did NOT drink with men in public taverns, and, damn it, Brydar knew it as well as she did.

One of the older mercenaries must have been having some fun with the green boy, needling him to prove his manhood by approaching the Amazon, amusing themselves by enjoying the rebuff he'd inevitably get.

One of the men looked up and made a remark Kindra didn't hear. The boy snarled something, a hand to his dagger. "Watch yourself, you—!" He spoke a foulness. Then he came to Kindra's table and said, in a soft, husky voice, "A good evening to you, honorable mistress."

Startled at the courteous phrase, but still wary, Kindra said, "And to you, young sir."

"May I offer you a tankard of wine?"

"I have had enough to drink," Kindra said, "but I thank you for the kind offer." Something faintly out of key, almost effeminate, in the youth's bearing, alerted her; his proposition, then, would not be the usual thing. Most people knew that Free Amazons took lovers if and when they chose, and all too many men interpreted that to mean that any Amazon could be had, at any time. Kindra was an expert at turning covert advances aside without ever letting it come to question or refusal; with ruder approaches, she managed with scant courtesy. But that wasn't what this youngster wanted; she knew when a man was looking at her with desire, whether he put it into words or not, and although there was certainly interest in this young man's face, it wasn't sexual interest! What did he want with her, then?

"May I—may I sit here and talk to you for a moment, honorable dame?"

Rudeness she could have managed. This excessive courtesy was a puzzle. Were they simply making game of a woman-hater, wagering he would not have the courage to talk to her? She said neutrally, "This is a public room; the chairs are not mine. Sit where you like."

Ill at ease, the boy took a seat. He was young indeed. He was still beardless, but his hands were callused and hard, and there was a long-healed scar on one cheek; he was not as young as she thought.

"You are a Free Amazon, *mestra?*" He used the common, and rather offensive, term; but she did not hold it against him. Many men knew no other name.

"I am," she said, "but we would rather say: I am of the oath-bound—" The word she used was *Comhi-Letzis*— "A Renunciate of the Sisterhood of Freed Women."

"May I ask—without giving offense—why the name Renunciate, *mestra?*"

Actually, Kindra welcomed a chance to explain. "Because, sir, in return for our freedom as women of the Guild, we swear an oath renouncing those privileges that we might have by choosing to belong to some man. If we renounce the disabilities of being property and chattel, we must renounce, also, whatever benefits there may be; so that no man can accuse us of trying to have the best of both choices."

He said gravely, "That seems to me an honorable choice. I have never yet met a—a—a Renunciate. Tell me, *mestra*—" His voice suddenly cracked high. "I suppose you know the slanders that are spoken of you—tell me, how does any woman have the courage to join the Guild, knowing what will be said of her?"

"I suppose," Kindra said quietly, "for some women, a time comes when they think that there are worse things than being the subject of public slanders. It was so with me."

He thought that over for a moment, frowning. "I have never seen a Free—er—a Renunciate traveling alone before. Do you not usually travel in pairs, honorable dame?"

"True. But need knows no mistress," Kindra said, and explained that her companion had fallen sick in Thendara.

"And you came so far to bear a message? Is she your *bredhis?*" the boy asked, using the polite word for a woman's freemate or female lover; and because it was the polite word he used, not the gutter one, Kindra did not take offense. "No, only a comrade."

"I—I would not have dared speak if there had been two of you—"

Kindra laughed. "Why not? Even in twos or threes, we are not dogs to bite strangers."

The boy stared at his boots. "I have cause to fear —women—" he said, almost inaudibly. "But you seemed kind. And I suppose, *mestra,* that whenever you come into these hills, where life is so hard for women, you are always seeking out wives and daughters who are discontented at home, to recruit them for your Guild?"

Would that we might! Kindra thought, with all the old bitterness; but she shook her head. "Our charter forbids it," she said. "It is the law that a women must seek us out herself, and formally petition to be allowed to join us. I am not even allowed to tell women of the advantages of the Guild, when they ask. I may only tell them of the things they must renounce, by oath." She tightened her lips and added, "If we were to do as you say, to seek out discontented wives and daughters and lure them away to the Guild, the men would not let any Guild-house stand in the Domains, but would burn our houses about our ears." It was the old injustice; the women of Darkover had won this concession, the charter of the Guild, but so hedged about with restrictions that many women never saw or spoke with a Guild-sister.

"I suppose," she said, "that they have found out that we are not whores, so they insist that we are all lovers of women, intent on stealing out their wives and daughters. We must be, it seems, one evil thing or the other."

"Are there no lovers of women among you, then?"

Kindra shrugged. "Certainly," she said. "You must know that there are some women who would rather die than marry; and even with all the restrictions and renunciations of the oath, it seems a preferable alternative. But I assure you we are not all so. We are free women—free to be thus or otherwise, at our own will." After a moment's thought she added carefully, "And if you have a sister you may tell her so from me."

The young man started, and Kindra bit her lip; again she had let her guard down, picking up hunches so clearly formed that sometimes her companions accused her of having a little of the telepathic gift of the higher castes; *laran.* Kindra, who was, as far as she knew, all commoner and without either noble blood or telepathic gift, usually kept herself barricaded; but she had picked up a random thought, a bitter thought from somewhere, *My sister would not believe . . .* a thought quickly vanished, so quickly that Kindra wondered if she had imagined the whole thing.

The young face across the table twisted into bitter lines.

"There is none, now, I may call my sister."

"I am sorry," Kindra said, puzzled. "To be alone, that is a sorrowful thing. May I ask your name?"

The boy hesitated again, and Kindra knew, with that odd intuition, that the real name had almost escaped the taut lips; but he bit it back.

"Brydar's men call me Marco. Don't ask my lineage; there is none who will claim kin to me now— thanks to those foul bandits under Scarface." He twisted his mouth and spat. "Why do you think I am in this company? For the few coppers these village folk can pay? No, *mestra.* I too am oath-bound. To revenge."

Kindra left the common-room early, but she could

not sleep for a long time. Something in the young man's voice, his words, had plucked a resonating string in her own mind and memory. Why had he questioned her so insistently? Had he a sister or kinswoman, perhaps, who had spoken of becoming a Renunciate? Or was he, an obvious effeminate, jealous of her because she could escape the role ordained by society for her sex and he could not? Did he fantasy, perhaps, some such escape from the demands made upon men? Surely not; there were simpler lives for men than that of a hired sword! And men had a choice of what lives they would live— more choice, anyhow, than most women. Kindra had chosen to become a Renunciate, making herself an outcaste among most people in the Domains. Even the innkeeper only tolerated her, because she was a regular customer and paid well, but he would have equally tolerated a prostitute or a traveling juggler, and would have had fewer prejudices against either.

Was the youth, she wondered, one of the rumored spies sent out by *cortes,* the governing body in Thendara, to trap Renunciates who broke the terms of their charter by proselytizing and attempting to recruit women into the Guild? If so, at least she had resisted the temptation. She had not even said, though tempted, that if Janella were a Renunciate she would have felt competent to run the inn by herself, with the help of her daughters.

A few times, in the history of the Guild, men had even tried to infiltrate them in disguise. Unmasked, they had met with summary justice, but it had happened and might happen again. At that, she thought, he might be convincing enough in women's clothes; but not with the scar on his face, or those callused hands. Then she laughed in the dark, feeling the calluses on her own fingers. Well, if he was fool enough to try it, so much the worse for him. Laughing, she fell asleep.

Hours later she woke to the sound of hoofbeats, the clash of steel, yells and cries outside. Somewhere women were shrieking. Kindra flung on her outer clothes and ran downstairs. Brydar was standing in the courtyard, bellowing orders. Over the wall of the courtyard she could see a sky reddened with flames. Scarface and his bandit crew were loose in the town, it seemed.

"Go, Renwal," Brydar ordered. "Slip behind their rear-guard and set their horses loose, stampede them, so they must stand to fight, not strike and flee again! And since all the good horses are stabled here, one of you must stay and guard them lest they strike here for ours . . . the rest of you come with me, and have your swords at the ready—"

Janella was huddled beneath the overhanging roof of an outbuilding, her daughters and serving women like roosting hens around her. "Will you leave us all here unguarded, when we have housed you all for seven days and never a penny in pay? Scarface and his men are sure to strike here for the horses, and we are unprotected, at their mercy—"

Brydar gestured to the boy Marco. "You. Stay and guard horses and women—"

The boy snarled, "No! I joined your crew on the pledge that I should face Scarface, steel in hand! It is an affair of honor—do you think I need your dirty coppers?"

Beyond the wall all was shrieking confusion. "I have no time to bandy words," Brydar said quickly. "Kindra—this is no quarrel of yours, but you know me a man of my word; stay here and guard the horses and these women, and I will make it worth your while!''

"At the mercy of a woman? A woman to guard us? Why not set a mouse to guard a lion!'' Janella's shrewish cry cut him off. The boy Marco urged, eyes blazing, "Whatever I have been promised for this foray is yours, *mestra,* if you free me to meet my sworn foe!''

"Go; I'll look after them," Kindra said. It was unlikely Scarface would get this far, but it was really no affair of hers; normally she fought beside the men, and would have been angry at being left in a post of safety. But Janella's cry had put her on her mettle. Marco caught up his sword and hurried to the gate, Brydar following him. Kindra watched them go, her mind on her own early battles. Some turn of gesture, of phrase, had alerted her. *The boy Marco is noble,* she thought. *Perhaps even Comyn, some bastard of a great lord, perhaps even a Hastur. I don't know what he's doing with Brydar's men, but he's no ordinary hired sword!*

Janella's wailing brought her back to her duty. "Oh! Oh! Horrible," she howled. "Left here with only a woman to look after us . . .''

Kindra said tersely, "Come on!'' She gestured. "Help me close that gate!''

"I don't take orders from one of you shameless women in breeches—''

"Let the damned gate stay open, then," Kindra said, right out of patience. "Let Scarface walk in without any trouble. Do you want me to go and invite him, or shall we send one of your daughters?''

"Mother!'' remonstrated a girl of fifteen, breaking away from Janella's hand. "That is no way to speak —Lilla, Marga, help the good *mestra* shove this gate shut!'' She came and joined Kindra, helping to thrust the heavy wooden gate tightly into place, pull down the heavy crossbeam. The women were wailing in dismay; Kindra singled out one of them, a young girl about six or seven moons along in pregnancy, who was huddled in a blanket over her nightgear.

"You," she said, "take all the babies and the little children upstairs into the strongest chamber, bolt the doors, and don't open them unless you hear my voice or Janella's." The woman did not move, still sobbing, and Kindra said sharply, "Hurry! Don't stand there like a rabbithorn frozen in the snow! Damn you, *move,* or I'll slap you senseless!" She made a menacing gesture and the woman started, then began to hurry the children up the stairs; she picked up one of the littlest ones, hurried the others along with frightened, clucking noises.

Kindra surveyed the rest of the frightened women. Janella was hopeless. She was fat and short of breath, and she was staring resentfully at Kindra, furious that she had been left in charge of their defense. Furthermore, she was trembling on the edge of a panic that would infect everyone; but if she had something to do, she might calm down. "Janella, go into the kitchen and make up some hot wine punch," she said. "The men will want it when they come back, and they'll deserve it, too. Then start hunting out some linen for bandages, in case anyone's hurt. Don't worry," she added, "they won't get to you while we're here. And take that one with you," she added, pointing to the terrified simpleton Lilla, who was clinging to Janella's skirt, round-eyed with terror, whimpering. "She'll only be in our way."

When Janella had gone, grumbling, the lackwit at her heels, Kindra looked around at the sturdy young women who remained.

"Come, all of you, into the stables, and pile heavy bales of hay around the horses, so they can't drive the horses over them or stampede them out. No, leave the lantern there; if Scarface and his men break through, we'll set a couple of bales afire; that will frighten the horses and they might well kick a bandit or two to death. Even so, the women can escape while they round up the horses; contrary to what you may have heard, most bandits look first for horses and rich plunder, and women are not the first item on their list. And none of you have jewels or rich garments they would seek to strip from you." Kindra herself knew that any man who laid his hand on her, intending rape, would quickly regret it; and if she was overpowered by numbers, she had been taught ways in which she could survive the experience undestroyed; but these women had had no such teaching. It was not right to blame them for their fears.

I could teach them this. But the laws of our charter prevent me and I am bound by oath to obey those laws; laws made, not by our own Guild-mothers, but by men who fear what we might have to say to their women!

Well, perhaps at least they will find it a matter for pride that they can defend their home against invaders! Kindra went to lend her own wiry strength to the task of piling up the heavy bales around the horses; the women worked, forgetting their fears in hard effort. But one grumbled, just loud enough to Kindra to hear, "It's all very well for *her!* She was trained as a warrior and she's used to this kind of work! I'm not!"

It was no time to debate Guild-house ethics; Kindra only asked mildly, "Are you proud of the fact that you have not been taught to defend yourself, child?" But the girl did not answer, sullenly hauling at her heavy hay-bale.

It was not difficult for Kindra to follow her

thought; if it had not been for Brydar, each man of the town could have protected each one his own women! Kindra thought, in utter disguest, that this was the sort of thinking that laid villages in flames, year after year, because no man owed loyalty to another or would protect any household but his own! It had taken a threat like Scarface to get these village men organized enough to buy the services of a few hired swords, and now their women were grumbling because their men could not stand, each at his own door, protecting his own woman and hearth!

Once the horses had been barricaded, the women clustered together nervously in the courtyard. Even Janella came to the kitchen door to watch. Kindra went to the barred gate, her knife loose in its scabbard. The other girls and women stood under the roof of the kitchen, but one young girl, the same who had helped Kindra to shut the gate, bent and tucked her skirt resolutely up to her knees, then went and brought back a big wood-chopping hatchet and stood with it in her hand, taking up a place at the gate beside Kindra.

"Annelys!" Janella called. "Come back here! By me!"

The girl cast a look of contempt at her mother and said, "If any bandit climbs these walls, he will not get his hands on me, or on my little sister, without facing cold steel. It's not a sword, but I think even in a girl's hands, this blade would change his mind in a hurry!" She glanced defiantely at Kindra and said, "I am ashamed for all of you, that you would let one lone woman protect us! Even a rabbithorn doe protects her kits!"

Kindra gave the girl a companionable grin. "If you have half as much skill with that thing as you have guts, little sister, I would rather have you at my back

than any man. Hold the axe with your hands close
together, if the time comes to use it, and don't try
anything fancy, just take a good hard chop at his
legs, just like you were cutting down a tree. The
thing is, he won't be expecting it, see?"

The night dragged on. The woman huddled on
hay-bales and boxes, listening with apprehension
and occasional sobs and tears as they heard the clash
of swords, cries and shouts. Only Annelys stood
grimly beside Kindra, clutching her axe. After an
hour or so, Kindra said, settling herself down on a
hay-bale, "You needn't clutch it like that, you'll only
weary yourself for an attack. Lean it against the bale,
so you can snatch it up when the need comes."

Annelys asked in an undertone, "How did you
know so well what to do? Are all the Free Amazons
—you call them something else, don't you?—how do
the Guild-women learn? Are they all fighting women
and hired swords?"

"No, no, not even many of us," Kindra said. "It is
only that I have not many other talents; I cannot
weave or embroider very well, and my skill at gar-
dening is only good in the summertime. My own
oath-mother is a midwife, that is our most respected
trade; even those who despise the Renunciates con-
fess that we can often save babes alive when the village healer-women fail. She would have taught me
her profession; but I had no talent for that, either,
and I am squeamish about the sight of blood—" She
looked down suddenly at her long knife, remembering her many battles, and laughed; and Annelys
laughed with her, a strange sound against the frightened moaning of the other women.

"*You* are afraid of the sight of blood?"

"It's different," Kindra said. "I can't stand suffering when I can't do anything about it, and if a babe

is born easily they seldom send for the midwife; we come only when matters are desperate. I would rather fight with men, or beasts, than for the life of a helpless woman or baby . . ."

"I think I would too," said Annelys, and Kindra thought: *Now, if I were not bound by the laws of the Guild, I could tell her what we are. And this one would be a credit to the Sisterhood* . . .

But her oath held her silent. She sighed and looked at Annelys, frustrated.

She was beginning to think the precautions had been useless, that Scarface's men would never come here at all, when there was a shriek from one of the women, and Kindra saw the tassel of a coarse knitted cap come up over the wall; then two men appeared on top of the wall, knives gripped in their teeth to free their hands for climbing.

"So here's where they've hidden it all, women, horses, all of it—" growled one. "You go for the horses, I'll take care of—oh, you would," he shouted as Kindra ran at him with her knife drawn. He was taller than Kindra; as they fought, she could only defend herself, backing step by step toward the stables. Where were the men? Why had the bandits been able to get this far? Were they the last defense of the town? Behind her, out of the corner of her eye she saw the other bandit coming up with his sword; she circled, backing carefully so she could face them both.

Then there was a shriek from Annelys, the axe flashed once, and the second bandit fell, howling, his leg spouting blood. Kindra's opponent faltered at the sound; Kindra brought up her knife and ran him through the shoulder, snatching up his knife as it fell from his limp hand. He fell backward, and she leaped on top of him.

"Annelys!" she shouted. "You women! Bring thongs, rope, anything to tie him up—there may be others—"

Janella came with a clothesline and stood by as Kindra tied the man, then, stepping back, looked at the bandit, lying in a pool of his own blood. His leg was nearly severed at the knee. He was still breathing, but he was too far gone even to moan and while the women stood and looked at him, he died. Janella stared at Annelys in horror, as if her young daughter had suddenly sprouted another head.

"You killed him," she breathed. "You chopped his leg off!"

"Would you rather he had chopped off mine, mother?" Annelys asked, and bent to look at the other bandit. "He is only stabbed through the shoulder, he'll live to be hanged!"

Breathing hard, Kindra straightened, giving the clothesline a final tug. She looked at Annelys and said, "You saved my life, little sister."

The girl smiled up at her, excited, her hair coming down and tumbling into her eyes. There was a cold sleet beginning to fall in the court; their faces were wet. Annelys suddenly flung her arms around Kindra, and the older woman hugged her, disregarding the mother's troubled face.

"One of our own could not have done better. My thanks, little one!" Damn it, the girl had *earned* her thanks and approval, and if Janella stared at them as if Kindra were a wicked seducer of young women, then so much the worse for Janella! She let the girl's arm stay around her shoulders as she said, "Listen; I think that is the men coming back."

And in a minute they heard Brydar's hail, and they struggled to raise the great crossbeam of the gate. His men drove before them more than a dozen good horses, and Brydar laughed, saying, "Scarface's men will have no more use for them; so we're well paid! I see you women got the last of them?" He looked down at the bandit lying in his gore, at the other, tied with Janella's clothesline. "Good work, *mestra,* I'll see you have a share in the booty!"

"The girl helped," Kindra said. "I'd have been dead without her."

"One of them killed my father," the girl said fiercely, "so I have paid my just debt, that is all!" She turned to Janella and ordered, "Mother, bring our defenders some of that wine punch, at once!"

Brydar's men sat all over the common-room, drinking the hot wine gratefully. Brydar set down the tankard and rubbed his hands over his eyes with a tired "Whoosh!" He said, "Some of my men are hurt, dame Janella; have any of your women skill with leech-craft? We will need bandages, and perhaps some salves and herbs. I—" He broke off as one of the men beckoned him urgently from the door, and he went at a run.

Annelys brought Kindra a tankard and put it shyly into her hand. Kindra sipped; it was not the wine-punch Janella had made, but a clear, fine, golden wine from the mountains. Kindra sipped it slowly, knowing the girl had been telling her something. She sat across from Kindra, taking a sip now and then of the hot wine in her own tankard. They were both reluctant to part.

Damn that fool law that says I cannot tell her of the Sisterhood! She is too good for this place and for that fool mother of hers; the idiot Lilla is more what her mother needs to help run the inn, and I suppose Janella will marry her off to some yokel at once, just to have help in running this place! Honor demanded she keep silent. Yet, watching Annelys, thinking of the life the girl would lead here, she wondered, troubled, what kind of honor it was, to require that she leave a girl like this in a place like this.

Yet she supposed it was a wise law; anyway, it had been made by wiser heads than hers. She supposed, otherwise, young girls, glamored for the moment with the thought of a life of excitement and adventure, might follow the Sisterhood without being fully aware of the hardships and the renunciations that awaited them. The name Renunciate was not lightly given; it was not an easy life. And considering the way Annelys was looking at her, Annelys might follow her simply out of hero-worship. That wouldn't do. She sighed, and said, "Well, the excitement is over for tonight, I suppose. I must be away to my bed; I have a long way to ride tomorrow. Listen to that racket! I didn't know any of Brydar's men were seriously hurt—"

"It sounds more like a quarrel than men in pain," Annelys said, listening to the shouts and protests. "Are they quarreling over the spoils?"

Abruptly the door thrust open and Brydar of Fen Hills came into the room. "*Mestra,* forgive me, you are wearied—"

"Enough," she said, "but after all this hullabaloo I am not like to sleep much; what can I do for you?"

"I beg you—will you come? It is the boy—young Marco; he is hurt, badly hurt, but he will not let us tend his wounds until he has spoken with you. He says he has an urgent message, very urgent, which he must give before he dies . . ."

"Avarra's mercy," Kindra said, shocked. "Is he dying, then?"

"I cannot tell, he will not let us near enough to dress his wound. If he would be reasonable and let us care for him—but he is bleeding like a slaughtered *chervine,* and he has threatened to slit the throat of any man who touches him. We tried to hold him down and tend him willy-nilly, but it made his wounds bleed so sore as he struggled that we dared not wait—will you come, *mestra?*"

Kindra looked at him with question—she had not thought he would humor any man of his band so. Brydar said defensively, "The lad is nothing to me; not foster-brother, kinsman, nor even friend. But he fought at my side, and he is brave; it was he who killed Scarface in single combat. And may have had his death from it."

"Why should he want to speak to me?"

"He says, *mestra,* that it is a matter concerning his sister. And he begs you in the name of Avarra the pitiful that you will come. And he is young enough, almost, to be your son."

"So," Kindra said at last. She had not seen her own son since he was eight days old; and he would, she thought, be too young to bear a sword. "I cannot refuse anyone who begs me in the name of the Goddess," she said, and rose, frowning; young Marco had said he had no sister. No; he had said that there was none, now, that he could call sister. Which might be a different thing.

On the stairs she heard the voice of one of Brydar's men, expostulating, "Lad, we won't hurt ye, but if we don't get to that wound and tend to it, you could die, do ye' hear?"

"Get away from me!" The young voice cracked. "I swear by Zandu's hells, and, by the spilt tripes of Scarface out there dead, I'll shove this knife into the throat of the first man who touches me!"

Inside, by torchlight, Kindra saw Marco half-sitting, half-lying on a straw pallet; he had a dagger in his hand, holding them away with it; but he was pale as death, and there was icy sweat on his forehead. The straw pallet was slowly reddening with a pool of blood. Kindra knew enough of wounds to know that the human body could lose more blood than most people thought possible without serious danger; but to any ordinary person it looked most alarming.

Marco saw Kindra and gasped, "*Mestra,* I beg you —I must speak with you alone—"

"That's no way to speak to a comrade, lad," said one of the mercenaries, kneeling behind him, as Kindra knelt beside the pallet. The wound was high on the leg, near the groin; the leather breeches had broken the blow somewhat, or the boy would have met the same fate as the man Annelys had struck with the axe.

"You little fool," Kindra said. "I can't do half as much for you as your friend can."

Marco's eyes closed for a moment, from pain or weakness. Kindra thought he had lost consciousness, and gestured to the man behind him. "Quick, now, while he is unconscious—" she said swiftly, but the tortured eyes flicked open.

"Would you betray me, too?" He gestured with the dagger, but so feebly that Kindra was shocked. There was certainly no time to be lost. The best thing was to humor him.

"Go," she said, "I'll reason with him, and if he won't listen, well, he is old enough to take the consequences of his folly." Her mouth twisted as the men went away. "I hope what you have to tell me is worth risking your life for, you lackwitted simpleton!"

But a great and terrifying suspicion was born in her as she knelt on the bloody pallet. "You fool, do you know this is likely to be your deathwound? I have small skill at leechcraft; your comrades could do better for you."

"It is sure to be my death unless you help me," said the hoarse, weakening voice. "None of these men is comrade enough that I could trust him . . . *mestra*, help me, I beg you, in the name of the merciful Avarra—I am a woman."

Kindra drew a sharp breath. She had begun to suspect—and it was true, then. "And none of Brydar's men knows—"

"None. I have dwelt among them for half a year, and I do not think any man of them suspects—and I fear women even more. But you, you I felt I might trust—"

"I swear it," Kindra said hastily. "I am oath-bound never to refuse aid to any woman who asks me in the name of the Goddess. But let me help you now, my poor girl, and pray Avarra you have not delayed too long!"

"Even if it was so—" the strange girl whispered— I would rather die as a woman, than—disgraced and exposed. I have known so much disgrace—"

"Hush! Hush, child!" But she fell back against the pallet; she had really fainted, this time, at last; and Kindra cut away the leather breeches, looking at the serious cut that sliced through the top of the thigh and into the pubic mound. It had bled heavily, but was not, Kindra thought, fatal. She picked up one of the clean towels the men had left, pressed heavily against the wound; when it slowed to an ooze, she frowned, thinking it should be stitched. She hesitated to do it—she had little skill at such things, and she was sure the man from Brydar's band could do it more tidily and sure-handed; but she knew that was exactly what the young woman had feared, to be handled and exposed by men. Kindra thought: *If it could be done before she recovers consciousness, she need not know* . . . But she had promised the girl, and she would keep her promise. The girl did not stir as she stepped out into the hall.

Brydar came halfway up the stairs. "How goes it?"

"Send young Annelys to me," Kindra said. "Tell her to bring linen thread and a needle; and linen for bandages, and hot water and soap." Annelys had courage and strength; what was more, she was sure that if Kindra asked her to keep a secret, Annelys would do so, instead of gossiping about it.

Brydar said, in a undertone that did not carry a yard past Kindra's ear, "It's a woman—isn't it?"

Kindra demanded, with a frown. "Were you listening?"

"Listening, hell! I've got the brains I was born with, and I was remembering a couple of other little things. Can you think of any other reason a member of my band wouldn't let us get his britches off? Whoever she is, she's got guts enough for two!"

Kindra shook her head in dismay. Then all the girl's suffering was useless, scandal and disgrace there would be in any case. "Brydar, you pledged this would be worth my while. Do you owe me, or not?"

"I owe you," Brydar said.

"Then swear by your sword that you will never open your mouth about this, and I am paid. Fair enough?"

Brydar grinned. "I won't cheat you out of your pay for that," he said. "You think I want it to get round these hills that Brydar of Fen Hills can't tell the men from the ladies? Young Marco rode with my band for half a year and proved himself the man. If his foster-sister or kinswoman or cousin or what you will chooses to nurse him herself, and take him home with her afterward, what's it to any of my men?

Damned if I want my crew thinking some girl killed Scarface right under my nose!" He put his hand to sword-hilt. "Zandru take this hand with the palsy if I say any word about this. I'll send Annelys to you," he promised, and went.

Kindra returned to the girl's side. She was still unconscious; when Annelys came in, Kindra said curtly, "Hold the lamp there; I want to get this stitched before she recovers consciousness. And try not to get squeamish or faint; I want to get it done quick enough so we don't have to hold her down while we do it."

Annelys gulped at the sight of the girl and the gaping wound, which had begun to bleed again. "A woman! Blessed Evanda! Kindra, is she one of your Sisterhood? Did you know?"

"No, to both questions. Here, hold the light—"

"No," said Annelys. "I have done this many times; I have steady hands for this. Once when my brother cut his thigh chopping wood, I sewed it up, and I have helped the midwife, too. You hold the light."

Relieved, Kindra surrendered the needle. Annelys began her work as skillfully as if she were embroidering a cushion; halfway through the business, the girl regained consciousness; she gave a faint cry of fright, but Kindra spoke to her, and she quieted and lay still, her teeth clamped in her lip, clinging to Kindra's hand. Halfway through, she moistened her lip and whispered, "Is she one of you, *mestra?*"

"No. No more than yourself, child. But she is a friend. And she will not gossip about you, I know it," Kindra said confidently.

When Annelys had finished, she fetched a glass of wine for the woman, and held her head while she drank it. Some color came back into the pale cheeks, and she was breathing more easily. Annelys brought one of her own nightgowns and said, "You will be more comfortable in this, I think. I wish we could carry you to my bed, but I don't think you should be moved yet. Kindra, help me to lift her." With a pillow and a couple of clean sheets she set about making the woman comfortable on the straw pallet.

The stranger made a faint sound of protest as they began to undress her, but was too weak to protest effectively. Kindra stared in shock as the undertunic came off. She would never have believed that any woman over fourteen could successfully pose as a man among men; yet this woman had done it, and now she saw how. The revealed form was flat, spare, breastless; the shoulders had the hardened musculature of any swordsman. There was more hair on the arms that most women would have tolerated without removing it somehow, with bleach or wax. Annelys stared in amazement, and the woman, seeing that shocked look, hid her face in the pillow. Kindra said sharply, "There is no need to stare. She is *emmasca*, that is all; haven't you ever seen one before?" The neutering operation was illegal all over Darkover, and dangerous; and in this woman it must have been done before, or shortly after puberty. She was filled with questions, but courtesy forbade any of them.

"But—but—" Annelys whispered. "Was she born so or made so? It is unlawful—who would dare—"

"Made so," the girl said, her face still hidden in the pillow. "Had I been born so, I would have had nothing to fear . . . and I chose this so that I might have nothing more to fear!"

She tightened her mouth as they lifted and turned her; Annelys gasped aloud at the shocking scars, like the marks of whips, across the woman's back; but

she said nothing, only pulled the merciful concealment of her own nightgown over the frightful revelation of those scars. Gently, she washed the woman's
face and hands with soapy water. The ginger-pale
hair was dark with sweat, but at the roots Kindra
saw something else; the hair was beginning to grow
in fire-red there.

*Comyn. The telepath caste, red-haired . . . this woman was
a noblewoman, born to rule in the Domains of Darkover!*

In the name of all the Gods, Kindra wondered,
who can she be, what has come to her? How came
she here in this disguise, even her hair bleached so
none can guess at her lineage? And who has mis-
handled her so? She must have been beaten like an
animal . . .

And then, shocked, she heard the words forming in
her mind, not knowing how.

Scarface, said the voice in her mind. *But now I am
avenged. Even if it means my death . . .*

She was frightened; never had she so clearly per-
ceived; her rudimentary telepath gift had always,
before, been a matter of quick intuition, hunch, lucky
guess. She whispered aloud, in horror and dismay,
"By the Goddess! Child, who are you?"

The pale face contorted in a grimace which Kindra
recognized, in dismay, was intended for a smile. "I
am—no one," she said. "I had thought myself the
daughter of Alaric Lindir. Have you heard the tale?"

Alaric Lindir. The Lindir family were a proud and
wealthy family, distantly akin to the Aillard family of
the Comyn. Too highly born, in fact, for Kindra to
claim acquaintance with any of that kin; they were of
the ancient blood of the Hastur-kin.

"Yes, they are a proud people," whispered the
woman. "My mother's name was Kyria, and she was
a younger sister to Dom Lewis Ardais—not the

Ardais Lord, but his younger brother. But still, she was high-born enough that when she proved to be with child by one of the Hastur lords of Thendara, she was hurried away and married in haste to Alaric Lindir. And my father—he that I had always believed my father—he was proud of his red-haired daughter; all during my childhood I heard how proud he was of me, for I would marry into Comyn, or go to one of the Towers and become a great and powerful sorceress or Keeper. And then—then came Scarface and his crew, and they sacked the castle, and carried away some of the women, just as an afterthought, and by the time Scarface discovered who he had as his latest captive—well, the damage was done, but still he sent to my father for ransom. And my father, that selfsame Dom Alaric who had not enough proud words for his red-haired beauty who should further his ambition by a proud marriage into the Comyn, my father—" She choked, then spat the words out. "He sent word that if Scarface could guarantee me—untouched—then he would ransom me at a great price; but if not, then he would pay nothing. For if I was—was spoilt, ravaged—then I was no use to him, and Scarface might hang me or give me to one of his men, as he saw fit."

"Holy Bearer of Burdens!" Annelys whispered. "And this man had reared you as his own child?"

"Yes—and I had thought he loved me," Camilla said, her face twisting. Kindra closed her eyes in horror, seeing all too clearly the man who had welcomed his wife's bastard—but only while she could further his ambition!

Annelys' eyes were filled with tears. "How dreadful! Oh, how could any man—"

"I have come to believe any man would do so," Camilla said, "for Scarface was so angry at my

father's refusal that he gave me to one of his men to
be a plaything, and you can see how he used me.
That one I killed while he lay sleeping one night,
when at last he had come to believe me beaten into
submission—and so made my escape, and back to
my mother, and she welcomed me with tears and
with pity, but I could see in her mind that her
greatest fear, now, was that I should shame her by
bearing the child of Scarface's bastard; she feared
that my father would say to her, *like mother, like daughter,* and my disgrace would revive the old story of her
own. And I could not forgive my mother—that she
should continue to love and to live with that man
who had rejected me and given me over to such a
fate. And so I made my way to a *leronis,* who took pity
on me—or perhaps she, too, wanted only to be certain I would not disgrace my Comyn blood by becoming a whore or a bandit's drab—and she made
me *emmasca,* as you see. And I took service with
Brydar's men, and so I won my revenge—"

Annelys was weeping; but the girl lay with a face
like stone. Her very calm was more terrible than hysteria; she had gone beyond tears, into a place where
grief and satisfaction were all one, and that one wore
the face of death.

Kindra said softly, "You are safe now; none will
harm you. But you must not talk any more; you are
weary, and weakened with loss of blood. Come, drink
the rest of this wine and sleep, my girl." She supported the girl's head while she finished the wine,
filled with horror. And yet, through the horror, was
admiration. Broken, beaten, ravaged, and then rejected, this girl had won free of her captors by killing
one of them; and then she had survived the further
rejection of her family, to plot her revenge, and to
carry it out, as a noble might do.

And the proud Comyn rejected this woman? She has the courage of any two of their menfolk! It is this kind of pride and folly that will one day bring the reign of the Comyn crashing down into ruin! And she shuddered with a strange premonitory fear, seeing with her wakening telepathic gift a flashing picture of flames over the Hellers, strange sky-ships, alien men walking the streets of Thendara clad in black leather . . .

The woman's eyes closed, her hands tightening on Kindra's. "Well, I have had my revenge," she whispered again, "and so I can die. And with my last breath I will bless you, that I die as a woman, and not in this hated disguise, among men . . ."

"But you are not going to die," Kindra said. "You will live, child."

"No." Her face was set stubbornly in lines of refusal, closed and barriered. "What does life hold for a woman friendless and without kin? I could endure to live alone and secret, among men, disguised, while I nursed the thought of my revenge to strengthen me for the—the daily pretense. But I hate men, I loathe the way they speak of women among themselves, I would rather die than go back to Brydar's band, or live further among men."

Annelys said softly, "But now you are revenged, now you can live as a woman again."

Again the nameless woman shook her head. "Live as a woman, subject to men like my father? Go back and beg shelter from my mother, who might give me bread in secret so I would not disgrace them further by dying across her doorstep, and keep me hidden away, to drudge among them hidden, sew or spin, when I have ridden free with a mercenary band? Or shall I live as a lone woman, at the mercy of men? I would rather face the mercy of the blizzard and the banshee!" Her hand closed on Kindra's. "No," she said, "I would rather die."

Kindra drew the girl into her arms, holding her against her breast. "Hush, my poor girl, hush, you are over-wrought, you must not talk like that. When you have slept you will not feel this way," she soothed, but she felt the depth of despair in the woman in her arms, and her rage overflowed.

The laws of her Guild forbade her to speak of the Sisterhood, to tell this girl that she could live free, protected by the Guild Charter, never again to be at the mercy of any man. The laws of the Guild, which she might not break, the oath she must keep. And yet on a deeper level, was it not breaking the oath to withhold from this woman, who had risked so much and who had appealed to her in the name of her Goddess, the knowledge that might give her the will to live?

Whatever I do, I am forsworn; either I break my oath by refusing this girl my help, or I break it by speaking when I am forbidden by the law to speak.

The law! The law made by men, which still hemmed her in on every side, though she had cast off the ordinary laws by which men forced women to live! And she was doubly damned if she spoke of the Guild before Annelys, though Annelys had fought at her side. The just law of the Hellers would protect Annelys from this knowledge; it would make trouble for the Sisterhood if Kindra should lure away a daughter of a respectable innkeeper, whose mother needed her, and needed the help her husband would bring to the running of her inn!

Against her breast, the nameless girl had closed her eyes. Kindra caught the faint thread of her thoughts; she knew that the telepath caste could will themselves to die . . . as this girl had willed herself to live, despite everything that had happened, until she had had her cherished revenge.

Let me sleep so . . . and I can believe myself back in my mother's arms, in the days when I was still her child and this horror had not touched me. . . . Let me sleep so and never wake . . .

Already she was drifting away, and for a moment, in despair, Kindra was tempted to let her die. *The law forbids me to speak.* And if she should speak, then Annelys, already struck with hero-worship of Kindra, already rebelling against a woman's lot, having tasted the pride of defending herself, Annelys would follow her, too. Kindra knew it, with a strange, premonitory shiver.

She let the rage in her have its way and overflow. She shook the nameless woman awake, knowing that already she was willing herself to death.

"Listen to me! Listen! You must not die," she said angrily. "Not when you have suffered so much! That is a coward's way, and you have proven again and again that you are no coward!"

"Oh, but I am a coward," the woman said. "I am too much a coward to live in the only way a woman like me can live—through the charity of women such as my mother—or the mercy of men like my father, or like Scarface! I dreamed that when I had my revenge, I could find some other way. But there is no other way."

And Kindra's rage and resolution overflowed. She looked despairing over the nameless woman's head, into Annelys's frightened eyes. She swallowed, knowing the seriousness of the step she was about to take.

"There—there might be another way," she said, still temporizing. "You—I do not even know your name, what is your name?"

"I am nameless," the woman said, her face like stone. "I swore I would never again speak the name given me by the father and the mother who rejected me. If I had lived, I would have taken another name. Call me what pleases you."

And with a great surge of wrath, Kindra made up her mind. She drew the girl against her.

"I will call you Camilla," she said, "for from this day forth, I swear it, I shall be mother and sister to you, as was the blessed Cassilda to Camilla; this I swear. Camilla, you shall not die," she said, pulling the girl upright. Then, with a deep resolute breath, clasping Camilla's hand in one of hers, and stretching the other to Annelys, she began.

"My little sisters, let me tell you of the Sisterhood of Free Women, which men call Free Amazons. Let me tell you of the ways of the Renunciates, the Oath-bound, the *Comhi-Letzii* . . ."

FRIENDS OF DARKOVER

The Friends of Darkover is an organization which first came into being among close friends of Marion Zimmer Bradley, and has since expanded to include many readers of the Darkover novels, as well as other self-contained fantasy worlds.

We publish a Friends of Darkover Newsletter (which over the years has become a magazine of substantial size) and function as a discussion group about fantasy worlds in general and Darkover in particular.

For further information regarding the organization send a self-addressed stamped envelope to

FRIENDS OF DARKOVER
Box 72
Berkeley, CA 94701

Include $1.00, and a sample Newsletter will be enclosed along with the information.